A
VIEW
ACROSS
THE
ROOFTOPS

Published by Bookouture in 2019

An imprint of StoryFire Ltd.

Carmelite House
50 Victoria Embankment
London EC4Y 0DZ

www.bookouture.com

Story based on the original screenplay *Held* by
Susannah Rose Woods and Suzanne Kelman.

ISBN: 978-1-83888-034-7
eBook ISBN: 978-1-83888-033-0

A VIEW ACROSS THE ROOFTOPS

SUZANNE KELMAN

bookouture

Dedicated to all the unsung heroes of Holland, who risked their lives during World War Two by hiding 30,000 Jewish people, the *onderduikers*, in their barns, attics, and basements. We may never know your names, but the legacy of your bravery will live on forever.

I looked out of the open window, over a large area of Amsterdam, over all the roofs and on to the horizon, which was such a pale blue that it was hard to see the dividing line. As long as this exists, I thought, and I may live to see it, this sunshine, these cloudless skies, while this lasts I cannot be unhappy.

—Anne Frank

Prologue

Holland, April 1921

Elegant white clouds floated in a perfect blue sky, casting shadows over fields of scarlet and gold tulips. A rippling wind moved through the fields, the only thing daring to intrude on perfect stillness. Its fearlessness caused the flowers to bob and weave like maids in a row. In the distance, along a well-worn path, an ancient windmill stood solemnly guarding the field. It towered above its budding subjects, its brown clapboard walls strong but worn, peeling and relentless against the passage of time. The red sails, now faded to time-worn pink, caught the wind and groaned a rhythmic chant as they creaked and toiled.

Bounding toward the windmill, a new bride ran ahead in playful chase away from her bridegroom through the rows of nodding tulips. Sarah, barely twenty-two, was already dressed for her honeymoon. A simple cream-colored cotton dress hung loosely from her delicate shoulders. Cream sandals emphasized her shapely ankles and her long legs, kissed generously by the early spring sun as she sprinted ahead of her husband.

Just a few short hours since exchanging vows, much of Sarah's wedding finery had already been carefully packed away in sheets of soft, white tissue paper. The satin shoes that buckled at the ankle, along with her dropped-waist, calf-length, silk dress, had been reverently tucked and folded by elderly female relatives and young unmarried friends. It was all nestled now in her mahogany chest, ready to delight the expected stream of family brides ahead of her.

Everything put away except the one thing she couldn't yet bear to surrender. Apart from the gold wedding band on her left hand, the only thing distinguishing her as a newly married woman streamed out behind her, waltzing on the wind—an antique lace veil, trimmed by her grandmother's aged and gnarled fingers, the exquisite fabric a bouquet of intricate daisy-chain stitches and miniature cream pearls.

As she ran along the colorful path, the wind picked up, a foil in the young couple's romp. All at once, a mischievous gust bridled her, tugging at the train and twisting it into a carefree, corkscrewed spiral that danced up into the sky. Josef caught up, through the lines of flowery guards, and leaped out in front of her. He was dressed in pleated linen trousers, and a blue linen shirt rolled to the elbows, exposing long, athletic forearms. His body was willowy but strong, and a shock of raven hair framed a face with piercing, expectant blue eyes.

He reached out, grabbing her around the waist, and pulled her toward him, playfully pinning her arms behind her back to gather her even closer. Her hot breath came in sharp, short gasps that warmed his cheek.

"Finally," he said triumphantly.

Sarah responded by giggling and trying to wriggle free as Josef attempted to unpin her veil. "I'm not giving it up, Josef. I plan on wearing it through the whole of my first year of marriage!"

Josef's eyes widened in amusement. "My mother would be horrified, since she already has plans to use it to trim our children's baptismal gowns."

"Children?" Sarah echoed. "We've only been married for four hours."

"Well, then," he said, in a decisive tone. "There is no time to lose!" Releasing her hand, he cupped her face, kissing her eyes, lips, and neck as she giggled in an attempt to squirm away from his advances.

"Not my neck, Josef. You know what that does to me."

Flashing her an all-knowing smile, he wrapped his arms around her, his mouth finding hers in a passionate kiss. In the distance, a voice called for them.

Sarah grabbed Josef by his shirt collars and pulled him down into a dip among the tulips as the long veil, whipped up by the wind, entwined the pair of them.

"Shhh," she whispered. "If we stay still and out of sight, Mama will not find us."

"I'm not complaining," Josef whispered, pulling down the billowing fabric that had encircled his face. He adjusted their position, laying an arm beneath her to protect her head from the stony earth.

They lay facing one another, waiting wordlessly for the footsteps to fade, their breath slowing into a unified rhythm. Deep in the heart of the field, the scent from the tulips was intoxicating. Sarah rose on one elbow and looked down at Josef with thoughtful eyes.

"I loved your father's gift," she whispered.

Josef shook his head and smiled. "My father is a romantic and always has been. He puts all his faith in the power of words of love." Josef rolled onto his back and interlinked his hands behind his head, looking up toward the wispy clouds. "I can't believe he read poems at our wedding. When I'm a mathematician! What do I need with such things? I think he holds out hope that one day, somehow, his precious poetry will find room in my heart. Even now at the age of twenty-eight."

Sarah pressed her lips together and thrust out her chin. "How can you say that? What is life without art, music, or poetry? It helps us know how to feel, love, and live!" She rolled onto her back and focused on a cloud that looked like a cantering pony. Coyly, she added, "I started to fall a little bit in love with your father as I watched him reciting. The way he looked at your mother showed all the love they'd shared for so long."

A look of real surprise crossed Josef's face.

Sarah continued, sighing, "I'm not sure how long our love will last if you don't know how to keep love alive like that. I can't see mathematical equations making me feel quite the same way."

Rolling toward her, he brushed aside an auburn curl from her heart-shaped face. "What do you mean? Mathematics can be beautiful. Euler's Identity is said to be the most beautiful equation in the world." He continued with intense romantic emphasis, "$e^{i\pi} + 1 = 0$."

Sarah closed her eyes and wrinkled up her nose as she shook her head, flicking her copper curls to flash her displeasure.

He pulled her in close again and whispered into her ear, "How shall I keep my soul from touching yours? How shall I lift it out beyond you toward other things?"

Opening her eyes fully, Sarah broke into a broad smile as he continued to recite the poem "Love Song" by the contemporary poet, Rainer Maria Rilke. She showed her appreciation by covering his face with tiny birdlike kisses and then slowly unbuttoning his shirt.

He continued to whisper the words of the poem as he nuzzled her neck and caressed her body.

"All right," she whispered, "you can have the veil. What shall we call our son?"

He looked deep into her eyes before answering. "Sarah." He smiled assuredly. "It will be a daughter and we will call her Sarah."

She started to protest before he silenced her by covering her mouth with a lingering kiss. As their lovemaking fell into a gentle rhythm, all that could be heard was the soft creaking of the windmill as its sails lifted toward the darkening sunset sky.

PART ONE

Chapter One

His vision, from the constantly passing bars,
has grown so weary that it cannot hold
anything else. It seems to him there are
a thousand bars; and behind the bars, no world.
—*Rainer Maria Rilke, "The Panther"*

Amsterdam, February 1941

Relentless, biting snow fell in icy sheets upon the war-torn streets of occupied Holland, forging heaps of gritty gray slush, suffocating a town already stripped of its humanity. The steely mounds of snow were pockmarked by ugly splatters accumulated from a week of frigid temperatures, dirty roads, and ricocheting stones splayed by hapless drivers. Gray snow on gray streets smothered by a bilious sky of the same dispiriting color. To the Dutch, this bleak weather reflected a world that felt the same.

Down a dark residential street came the hollow echo of hobnailed boots, the now-familiar sound of a column of marching Nazis. As the feet pounded the roadway, the cadence grew ominous in its rhythmical element, each hammered step casting forth a web of piercing foreboding, like a pound of steel nails shaken aggressively in a tin box. In the nine months of occupation, the Third Reich had already proven itself an evil beast not to be trifled with, a bloodthirsty jackal, primed and alert, ready to take down and devour whatever stood between it and conquering for the Führer.

Amsterdam, once lively and carefree, with an opulent brilliance, the apple of the Netherlands' eye, had high hopes of defeating the invading forces, but instead, as the rest of Holland, fell to German Blitzkrieg in just four days. Its heart now stood wrenched open and forever wounded. Its previously unblemished optimism, not unlike the heaps of ice on the ground, forever tarnished, pebble-dashed and smothered by the dark forces of evil that had also arrived in gray.

As the sound became deafening on the quiet city street, behind locked doors and shuttered windows, fearful faces froze, eyes closed in silent prayer. Chilled souls hoping that their one defiant act of un-parted curtains would signal their united scream of resistance, allowing them to hang onto the last strands of their civility. The footfalls faded, but the fear lingered much longer than the echoes. Only once there was total silence did they allow themselves the luxury to breathe and return to the business of surviving. Thanking God once again—not this street, not this day.

Across town, a ticking clock matched the rhythm of the marching feet. Professor Josef Held stared at its white face and sharp, black hands, unaware of the dangerous rhythm it marked time with. The clock hung high on a wall, watching over a large classroom filled with rows of students. A high ceiling held aloft by ornate limestone cornices gave way on one side to dusty but ordered bookcases, and on the other to an elegant bank of windows.

Professor Held worked wordlessly, grading papers at his desk. An awkward middle-aged man of forty-seven, seemingly uncomfortable in his own skin, he rarely looked up. When he did, a ghost of handsomeness lingered about him. It seeped out through his perfect blue eyes and striking black hair, only beginning to gray at the temples. And even though he had spent his life bent over this one desk, somehow his body managed to retain a semblance of youthful tautness more suited to a retired athlete than an unassuming mathematics professor.

In his classroom, the regime of marching soldiers seemed far away as diligent students set their minds to work, with shirtsleeves rolled to the elbows and heads bent over heavy oak desks. Other than the ticking of the clock, there was nothing to hear except the occasional hushed cough or a busy pencil scratching dry paper. The room seemed timeless, and the hours endless. As the hands of the clock finally met at the midday hour, a weak sun fought its way through the hopeless slate sky and grazed the high windows.

Held exchanged one math paper for another, and stopped. Upon the sheet in front of him there was no math, no answers to the numbered problems. Instead the page was covered with a poem, "Panther," written by Rilke, his late wife's favourite poet. Shaking his head, he sighed, exasperated, not wanting to think about Sarah today. He took off the silver-rimmed glasses that were a well-chosen prop for a man who wanted to buffer himself from the outside world. Gently he placed them on the desk and rubbed his eyes before replacing them, one loop of hooked wire at a time, back on his face. He looked at the clock and cleared his throat. "Class dismissed. Mr. Blum, I need a moment of your time."

University students quietly filed out the door, escaping the stifled silence of the room. One student, Elke Dirksen, her lovely eyes filled with concern, lingered in the doorway as she watched Michael Blum stride toward the front. With his good looks, Michael seemed like the best of what youth could offer. Twenty-two years old, vibrant, and with a restless charisma. Michael's eyes sparkled with defiant humor as he winked at Elke in the corridor.

Professor Held waited at his desk for the classroom to empty while he stacked his papers into an orderly pile. As the room grew silent and the door closed, he pulled Michael's paper to the top. He spoke directly to him without looking up. "You are aware, Mr. Blum, that this is an advanced mathematics course."

Michael laughed.

After many years of teaching, Held was unaffected by insolence. "This is not the first time we have had this discussion. You have written on your assignment again rather than solving the formula as requested."

Michael balked. "What? You don't like Rilke?"

Professor Held continued, "That has nothing to do with it. Poetry belongs in books, not on mathematics papers."

A sharp intake of breath from Michael lasted a split second before it dissolved into a tone of controlled bitterness that brimmed just under his words. "It's no longer so easy for me to just buy… books. Do you even know who he is?"

For the first time, the older man looked up. "I beg your pardon?"

Michael became animated, enthusiastic even. "Rainer Maria Rilke. The poet? He is considered one of the most romantic—"

Professor Held tried to stop Michael short with a raised hand.

Michael's face registered angry frustration. Then he continued, "Look, none of this matters anyway, because today is my last day."

Professor Held lowered his eyes and dragged a new pile of papers toward himself. As he did, he pushed Michael's paper across his orderly desk. "Please complete the assignment."

Michael shook his head. "Today. Is. My. Last. Day. I am not going to sit here waiting for them to come after me. And I will not be forced into the Arbeitseinsatz."

Held looked up briefly. So many of the young men were being forced into working in German factories; resisting could be dangerous. He wanted to say as much, but instead he retreated back behind the safety of his wall.

"Still, you need to complete this assignment."

Michael snatched up the paper. As he leaned forward, a flyer fell out of his satchel onto the desk. The corner was torn off. Michael had obviously ripped it down, probably in anger. It was instructions ordering all the Jewish people to register. Both men stared at it and froze. The ticking clock and muffled sounds in the hallway filled the deafening space between them. Held realized all at once that Michael was Jewish, and he felt helpless, wordless. Wanted to take back his severe manner, but before he could say anything, Michael picked up the math paper and slowly and defiantly crumpled it into a ball and dropped it on the professor's desk.

"Do you honestly think that any of this is important? The courage to fight and to love—that's all that is important right now. And you won't find any of that in a mathematical formula."

Slowly pushing his glasses farther up his nose, Professor Held stared at the ball of crumpled paper.

Elke opened the door. "Michael! Come now!"

The sound of marching feet echoed down the hall toward the classroom. Michael moved swiftly toward the door.

Held opened his desk drawer and pulled out a book. It was a well-worn copy of Rilke's *New Poems*. He signaled to his young student. "Before you go, Mr. Blum—"

Michael turned and Held pushed the book across the desk. Michael approached, curious, in spite of himself. Noting the title, he opened it reverently. Held watched him read the inscription on the first page, handwritten by his father.

"To Josef. Sometimes the most courageous love is whispered in the quietest moments."

Meaningless words from a very long time ago, Held mused. He returned to his papers and with a dismissive wave of his hand muttered, "Keep it."

Michael clasped the book to his chest. "Really? Thank you. Thank you, very much."

Uncomfortable with this show of emotion, Held pushed his spectacles higher up his nose and nodded, shuffling papers awkwardly about the desk.

Michael turned to leave and then stopped at the door. "I guess it's safe to tell you now that I hate mathematics."

Held scoffed, then muttered, more to himself than to Michael, "So I have surmised."

As Michael reached the door, Elke pulled him quickly by the arm into the corridor.

Held noted the empty place where the book had sat unopened for many years. He took a deep breath and closed the drawer. He was about to return to his grading when he noticed something on his desk. Gingerly, he picked up the flyer Michael had dropped.

The classroom door opened, and Held called out, "Mr. Blum, you forgot…"

But instead of Michael, he was surprised by Hannah Pender. The new university secretary, a striking woman with fine cheekbones and thoughtful blue eyes, was rarely seen away from the front desk. Her clothes today, he noticed, were a dark blue A-line skirt, that hugged her hips and emphasized her shapely legs, and an ivory-coloured blouse with a lacy neckline. As she walked in, she spoke in perfect German to a serious-looking Nazi officer who followed.

A small group of soldiers accompanied him and stood to attention outside the door, their severe gray uniforms sharp-edged and out of place against the elegant high-banked windows and pleasant wood-paneled hallway.

"This is Professor Held," Hannah said. "He tutors advanced mathematics." She approached his desk. "Hello, Professor. We are just checking on your students."

Held responded, bewildered, "My students? My room is empty." Under his desk, he clutched the census notice in his hand. He didn't need any questions about why he had it or why it had been torn down.

Hannah smiled nervously and nodded.

The Major walked purposefully around the classroom, taking in every detail. Stopping at the large arched windows, he looked up, seemingly mesmerized by a spider building a web in a high corner outside. As the spider bobbed and wove its gossamer threads, a gentle breeze captured its work and rocked it like a hammock at sea. In the classroom, the only sound, the ticking clock, built its own tension with each stroke marking time. A bead of sweat formed across the bridge of Held's nose under the rim of his glasses, and he quickly swiped it away with his free hand. The Major turned slowly to face Held.

"Professor Held? Interesting name."

The professor nodded slightly.

The soldier approached the desk, speaking in German. "I believe that word is the same in Dutch as it is in German, meaning 'hero.' I hope you are not planning on being one."

Held methodically pushed his spectacles farther up his nose and looked up at the officer, answering him in Dutch. "I'm afraid I am."

A curious expression crossed the soldier's face, accompanied by a forced smile; he knotted his eyebrows as if he were weighing up the professor.

Held continued with his well-versed return. "I teach literature students who would rather be learning the classics how to understand algebra."

The soldier realized the professor was joking and laughed. A forced, overblown laugh meant for show, controlling and demanding attention. He recovered quickly and took a long, hard moment to scan Held's desk as he nodded slowly.

Professor Held shifted in his seat and glanced at the wall clock. "Is there anything else? If you don't mind, Mrs. Pender, I do have to prepare. I have another class arriving soon."

Ignoring him, the Major walked back toward the window and looked out at the icy view once more. Through the feeble shafts of sunlight, columns of sleeted snow started to fall again. Mrs. Pender smiled awkwardly at Professor Held. As they waited, the air between them felt like it tightened. Eventually, the captain turned. "I think teaching is a fine profession and, as long as you keep your heroics to algebra, things will go well for you."

With that, the Major nodded before striding out of the room. Mrs. Pender followed. Held waited until the footsteps faded before letting out a ragged breath. He screwed up the census notice and dropped it into his wastepaper basket.

He stood and stretched before walking to a cupboard at the back of his classroom, where he took out a small key from his waistcoat breast-pocket to unlock the door. The cupboard was completely empty except for a pristine wireless with a rich, mahogany veneer. Held reached in and turned the large dial. The display glowed, and the wireless crackled into life. Lilting classical music filled the dry space and cut through the suffocating air. Sitting back down at his desk, he removed his glasses, closed his eyes, and took a deep, slow breath.

At the end of the day, Held added a new equation to the blackboard to be solved by his first class, wrapped a wool scarf tightly around his neck, and put on his coat. With his hat and satchel in hand, he exited the classroom. Moving wordlessly through the corridors, his eyes cast down, he gave an air of deliberate aloofness. As a result, no one talked to him or even acknowledged him. It was as if he were invisible. Making his way to the university's main desk, he noted Hannah Pender instructing a young woman about her duties.

Mrs. Pender turned and spoke. "Oh, and here is Professor Held," she said to the young girl. "Good evening, Professor. You will want your mail."

Held nodded.

Hannah turned to instruct her protégée about which pigeonhole to fetch it from. As she moved around behind her desk Held pretended to be focused on the mathematics book he was holding, but couldn't resist giving her a sideways glance. She was very attractive, he mused, more attractive than the woman who had just retired from the same job. She had been square-built, with wiry hair, a constant look of disappointment, and the beginnings of a mustache. This new secretary, this Hannah Pender, was very different.

"So sorry about the intrusion today, Professor," she continued, turning to him as he looked down quickly toward his hands. "We have so much to do, and we have the German Army to answer to as well. As if I weren't busy enough. And now I have this young girl, Isabelle, all they could spare me, who I have to train, and as you know I have only been here a few weeks myself…"

As she chattered on, Held waited, watching her, trying not to draw attention to the fact he was studying the shape of her face and her soft brown curls.

Isabelle, a mousy girl with wispy, brown hair tamed into a hairclip, appeared at Hannah's side and handed her a bundle of mail, which Hannah then presented to Held. Hannah continued to chat about the weather, her workload, and the drop in enrollment as he quietly shuffled through his letters. As she leaned forward to await his instructions he caught a wisp of her perfume, violets or maybe it was lilac. Not wanting her to see how much of a distraction it was to him he hastily replaced a couple of pieces of mail on the desk and put the rest in his bag, turning quickly and saying, "Good evening, Mrs. Pender."

Hannah took his discarded mail and smiled. "Good evening, Professor."

Held nodded, put on his hat, and walked quickly toward the main door.

Out on the street, the morning chill had returned to herald the evening. Pulling his hat down farther on his head, he moved mutely through the streets on a well-worn route toward home. After picking up his evening groceries, he turned into Staalstraat, where a commotion of angry, volatile voices confronted him. A young couple were having an altercation with a German officer. People everywhere stopped, watching from a safe distance. Helpless despair hung in the air as thick as the blanket of cold around them.

Held noted people's faces—the shock and the horror, but also the fear, as if any of them could be next.

The soldier was yelling something about *identiteitsdocumenten* and the young woman started to cry, pleading she was on the way to the doctor and just forgot to pick them up. Held turned and kept moving, keeping his head down, deliberately looking in the opposite direction as the woman started to scream. He assured himself this would all be over soon. It had to be. He picked up his pace as he turned into his street. Still able to hear the echoes of the Jewish woman screaming, he tightened his scarf around his ears to block it out.

He pulled out a key as he reached the stone steps that led to the simple brown door of his three-story house. Behind him, the sound of two soldiers marching encouraged him to unbolt the lock and step inside without hesitation.

Putting down his satchel and small cloth shopping bag, he turned on the light. It illuminated a life that was neat and functional but devoid of warmth. A young gray cat raced up the hall to meet him, meowing incessantly. Held came to life. "Hello, Kat, I brought you a little something from the market. How was your day? Mine was interesting."

Following Held up the hallway and into the kitchen, Kat watched intently as he put out scraps of fish in a bowl and then made himself a cup of tea.

He looked at the clock on his kitchen wall. "It is almost time," he informed Kat. "I wonder what it is going to be tonight."

Above the sink in his kitchen, he unlatched the heavy shutters and opened the windows wide. Methodically, he began his nightly ritual. First, he carefully arranged a chair to face toward the window, then he sat, added a plain woolen blanket to his knee and, with tea in hand, waited expectantly.

The cat jumped up into his lap. The last weak rays of evening light illuminated the darkness and streamed across his face. All at once, the awaited event began. Delightful piano music from next door danced through the window.

He educated Kat as he stroked his lean body. "Ah, Chopin, one of the nocturnes."

He closed his eyes and took a deep breath.

Chapter Two

Michael gazed down at Elke; her eyes were closed and her soft brown lashes still. Her long, chestnut hair, ends damp with perspiration, lay heavy upon her chest, masking her bare breasts. He leaned down and kissed her lips. As he pulled away, dragging the sheets to just under her chin, she moaned.

"No more, Michael, I'm tired."

Moving his hands below the sheets, he started to stroke the length of her body with just the tips of his fingers.

"Stop." Her eyes flashed, confrontational. "Don't you know there is a war on? We should conserve our energy."

Michael lifted himself gently on top of her, enjoying the feel and weight of their naked bodies pressed together as he whispered into her hair, "That is exactly why we should be making love. Who knows how long we have left."

Playfully, she pushed him off her and returned the sheet close to her chest. She sat up and ran her hand through her messy hair. "Do you want some coffee?"

Michael sighed, rolled onto his back, and nodded. "If that's the best you can offer."

Giggling, she jumped up, taking the sheet with her and wrapping it around herself toga-style, leaving him naked on the bed.

As she moved toward the front of her houseboat, she looked back at him stretched out the length of the bed, as he pretended not to care he was naked and sheet-less.

"I am just going to lie here until you are overcome by my incredible body and beg me to make love to you again," he informed her.

She shook her head before moving to the kitchen to make coffee and, standing waiting for the kettle to boil, looked over at her latest painting—an unfinished vase of sunflowers she'd been working on—with a self-critical eye. Michael noticed her shiver, her body reacting to a night that had descended into bitter cold again. When he heard the kettle boiling, he stood and dressed himself in her orange robe that he had found on the back of the bedroom door. He grabbed the book of poetry, the one Professor Held had given him, from the nightstand and joined her in the small galley kitchen.

Elke smiled at his ensemble, but her look changed to concern as she noted what he was carrying. "You should be careful. You know you're not supposed to have books."

Michael puffed out his cheeks as he flicked through the pages. "Let them try and take it from me. They can take away my freedom, but they can't suppress my thoughts or mind. I refuse to give them either of those."

Worry crept into her tone. "What will you do now though? These new laws are saying you can't go out after 9 p.m., read books, study…'

Michael shut the book thoughtfully. "I haven't given it much consideration, but maybe I'll stay here, write poetry, and cook food for you all day. Imagine the sheer luxury of hiding away writing poems day after day."

"No, seriously. Have you thought of leaving? I'm not sure how difficult it would be, but maybe you need to try."

"And go where? I am Jewish. And even though I haven't practiced my faith since my grandmother's death, still that's how our new German guests see me. There is no place for me right now. Besides, I would never leave my beloved Amsterdam, nor you."

She smiled and interlocked her fingers with his. "This is the first time I have really heard you talk about your faith. Does it worry you that I am not Jewish?"

He looked at her with surprise. "I barely feel Jewish myself. Yes, it is my race. And yes, when I was young I went to the synagogue. And I suppose I liked the way the Rabbi recited the Torah, but I stopped believing in God, when He took all of my family from me." He found it hard to keep the pain from his voice as he continued. "As you know, my father was in the Great War, so it wasn't exactly a shock when he died because of his injuries, but when my mother was struck down with tuberculosis a year later and I had to watch her fight for her every breath, and my grandmother died just weeks after, I knew I could never believe in a just and kind God again. Even less so as this war goes on, and my people are persecuted."

His voice petered out, with the emotion it still aroused in him, as once again he felt the isolation and loneliness that he'd experienced when he'd lost all of his family before the start of the war.

"You will always have me," Elke whispered. "And if our relationship progressed to something more…'—she blushed slightly—"permanent, then I would be willing to convert if you wanted me to."

"More permanent," he repeated with a tone of mock surprise, as he reached forward to take her in his arms. "That sounds rather lovely. Though I would be surprised if there is a Rabbi left to marry us. I think they've all already gone into hiding." He leaned forward and brushed her chilled lips with a kiss. "Don't worry so much. This thing has to end soon, and in the meantime, we will continue to fight hate with love."

He attempted to cup her breast again, but she took hold of his wandering hand and placed a mug of coffee in it. "You are incorrigible."

Chapter Three

That same evening Hannah Pender made her way home from her job at the university, clothed in her navy-blue felt hat and coat, leather gloves, her tiny waist emphasized with a wide, black, patent-leather belt. She moved at a fast clip through clouds of her own icy breath that numbed the side of her face as she walked. On the corner of her street, she stopped. Even in the cold weather, she took a moment to look up. Though chilly, it was a beautiful twilight evening. She admired a chevron of birds returning for the spring, forming long dark streaks across the red-marbled sky that stretched above her.

"Red sky at night, shepherd's delight," she said out loud to herself and smiled. Her great-grandmother had been British, and she'd heard her say that many times. As she continued to stare up, a young boy came running toward her.

"Hannah, Hannah, it fell out!" he yelled with gusto as he beamed at her. He pointed to a gaping hole in the front of his mouth, where a tooth had been the day before.

She smiled and crouched down to meet him on his level. "Let me see," she said, a glint in her eye.

Even with his mouth wide open he continued to talk. "I found a five cent coin; it was under my pillow this morning."

Hannah stood to her feet. "Well done, Albert. Did you have to force it?"

Albert shook his head a little too vigorously. Then, sensing her lack of belief, added reluctantly, "Well, maybe just a little."

Hannah ruffled his hair, and then he ran off to announce his achievement to someone else. She was charmed, reminded that not everything was swept away by such desperate times; innocence still prevailed. Teeth fell out of children's mouths, and swallows still built spring nests.

She turned the corner and noticed a woman standing in a doorway, waving vigorously to her. It was her mother's old friend, Mrs. Oberon, whom all the neighborhood children called "Oma", meaning "Grandmother". She was a tiny older woman bundled into a fringed shawl and a dark, heavy skirt. Upon her feet, thick black stockings and traditional wooden clogs. As Hannah made her way up the path, the woman tucked a few strands of gray, greasy hair back under her threadbare headscarf and fingered a brown paper package clasped in her dark, wrinkled hands. At five foot six, and in her high-heeled shoes, Hannah towered over her.

"Wool for your mama," Mrs. Oberon said with a full gummy smile, thrusting out the parcel. "I would take it myself, but I have stew boiling on the stove."

Hannah took it and and bent down to hug the woman. "Thank you, Mrs. Oberon. You shouldn't have. She'll be so grateful."

Oma shook off the thanks with a flick of her hand. "Clara has done so much for me over the years, especially when my husband died. It's the least I could do. Besides, I had to wait in line anyway."

She kissed Hannah warmly on both cheeks. As Hannah moved off down the road, Oma shouted after her, "Give her my love."

Hannah waved back her response.

As she stood waiting to cross the street, a truck pulled in front of her and came to an abrupt stop in traffic. Sooty, angry smoke and the putrid smell of gasoline fumes caused Hannah to take a step back as the idling truck rocked in front of her. It was German. Heaped in the back were piles of bicycles.

Hannah sighed as she thought of the waste. The metal and rubber were apparently needed for the war effort, but everyone knew it was just another ruse the Germans were using to suppress them and take away every aspect of their independence and freedom.

As the truck pulled away, something flew off the back and clattered to the ground. It was a pedal that had worked itself loose from an overhanging bicycle. Instinctively, Hannah reached down and picked it up. She slipped it into her pocket and continued down the street to her door.

Walking up the path, she admired the indomitable boldness of crocuses springing up either side, fighting their way up through the frozen earth. Beside her door, a red-and-blue painted milk jug had been turned into a home for a nest of daffodils.

She placed the key in the lock, and her cheery, warm home was a welcoming sight to her as she stepped inside. Her paneled hallway was painted a soft, muted lemon, and hand-painted blue plates were displayed with honor on high shelves. As she closed the door behind her, the mahogany grandfather clock that dominated the hallway pounded the five o'clock hour in deep dulcet tones, wrapping its familiar arms around her to welcome her home.

From the sitting room, a strained, older voice called out to her, "Hello, dear."

Hannah took off her coat and hung it on a wooden peg. "Hello, Mama," she sang back.

She found her mother in her usual chair in the sitting room, bent over her latest knitting project. Her hair, like fluffy cotton wool, framed her wrinkled face, which broke into a broad smile, not unlike her daughter's. She looked up to her with pensive eyes reflecting the same shade of blue.

"Still so cold," she said, shaking her head.

"Yes, it is." Hannah nodded as she picked up the thick woollen shawl that had slipped to the floor and placed it around her mother's shoulders. Then she added wood to their fire.

"Did you get anything new today?" asked Clara, spotting the package Hannah had temporarily laid at her feet while she fixed the fire.

"Yes, I have something for you from Mrs. Oberon."

Clara dropped her knitting needles to her lap and her eyes danced with anticipation. Hannah loved to see her mama so excited.

"Well," said Clara, impatiently, "do I get to see it?"

Hannah moved across the room and dropped the wrapped bundle into Clara's upstretched arms. Even though they were twisted with arthritis, her mother's hands still managed, somehow, to undo the package in record time. Then she clasped them together with joy.

"Green. Perfect. It will do so well for a new hat for Pieter, if I can get that scoundrel to keep a hat on!"

Hannah looked down at the soft skeins of forest-colored wool as Clara's artful fingers smoothed them out on her lap. "Mama," she laughed, "are there any Dutch children left in Holland who aren't wearing one of your creations?"

Clara chuckled to herself and returned to her discarded project. "It's my own personal act of resistance," she confessed. "I plan to keep all the young boys in Holland warm even if I can't keep them safe."

Hannah shook her head and moved to the kitchen to place the kettle on the stove. As she returned to the sitting room, she noticed her mother's hands gripping the chair arms.

"I need to stand, I'm getting stiff," she announced, shooing away her daughter's attempts to help her as she slowly pulled herself up. Her body took a few moments to uncurl, and she hobbled her first few steps. Then she straightened and walked stiffly on her cane toward the window. "How was the university, dear?"

Hannah was pensive; she wondered how much to tell her mother. She settled on, "More of the same. Fewer students, more rules."

As Clara tugged at the curtains, she looked out into the twilight and became thoughtful. "It's hard for anyone to breathe in all of that, so much sadness in the air. Sometimes I'm glad I'm house-bound. I'm not sure I could take it. I'm sure if I ever get out I'd be locked up in a cell the very first day for selling secrets to the British or knocking down one of those German soldiers with my cane."

Hannah smiled as she moved about the room, straightening things. "You would be Amsterdam's greatest secret weapon for sure, Mama. Who would expect a white-haired knitter of espionage? I don't doubt you'd take out the whole German Army single-handedly if you had the chance."

Clara agreed by waving her cane in the air. She made her way to the other curtain and steadily pulled it closed.

Hannah removed the kettle from the boil and steeped tea, then unwrapped a thin sliver of meat from brown paper and added dark bread and fruit, for their dinner. After they finished eating by the fire, Hannah went into the hallway to retrieve the Underground newspaper *Het Parool* from her satchel, which one of the teachers had given her at work so Clara could read it. As she fished in her coat pocket for a pen, in case her mother wanted to circle articles for Hannah to read later, she found the pedal she'd slipped in there. Picking it up had been instinctive, like taking something back from the Germans, something that belonged to them. But now as she looked at it, a thought struck her.

"I'm just going out to Poppa's shed," she shouted over her shoulder after she'd delivered the newspaper to her mother's eager hand. Clara now hunched even closer to the fire, nodded as she started to scan the headlines.

Pulling on a coat, Hannah went through her back door and down a narrow stone path to the bottom of their tiny garden. It was unusual for Dutch homes to have back gardens, but their house edged onto a small area of woodland and her father had negotiated a deal for a tiny lot when he'd bought it. Opening the two large wooden doors to her father's workshop, she was transported back in time. The smell of oil and dust greeted her as it had ever since she was a little girl. Reaching up, she pulled on a light just inside the door. A single light bulb swung back and forth, clanging against its own metal chain as it illuminated the whole room. A wayward moth flew inside, drawn toward the light, and its wings brushed against the bulb, creating a crisp, ruffling sound. She looked around, breathing in deeply, allowing the memories that cradled her to fill her with the awe she always felt every time she walked inside. Her father's presence, large and looming, still felt as if it occupied all this space. She looked down at her hands then opened her fingers one at a time to offer up the pedal to the room itself.

She was surprised to feel tears run down her cheeks. The time they were in right now, this war, could do that to her with memories of her late husband and her father. It was like her feelings were always just beneath the surface.

She closed her eyes and imagined her father's large bear-like hand reaching forward and taking the pedal from her, his thick dark eyebrows knotting as he peered over his reading glasses to see what she'd given him. His deep rolling voice would say, "What do you have here for me, Hannah Bear?" Carefully he would have rolled it around in his considerable hand, inspecting it as if she'd brought him a treasure from a far-off place. Then, no matter how insignificant the gift, he would have placed both his hands around hers, saying, "Thank you, darling."

Hannah swept away the tears and made her way farther into the shed, to the workbench that had been left just the same as when he had died. She placed the pedal on the desk next to the last project he'd ever worked on, a tricycle for one of the children down the street.

As she walked around surveying all the workshop had to offer, she shivered and pulled her coat tighter around her shoulders. Her father had been a bicycle enthusiast. There were chains and deflated, flabby inner tubes hanging on the walls, spoked wheels and discarded leather seats stacked in one corner. Yellowing posters of bicycle events and advertisements covered every available wall. Rickety, dark-green shelves overflowed with cans of paint, lubricating oils, and saddle glue.

As she continued to circle the room, she became transfixed by a bright-colored poster of a heavily-mustached man in knickerbockers and a bowler hat balanced precariously astride an elegant penny-farthing bicycle. As she read the words—*Just what he needs!*—under the advertisement, she was struck with an idea, the thrill of it taking hold of her all at once.

She moved over to her father's dusty, but ordered, bookshelves and looked for the book she wanted. Smiling to herself, she pulled it down from the shelf, rubbing the dusty cover with satisfaction. Turning on her heels, she left the shed and turned out the light. Maybe there was something she could do with all this sadness.

Chapter Four

Held left his house the next day, on Saturday morning, locked the door, and made his way to the centre of Amsterdam. Every weekend, he met his niece, Ingrid, for lunch. The only daughter of his late brother, Marcus, he felt he owed it to him to be involved in Ingrid's life. She had been through so many hardships. Losing both parents to influenza at a young age had been a devastating blow for her. She'd been sent by her mother's well-meaning relatives to well-chosen schools, only to be told she wasn't quite the right fit when she habitually didn't complete her studies, having no care for her education in the least. She had struggled to make friends and to find her place in the world all through her turbulent childhood. Now in her twenties, all of that rejection had built up inside her and left a harsh, toughened exterior. But Josef still had a hope that one day she would soften into a sweeter person, more like his dear, mild-mannered brother.

His walk through Jodenbuurt revealed that the line for the bakery was long this morning. Downcast women huddled, wearing tightly wrapped headscarves and shawls, and clinging to empty shopping baskets as they talked in hushed, solemn tones. He turned the corner and walked past a blackened building that used to house the kosher butcher. The shop was boarded up after it had been abandoned and then set on fire. Newly splashed across the wooden front in black paint was the word "Juden." Held sighed. He missed the jolly butcher, Mr. Wolff. He'd been a large, happy man with a buxom wife and two lovely daughters. He would whistle while he separated generous beef shanks from their bones before carving them expertly with long, sharp blades, and entertain his customers with one more re-telling of his latest joke while he filled his immense scales with chunks of red flesh.

Held wondered where Wolff and his family were now. He tried not to think the worst or to believe the rumors. He preferred to believe the pleasant man was telling his jokes to a new crowd, in a safe place called Manhattan or maybe Cincinnati.

Turning into Amstelstraat toward Café Schiller, he noticed that the grubby piles of ice along the roadways were finally starting to melt. The weather must have climbed a few degrees higher. Though as he blew out thick, icy breath, the chill that set hard in his cheeks seemed to disagree.

When he arrived at the blue-and-white awning of the café, he looked through the window. Ingrid was already inside, with a cigarette held high in one hand, one leg crossed seductively over the other, which allowed her skirt to ride up more than was necessary. She sat posed at a table, thick blonde hair in a fashionable wave. Her overly made-up face made her stand out among the rest of the bleak, miserable clientele.

When he entered, she jumped up to meet him and kissed him on his cheek. "Uncle Josef!" She then flashed her eyes at two young German soldiers who had arrived behind him.

Held automatically pulled a clean handkerchief from his waistcoat pocket to wipe away the red lipstick mark he knew would be there.

They sat, and she dived straight into a conversation about her life and the new job she had just got. Changing jobs was not unusual for Ingrid, who never settled and somehow seemed to upset people wherever she went. Held listened as a dreary-looking woman brought him a glass of water and his usual sandwich.

As she trilled on, Ingrid's enthusiasm about her latest job was unmistakable. "I have my own office and everyone, especially Major Heinrich von Strauss, has been so nice to me."

Held, who had only been half-listening until that moment, stopped eating. When she took a second to draw from her cigarette, he broached his worst fear. "Ingrid, are you working for... them?"

She blew out a blue plume, responding indignantly, "Oh for heaven's sake. There's no 'us' and 'them' anymore. And don't tell me you've been listening to all the rumors and gossip. You are a professor, and I thought you'd have more sense. These are just ordinary people. Besides, they like the Dutch, and we're just like them."

The two German soldiers who had seated themselves close by laughed loudly, and Held shifted in his chair. Ingrid glanced across at them and flashed a bright smile.

He took a minute to steady himself. He looked out the window and observed a young family with heads downcast, who he pondered may well be Jewish, were obviously trying to not draw attention as they made their slow amble down the street. What would Marcus tell his daughter if he were still alive? Held knew she had a strong will and could be very stubborn. If he wasn't careful, he could push her in the wrong direction if he attempted to control her. Closing his eyes, the voice of the screaming Jewish woman from the day before came back to haunt him. No, he had to say something. Lowering his tone and looking directly at her, he nodded toward the young family.

"How can you condone this?"

She batted away smoke from her face. "Uncle Josef! It's all going to be all right! I'm thinking of joining the party myself. If we all just do what they want, everything will be fine. Heinrich told me so."

Held continued with concern, knowing how gullible his niece could be. "Jewish students are unable to go to school."

Ingrid became defensive. "Heinrich says they have their own separate schools."

Held was mute.

Ingrid took a sip of her own tea and pouted. They sat for a long moment. Then to break the awkward silence between them, she added, "We have nothing to worry about. *You* have nothing to worry about. You are not," she lowered her voice, "one of them."

Held tried to understand. "I'm not one of *them*?"

Ingrid's tone became tiresome; she continued as if talking to a small child. "Our heritage is clean! We are pure! We are not vermin."

Held could hardly believe what he was hearing, and his concern shifted to anger. "Vermin? People like my neighbor... a kind woman... a piano teacher... Why would anyone think someone like her was vermin?"

Ingrid crushed her cigarette into a battered metal ashtray and automatically lit another one as she became interested. "She is Jewish? And still living in your neighborhood? Has she registered? She could go to prison or worse if she hasn't."

Held felt his anger move suddenly to fear. As he lifted the glass of water to his lips, his hand trembled slightly. He allowed himself a second to answer, watching a wayward fly land between them on the table and start to rub its back legs together. He added, quietly, "She teaches music to local children. She has an illness that means she is afraid to leave her home, afraid of the outside world."

Ingrid screwed up her eyes in thought. "Still, she should have been moved by now."

Held desperately wanted to change the subject. "I don't know anything about that."

Ingrid took on a condescending air. "Well, why would you?" she bristled. Then, catching the attention of the German soldiers, she blew smoke in their direction and one winked at her in return.

Held pushed his uneaten plate of food away in quiet disgust. He suddenly felt sick and hot, as if the walls of the café were closing in on him. He should say something more about Mrs. Epstein, but he didn't know what. He could tell Ingrid that he had made a mistake, but he was a terrible liar, and she would surely know. Besides, that would bring more attention to their conversation. He looked at her warily; she was preoccupied, flirting with the soldiers. She was flighty and would probably forget what they had spoken of. Besides, he was sure Ingrid wouldn't say anything to anyone. She wasn't callous after all. She was Dutch, like they all were. Naïve, perhaps but not cruel.

He stood up. "I must go."

Ingrid seemed relieved and smiled in a placating kind of a way. "Oh, Uncle Josef! I wish you'd found someone to take care of you since Aunt Sarah died. Remember, just keep your head down, as you always do, and stay cheerful. I think if you give it a chance, you'll like the new Amsterdam."

Held placed money on the table. The continued searing heat coursing through his veins made his overcoat unusually heavy as he pulled it on and his mouth bone dry.

Ingrid jumped up and kissed him on the cheek, apparently leaving another bright red lipstick mark because she giggled at her handiwork. "I better wash that off, or someone might think you have a girlfriend!" She took a napkin, licked it, and scrubbed his cheek to his significant discomfort, but Held stood there somberly, reeling from the conversation and utterly demoralized.

Finally, he was able to move his feet and slowly make his way out to the street. As he stepped into the chilly day, the cold gave him no comfort. He turned to look back at Ingrid. He should go back, say something more. But before he could act, he noticed she had moved over to the table of the German soldiers and started to flirt openly.

Held walked home, preoccupied as a sickening concern took hold of him. There was so much evil around. Could it be coming to darken his own front door? He thought about Ingrid, the frightened child who had visited him not long after she had lost her mother. Wearing a simple checkered blue dress and a brown cardigan with a tiny hole in the elbow, she'd clung to her doll in his kitchen, looking for a hero. But he had been ill-equipped to take care of a young girl, too sad, still grieving Sarah's death. He had been more than happy to have other relatives step in and take her away. The hollow pain of his own sorrow was too great to bear when reflected through the grief in the eyes of a child. He remembered holding her small hand in his before she boarded a train, taking her away to another family member. As she waved goodbye through the window, he'd wondered who would repair the hole in her cardigan now.

What if his complete inability to care for her had let her down? Was it his fault there was such a huge hole inside her that she could only fill it with the evil that now waited for them around every corner? Was this how it started, the disillusionment of one's soul, an easy target for evil that came disguised as elitist acceptence?

As he turned into his street, his pace quickened. He needed to get home, needed to breathe, needed to feel safe again.

He entered the house, took off his coat, and walked straight into the kitchen. Ignoring Kat's plaintive meows, he opened the large wooden shutters. Icy air swirled in and filled the whole room. He stood with his eyes closed, desperately wanting relief. As the chill finally found its way through the thick fabric of his trousers, it took hold of his bones and calmed them, and he started to think clearly.

He would talk again to Ingrid. She would listen. After all, he was her uncle. He would explain about the danger in the simplest of terms. He would make her see. He *had* to make her see. Poor Ingrid with her simple, gullible ways. All she really wanted was to be loved. No wonder the striking officers with their slick boots and glossy propaganda had lured her. She was easy prey for evil.

A blast of frigid air moved through the kitchen, lifting the corners of a pile of student papers stacked on his table. It ruffled his hair, causing him to shiver. Then Mrs. Epstein's music began. Its familiar presence pacifying him like a child hearing a favored lullaby. He opened his eyes, and tears brimmed for the beauty of the music that filled his kitchen and gave him hope. It was a tune she'd been practicing for weeks, he didn't know it, but the notes were soothing and lyrical, rocking and comforting him. As he absorbed the music, a wave of reassurance flowed over him. It would be all right; it had to be.

All at once, sharp claws extended and retracted through the thick woolen fabric of his trousers, and he couldn't help but smile at the expectant, purring gray head. He reached down to pick up Kat.

"I guess you are hungry, my friend."

Slowly, he moved about the kitchen as the music turned his soul from night to day, hopelessness to quiet strength. He placed food in Kat's bowl then made himself a cup of tea. By the time Mrs. Epstein had moved on to Beethoven, he had settled in his chair by the window as the gentle strains surrounded him once more. He closed his eyes again, his heart and senses smoothed to an even keel.

Chapter Five

Professor Held observed his diminished classroom. So many empty desks. How was it that so many people were now unacceptable to the Nazis? He thought of some of the students who were now gone, good students, quiet, pensive souls who had only wanted to learn. What was so threatening to the Third Reich about someone wanting to understand the fundamentals of calculus? What terrible threat could a young person educated in adding and subtracting be to the world?

He thought of Michael Blum. Opening his desk drawer, he pulled out Michael's assignment, carefully smoothed it out and puzzled over the poem he'd transcribed, which was about a powerful animal being kept behind bars. In that instant, something in Rilke's words struck a chord in him—after many years of feeling trapped in his own emotional cage, he found himself understanding the plight of this panther Rilke had written about.

He placed the paper back in the spot where the book had been and closed the drawer. He wasn't sure why he had kept it. Perhaps some vague hope of satisfaction that would arise from giving it back to the student when this was all over, when everything was back to normal and the assignment could be finished. Somehow that appealed to him, being able to make things right in his own world. He closed the drawer and looked out once again at the empty desks. Taking off his glasses, he rubbed his eyes, then carefully replaced the glasses, and cleared his throat.

"Class dismissed."

The classroom emptied, and the room fell silent. There was a gentle knocking at his door, and he thought that maybe one of his students had forgotten a math book or pencil, but was surprised instead to see Hannah Pender hovering in the doorway. He beckoned her to enter.

She strode into the room, and once again he was struck by her beauty, her dark hair had recently been cut into a new shorter style and it emphasized the loveliness of her blue eyes. As she entered, he was quite captivated by their color and realized he had not looked into a woman's eyes in a very long time. He stood respectfully to greet her and there was that scent again. Definitely lilacs.

"Professor."

"Mrs. Pender." He noted his voice sounded strange, almost high-pitched and shrill. He coughed to clear it and disguise his discomfort.

She hesitated for a few seconds, as she weighed her words before she spoke.

"I believe you have a wireless."

Held drew himself up to his full height before answering. "Yes, why?"

Hannah shifted her weight her eyes cast downwards. "We have been ordered to collect all wirelesses."

For a second Held was speechless. "Ordered?"

"By the Third Reich."

Held continued to stare. "Why do they need my wireless?"

Nervously Hannah smoothed her skirt with her hands. There was an intense moment between them as their eyes met and he tried to process the information and the implications of giving up something so precious to him. He noted she looked—or perhaps was pretending to look—just as sad to be asking.

Hannah continued, "I'm sorry."

Slowly, he walked to the back of the classroom. His hands shook as he found the appropriate key, not only with what she was asking of him but also with the encounter; he reminded himself she was a married woman.

Turning the key in the lock, sadness struck him. Opening this one door had always been preceded by joyous expectancy until now. He pulled it open and lifted out the wireless. He could smell its polished wood as he carried it to Hannah and placed it in her expectant arms.

As he handed it over their hands grazed each other momentarily and he tried not to think about it as she started to apologize again. "I know how much your wireless means to you."

He shook his head, unable to speak. Unwilling to connect with the pain of losing his wireless, and thrown off balance by the softness of her skin brushing his and how aware he seemed of her.

He turned quickly, walking to his desk, and sitting down, he pretended to be busy marking papers.

Hannah followed him and appeared to want to say more but seemed lost for words. She hovered above him nervously, that scent of spring flowers permeating his whole space. He glanced up and she gave him a reassuring smile. It was as if she wanted to say something more, but for whatever reason didn't seem to have the courage. He looked back down and tried to focus all of his attention on his desk as she lingered a little longer than was necessary before finally leaving, and he breathed a sigh of relief.

As Held walked home that evening, he bought a bottle of wine with his groceries as he dwelled on his day. The loss was acute. He knew it was just a wireless, a thing, an object, but it was what it represented to him. Hadn't the Nazis already taken so much? Their town, their way of life, their hope. Why was one more thing so important? They were already stripped and surrendered. What was the point of taking even more? And what would they do with his wireless? The sting of resentment coursed through him as he imagined it taking pride of place in some Nazi's home or, worse, getting dusty on some German requisition shelf. What harm could come to Germany from a mathematics professor with a wireless tuned to a classical music station?

As he rounded the bend of his road, a German soldier approached and asked for his papers. For a second, he wondered if the officer had read his mind, sensing the seething anger he felt for that uniform right then. But the tired-looking soldier just inspected his papers as he waited, sickened by this day. He wanted to be home. After passing inspection, he walked to his door and thought of the bottle of red wine he carried in the cloth bag by his side. Not a regular wine drinker, he had decided he needed a glass or two this evening.

He was fumbling for the keys at his door when he heard a piercing scream coming from close by. Turning quickly on his heels, he could see nothing. Then, bursting through the hedge came his neighbor, Mrs. Epstein, clutching a pile of papers to her chest. The look of panic in her eyes was terrifying. Running straight up his steps toward him, she threw the whole weight of her body at him, grappling for his arms with her free hand. Held was frozen in terror. With her great fear of the outdoors, he had never seen her outside in the street before and knew that the situation had to be desperate in order for her to leave the safety of her home.

Then, in a frenzied attack, she snatched the lapel of his coat, jerking him so aggressively that he stumbled down his two steps as she pulled her face close to his. "Help me, please," she screamed. "Please help me!"

Before Held could even respond, someone was upon her. It happened so fast that over the many times he would recall the event, it would still have the turbulent confusion of a frantic nightmare; a fractured vision of jarring and maniacal memory. An arm around her neck, a gray-sleeved arm, wearing a black leather glove. Her petrified eyes imploring him like desperate prey caught by a bloodthirsty predator. The screaming, shrill and constant, desperately piercing his world over and over again.

And finally, her words high and frantic, the words that would remain with him forever. "No, let me go, please, please let me go."

Then with a final violent jerk of his collar, her white fingers, which had locked on and refused to let go, were aggressively torn from him. There was a stunned look of desperate futility on her face as she was dragged back through the bushes. His last image was a blur of a blue wool skirt and one black shoe left turned on its side on his path. And then, from just behind his shrubbery, the crack of a bullet, followed by deafening silence. And with that one sharp sound, the whole of Held's world fractured open.

He was unaware of the bag slipping from his hand, didn't hear the bottle smash or see the wine pour forth onto his step. He realized afterward that he must have closed his eyes because when he opened them again, the sky was filled with fluttering white paper. Sheet music raining down all around him. He remembered thinking how mesmerizing it was, like white rose petals stirred up by a mighty wind. Watching stupefied, incomprehensible horror was paused to anchor him to beauty. A hairbreadth of time to allow a chink of exquisiteness to drift through the cracks of weighty realization and the acrid smell of cordite that lingered heavy on the air.

Through the flurry of papers, he saw German soldiers coming toward him. In a moment of blind panic, he thought he would be next.

He couldn't move, his legs locked in cement. He willed them to move, looked down at them. His shoes were covered in red liquid. Was it wine or blood?

He looked up at the officer who was speaking but Held couldn't hear the words. The soldier repeated himself, and slowly sound filtered through.

"You are the professor?"

Without even being aware of doing it, he nodded. Held didn't have control of his own body; someone else appeared to be working it for him. He was just the observer watching from a safe place.

The soldier continued. "Held?"

Again, he nodded. Words were out of the question. Held caught sight of something on his shirtsleeve. Tiny red specks along the cuff where the arm of his coat had ridden up. He took a moment to process; it was blood.

The officer lit a cigarette and offered one to Held. He managed to shake his head.

The soldier continued in a tone the same as if they were discussing the weather. "Yes, Ingrid described you. You're her uncle, yes? We had been given a tip-off about this particular Jewess already, but I thank you anyway for your confirmation that she was here."

Held registered his niece's name. It sounded foreign and ugly coming from the mouth of this animal, a deplorable creature who had just casually taken the life of another human being a few feet away. A human being the enemy knew nothing of, blind to everything except that to them she was vermin. What confirmation was this man talking about?

Held became light-headed from holding his breath. The words of the soldier continued to reverberate as if he were yelling into a deep well and Held was imprisoned at the bottom. From the shattered shards that were his thoughts, one rose to the top, something so fearful and unimaginable that he felt he might throw up. A terrible realization, piercing his heart and soul with such acute precision the pain was even worse than what he had just witnessed. The officer was talking about Held's conversation with Ingrid.

The soldier continued, oblivious to the fact Held was about to pass out. "Yes. The sneaky Jews are the hardest to find. But we will find them thanks to the good Dutch, like Ingrid. Like yourself."

The German soldier picked up the wet cloth bag, now just a bag of broken glass, and handed it to Held.

His hand shook violently as he put the key into the lock and entered. Inside the house, he closed the door on the horror, fighting again for his breath. He slumped against the doorframe and then slid to the floor. Kat climbed onto his lap, purring and meowing his welcome.

Reaching out absentmindedly for any fragment of comfort, Held petted his friend. "Oh, Kat, what did I do?"

Held did not remember much of what happened in the next two hours, but he did remember pouring water on his front step in an attempt to wash everything away. He stood there in the dark night, uncaring of the blackout or the curfew, pouring pails of clear, cold liquid in a steady stream. The water bounced down the concrete steps onto his path, swelling and swirling, gathering mud and debris as it turned the red into pink. As he finished the task, he heard a fluttering, like a bird trapped in his thick hedge. The moonlight illuminated crumpled sheets of music, most of it caught and wrapped around a bush in his tiny front garden.

He took his time gathering all of them, straightening out the sheets the best he could. Then he placed them on his kitchen table. He wasn't sure why, but somehow it felt important. A physical reminder that what had happened to Mrs. Epstein had been real. He stared at the musical notes and saw this was a lively, upbeat piece, marked to be played *allegro*. He instantly recognized the placement of the notes, the music she'd been practicing for weeks now. It appeared to be a piece she had written herself. He pulled the title page close to his face to be able to read the two words written at the top in Mrs. Epstein's spidery hand. He whispered them to himself, "Mijn Amsterdam."

Chapter Six

As the cold day turned to night that evening, Elke lit long red candles around the houseboat. They bounced light off the windows into the overhanging eaves, casting a rich warm shadow across the boat. She stood barefoot on the red-tiled floor that she had painted herself, her hair was swept up in a messy bun and a thick woolen shawl draped around her shoulders. Humming in front of her stove, she stirred the pot of warm food that was to be their dinner. Elke always loved to make soup; it reminded her of her grandmother.

She had just finished painting and she could hear Michael playing her guitar on her bed. He was composing a song and was not to be disturbed, he'd reminded her in a severe, artistic fashion. Then, to soften his declaration, he'd added that it was a love song for her.

Elke continued to stir the wooden spoon around the blue enamel pot, listening to his gentle strumming. The soup started to erupt into tiny bubbles at the base of the pan that soon gave way to larger syrupy ones at the top. The smell of the carrots and potatoes cooking became intoxicating. Replacing the lid, she moved the pot to simmer and took time setting her tiny galley table for dinner. A vase of paper flowers she had made years before in art class anchored a Van Gogh-inspired tablecloth in vivid yellows and blues. Spoons sat arranged beside wide-brimmed purple soup bowls she had turned herself. Elke completed the arrangement by placing two oversized, mismatched wine glasses and a candle.

Going to a shelf, she took down a cheap bottle of red wine. Since the occupation, certain foods were hard to come by, but at least wine always seemed to be available. She turned the corkscrew, removing the cork and leaving the wine to breathe on the table. It would be a surprise for Michael, a frivolous indulgence from some extra money she made doing French translation work, a sideline she pursued to help fund her university education.

Next, she returned to the stove and wrapped the hot panhandle in a tea towel. She carried the pan to the table and filled the wide misshapen bowls with steaming orange liquid. She knew it was a little spicy, but she hoped the heat would help compensate for the lack of substance.

Elke called to Michael. The music stopped, and he padded barefoot into the kitchen.

"Umm." His eyes lit up as he caught sight of the table. "What do we have here?"

"My grandmother's soup. Well, half of the recipe," she added.

"I was talking about this," he said jokingly, winking at her as he picked up the bottle of red wine and started filling their glasses.

Sitting down on one of her hand-painted blue stools he looked like a young boy with his dark hair swept untidily about his face. Taking the spoon, he carefully blew, then sampled her offering.

"Oh my God, it is delicious. How did you know lobster soup was my favorite?"

She giggled at his joke as she brushed a stray hair from her forehead and drew herself closer to her bowl. Suddenly she remembered something. "I forgot we have bread," she said with wild enthusiasm. Jumping up, she went to a small cupboard painted red with blue handles and opened it, pulling out a dry-looking loaf. She placed it on a breadboard on the table along with a blunt-looking knife. "It's a little crusty, three days old, and we have no butter. But it was free."

Michael attempted several times to cut a slice, but to no avail. The blunt knife just slid around the rubbery crust, not even breaking the surface. Giving up on the knife, he ripped off a ragged chunk and handed it to Elke.

"For you, my lady."

Elke bobbed her head. "Why thank you, kind sir," she joked as she took the wedge of bread and attempted to soften it by dunking it in the soup.

"How were things out there today?" he asked, watching her spoon in a softened chunk and then catch drips of the thick soup with her fingers as the liquid ran down her chin.

"Fine," she said, then lowered her eyes.

He stared at her for a long moment.

She sighed. Michael could always read her; she had been attempting to put this from her mind. "Mr. Meir the shoe repairer had his windows smashed again today, by Dutch people who support Hitler, and no one did anything. I think even the police are afraid to stand up to the injustice now. All because it was rumored that maybe his father was half-Jewish."

Dropping another lump of the hard crust into her bowl, she picked up her spoon and attempted to smother it by scooping soup from around the edges. When she reached for her wine glass, tears blurred her eyes.

Michael reached forward and covered her hand with his own. "I am going to be okay. You have to stop worrying."

As she stretched her hand toward him, he gently held it in his, stroking the back of her hand with his thumb.

Elke waited to regain control of her emotions before she spoke again.

"How do you know? Every day they are finding more and more Jewish people. I cannot believe that our friends and families, the people we have known all our lives and trusted, are telling the Germans where to find them. Then, once they arrest them… I have no idea where they are taking them, but the rumors are awful. I can't sleep with the nightmares." Her voice cracked as she finished her thought.

Michael moved to her side and crouched down beside her.

"People are scared. They hope by giving the Germans what they want, things will be easier for them here. You must stop worrying. It will destroy you. You need to stay positive and strong. Otherwise, you will go mad. I am going to be okay, I promise you. You have to believe me. I don't know how I know, I just do."

He reached up, gently taking her in his arms and releasing her hair from its messy bun so he could stroke it. Michael comforted her as she silently allowed the emotions of the day to sweep over her. He pulled her closer and rocked her gently until her sobbing slowly subsided.

He spoke again, and a defiant resilience underscored his tone. "I am not afraid. I am going to find a way to fight this. I don't know how, but I will. So I can make your life safe again." He gently drew her back in his arms so he could look into her eyes and wipe the last of the tears from her cheeks with his thumb. "Then one day I can marry you and give you two plump Jewish children. Though I suppose maybe you would need to convert, if you wanted them to be Jewish. But either way we will call them Hansel and Gretel!"

Elke buried her head deep in his shoulder, smothering her laughter before making a muffled response. "But we are Dutch. Those are German names."

"Ah, good point," said Michael, pulling away from her to reach for a handkerchief in his pocket. "We need good Dutch names. How about Ot and Sien then?" Making a reference to her favorite Dutch children's story.

Elke continued to giggle as she blew her nose on the handkerchief he handed her.

"Sounds great," she said sarcastically, relaxing a little. "The perfect names for twins."

They returned to their dinner, devouring every bit of the warm soup as their conversation returned to other things, like the song he was working on and the terrible flu that was going around.

Once they had cleared the table, he announced there would be a special bedroom concert in her honor. With dirty dishes stacked haphazardly in the sink, he took her by the hand to the bedroom, and she sat down at the head of the bed as he picked up the guitar. Elke grabbed two pillows to lie across as he strummed gently and recited one of his poems that he'd set to music. She listened, enthralled as his dark eyes danced in the flickering candlelight.

When he finished, she clapped her hands enthusiastically. "Wonderful, but unfortunately I have nothing to pay you with."

Putting down the guitar, he prowled cat-like toward her on the bed. Then, in one swift move, grabbed her around the waist. It knocked her off balance, and she fell flat on her back, giggling.

His eyes shone as he brushed back stray wisps of hair from her brow and whispered, "I can think of something." He paused then, looked at her intensely, without the usual mischievous glint that always danced in his eyes. "You are so beautiful."

She dismissed him with a wave of her hand. "Oh, Michael."

"No, seriously. You are so incredibly lovely, a goddess. I have no idea how I got to be this lucky."

Her heart softened. "I wish we had met in an easier time," she whispered back. "I feel as if so much of our love has been corroded and corrupted by this awful war. Every time I see or hear anything about the Jewish people, my stomach knots and I can't imagine what I would do if you were taken from me."

"Shh," he said to quell her fears again. "You can't worry, my sweet Elke. I want you to be happy. Listen to me. If for some reason I have to leave, then you have to find your own path to peace and happiness. You cannot live with this fear. It will destroy your beauty from the inside out." And then he added with a mischievous smirk, "And then what will I have to come back to? This crazy old woman with wild hair who lives on a houseboat talking to herself."

Playfully, she punched him on the arm. "Don't even joke about such things, you are not going anywhere. You have to stay here with me, forever."

He pulled her close again, touching his warm lips against her cheek, the clean smell of his soap lingering on her skin. "Of course not. Just promise me, Elke, that you will not look back if for some reason we are separated? But that you'll find a way to be happy. Promise me."

She nodded slowly.

He became more intense. "No, say it. That's the only way I can stand being away from you for even one day. I have to know."

"I promise to find a way to be happy if... we have to part."

"Okay," he said, returning to a lighter tone. Rolling her gently on her back he kissed the palm of her hand. He caressed it, tracing tiny circles on it with his fingertips, before drifting up to her face. He took in every detail before kissing her lips then her cheek and starting to work his way gradually down the side of her neck.

"Now," he said as he slowly unbuttoned her blouse, "let's see about that payment for my song, shall we?"

Chapter Seven

As they pulled up in front of the Nazi Lieutenant Colonel's home, Ingrid couldn't believe the grandeur on the other side of the gleaming black Mercedes window. Since the war had begun, the scarcity around her had disgusted her, but now she felt as if she were dreaming. Once the car came to a stop, she noted the well-lit, majestic, white marble pillars. From their arches, a long line of bright red flags emblazoned with swastikas rippled gently in the cool night breeze.

A young officer saluted and opened the car door. Ingrid looked across at her companion. He was attired impeccably in his black dress uniform; his silver buttons shone, as did the high-topped boots. Every time she looked at him, her heart skipped a beat.

The young officer held out his hand and helped her out of the car. As she stepped into the night, she felt like a Hollywood movie star. All around her were officers dressed in the same smart uniforms. They stood talking and laughing in small groups, and more than one of them eyed her with delight. She loved the attention. She had worn an ankle-length black sequin dress with a tiny white fur stole that Heinrich had given her. He towered above her, and once again, pride swept over her.

A group of Nazis joined them, shaking hands and talking rapidly in German to Heinrich. They all laughed heartily and nodded respectfully to Ingrid as Heinrich introduced her.

Taking her by the arm, he then escorted her up the white stone steps and into the mansion. The inside was even more dazzling than the outside. A capacious, ornate white marble staircase dominated the entrance hall, and between each elegant crystal chandelier hung more banners of swastikas, swaying, ruffled by the heat rising from the room. As she fluttered about by Heinrich's side meeting people, she took in the affluence of the home. Heinrich would always introduce her as, "Ingrid, one of the good Dutch." This announcement would undoubtedly bring smiles and remarks such as, "Good for you" or, "Wonderful." She liked the idea of being popular, being one of the "good Dutch."

At one point Heinrich excused himself, letting her know he would be back with her shortly and he moved away to talk in a hushed tone to another officer.

While he was gone, she wandered about the room, looking at all the beauty, imagining a life with Heinrich and everything that would be hers. Because of him, she knew some of the wealth the German Army was acquiring, including the lovely fur stole she was wearing, and it excited her to think a life of struggle was behind her. She had been made for a life like this.

As she scanned the room, a young woman in a black uniform with a white apron moved toward her. The maid held a large silver tray in her hand, its crystal glasses filled to the brim with a sparkling, golden liquid. As she approached, Ingrid felt uneasy. The girl peered intensely at Ingrid in an odd manner before offering the tray while speaking in perfect Dutch. Ingrid vaguely recognized her from a school she had attended.

"Would you like champagne?"

As she spoke, Ingrid's hackles rose, not by the words but by how they had been said, with severe disdain.

Ingrid straightened to her full height. She had met jealousy before, and she was pretty sure this was what this was. Ingrid responded back in her own cold, condescending, tone. "Yes, I would." She swept a glass from the tray and gave the girl a small smile, hoping that would be the end of it.

As Ingrid turned her back, the girl continued. "I heard it is very good," she spat. "I hope it is worth it."

Ingrid turned again to face her, but the girl just stared back at her with hate, and then she was gone.

What had she meant by saying she hoped it was worth it? Ingrid was livid. How rude. She had heard that many were unhappy about being forced to work for the Germans, but why was she so hostile? Surely she saw the honor it was? As she sipped at her champagne, she decided she would make sure to vet all the girls that would attend to her and Heinrich at their own dinner parties.

Heinrich re-joined her, and they continued to make the social rounds. The thin, spidery Lieutenant Colonel with a hooked nose and hair slicked in a side parting sidled up to her and introduced himself as the host of the party. Taking her hand in his, he kissed it, lingering far longer than was necessary, flirting openly.

"So, Ingrid, how are you enjoying the new Holland, and my new home?" he asked casually, sweeping his hand about the room.

Ingrid smiled. "Very much," she answered. "I think this occupation is the best thing to happen to this country."

He ran his eyes up and down her slowly. "You look very beautiful tonight; I am honored to meet such a lovely young lady." Ingrid beamed. She didn't find him desirable in the least but it was still lovely to be flattered. Then, firmly taking hold of her arm, he whispered close to her ear, "Are you exclusive to Heinrich?"

The insinuation of his comment shocked her, and she laughed nervously, believing it to be aggressive flirting. Pulling away, she changed the subject. "I do love your home," she stated merrily. "I would love to see more of it."

The Lieutenant Colonel's eyes lit up, and he asked something of Heinrich in German too softly for Ingrid to quite follow. Heinrich, who was engrossed in an intense conversation by her side, nodded his consent.

The officer took her arm and tucked it under his own. "Let me give you the grand tour then."

Uneasiness gripped her, but she put it down to the fact she was new to all this, men escorting her around mansions. He led her up the wide marble staircase, slowly taking her room by room. She tried tactfully to move away, but at every chance, he pawed at her or rubbed the hollow of her back. Now that she was alone in such an intimate setting, she wished she had asked Heinrich to join them. She tried to pull away from his advances and move about the rooms instead. The sheer beauty was staggering. High arched windows with a magnificent view of the Herengracht canal. Upholstered gold-fringed bedroom chairs. Rich mahogany desks. Walls adorned by many exquisite tapestries or magnificent murals.

"Did you furnish this yourself?" she asked, running her hand along a smooth marble-top desk.

The officer looked a little irritated at her question. "The place came with many of the furnishings you see here, but I have added a few pieces myself, of course."

"How wonderful," observed Ingrid, taken by the beauty of red velvet curtains that hung in front of a group of floor-to-ceiling windows. "How considerate of the previous occupants to let the house with all this furniture for you to use."

The officer bristled. "They were going away and no longer had need of it." Then he quickly changed the subject. "Come, I want you to see the best room in the house," and he took her stiffly by the arm again.

He walked her into an immense bedroom with a full marble ceiling, its circular center design an exquisite mural of plump cherubs playing gold harps. A magnificent ornately carved bed with an abundance of tasseled red-and-gold pillows dominated the room. Escorting her to the bed, he sat down. She managed to extract herself from his grip and tried to appear interested in the ceiling.

"My bed is very comfortable," he purred, and smiled in such a way it peeled his lips back, showing his teeth and making his hooked nose appear even more prominent. He patted a spot beside him. "You should try it," he whispered, looking her up and down, hungrily.

She ignored him and turned her head away. In one swift move, he reached out, yanking her arm and pulling her to the bed, jerking her down beside him. She bit her lip to stop herself from yelping in pain. She willed herself to retain an appearance of sophistication.

"You see?" he said, leering toward her so closely she could smell the alcohol on his breath.

As he released her arm to brush her thigh with his hand, she saw her opportunity. She jumped to her feet and hurried toward the bedroom door. "I really should get back to Heinrich. He will be wondering about me."

She didn't look back, but dashed out of the bedroom and down the hallway toward the stairs. On the way, she decided not to tell Heinrich about the incident since she didn't want to spoil their perfect evening. Besides, she thought as she caught sight of herself in a large gilded mirror at the top of the stairs, it was hardly the officer's fault. She *was* looking decidedly lovely tonight. She smiled to herself and darted down the marble staircase and back to Heinrich's side.

He nodded to her, and she grabbed another glass of champagne from a passing tray and knocked it back in one gulp. Taking another one immediately after, she drank it a little slower as the bubbles started to do their work.

The rest of the evening she followed Heinrich around, meeting more guests until they found themselves in an elegant ballroom. Someone was playing traditional German drinking songs on the piano as inebriated soldiers drank and swayed, singing raucously around her, and she felt more relaxed. Heinrich lit them both a cigarette and pulled her down onto his lap. A small, adoring group had formed around them. As she took yet another glass of champagne, one of them asked her if she liked the house, and already forgetting the unfortunate incident in the bedroom, she gushed about the beauty of all the rooms she had seen. Then added what she planned to do in her own home when the new Amsterdam was completely established.

Enjoying the attention, she returned to her flirtatious self, crossing one leg seductively over the other, allowing her evening dress to creep up in a way she knew showed off her curvaceous legs to their best advantage. She held a glass of champagne high, saying, "And I will have red velvet curtains."

They had all cheered at that, and Heinrich kissed her neck playfully. "And so you shall, mein liebling."

Chapter Eight

Just after midnight, Michael and Elke were violently awoken from their deep sleep by frantic knocking on the houseboat door. Michael's eyes flashed open, aware the world around him was rocking. Elke uncoiled herself from him and sat upright. Shock penetrated her whole body. Someone must have jumped onto the boat.

As they leaped out of bed, angry shouting came from afar, repetitive German words that they couldn't make out, echoing across the silent, inky darkness of the canal.

Michael grabbed his trousers and ran to the door to look out the window at a lone dark figure hunched by the houseboat door. He couldn't make out who it was, but it certainly was not someone in any sort of uniform.

The banging continued, then a frantic hushed voice came through the woodwork. "Michael, hurry! It's me, David!"

Relief swept over Michael as he recognized the voice of his childhood friend from synagogue. A panicked Elke rushed into the galley, pulling a sweater frantically over her head, her legs still bare.

"Who is it?" she whispered, her voice trembling.

"It's okay. It's okay. It's David."

Michael pulled his clothes from the bedroom and threw the rest of Elke's clothes at her as they both started dressing hurriedly in the kitchen.

The urgent voice came again. "Michael, are you there?"

Michael hissed back, "Yeah, hold on." He buckled his trousers and then turned to make sure Elke was covered before he opened the door.

David practically fell in, terror evident in his eyes. "They are coming for you, Michael. You have to go. My father overheard Mr. Kratz from the bakery telling the Gestapo about you staying here, unregistered. I ran here as soon as I could, but soldiers watching the curfew saw me and chased me. We have to go. Now!" David started to cough.

For a wild second everything in the room froze.

As Michael threw on the rest of his clothes and shoes, a look passed between him and Elke. They knew this was it. The war had finally found its way to their precious houseboat, and this was just the beginning. The running, the hiding, the constant fear. It was as if, in that instant, he knew—and by the look in her eyes, so did she—that once they left the houseboat, the whole world as they knew it would change.

As Michael pulled on his jacket, he did something he would question for years to come. Why he did it, he wasn't sure. Instinct, some higher sense, or maybe God. Like a person running from a burning building able to snatch up just one last thing, he grabbed Professor Held's book of Rilke's poetry from the table and stuffed it into the pocket of his jacket.

Elke was putting on her jacket too, and the pain of seeing her dragged into this was overwhelming. "You don't have to come. You'd be safe. You're pure Dutch."

She snapped back at him, "Who's in love with a Jew!"

It landed hard in his soul; he had caused this. In his selfish need to have her, be with her, he had put in danger the one thing that made life worth living for him. His sweet, wonderful Elke.

She appeared to read it in his eyes as they moved toward the door. She practically pushed him through it. "Don't worry about me. I will go to my sister's place for a while. I will be fine, but you have to go."

They moved out into the night. Farther up the towpath, two German soldiers were searching some bushes a little way off. As all three of them started to run, one of the soldiers spotted them and shouted, "Halt!"

Sprinting along Oudezijds Voorburgwal, they didn't look back but could hear the soldiers giving chase. The clatter of their hobnailed boots followed closely behind.

Cutting away from the towpath, they raced over the Armbrug bridge heading toward the residential part of town, where it would be harder for them to be followed. The snap of bushes breaking behind them and then the cracking of a gun kept them running. As they arrived on the main street, the group raced down a dark passageway hidden from the road. It was a shortcut for Dutch schoolchildren. Stopping halfway down the alley overshadowed by a row of houses, they flattened themselves against the damp wall. They waited with their breath coming thick and fast as the clash of the metal-studded boots grew louder and then slowed to a clip behind them. They heard the soldiers searching gardens and thrashing at bushes with the barrels of their rifles near the alley's entrance.

All three of them continued to remain still, their bodies close to the wall. Michael knew that as they came out the far end of the passageway, they would be in the street again and able to be easily spotted, but he had to make sure Elke was safe.

He whispered to her, "Stay here. David and I will run out the other end. They will see us and follow, and once they are chasing us, slip out of the opening and go to your sister's."

Elke became frantic, and he could hear the panic even in her whisper. "Michael, I don't want to lose you. I want to go with you."

He grabbed her ice-cold hand and pulled her face close. "You have to do this, Elke. You have to be brave. I will find you, I promise. Meet me in our special place, tomorrow, right before curfew, okay?"

Elke squeezed his hand so hard it was as if she was somehow trying to take the last of what they had between them with her.

His hand stung with her grip and the cold. He gathered a handful of her brown hair and pulled her in for an intense kiss.

"You have to do this, Elke. You have to be strong and remember what you promised me."

The footsteps approached the end of the alley. As torch light probed the dripping walls, they all automatically dropped to a squat. The flicker of frantic torchlight illuminated the wild fear in her eyes. Michael shook his head, reminding her to not give up. Grabbing David's arm, he signaled that they should run out the other end of the alley. David nodded. Michael turned to Elke, gesturing her to stay put.

He sprang to his feet and raced to the end of the alley, his steps echoing as he exited into full view farther up the road. The soldiers spotted him with David following close at his heels. As Michael had hoped, the soldiers gave chase along the roadway, trying to head them off as they exited the passageway.

One soldier's voice echoed through the night, "Halt." Then in crude Dutch, "Or we will shoot."

Chapter Nine

That same evening Josef stood in his dimly lit kitchen, bent over the sink, sleeves rolled up, arms turning red in the scalding water. He couldn't believe so much had happened in one day. He scrubbed at the spots of Mrs. Epstein's blood on his shirtsleeve with a kind of desperation. It was very late and the whole house was silent, as if holding its breath, waiting to see if Held could remove the gruesome memories of the day by frantically scraping blood off the stiff fabric. As the water in the sink turned a faint pink, Held fought to keep at bay the one vision that kept wanting to haunt him. Ever since the incident with his neighbor, it had resurfaced. He had not thought about his beloved Sarah for so long, managing to keep it locked away in a dark place. Never to be revisited. He had packed away the memory as he had packed away her clothes. But since that afternoon, and Mrs. Epstein's death, reminiscence of her hovered dangerously at the threshold of his thoughts, ready to break in and devour him.

As if his thoughts had come to life, there was an urgent knocking at his kitchen door. For a minute Held thought it was his imagination, but the rapping came again in quick succession. Dropping the sleeve into the sink, he turned off the kitchen lamp, fearful that light had leaked out into the night and he was about to get another visit from the enemy. He just couldn't face dealing with one more soldier this evening.

As the frantic knocking continued, he took a deep breath and opened the back door. Like a fox with a pack of hounds on its tail, Michael Blum bolted past him into the kitchen. He wrenched the door from Held's hand and slammed it shut behind him.

Flicking on the light, Held struggled to put all the pieces together. This was one of his students, the Jewish boy. Why was one of his pupils here at his house? As he tried to make sense of this highly unconventional situation, he looked questioningly at Michael, who stared back, silent, but with frantic eyes.

Finally, between gasping breaths, Michael spoke with a bravado he clearly did not feel. "Well, hello, Professor!"

"Mr. Blum."

Michael continued in his cavalier way. "Would you believe that I thought you might have missed me?"

"What are you *doing* here?"

"I… wanted… to… return your book."

Held was confused. "What are you talking about?"

"The Rilke poems," Michael said as he paced the room, eyes darting about, his breathing still frantic. He looked as if he were making this up as he went along. Held knew the look; he had seen it on many students' faces over the years when they were fearful of getting a low grade for not turning in a paper on time.

Held shook his head. "How did you find me?"

Michael opened his jacket and held up the book. "Your address was inside."

"What?"

"Inside the front cover."

"What?"

"Your address. In the book."

"That still doesn't explain…"

A reddish-brown smear across the front of the book caught Held's eye. He noticed a similar smear on Michael's hand and arm. And in that instant, Held knew. Once, he'd had the same dark smears on his own body. As his eyes took in the young man's clothes, he noted the dark sticky red patches on his shirt were also clinging in maroon-tufted clumps to his thick woolen jacket. Blood.

Everything around Held stopped, and that one memory, the one he had been fighting to suppress all night, the one from so long ago, came back with such force, it was as if he had been hit in the face with a hammer. It split his mind, gripped his heart, took his breath. Sarah's face, blood everywhere, her emerald eyes cold and still, as if somewhere behind them the light had just been snuffed out.

Abruptly, Held was shaken from his waking nightmare by more pounding on his front door. Both men were startled. As Held took in Michael's fearful stare, he suddenly seemed very young.

Wordlessly, he pointed to the closet in the hallway as Michael ran in and crouched down inside. Held grabbed a red plaid blanket from the shelf and covered him.

Taking a minute to steady himself, Held picked up Kat and, with a long, slow breath to calm himself, opened the door.

On his doorstep stood the same German officer from earlier that day. But gone was the polite familiarity. Instead, his tone was clipped and professional. "Professor Held. Sorry to disturb you at this late hour."

Held forced himself to sound nonchalant. "Good evening. What can I do for you?"

Without being invited, the officer stepped inside. "We are having trouble with some runaways, whom we believe to be Jewish. We dealt with one of them."

Held's breath caught in his throat and a knot tightened his stomach, the experience of just what that phrase could mean still a little too raw in his memory.

"Two of our patrol officers tracked the last one down to this neighborhood. We have soldiers blocking the roads, which means he must be hiding somewhere very near here."

He forced himself to remain calm as Kat squirmed in his arms, apparently annoyed at being held for so long. "I do not understand how I can help."

The officer looked around the hallway. "Have you seen or heard anything this evening?"

Kat finally had his way and jumped down from Held's arms and approached the closet sniffing, obviously intrigued by the fresh scent of blood.

The professor shook his head with conviction. Hoping that would be the end of it. "No. Not at all."

The soldier nodded, looking concerned. "We would like to search your house, to make sure you are safe."

Held wanted to stop him but was at a loss for words. Before he could say any more, the officer motioned to four soldiers standing in the shadows. He shouted gruff commands in German.

Held finally found words. "I don't think—"

The soldier reassured him. "It won't take long. We are under strict orders from Major von Strauss to make sure you are kept safe."

The soldiers rushed past him and into the hallway. They moved quickly upstairs and could be heard searching efficiently, relentlessly.

In the hallway, the German soldier took out a cigarette. "May I?"

Held was flustered. "Of course."

Mechanically, he moved to the kitchen to retrieve an ashtray he kept in the cupboard, making sure to pick up Kat on the way, who still had his nose pressed against the hall closet. He reached for the ashtray on its shelf but turned back toward the hallway when he noticed long blood smears leading to the closet from the kitchen. Probably from Michael's shoes. Thinking quickly, he snatched up a bottle of dark vinegar from the open cupboard and smashed it on the floor, covering the stain. Kat leaped from the professor's arms in terror as the soldier approached the kitchen.

"Professor Held?"

"I am so sorry!" muttered the professor. "I knocked it from the shelf while getting you an ashtray."

The soldier surveyed the pool of dark liquid and broken glass and shrugged.

On his hands and knees, Held mopped up the spill as the other soldiers came downstairs and started to search the ground floor, moving around him in the kitchen. One soldier reached for the handle of the hall closet door.

Held stood silently with the dripping cloth in his hand, the stench of vinegar hanging heavy in the air. The soldier pulled open the door and pushed the plaid blanket aside with a gun. Held girded himself, trying to think of what he would say. He prepared for the worst. But after a minute, the German stepped back into the hallway and closed the closet door.

As the rest of the soldiers filed back outside, the young officer nodded at Held. "Sorry to have bothered you, Professor."

Held dropped the cloth in the sink and followed them to the front door. He was trembling so hard he had to grab the edges of his trousers to hide it, though he somehow found an easy tone to reply, "That's all right."

As the officer descended the front steps, he shouted back toward Held, "Be sure to lock your door."

The professor waved stiffly and nodded. "Yes, yes, of course."

Silently, he closed and bolted it. Placing both palms against the panel of the door to ground himself, he shut his eyes and took a moment to breathe. Held steadied himself and moved to the closet. Opening the door, he drew aside the coats and then picked up the red plaid blanket. Michael wasn't there. Following him into the closet, Kat started to paw at the red wool. The professor looked through the coats in the dark cupboard. From above his head, a large box began to move, then dropped to the floor. Somehow Michael had managed to cram himself up behind three boxes on the high shelf, which couldn't be more than three feet wide.

Held shook his head in disbelief. "How…?"

He helped Michael extract himself, and they both moved into the kitchen, the smell of vinegar still heavy in the air.

He looked again at Michael's bloodstained shirt. "Where are you hurt?"

Michael's eyes revealed an overwhelming pain. "It's not mine."

They both took a moment.

Held moved toward the kitchen door. "You need to change your clothes."

Michael started to protest.

"I'll get some," Held continued. "Throw those on the fire."

He went to his bedroom and brought down clean clothes. When he came back, he found Michael, who had moved into the sitting room, staring blankly at the fire. Held handed a pair of trousers and a shirt to him, and Michael nodded his thanks.

"Do you need anything else?"

"I could use a drink."

"Yes, of course."

"Thank you, Professor, thank you so much." Michael sounded exhausted.

Held went to the kitchen, where the sleeve of his own blood-stained shirt still sat in the pink water. He snatched it up and, taking out all of his own frustration, squeezed out every last drop of the water. Pouring two large glasses of brandy, which he kept for medicinal purposes, he returned to Michael and handed him a drink. Then he tossed his own damp, soiled shirt onto the fire with Michael's clothes. The fire hissed and smoldered for a minute before erupting back into a blaze once more.

Held picked up his own glass of brandy and joined Michael, who now sat buttoning up the shirt Held had given him. They drank in silence.

Staring numbly at the fire as it hungrily licked yellow flames around the fresh kindling, Michael quietly asked a question. "Why didn't you turn me in?"

Held was silent for a moment, overcome with the exhausting emotions of the day.

Michael looked across at him. "You could have."

"No. I couldn't. I have seen enough blood today."

Michael nodded, his eyes showing fresh pain. "Me too."

After they both had finished another glass of brandy, Held got up and fetched a neat pile of folded blankets. "Come."

Held showed him to the bathroom, where Michael cleaned himself, then had the young man follow him up a flight of stairs to a door on the first-floor landing. Held opened it and revealed another steep, thin wooden staircase. At the top of that was another door into an attic.

"You should be safe up here, even if they come back to search, this room is often overlooked."

The door looked more like a closet, and was tucked out of sight from the staircase meaning they both had to duck their heads to enter. The professor turned the key and opened the door into an airless, dusty space. At one end was a small window with a cracked pane, where a sliver of moonlight shimmered through, illuminating a tiny patch on the wooden floor. There were boxes stacked at the back and against the other walls and a gray camp bed folded neatly away, a relic from the professor's childhood when he would camp with his father. Held handed the blankets to Michael, who stood despondently watching him put the bed together. Once he was finished, he nodded and moved toward the door.

Michael's voice reached out to him through the darkness. "Professor?"

He stopped and turned. "Yes?"

"Thank you. I'll be gone tomorrow."

Held nodded. "Goodnight."

Closing the attic door, he moved back down the stairs, realizing how ridiculous his parting word had sounded. What could be good about this night? Once again in his kitchen, he sat in a chair and put his head in his hands.

Chapter Ten

After a night of troubled sleep, Held lay staring at the stark white ceiling, thinking about both Michael and Mrs. Epstein. As he focused on the tiny crack that snaked its way across the plaster, her terrified face swam into his consciousness once again. He attempted to calm his rapidly beating heart by taking long, slow, deep breaths and squeezing his eyes shut once more.

Listening to air moving in and out of his lungs, he felt exhausted, having fought and lost an endless night of gruesome nightmares, filled with fearful faces, and the sound of screaming. He tried to sort through the onslaught of feelings that assaulted every one of his senses, but the graphic images ran wild and untethered through his thoughts as he tried and failed to file them tidily away in his usually ordered mind.

As he attempted to focus on anything else, he still kept hearing the piercing sound of gunshots. Caught in a manic loop in his memory, it was only intensified by the smell of the vinegar that still clung to his clothes and his hair. Its strong putrid scent pulled him back to the horrors of the day before.

He reassured himself over and over again that he was okay as he tried and failed to make any sense of it all.

He rose from the bed and moved to the bathroom, reassured by the rhythm of his morning routine. He washed and dressed, fed Kat some breakfast, and forced a little food down himself before gathering some supplies. Then he made his way to the attic.

Michael, already awake, sat on a trunk, staring numbly at the cracked window, where weak morning sun managed to force its way through the dusty pane. He looked quite ridiculous in the professor's clothes. Held was reminded again that, despite his cavalier manner, Michael Blum was still so young.

Held closed the door behind him, but still Michael didn't move.

"I am going to the university."

Michael nodded.

On a wooden chest, Held put a jug of water, a few crackers, nuts and an apple. On the floor, he placed a chamber pot.

"Best to stay out of sight just in case." He nodded toward the supplies. "This should keep you for today."

Only then did Michael turn to look at him. "Thank you, Professor. I'll leave tonight just before dark."

Held nodded. "Yes. That would be best. I will be home later." Held moved toward the door.

"Professor?" He turned. Michael's tone was sincere. "I know we've never exactly got along that well—"

Held put up a hand before he left. "I will see you this evening."

Downstairs, the professor put on his overcoat, hat, and scarf, picked up his satchel, and left the house, carefully locking the door.

Trying to find his equilibrium, he followed his impeccable routine and took the usual route to work with his head down. As he concentrated on the hollow, echoing sound of his footsteps, he tried once again to desperately control the memories of the day before, memories that seemingly now sat on the edge of every part of his reality. He felt vulnerable. Years of a carefully constructed wall, trying to feel nothing at all, had been laid to waste in just one day. It took all his strength to stop the overwhelming thoughts taking hold and crushing him.

Arriving at the university early, he attempted to ground himself by paying attention to every detail, craving the comfort of the familiar—the usual creak of his classroom door as he opened it, the smell of wood and dry air mingled with chalk dust. He took off his coat and hung it on a hook with his hat and scarf. As he walked to his desk, he noticed the equation he had placed on the blackboard. Had it only been the evening before? So much had happened.

Anger brimmed inside his heart. Anger at the Germans and anger for the senseless waste of life, but mainly anger toward himself. How could he have been so foolish? Now a woman was dead; a sweet, simple soul who just wanted to bring music to the world. He swallowed down the hot rage and tried to stomach his own bitter guilt.

Unconsciously he walked to his cupboard and unlocked the door. The empty space inside was raw and shocking. He had completely forgotten he no longer had his wireless. His heart ached for the music that could have soothed his spirit and helped with this pain. Replacing the key in his pocket, he left the doors of the cupboard swinging open, not bothering to lock them again.

The day passed excruciatingly slowly as he seesawed between a heightened sense of fear and the weight of crushing pain. He had spells when he would forget the horror, though briefly, moments of disappearing into the refuge of his mathematics. Then he would remember, and his conflicting feelings would slam into him once again like a stone wall. At one point, in a wave of panic, he opened the drawer and pulled out Michael's assignment and stuffed it into his pocket. He wanted nothing to be there that could link him and that particular student.

Late in the afternoon, Held looked up at the clock and couldn't believe there was still an hour more of this final class before the end of his day. Outside the high windows, rain had started to fall in long, sleeting sheets, its presence sure to remove any last traces of the lingering ice. For the first time he could ever remember, he couldn't wait to get out of the classroom after this last class. He had been desperate to escape his home that morning, and now the same desperation compelled him to leave the university.

As he scuttled down the cold hallway toward the main door, a familiar voice called after him, "Professor Held! Your mail."

Held turned. Hannah Pender's attractive, worried face looked across at him from her desk.

"Yes. Of course, Mrs. Pender." He approached her.

Hannah observed him carefully, her tone more concerned than friendly. "How are you, Professor?"

He nodded.

"I am sorry about yesterday."

Held was taken back by how she had found out what had happened to him, before realizing she was talking about the wireless, nothing else. Afraid of the weight of emotions brimming just under the surface, he fought his feelings down by striking a serious tone. "My mail, please."

As he watched her retrieve his letters, he wanted to tell her that his inability to meet her eye wasn't about a wireless, but because he was afraid if he started to speak he would break down right in front of her. He also wished he could share the burden he was carrying with someone, especially a person with such kind eyes. But how could he trust her? His thoughts flashed back to before when he had seen her speaking in German so comfortably with the Major. Telling anyone was too dangerous. He couldn't risk putting Michael in jeopardy.

Sheepishly, she handed letters across the desk, speaking in rapid sentences. "I really am sorry about your wireless. If I could have stopped them taking it, I would have, believe me. I felt awful asking you for it. I know it means a great deal to you. I can't understand what on earth they would want with them..."

As she rattled on, Held looked into her lovely face and was struck by the ridiculousness of it all. She was talking about the wireless. Just twenty-four hours before, he had been so upset by an object, and now... His thoughtful silence provoked Hannah to reach forward and cover his hand with her own to comfort him. Her eyes were filled with warmth.

Shocked by the sudden effect of her touch, he withdrew his hand quickly and collected his letters. "Yes, well then. Good day, Mrs. Pender." He moved hastily toward the university doors before Hannah could say another word. Looking back swiftly over his shoulder, he noticed she was watching him intently as he exited the university.

Striding into the street, he pulled his scarf tightly around his neck to protect himself from the pelting rain pouring down with a vengeance. The sheer deluge, coupled with the bleak temperatures, lashed down on him in long, wet, icy streaks, slicing into his body and thoroughly soaking every piece of clothing. It matched his mood exactly.

Gripping his hat and the lapels of his coat, he put his head down and steered a course toward home. His nightly journey felt endless as he put one foot in front of the other. Not unlike the torrential rain that, even in his heavy overcoat and clothes, seemed to seep right down into his bones, so too the shock of the evening before sank in ever more deeply. The true weight of the injustice felt as if it would devour him from the inside out.

As he passed two Nazi-uniformed patrol officers, vehement anger coursed up his spine and vibrated through his whole body. Every soldier was now a representation of the one who had taken Mrs. Epstein's life. He wondered how he'd managed to avoid seeing it before. How he'd not been aware of the blatant evil living alongside him in the city.

Preoccupied with his new emotions, he crossed the street and a blaring horn shook him to the core. He realized he'd walked right in front of a Nazi officer's car. Through water cascading across a windscreen and manic black wipers, the uniformed driver glared at him before swerving and pulling away at speed. Held stepped back onto the curb and waved his apologies. Dazed and exhausted, he leaned against a lamppost to recover.

As he stood, rigidly waiting for the strength to move, he couldn't fight the frigid rain that rolled in a steady stream from the brim of his hat, down his nose, and off the end of his chin. Through the icy shroud, he saw his world with newly opened eyes, and it was raw and rancid. The boarded-up butcher's with the anti-Jewish slur painted across its door was highly offensive. The hopelessness in the eyes of two pale, thin Jewish men, sheltering in a doorway, gut-wrenching. The gray uniforms and rifles on every corner, truly terrorizing. And in the distance, rain-soaked swastikas flapping manically over their town hall, utterly suffocating.

Why had he not felt the true weight of what was happening around him? As he stumbled along the rest of his journey home, he was obsessed with just one thought. When had all of this become normal?

After the initial shock of Occupation nearly a year before, there had been a cowering; a nation victimized, a collective holding of their breath, their only hope a stoic wait-and-see attitude. But the daily erosion of their way of life had been constant, like drops of acid rain, each small but adding up to something deadly. For him, the changes had been minor enough that he had learned to sidestep each new reality, readjust, then find his new set point. But now, as he passed each corrupted building and each familiar, yet barely recognizable street, he realized how the German occupiers had devoured the city.

A group of rowdy Nazi soldiers in a *Kübelwagen* passed by him, laughing and joking with each other. Their frivolity sickened him. He increased his pace and focused on the forced breath that disappeared in chilly, damp clouds in front of him, knowing one thing: He needed to get home.

The storm finally eased as he reached his street, and the sweet smell of the smoky earth after the rain rose heavily in the air. Soaking wet and bone-weary, he stepped into his tiny front garden, averting his eyes from the darkened stain of the wine he had been unable to remove completely still visible on his step. As he placed his key in the lock, he vaguely became aware of a car drawing up behind him. Two car doors slammed, and a familiar voice rang out, "Uncle Josef!"

Rapidly, he turned around. Ingrid so rarely visited him at his home that he was disoriented, but he was sure it was her voice. As he looked toward the road, he saw a long, black sedan parked in front of his house. He was confused. Ingrid didn't own a car. Then, he saw who she was with. A tall, broad, impeccably dressed Nazi was walking toward him. For one second, Held thought this was a nightmare, some wild flashback from the day before, but that illusion was shattered when he saw the smiling face of his niece by the Nazi's side.

Warily, Held watched them march through the puddles on his path to greet him. Ingrid clipped along in a pair of glossy, red high-heeled shoes, her partner striding confidently by her side in black jackboots. Reaching the door, she greeted her uncle exuberantly, giving the appearance that they were being reunited after a long absence. "Uncle, darling, I'm so glad to see you."

Held was only barely aware of her gushing because all his animal instinct was heightened, focused on the tall, fair-haired man standing by her side.

Ingrid introduced her companion. "This is Major Heinrich von Strauss."

Held shivered and continued to stare, focused on only one thought: Why is there a Nazi at my front door?

Embarrassed by the silence, Ingrid continued, "Remember I told you about him?"

The officer extended his hand, crushing Held's own. "How do you do, Professor Held?"

Held removed his hand as he continued to drip, looking up at the man who towered above him. Under his officer's cap, he had neat blond hair, his eyes close and shrewd. He was almost painfully well-groomed, making it apparent this was a vain man who took a great deal of care in his appearance. As he spoke, he had a deep, forceful resonance. The voice of someone in charge.

Held answered automatically, "How do you do?"

They all stood for a moment, then Ingrid looked embarrassed again. "Aren't you going to ask us in?"

Held froze. He had utterly forgotten about Michael Blum for a moment. What was he to do? The two expectant faces before him gave Held no choice. If he appeared reluctant, that would surely throw suspicion on what he might be hiding.

He found himself saying, "Of course, forgive me."

Praying Michael was still in the attic, he took a deep breath and opened the door. Ingrid stepped inside and looked about her, clearly embarrassed by what she saw. "Oh, you really need to redecorate, Uncle. I could help." Turning to her companion she added, "Uncle Josef's wife Sarah died nearly twenty years ago. I'm afraid he's turned into a terrible bachelor."

Held was only half-listening as he removed his sodden coat, hat, and scarf. He craved to start a fire to warm the chill threatening to set in his bones, but the awareness of Michael's presence somewhere in his home overpowered any thought for comfort. His eyes darted around the hallway. Was anything out of place? Anything that would reveal who was just a few feet above their heads?

Heinrich stooped to enter the house, responding to Ingrid in his booming tone, "Ah, a man doesn't have time for decorating! Right, Professor?"

Held continued to move through the house, acutely aware, observing every corner as rapidly and as thoroughly as he could, muttering behind him, "I work at the university."

Ingrid removed her own coat and hung it in the closet, adding, "All the time!"

Heinrich nodded his approval. "Yes, we know. We need good teachers like you!"

As Held dropped his satchel on the table, he heard a soft noise above him. He started and then caught his breath. Glancing toward the ceiling, he hoped it was just Kat.

Ingrid came into the kitchen with Heinrich proclaiming, "We brought you some presents!"

Heinrich opened a large bag he was carrying. It was filled with wine, meats, and cheese. A bounty!

Held stared at the food in disbelief. "I don't know what to say. How is all this possible?"

Throwing the bag on the table, Heinrich slammed a heavy hand on Held's shoulder and drew him closer. "Your little niece worries about you."

Ingrid moved about the kitchen, opening drawers until she found a corkscrew. She handed it and the bottle of wine to Heinrich, who popped it open easily and poured glasses that Ingrid placed on the table. Gathering plates and cutlery, Ingrid began to lay out the food while exchanging intimate glances with Heinrich. As the two of them moved around him, Held felt like a stranger in his own home.

Ingrid continued to prattle on. "Actually, Uncle Josef worries about me and always has."

Heinrich sat down at the table, making himself at home. "Tell me more."

Held sat down in a chair and tried to engage. He couldn't think of one thing to say. Ingrid joined them at the table and filled in the aching silence.

"My parents died when I was young, as I told you already, Heinrich." He nodded as she continued. "And after a lot of moving about, I came back here to settle in Amsterdam, the city of my birth. I have no real family left here though, except my Uncle Josef." She planted a kiss on Held's cheek.

Heinrich recoiled, half in jest. "Do I have something to worry about here?"

Ingrid flashed her eyes playfully at him and hugged her uncle. "Don't be silly, Heinrich. He's my wonderful uncle, that is all, and he watches out for me."

Heinrich reached forward and slapped Held on the back. "Good man!" Heinrich continued the conversation as Ingrid started to nibble on a piece of cheese. "You should be very proud of her. She's a great help to the Third Reich and me. She is well-liked at our offices."

Held nodded absently. "Ah."

While they both ate heartily around him, Held hadn't touch the food and Heinrich noticed. "Eat up, Professor."

He forced himself to eat a little and drank the wine swiftly then responded with a forced, unconvincing, "Thank you. This is very... kind."

As Ingrid gathered their plates in the sink, Heinrich put an arm around Held, lowering his voice, speaking man to man. "I heard about last night, and I wanted to let you know how much we appreciate your help."

Held tried to swallow a piece of cheese that stuck in his throat.

As Ingrid returned to the table, a noise came from down the hall. Heinrich looked over Held's shoulder, and his face became grave. "I thought Ingrid told me you lived alone."

Paralyzing fear gripped him as he stalled for time. "I beg your pardon?"

Heinrich continued to look at him sternly with questioning eyes. "You don't live alone at all, do you?"

All the air left the room.

Heinrich stood up and strode into the hallway. "What a nice cat." He brought Kat into the kitchen and placed him in his large lap, stroking him.

Held managed to splutter out, "Oh. No. Not quite alone."

Kat meowed as Ingrid and Heinrich laughed. Held mopped his brow and thrust his spectacles into the bridge of his nose.

"Well, meine geliebte," Heinrich finally said, throwing down his napkin on the table and standing up, "we have to go."

Ingrid nodded. As she clipped into the hallway to retrieve her coat, Heinrich pulled Held aside. "A word of caution, my friend." Held looked up at the officer. "There are some scheduled… events over the next few weeks, mainly at night. Best to stay off the streets, inside, with the doors locked."

Held nodded thoughtfully. "Ah."

As Ingrid re-joined them, Heinrich put his arm around her. "We don't want little Ingrid to worry about you."

Held nodded again. "Of course. Inside. Doors locked."

As he escorted them to the door, he began to feel quite ill. After they had left, he closed it behind them and locked it, barely making it to the bathroom in time to vomit. Weary and shivering, he changed into dry clothes then lit a fire in the sitting room. While it was crackling in the grate, he went into the kitchen and automatically opened the large shutters, needing his usual evening's peace. Horrified awareness washed over him as he remembered there would be no more music.

He shut and bolted the window. With new determination, he picked up the leftover food and climbed the attic stairs. When he opened the door, he was surprised to see the attic was empty. As he turned to leave, he heard a rustling behind him. Michael had burrowed himself behind some boxes.

Held sighed with relief. "Mr. Blum?"

"I heard voices."

Michael extricated himself and sat on a large chest, watching him lay out the abundance of food on an upturned box before sitting down on the trunk opposite Michael. There was a long silence as Held struggled to speak, and then finally said, "I think it would be best if you didn't leave right now."

Michael was shocked. "But…"

Held was adamant. "No. You will stay."

Michael responded defiantly, "I can't! You don't understand. I have to be somewhere."

"It isn't safe out there."

"You can't force me to stay."

Held, with his mind made up, walked to the door. "It's for your own good."

Michael got up, obviously exasperated. "You don't even like me!"

Held nodded before continuing. "That's immaterial." Michael moved toward the door. The professor put up a hand. "It is going to be very dangerous out there over the next few weeks. A Nazi just told me so. You will stay here until this horror passes."

"A Nazi was here?" Michael appeared shocked.

"He was not looking for you. You are still safe, as long as you stay up here."

The student shook his head. "Professor, I'm sorry. I have to go! I promised to meet someone!"

Before Michael could say any more, Held stepped through the door and locked it.

Michael reacted in utter disbelief. "I can't believe it. You're locking me in!?" As Held descended the stairs, he heard Michael pacing his tiny room like a caged animal. He thought again about the poem, "The Panther", and felt conflicted. Was it fair to imprison someone for their own good, and what could that really accomplish? But a stronger sense took over him. The need to keep someone alive—at any cost.

Held placed the key in his pocket. This time he would do the right thing. This time there would be life instead of death. This time he would stand up for what was right. It was the least he could do. It was the least he could do for Mrs. Epstein and for Sarah.

Chapter Eleven

The morning after the raids Professor Held woke up and stared once again at his bedroom ceiling. He sighed, exhausted and glad he didn't have to be at the university until later. His home was fairly close to the Jewish ghetto of Jodenbuurt and he had been kept awake most of the night by the sounds of sirens, gunshots and screams streaming in through his bedroom window as the Jewish roundups had continued all night. Even with thick curtains and wooden shutters firmly locked, anguished cries and high-pitched screams had still pierced the muted stagnancy of the night.

He'd repeatedly tried not to speculate about what was happening. But there were raised, angry German voices and trucks moving in the streets and occasional bursts of gunfire. He'd prayed that they were just warning shots, but every sharp crack that defiled the night's silence took him straight back to the moment Mrs. Epstein had been murdered. Each startling shot had shaken him to his core and he'd felt so powerless.

As he'd tossed and turned, he'd thought of Sarah, his raw emotions exposed for the first time in years. A meticulously bolted door that had kept everything locked away had seemingly been wrenched opened by Mrs. Epstein's death. But now it refused to shut and he had no control over the thoughts that assaulted him in an ever-flowing discourse. As he'd tried to distance himself from them, instead of subsiding, they'd just intensified in focus; his dreams becoming more vibrant and jarringly real as the night wore on, speeding his heart and stealing his breath in gasps as he'd found himself reliving the last moments of Sarah's life over and over again.

At 3 a.m., unable to cope with the terrifying visions any longer, he'd got up to fetch a glass of water. A sleepy Kat had followed him downstairs, seemingly confused by the disturbance in their usual routine. As he'd hunched over the kitchen sink, drawing water, his reflection in the darkened window had showed the full weight of his foolishness crashing down upon him.

Why had he locked Michael in the attic? The boy had come for help and he was treating him like a criminal. He'd felt estranged from his actions, though he knew he had acted out of fear and instinct; there had been a compulsion, a need to have control over something uncontrollable. As emotions had weighed in again and overwhelmed him like an angry tide, he'd tried once more to put his thoughts and emotions into their place, find a tidy space in his mind to collect them and file them away. But nothing seemed to help. He was free-falling, and there was nothing he could do to stop it.

Slowly, he had finished his water and washed up the glass. Walking back upstairs, he had hesitated on the landing before quietly walking to the attic. Putting his ear to the door and closing his eyes, he'd listened. Soft, rhythmical sounds of breathing had come from inside, a reassuring presence that calmed him. With a grateful heart, he'd turned and walked down the stairs to bed. Later in the morning he'd unlock the attic and Michael could make up his own mind about whether he wanted to stay or go, live or die. He had to give him that.

Held had finally managed to fall asleep around four, just as the cries from outside started to subside.

Finally awake again, the sun was already streaming through cracks in his shutters though it created no heat for the icy day. He again rolled over and looked at the clock—8 a.m. The chill of the bedroom floor was striking and stung the soles of his feet. He dressed quickly, the fabric of his shirt feeling raw and cold as he shivered under it. Once dressed, he climbed the attic stairs and placed his hand upon the handle. A face flashed into his mind, one he had imagined many times. How old would his son have been had he lived? He shuddered with the thought. Where had all those years gone?

The door creaked open. A shaft of early-morning blue light streamed through the cracked window pane. It cast a long dust-filled shadow across the wooden floor and one perfect rectangle of light across Michael's bed.

Michael lay with his back to him and was naked from the waist up, which seemed ludicrous in the frosty chill of the morning. His broad shoulders rose and dropped as he breathed. His black, curly hair splayed across the pillow. A gray woolen blanket was in disarray and a white sheet was knotted in a bunch at Michael's feet. Evidently, Held wasn't the only one who had had a restless night.

"Mr. Blum," he whispered. Michael was still. Held coughed and cleared his throat and repeated it a little louder. "Mr. Blum, are you awake?"

Michael started to stir. Taking in a full breath, he rubbed his face and turned over to acknowledge the professor. Held didn't know what to say. He shifted his weight from foot to foot and slid his spectacles farther up his nose.

"Did you hear? Did you hear the…?" Held didn't know how to finish the sentence.

"Yes," Michael responded abruptly, sitting up and gathering the gray blanket around his shoulders.

Held walked to the corner of the attic, pulled out a dusty tea chest, and sat down awkwardly on it. As he sat, Michael spoke, unable to keep the ice from his tone. "I can't believe you locked the door. My friends were out there. They might have needed my help."

Held wanted to respond to Michael's frustrations but he couldn't remember how to have this kind of conversation. It had been so long since there had been anyone in his life with whom he'd had a chance to have a real and honest conversation. There had only been

Ingrid and she just talked at him. He wanted to explain everything. He wanted to explain that there was very little help for Jewish people these days, but those words sounded coarse and heartless. He wanted to clarify why he had locked him in the attic, but then he would've had to talk about his son and Sarah, and the thought of exposing his own losses made him feel much too vulnerable to even contemplate sharing them. Now, in the light of the day, it really did seem absurd that he had locked the door.

So, he retreated behind safe words. "I have a little food if you're hungry." He got up and started to make his way to the door. Then stopped, forcing himself to say more. "You are free to leave if you want, it would be safer after dusk. I'm going to the university in a little while. Is there anything else you need?"

"Need?" said Michael, rolling back on his bed and putting his hands behind his head. "Yes. There are many things that I need. I need to be free. I need this war to be over. I need to be able to walk on the street and be treated like a human being instead of the animal they call Jew."

Held blinked behind his glasses, rendered speechless.

Michael must have sensed his discomfort as he met the professor's eyes, because he added, "But I'd be happy to start with some water if you've got some." A faint smile crossed his face.

Held nodded. By the time he made his way downstairs, put together a small tray of food, and brought it back to the attic, Michael had dressed. He stood at the window looking across the red rooftops that stretched as far as the eye could see and flicked through his book of poetry.

Held placed the tray on the tea chest. "There is a desk in the corner," he stated. "It's old, but you can sit and write or read at it. I have a little scrap paper that I haven't had taken off me that I keep for students," he offered, pulling a few sheets from a box in the attic.

Michael nodded. "Thank you."

Held stood awkwardly for a second, then moved toward the door.

"There's actually something that you can do for me, Professor." Michael turned to face Held. "Remember the girl with me the other day? The girl who met me after the class? She only took the class so we could be together. She is the girl I will marry one day."

Held thought for a moment and then remembered the girl with the concerned eyes. "Miss Dirksen? But she is not Jewish—"

Michael became defensive. "Her name is Elke. And why does that matter?"

Held was shocked—knowing it was very unconventional for Michael to date a Gentile, especially in these times—but just nodded his head.

"Well, I wonder if you could get a message to her. Will you tell her that I'll try and meet her in a few days' time when these raids are over?" Michael went to the bed and scribbled on one of the pieces of paper that the professor had just given him and held it out.

Held stiffened. "It's very dangerous," he said, stepping back, his hand moving nervously to his spectacles. "You know, now that you're on the run, it is dangerous for her, too. I don't think it would be wise."

Michael threw the note down on the bed and slammed the poetry book shut. "I have to see her. She is waiting. She is already worried. I can't imagine not seeing her. Please, you have to at least try. She means so much to me." Michael's voice cracked.

Held took a couple of steps forward to reassure him, but he didn't know what to do. It struck him that he didn't really remember how to be physical with someone. Did he put an arm around him? Should he put a hand on his shoulder? It had been so long since Held had touched anyone with intention. He ended up just nodding his head and doing the only thing he was capable of. He picked up the note from the bed. "I will see what I can do."

For a second Held saw the weight of the world lift from the young man's shoulders.

Leaving the attic, the professor's heart was troubled with something new. The realization of what he'd become. Who had he last touched apart from Kat? Even Ingrid just forced her affection on him and he could not reciprocate it. He couldn't even remember the last time he'd reached out for someone's hand, let alone held it. After Sarah's death eighteen years before, there had been many arms of comfort—sisters, parents, well-meaning friends. But none of them were Sarah's, so the comfort had felt hollow, unfamiliar, painful even. Intentionally, one person at a time, one pair of arms at a time, he had pushed them all away. Now he had become this. Before he could close the attic door, Kat arrived and forced his way in. He leaped onto Michael's bed and rolled himself into a ball.

Michael's eyes lit up. "At least I have one friend to keep me company," he acknowledged, a little more cheerfully.

Held nodded. "I have a class. I'll be back later." He stopped. It needed to be said. "Michael." Michael looked up. "I'm sorry I locked you in."

Michael shrugged his shoulders. "You probably saved my life," he said, sitting down on the bed and starting to stroke Kat. As Held shut the door, he heard Michael say quietly to Kat, "Whether it is worth saving remains to be seen."

With a heavy heart, Held walked downstairs, put on his coat, and went to the university.

Once in the safety of his classroom, Held looked down at the class register, looking for Elke Dirksen's name. She would be with him late this afternoon. As the day went on, he waited for the fourth lesson. But Elke didn't show up. Maybe she was ill or maybe she, too, had been caught like Michael. He debated whether to tell Michael and thought it was best he confirm his suspicions first.

At the end of his day, he put on his heavy overcoat, hat, and scarf, paused to add his last math problem to the blackboard, and moved out of the classroom.

He made his usual stop in the hallway, and Hannah Pender nodded to him cheerfully. "I have your mail, Professor," she sang out.

He nodded, then paused, wondering for a second if he would be causing more problems if he asked about Miss Dirksen. Bringing attention to any person in these times was dangerous. But he needed to know, for Michael's sake. He owed him this.

"Mrs. Pender, I wonder if I can ask you something?"

Her eyes lit up, expectantly.

"It's about a student."

She couldn't hide her disappointment. "Oh, of course, Professor Held."

He was surprised by her reaction, but nevertheless continued. "She is a student and didn't attend today. I wondered if she is unwell." He tried to sound nonchalant.

Hannah studied his face before nodding. "Let me get the main register." She disappeared beneath her desk. She pulled up a heavy, leather-bound book and turned to Professor Held's classes. "What is her name?"

"Elke Dirksen," he responded, swallowing down the tremble in his voice. His hand went to his pocket and he fingered the note he had placed there that morning.

He watched her forefinger move swiftly down the page until she was under the letter D. "Elke Dirksen... Oh."

Held's breath caught in his throat. "Is there a problem?"

Her eyes looked up to meet his, filled with concern.

"Yes, I'm afraid there is, Professor. There is a note in here, to say that she will no longer be enrolled in the university. She's had to move on. I remember her now. She seemed very nervous and looked exhausted. I wondered if she had—" Hannah paused, trying to find the right words. "Personal problems."

A gaze lingered between them as they both contemplated her words. "Personal problems" was the phrase often used to describe the peril all around them now. It could mean her family had been moved or taken, or their business had been destroyed. Personal problems never meant anything good.

Held nodded and pulled his scarf tightly around his neck. Slowly, he took his letters from the counter and slipped them into his bag without even looking through them. Once again he felt Hannah watching him as he made his way out into the night.

He thought about her again as he followed his usual route home, he knew so little about her and her husband. Held stiffened at the thought of her with him, the two of them eating dinner, talking, laughing, making love. He was shocked that this last thought didn't sit comfortably with him. He must be confusing his resurfacing thoughts of Sarah with the woman with the beautiful eyes that watched him leave the building every evening. He shook the thoughts from his mind and concentrated on the things around him on his journey home; noticing the first hints of spring. Winter had felt endless, but now the beginning of buds appeared on the trees. Anything positive was worth noting in these dark times, he reassured himself. Surely things would feel better with brighter days and warmer weather.

Held sighed as he crossed the street. How much longer would they have to endure the Germans? How much longer would they have to put up with a life of holding their breath? And then a new thought. How much longer might Michael need to stay in his attic? Surely not too long. Even if the war continued, he would presumably need to leave the attic to find somewhere safer.

He stopped at the store and picked up what little food was available with his ration coupons for the day and then made his way home. He dreaded telling Michael that Elke was gone. Hopefully this war would be over in a couple of months and they could all get back to living their former lives.

Chapter Twelve

Ingrid opened her eyes, and for a second she couldn't remember where she was. As she took in the immense opulence around her, she knew she wasn't in her own bed. Not in her dark, dank flat on Bloedstraat. Her eyes focused on her red dress and white fur stole laid across a gold brocade chair, her high, strappy red shoes slung haphazardly across the Persian carpet. Then she remembered she was with Heinrich.

With the sheer thrill of that wonderful thought, she stretched out in the vast, comfortable bed then rolled onto her side and curled her legs up, catlike, under her, reveling in the luxuriousness as she skimmed the soft, silk sheets. Ingrid stretched her arm across the expanse of the bed to find Heinrich. But though the sheets were still warm, she was disappointed to find he wasn't there. She was alone. Ingrid felt a sudden sadness in that loss. A moment of connection missed. This had been their first time making love and her first time ever. Selfishly, she had hoped to lie leisurely in his strong arms before they started their day.

He had taken her to heights and places that she could only have imagined before. He had been eager to consummate their relationship, and she had been happy to satisfy his urgent need for her. She loved the power she had felt over him, the way he had watched her undress, the way he had looked at her with such desire.

As she became fully awake, she was aware of a far-off voice and realized it was Heinrich's; he was talking to somebody in the hallway. Ingrid propped herself up into a sitting position and stretched. This was how it was going to be, she thought as she looked around his stylish apartment. It was filled with expensive furniture and bathed in full morning light. This was how it was going to be being married to Heinrich. She smiled to herself for having finally got what she had always wanted. The love of a strong, handsome man who would take care of her.

From her new position, Ingrid could see through French windows onto Noordermarkt below, illuminated by the early morning sun. She had thought she would wait, wait at least until they were engaged, but last night had been the perfect moment. After visiting her uncle, they had been out at a dinner party with some of his friends and he had brought her here for a nightcap. Before long they had started kissing passionately, and he had pushed her, coaxed her, telling her how beautiful she was, making it obvious he wanted more. Ingrid had been unsure at first, wanting to go home, but Heinrich had used all his powers of persuasion, reminding her they were in love. And now, here she was, in her slip, waking up in Heinrich's bed.

Sliding out of the sheets, Ingrid moved to the windows. It looked like it wasn't going to rain for a change. She sauntered toward the bathroom. As Ingrid glanced down the hallway, she caught sight of Heinrich. He had his back to her, dressed in his trousers and shirt. She liked seeing him in a state of undress. It felt personal, intimate. Rarely seeing him without his jacket, Ingrid looked forward to the times that she would be his wife and would see him like this every day before cooking his breakfast.

She tiptoed into the hallway. Heinrich continued to talk on the telephone, all of his attention focused and intense. He was speaking very quickly in German so she only caught a couple of the words—she heard "Jew" and "underground." He didn't hear her as she came up behind him and slipped her arms around his waist.

Heinrich flinched, turning and communicating by his stern expression that this was unacceptable. Ingrid felt belittled, deflated. She forced a smile and withdrew her arms. He shifted uncomfortably, appearing uneasy at the proximity of her presence. He eyed her intently and, covering the receiver, whispered, "You need to fix your face."

Ingrid was taken aback. Then she felt hot embarrassment rise to her cheeks as he turned his back on her again and continued his conversation uninterrupted.

Making her way to the bathroom, Ingrid berated herself for not checking her appearance in the mirror first before she approached him. Before shutting the door, she heard Heinrich swear and reasoned that there were obviously problems at work.

As she turned on the light, she thought about how much better their life would be once this stupid war was over. Seeing her reflection, she gasped. Her makeup, so meticulously applied the night before, was indeed in disarray. Her mascara had run in black rings under her eyes, and her red lipstick was smeared across her chin. No wonder Heinrich had rebuked her. She felt ashamed for not getting up first and cleaning off her face. Of course, Heinrich would expect her to be as impeccable as he was. After all, he was a very prestigious man. Always clean, always smartly dressed, and one day, as his wife, she would need to be the same.

Ingrid filled a sink with hot water, lathered up from a block of white fresh-smelling soap, and scrubbed at her face until it was red raw. She reached for her open-clasp bag and makeup, which she had used to make herself attractive to him the night before, and pulled out what she needed. Once her face was clean, she took time to reapply fresh makeup, paying particular attention, making herself up as attractive as she could be. Ingrid didn't want Henrich's last impression of her as he headed out this morning to be as unfortunate as the first.

Re-entering the bedroom, she noticed Heinrich was off the telephone and she could tell by the way he was moving around the room that he was not in a good mood, slamming doors and drawers as he finished dressing.

"Good morning, Heinrich," she said, hoping to catch his eye again. Now that her makeup was reapplied, maybe she would be more acceptable to him.

Heinrich didn't turn to meet her gaze. Instead, he put on his jacket. "I have an issue this morning. There is talk of unrest. Now it is spreading through Amsterdam. Apparently they are all talking about a strike. Can you believe it? All over the city, people are talking about marching in the streets." He swore under his breath again. Tightening his belt, he turned to her. "You must dress quickly and go home."

Ingrid deflated. "But you said that we could maybe take the morning off and go for a walk, maybe get some breakfast."

Heinrich shot her a look. "That's not possible today."

Placing his cap on his head, he strode into the hallway.

"How will I get home?" Ingrid enquired meekly, not wanting to walk through the streets in the morning in her evening attire.

"My driver will take you," he stated over his shoulder. "I will get him to come back for you once he has dropped me at work." He turned to her and continued, "You must come to work as soon as you have changed. I expect to see you there no later than ten o'clock."

Ingrid stopped just short of saluting. Sometimes she felt that Heinrich seemed to think of her as just another soldier. Someone to obey him, to do his bidding.

He must have read the wounded expression on her face because as she turned and walked to the bedroom, he softened his tone. "We will have time for walking the canals at the weekend, I'm sure, liebling. But now we have to work."

With her back to him, Ingrid nodded as she gazed out the French windows. Across the square, there was a group of people, a mob, massing and walking toward their building. They held up signs and placards supporting the Jewish people, demanding that the German Army stop the roundups, and expressing outrage at the unfair treatment of Dutch Jews in Amsterdam. As the group approached, their voices raised, it caught Heinrich's attention. Joining her at the window, he looked out at the gathering crowd over her shoulder.

"Can you believe it?" His tone was once again harsh and bitter. "These are Dutch people. Holland is one of the Aryan nations. They should be with us, not against us. Who cares about Jews? Everyone knows they are untermensch and that they need to be dealt with. Well, there'll be severe repercussions. We will not let people get away with this."

Ingrid nodded. "Of course. I'm so sorry, Heinrich. I can't believe that my people do not see the benefit of the Third Reich. They do not see the good that you are doing. They do not see all the wealth that you will bring, and the peace. I'm embarrassed to be Dutch," she added, with disgust. "I will help you in any way that I can."

Heinrich turned Ingrid toward him. "You are one of the good Dutch for sure, meine liebchen." The kind tone from the night before had returned. The gentleness in his eyes, the softness of his voice. He caressed the side of her face. "Now, I have to go. I must deal with this."

His lips grazed her cheek. Then he was gone, out the door and away in his staff car.

Ingrid put on her evening gown once again, feeling awkward and self-conscious. Surely people in her building would know she had stayed out, probably with a man. She rolled back her shoulders. What did she care? No one really cared about her. Only Heinrich. She was his girlfriend now, and the Third Reich was her new family.

Ingrid sat waiting on a chair in the hall, her fur stole on and her sequined clasp bag on her lap. Heinrich's driver returned about fifteen minutes later and escorted her to the car. Stepping out into the street, she couldn't believe what greeted her. Hundreds and hundreds of people were amassed in the square, chanting and shouting and singing. They held up signs supporting the Resistance and signs supporting Queen Wilhelmina and the royal family, though they were now in exile in England. Ingrid felt sick to her stomach. These people were making Heinrich's job so hard.

As she moved toward the car with its swastikas, accompanied by Heinrich's driver, she heard somebody yell something about being a Nazi lover. Suddenly Ingrid felt afraid, as if she were the enemy. It shocked her to think that they could be so hostile toward her. Somebody else screamed and swore at her, and a woman close by spat in front of her. Shaken, she hustled into the back seat.

The mob surrounded them and began banging on the car roof. The driver wasted no time jumping into the front seat and trying to inch his way through the furious crowd. Ingrid huddled in the back corner of the car, wanting to be taken home.

Chapter Thirteen

Hannah carried two heavy shopping baskets, glad for a morning off work. She was pleased with her shopping expedition, and her ration coupons had stretched to allow her a good week of groceries for her and her mother. However, her thoughts were full of what she had witnessed earlier that morning.

As she'd turned the corner into Noordermarkt, she had been amazed to see that the normally quiet market square surrounded by cafés and shops was alive with people. Someone standing at the front of the crowd was rallying them as they cheered and yelled their support. She'd decided on turning around and taking a different way home when she'd been caught up by the words being said. A passionate speaker talked about raids that had happened the night before and encouraged people to attend a meeting that evening.

Hannah stopped to listen more intently. She didn't live far from Jodenbuurt and had already seen the barbed wire and blockades that had gone up around the Jewish neighborhood. There were also awful tales she had heard while waiting in line at the butcher's that morning; hundreds of Jewish men being rounded up. And this happening here in her precious Holland.

Wanting to hear more, she quickened her pace and made her way into the center of the square to join the crowd thronging there. She listened to the passionate speaker express their need to strike, to protest the treatment of the Jewish people and particularly the raids and roundups. There must have been hundreds of people listening. On the perimeter, bewildered German soldiers stood in nervous groups gripping rifles, unsure how to contain the frothing crowd of angry supporters.

As Hannah continued to listen to the speaker, someone handed her a flyer. On it, the words, "Strike! Strike! Strike!" She read through it and noted it had been handed to her by a member of the Communist Party. She had read that the Germans had now made the Communist Party illegal in Amsterdam, and it appeared they wanted to fight back.

Suddenly, a car drove away from the corner of the square, where angry voices were directed at it. Hannah caught a glimpse of a pretty blonde woman with a German soldier driving. From what the crowd was shouting around her, it appeared she was Dutch. The crowds continued to chase after the car and scream their displeasure. Hannah sighed and, despite herself, felt sorry for the young woman. Who knew her story? Anger was an easy emotion, quickly accelerated to rage.

As the car sped away, she turned back to listen to the speaker, an enthusiastic man in a heavy gray coat and cloth cap, who talked about the need for Amsterdam to be free. He then went on to protest the forced labor in Germany that the Nazis had also inflicted upon them. She listened to him finish, then popped the leaflet into her pocket and made her way home.

Her mother was standing nervously at the window, awaiting Hannah's return. Before she could even put the key in the lock, Hannah could hear Clara hobble into the hallway on her cane. Hannah opened the door and Clara snapped at her.

"Did you hear? Have you heard about the treatment of the Jewish people in Jodenbuurt?"

Hannah closed the door and put her basket down to take off her coat. "Yes, Mama, everyone in town is talking about it."

"What about Little Eva?" asked Clara. "Have you heard from her? Is she okay? She should have been here hours ago for her knitting lesson."

"I went by their street but there are Nazis everywhere," said Hannah, moving into the kitchen with her heavy baskets.

Clara followed her daughter, speeding along on her walking stick. "It is so awful," she said. "I cannot believe this is Holland. These people are our friends, our families."

"I know," said Hannah, nodding her head. "I promise I will check, Mama. But there are barbed-wire fences, and soldiers are guarding their street. As soon as it is possible, I will walk over there. Until then, please don't worry."

Clara did not seem content with that. She moved back to the window, hobbling backward and forward on her stick to look up and down the street, as if that was going to give her some answers. Hannah made her mother a cup of tea, placing it in the sitting room on her favorite tea tray to entice her away from the window.

"I'm sure Eva will come by when she is able," Hannah reassured her mother. "I'm sure they're fine. Let's have a cup of tea, and if we've not heard anything soon, I promise I will go and check this afternoon."

Clara sighed a deep sigh and slowly worked her way back to her chair. Sitting down with another heavy sigh, she asked, "Is there any other news? Any other news out there that's good?"

"Actually, I do have some news," said Hannah, handing over the leaflet from the protest. "It appears that Amsterdam is fighting back."

Her mother read it and smiled.

"Good, good," she said, nodding. "I was hoping that somebody would do something like this."

"Yes, they were all congregated in Noordermarkt," explained Hannah, taking a gingerbread biscuit from a plate on the tray. "Apparently, the strike continues tomorrow." She paused. "I saw a young woman," she continued, taking a sip of her tea. "A young Dutch woman getting into one of the German officer's cars today. She was on the edge of the square. People reacted so vehemently that I worried for her safety, but I understand their anger. How can anyone be friendly with these people? They have brought such oppression and sadness to our town."

Clara nodded. "I fear for that young woman, too. She will probably come to a very sad end if she continues on the track she is on. Now the Germans have mighty strength, but one day, because I believe in goodness, we will have our town back. Then she will pay a terrible price for befriending the enemy."

Hannah agreed, feeling concerned. "Everybody is just trying to get by the only way they can."

All at once, there was a knock at the front door.

Clara clattered down her cup onto its saucer. "Go see who it is. See if it is Eva at last."

Hannah nodded, replacing her own teacup before going. She opened the door to the tiny figure of Eva Herzenberg, and even though she was wearing a thick coat, she was visibly shivering on the doorstep.

"Come in, come in," said Hannah. "My mother will be so glad to see you."

As she helped Eva off with her coat, she marveled at how big she was becoming. Having attended school with Greta, Eva's mother, Hannah had known Eva all her life, and this sweet ten-year-old had become an instant favorite with her mother. She visited a couple of afternoons a week to keep Clara company, which seemed to be good for both of them. As Hannah hung her coat on the hook, she remembered Greta's overjoyed face at Eva's arrival as if it were yesterday. The sheer joy of finally giving birth to the baby girl that she had so wanted, after having three boys.

"I'm sorry I didn't come earlier," Eva apologized. "I'm sorry it's so late. A horrible thing happened last night."

Hannah shut the door behind her, softly. "We know all about it," she reassured. "Why don't you come in and get warm by the fire?"

Eva continued all in one stream. "I couldn't leave, Mama wouldn't let us leave the house, she was afraid we would get taken like Papa got taken to those work camps last year, she didn't want them to take us, to take my brothers."

"Yes, yes," agreed Hannah, stroking the girl's hair and rubbing comforting circles in the center of her back. "Your mother was right to wait. Come now, Clara is waiting impatiently for word of you."

Eva opened the sitting-room door to be greeted by her elderly friend from her chair, arms outstretched.

"Eva," she cried. "I am so glad to see you. I have been so worried. Tell me, is your family well?"

The young girl ran to the woman's arms and hugged her as if she would never let go. Then she told the whole tale. It tumbled out in one long jumble of words. Hannah stopped her before she got too far. "You will need some tea," she said smiling and went to the kitchen to get Eva's special cup. Once the tea was poured, they settled and as Eva warmed, the pink returned to her young cheeks.

What Eva told them was heart-wrenching. Nazis had come in the middle of the night, taking people randomly, pulling them from their beds, from their homes, from the arms of loved ones. They took anyone suspected of connections with the Resistance, rounding them up as if they were cattle.

Eva nibbled on a biscuit. "They even took Vince, the man who sharpens the knives in the corner square. You know Vince." Her small face crumpled into acute concern. "Where will they take him? Where has he gone? Why are they doing this?" she asked desperately, tears appearing in the corners of her eyes. Then quietly, almost to herself, "Who will sharpen our knives now?"

Clara pulled her small friend up into her lap.

"Shh, now, Eva, don't worry about everything all at once. You need to drink your tea and eat your biscuit. There are many things going on in the world that none of us understand, but you are safe here."

"But there is barbed wire and soldiers everywhere."

Clara nodded. "It is indeed a strange time that we are in, little one. Now, let us think of better things. Where were you in your knitting project?"

Eva's eyes lit up. "I just cast on the second row," she said, remembering the fact with joy.

"Well go and get the knitting basket and let's get going," said Clara. "We have much more important things to do. We have to fight with the Resistance. You and I will be the knitting resistance." She raised her teacup to her young friend.

Eva smiled a broad smile, revealing gaps in the side of her mouth where she was awaiting her adult teeth.

"Okay," she agreed, "I like that idea." She fetched the knitting basket from the corner of the room and dragged it over to her older friend's lap, pulling out both their knitting projects. From Clara's lap, Eva watched as the old woman put the needles together in her gnarly fingers and started to slowly loop wool. She looped a couple of stitches and then handed it to the young girl.

"Come on now, Eva, we have many hats to make. We have a lot of young boys whose heads need to be kept warm in this war," she chuckled.

Hannah poured tea as Eva nodded her agreement, took the needles, and started to knit.

Chapter Fourteen

Moving through the trees, Elke tried desperately not to make any sound. The Germans usually guarded the streets, but occasionally they ventured out into the woods. It was late afternoon, and she had only about an hour until she needed to leave to make the curfew in time.

As she walked, her heart ached. It had been three days of searching for Michael. Three days since she'd seen him disappear from the alleyway with David.

And now she knew David was dead. She still couldn't believe it. It had been too dangerous to visit the Jewish neighborhood for David's funeral, so she had grieved for her boyfriend's oldest friend alone at her sister's home, her emotions only intensified by Michael's absence.

Then there had been the raids. Jewish people being forced into the ghetto, interrogated, deported. A claw-like vice of fear gripped her chest every time she thought of it. How could Michael have escaped that? And if he had, where was he? She'd put out tentative enquiries to all their friends. But there was no word of him.

She was unable to return to her houseboat because Nazis were still patrolling all the canals vigorously, and it didn't feel like a safe place to be a woman alone, especially one whose neighbors might know her to be a Jew-sympathiser. She hoped it would feel safe for her to go back home soon.

Continuing her way over the sodden earth and through piles of decaying leaves, she turned down a dark pathway almost hidden from view by the undergrowth that had overwhelmed it. All at once, ahead of her, she heard a rustle in the bushes. Drawing her body close to a tree, she stopped and waited silently. After a few seconds, a badger lumbered across her path, unaware of the fear it was causing. Elke let go of a breath she didn't realize she was holding and continued stealthily into the heart of the woods.

She had known instantly what Michael had meant when he had said "their secret place." There could only be one such place—safe, away from the town, away from prying eyes. The first place they'd ever made love.

As she continued to creep through the bracken, she remembered that day the summer before and how she had not been impressed meeting him when he first turned up in her life. Lying out on the university lawns reading, she'd nibbled on an apple, cross-legged on a blanket, when someone stood between her and the sun, casting a long shadow across her page. Annoyed, she eventually looked up from her book and met Michael Blum.

"You're blocking my sunlight," she said.

"I'm struck by the beauty of something brighter than the sun," he'd quipped back to her.

Her inner voice had groaned at this flowery language. She had been about to reprimand him once more when he had stepped forward out of the light so she could see him clearly. It had stopped any harsh words from rolling off her tongue, as she was instantly hypnotized by his dark, curly hair, muscular build, and gorgeous brown eyes. She couldn't recall having seen him on campus before, even though she had been at the university for a year.

"What are you reading?" he asked, sitting himself down on her blanket before he had even been invited.

"Did I ask you to join me?" she half-heartily asked, protesting his brazen manner.

"You will when you get to know me," he responded, stealing the apple from her hand and taking a large bite from it. She was irritated again, but also curious. There was an intensity about his spirit, a restless energy, a playful boldness. He was striking, like someone who knew he was destined to do great things with his life.

Snatching back her apple, she stated, "I'm reading a book about art history."

"Ah, am I in there?"

"Are you a famous artist?"

"Absolutely. But maybe I wouldn't be in this type of book," he added, taking the book from her and scrutinizing it. "I'm more of a word artist than a paint artist."

Placing her open book on his chest, he stretched himself out on her blanket, tucked his hands behind his head, and closed his eyes, appearing to relish the sun on his face.

"A word artist?" she echoed. "Please don't tell me you're a poet."

"Why not?" he enquired, cocking open one eye, then the other, squinting back and forth, apparently trying to bring her into focus under the glare of the harsh sunshine.

"Because I detest poets. I've never met a poet that was sane."

"And wasn't hungry," he added, shifting up onto his elbows and taking her apple from her again.

"Hey! This is my lunch."

"This is your lunch?" he echoed back incredulously. "You obviously don't know how to dine."

She grabbed the apple. "I'm on a very tight budget, I am paying for my courses myself," she responded, trying to take a rather large bite before he stole it again.

"What has that to do with anything? You don't need money to eat in this town. Come with me." He lifted her to her feet before she had time to react.

"Where are we going?" she asked, feeling a little apprehensive. As gorgeous as he was, she'd only just met this man.

"You need to learn a few things about Amsterdam. For example, eating only apples for lunch is ridiculous."

"I really need to stay here," she protested. "I've got class in an hour."

"A whole hour? We could have feasted in that hour," he declared, grabbing hold of her bike lying on the grass. He encouraged her again. "Come on, we have no time to lose."

She hesitated. But there was something about him that intrigued her. He seemed harmless but intense and impulsive. She watched as he bundled up her blanket and put it into her bicycle basket. "You can give me a lift. I don't have a bike."

"You don't have a bicycle? Who in Amsterdam doesn't have a bicycle?"

"Michael Blum doesn't, that's who."

"I take it that's your name."

"Yes, I'm sorry." He bowed deeply, taking hold of her hand and kissing it dramatically, introducing himself with a fake British accent, as if she was a duchess, "Michael Blum, at your service." She shook her head as he continued, "And who do I have the pleasure of addressing?"

He turned her hand over and let his lips brush her wrist with a light kiss, sending a chill down her spine.

"My name is Elke."

"Elke," he whispered back, his gaze intent on her face. "Elke what?"

"I'm not sure I should give you my last name," she said curtly. "You might find me again."

"Oh, there are many ways to find you without knowing your name."

"Let's just start with Elke," she answered playfully. "We will see if I like you enough to let you know anything more about me."

"Okay, 'just Elke,' let's go." With that, he picked up the bike, sat on the saddle, and tapped on his leg. "You can sit on my lap."

"Sit on your lap!" She balked, raising her eyebrows.

Before she could say any more, he whipped his arm around her waist and hoisted her up onto his right hip and attempted to use his left leg to pedal and his left arm to steer.

"You're not going to get very far like that," she laughed, shaking her head.

"Okay then," he said. He gathered her up in his arms and lifted both her legs across his lap, so that she was facing him. She screamed with surprise. He could get to both pedals then and started to move at great speed through the university gardens.

"You're crazy!" she shouted to him as they whooshed past startled students who jumped out of their way as they careened out into the streets of the city.

"Aren't all poets?" he hollered back, smirking. "Somebody told me that once, someone without a last name."

As she clung to his neck for safety, she was acutely aware of their proximity. Every nerve and sense in her body heightened to the attraction. She tried to appear aloof as she fought the feelings that swelled up and coursed through her whole being. His breath grazing her cheek, his thick hair brushing her bare shoulder, his powerful arms on either side of her body steering the bike. And he smelled wonderful.

He cycled into the center of town and stopped in front of a very exclusive art gallery. It had a "closed" sign in the window and appeared to be hosting an opening.

"This looks promising," he told her, dropping her softly to the ground and parking the bicycle. "Let's go and look at art."

Elke peered into the window. "I don't really care for this kind of modern work. I much prefer the Romantics."

He grabbed her hand. "Oh, you'll appreciate it a whole lot more after you've had something to eat."

At the entrance, a doorman stepped in front of them.

"We're here for the opening," Michael announced. "We've been waiting for it all week. Haven't we, darling?" He squeezed Elke's hand, rendering her speechless.

"Does Mrs. de Haan know you?" the doorman asked suspiciously.

"Of course she knows us. Why would we be here if she didn't know us?" Michael answered, feigning irritation, seeming totally comfortable in his lie.

"Do you have your tickets?"

"No, we didn't bring our tickets," answered Michael with disgust. "We don't need tickets. We are very close friends of Mrs. de Haan."

The doorman seemed wary. "What are your names?"

Michael responded without hesitation. "Mr. and Mrs. Jargen Smit."

The doorman furrowed his brows. "Wait here. I will need to check." He walked away.

"Come on," said Michael, pulling Elke inside.

As he dragged her into the room, she cocked an eyebrow and asked, "Mrs. Smit? That was a fast courtship. When I left the university, I wasn't married."

"You weren't married but you were hungry. Besides, you didn't have a last name, so I decided to give you one," he stated, his face alight with his adventure. "Now, you will be married and well fed."

He raced her to a side room in the gallery. Inside was a splendid buffet of hors d'oeuvres set out on silver platters. He grabbed a napkin, handing one to Elke, and began to heap up pieces of delectable food.

"What are you doing?" she hissed, shocked as she watched the speed at which he could pile up food.

"Feeding my new wife. Quickly, Mrs. Smit, before we get caught."

She grabbed a few bites of food and wrapped them in the napkin, then he hustled her back out the door before the doorman returned. He stuffed their bounty into his pockets, grabbed hold of Elke's bike, and threw her across his lap again. They sped off, laughing uncontrollably, riding like the wind away from the scene of their crime. Breathless and windswept, they stopped close to a canal and sat down on a peeling wooden bench before unwrapping the stolen goods.

"You should see what I can do for dessert," he mused. "But this will do for starters." Appearing pleased with his haul, he inspected a rather large hunk of cheese and offered her a golden slice of peach.

She shook her head, instead picking up a delicious sliver of smoked salmon and devouring it in awe—not just of the swash-buckling food adventure, but also in awe of this human being.

Their meeting had a strange déjà vu quality to it. It wasn't like meeting someone new, but more like finding someone she had lost. Someone who had always been near, circling her, just not in human form until today. She didn't know why, but as she licked cream cheese from her fingers, she knew in some subconscious way she had been waiting for him, and it was shocking and comforting all at once. She sat peacefully by his side, eating their stolen bounty, watching the life along the canal banks, and she heard her soul whisper to her, "*He is the one.*"

From that day, their lives had been passionately entwined. There had been no talk of a second or even a first date; it just felt wrong to be away from each other. Her heart felt strained when they were apart, and it sighed with satisfaction whenever they were together. Even though she wasn't Jewish and she knew how controversial it was to be in love and sleeping with a Jew in peacetime, never mind occupied Holland, with both of their parents gone there didn't seem to be anyone to object. So they'd been inseparable, until now.

She shivered. It was growing cold in the woods. Her thoughts returned to the last time she had been with Michael, the last time he'd kissed her in that cold dark alley, his chilled lips on hers, and that memory stung all over again.

Waiting in their meeting place, she trembled as the weight of the realization gnawed at her: He wasn't coming. She would be able to sense him if he was. She could always sense him.

She huddled under their tree, her feet frozen into two blocks of ice. She stamped them to warm herself and ran her hand across the knobby trunk, finding where Michael had carved a crude heart into the bark with his pocket knife. Her fingers, moving like a braille reader, touched his words: "Mr. and Mrs. Smit." She felt a warm connection with him. This was her daily touchstone, the reminder that he was real, and he was out there somewhere.

She decided to wait for another thirty minutes, right up until the very last moment before she had to run for the curfew, as she had last night. She would wait here every night until he came for her. She wasn't going to believe that he'd been taken. She couldn't. She had to believe with all her heart that he was still in Amsterdam. And that he was still alive.

PART TWO

Chapter Fifteen

Spring 1943

As the war kept its chokehold on Europe, its ravaging fingers crept into all elements of civilian life. In Holland, where the Nazis had hoped to befriend an ally, relations continued to deteriorate. It seemed to Professor Josef Held that after three years of occupation, it was finally becoming evident to the invading forces that the Netherlands was a stubborn mule, unwilling to give in and bow to the Führer's bidding. In Amsterdam, on the street, Josef noticed his fellow Dutch covertly wearing orange flowers and ribbons to signify their united resistance against their foe. The Underground, too, was alive and well, with Resistance members creating printed papers on secret presses that were disbursed to the population, and Wireless Orange, the Dutch Resistance broadcast, was transmitted daily, to those who had retained wirelesses. Held had heard that even Queen Wilhelmina would send messages of encouragement from her haven in the British Isles.

But in Professor Held's world, everything and nothing had changed.

The lines for the bakery, the butchers, and the greengrocers had grown longer, while food supplies became shorter. Yet amidst it all, he had walked back and forth to the university daily, marking endless math papers, placing hundreds of math equations on his blackboard. Everything remained the same except for at home, where he still sheltered his secret—that Michael Blum slept night after night in his attic.

With Michael's days being long and endless, he had contemplated leaving, and both he and Held had discussed it, but there was never a moment that felt safe. Instead he had made his home in the attic the best he could and the two of them had survived together.

One day seemed to melt into another, and before they knew it, Michael's view was across snowy rooftops once more. Sometimes the two men went days without really speaking, sometimes they'd make idle chatter about the weather, or the university. One time Josef found Michael crying, and just closed the door without disturbing him.

At the start Michael would ask, "Is it any better?" and Josef would shake his head and respond, "Worse." Until finally, Michael stopped asking. As the months had worn on, it had become clear that there was nothing else that could be done. The treatment of the Jewish people had only grown harsher, and many had now left or been transported, leaving only a hollow echo of their many voices behind them. Josef felt anger when he thought of the injustice of this. He had become fond of Michael in their time together and treasured their conversations that often stretched late into the night. He envied the young man's passion for his poetry and felt a sense of pride as Michael's work became deep and enriched by the harsh seasoning of an unjust war.

One spring afternoon, like many others before, Josef picked up groceries before walking home. He was grateful for what he got. Food had become scarce, but still they managed to survive, though Josef had stopped trying too hard to keep kosher for Michael, who insisted he didn't mind what he ate. Three years of the Nazi regime had made life harder, and the people wearier as a sad acceptance crept in. An unspoken, collective need to preserve their energy for the long haul as the war dragged on with no end in sight.

Josef sighed. He could barely remember what peacetime felt like.

As he approached his street, two German soldiers moved toward him to check his identification papers then, recognizing him, waved and let him pass.

"Good evening, Professor," one of them greeted.

Josef nodded, thinking to himself, not for the first time, that this was the only good thing about having a niece who was in love with a Nazi.

Josef approached home and on passing Mrs. Epstein's house stopped to look at it for the first time in months. It had been painful for him at first to see her home, but now he stood and took in all that it was, remembering once again that experience that had so abruptly thrown him into the realities of war. A flashback stung him: The air filled with piano scores raining down on him. One of her shoes lying on its side on the ground. For the first time, he wondered what had happened to it.

She had named her house "Haven," as depicted by a hand-painted tile above the door. But its green-painted windowsills were starting to peel; the German soldiers had boarded it up; and with its tiny overgrown garden, it had become a sad, empty shell. Josef remembered the music, remembered how her playing made him feel, and he missed it terribly.

As he turned toward his own home, he noticed something on his front step. His curiosity piqued. He rarely got mail at home, never gifts. He picked up the parcel wrapped in brown paper and string. He looked around him, but no one seemed to be about. He put the key in the lock and hurriedly opened the door.

Kat did not come to greet him, probably with Michael, as usual. From a stand by the door he took a small umbrella and tapped on a pipe that ran right up through the house to the attic with a rhythmical code. There was a muffled tapped response; all is well.

Josef placed the package on his kitchen table and cut the string. He was surprised, yet delighted, to see it would be an excellent gift for his young friend. He left it on the table, though, wanting to check on him first and, more importantly, wanting to present it at a moment when Michael most needed it. He extinguished the lights, rechecked he had locked the door, and went upstairs.

As he opened the attic door, he acknowledged how much the dark, musky room had changed. Once a dry, functional space to store the outlived parts of his life, it had been transformed into a bohemian artist's space. A ramshackle bookshelf was stacked with books Josef had managed to get Michael from his own shelves and the university. Scraps of writing and sketches were pinned across every available space. A crude sitting area had been fashioned from trunks and pillows. The old table now a makeshift desk pushed up into one of the corners, the Rilke book that Josef had given him so long ago was open and propped up against the wall on the desk in pride. A full life crammed into a tiny space, yet full of warmth and frenetic energy.

Michael sat writing in a notebook at his desk, a gaunter version of his earlier self, with the insipid pallor of his skin more than a hint at his two years of captivity, though usually his eyes had the same unmistakable spark. Kat sat comfortably on Michael's lap. As Josef entered, Michael snarled then ripped the page from the book and flung it on the floor, which was littered with crumpled balls of paper.

Michael jumped to his feet, and the cat leaped down. "It has been a hard day. I am frustrated. I need *something* to do."

"Ah," said Josef, cocking one eyebrow.

"I would do anything," he implored.

"Anything?" Held repeated, allowing a small smile to creep across his face. "Then I have something for you," he announced, before turning to go back downstairs.

In the kitchen, from a dusty stack of papers, he pulled out a sheet he had kept for a long time. Returning to the attic, he handed it to Michael.

Michael opened it with a look of curiousity on his face. It was the assignment that he hadn't completed in Held's class over two years before.

"Professor, you can't be serious," said Michael.

Josef couldn't help but smirk as he looked around the attic and repositioned a trunk so he could sit down.

"When the war is over, you might appreciate mathematics," he informed him with some satisfaction.

Michael rolled his eyes. "Fantastic."

"Would you like tea?"

"No, tea won't help, thank you. How is it out there today?"

"Ah," said Josef, "about the same."

"Why do they keep letting you teach, do you think?"

Josef shook his head. "I don't know. So many have now been sent to work camps. I mainly teach girls and people who are too sick to be called up. What about your day?"

Michael shook his head. "We have had quite a day, Dantes and I."

"Who?" enquired Josef, confused.

"Professor, I named your cat a year ago. Do you not remember? I have told you many times."

"Oh, yes, he is still Kat to me, of course. Remind me—from Dante's *Inferno*?"

"No, Edmond Dantes, *The Count of Monte Cristo*, a novel."

"Ah." Not for the first time, Josef considered how different he and Michael were. How he just wanted to call a cat a cat, whereas for Michael the cat could exist both there, and in his imagination as a swashbuckling prisoner who—like him perhaps—would one day break free.

Michael continued, "Dantes and I played tag. We did laps around the room. I think he was trying to tell me the story of his life."

Josef looked at the cat, who was now curled up in a ball on the camp bed. "Yes, well, that seems to have rather tired him out. No prison break for him today, I think. Anyway, Mr. Blum, I have something I think you might really enjoy."

"Oh good, more mathematics no doubt."

Josef brought in the real present for Michael, which he'd rewrapped and left just outside the attic door, while he'd jokingly presented his young friend with the old math equation.

Michael ripped open the brown paper and discovered the small wireless inside. He stared a moment before a large grin broke out on his face. "What...? Where did you...? Where did you get this? I thought these were illegal."

"Everything seems to be illegal now."

"You, a renegade? I would never have believed it. How?"

Josef shook his head. "Actually, I don't know. Would you believe I found it on my front doorstep?"

Michael looked at him and narrowed his eyes. "Interesting. A friend or foe, do you think? Ingrid?" His eyes lit up. "No, maybe it's another woman."

Josef shifted uncomfortably in his seat. "Mr. Blum, you're always a romantic. A very frivolous occupation in such difficult times."

Michael became animated. "Isn't wartime the most important time to fall in love? Don't we need it more than ever? The warm thoughts of my Elke are what keep my heart beating. What about yours?"

Josef stood to his feet, uncomfortable with where this conversation was heading. "Well there is enough excitement out there every day to keep my blood pumping, that's clear, Mr. Blum."

Michael grinned. "You always have to change the subject, but I'm always going to try. You need love in your life, Professor. Everybody does. And my name's Michael, for the hundredth time. Call me Michael."

Josef rapidly changed the subject and pointed at the wireless. "You must keep it very quiet."

"Of course."

"And only listen to it when I am in the house—there cannot be music heard when I am not."

"Yes, sir." Michael turned his attention back to the wireless, swiveling the large black dial to search for a station. Finally, scratchy strains of Mozart came through, a piece that had been a favorite of Mrs. Epstein's.

Josef took a deep breath, the pain and pleasure too hard for him to stand. "Well, if that is all…" he whispered. His throat tightened, and seeing that Michael was engrossed in his new toy, he turned to leave.

The cat jumped down from the bed and followed Josef downstairs, ready for his dinner. As he reached the bottom stair on the landing, a paper airplane created from the math assignment came whizzing past Josef's ears and down the stairs in front of him. Josef couldn't help but smile and shake his head.

Chapter Sixteen

As soon as Hannah opened the front door, she knew her mother was not alone inside. The high-pitched, delighted voice of Eva met Hannah in the hallway. On the coat rack was the usual black woolen coat. Hannah's heart sank as she looked at the yellow star, so meticulously stitched on by Greta's hand. It was much more difficult for the Jewish people to move around the city, but Eva had found a gap in the chainlink fence that was just big enough for her to slip through.

"Nobody cares about little girls," she would state when Hannah and Clara showed their concern.

Hannah closed the door and moved into the sitting room, her suspicions confirmed. Kneeling on the floor next to her mother was their young friend. Two thick black plaits fell way below Eva's shoulders. She wore a simple gray tunic, also made by Greta. Her brown eyes were wide and round as she intently observed and listened to Clara's instructions for a new knitting project.

"I see we have company," said Hannah, trying to be cheerful.

"Why yes," responded Clara as she lifted her snowy head up to greet her daughter. "Eva is so skilled now."

Eva's excited eyes met Hannah's. "Yes, I'm going to knit another blanket. There are many people now who need them."

"Well, I think that sounds wonderful," chirped Hannah as she stoked the fire and moved toward the kitchen to put on the kettle. Hannah's heart stirred again as she thought about this child's life. She looked through her cupboards and managed to find a few nuts and a little dried fruit they had saved from Christmas. She bundled them up into tiny packets and stuffed them into Eva's coat pockets in the hall.

When the kettle had boiled, she poured the water into a teapot and brought a tray into the sitting room. "I think a teacup is in order."

The young girl's face lit up with excitement.

Hannah poured tea into three cups and added a spoonful of milk and sugar. She stretched out a cup toward Eva. "Here, Eva, why don't you sit and drink this tea?"

Eva gingerly took the bone-china cup." My mamma normally doesn't let me hold a teacup. I am quite happy with the cup I usually have."

"Well, you are nearly twelve now," said Clara. "It's time."

"It is?" Eva sat carefully in a chair, spreading out her skirt as she'd apparently been taught by her mamma. Then she crossed her legs, taking the teacup.

"How is your family?" asked Hannah.

Eva's eyes grew dark. She sipped at her tea as if she was trying to think of the right words to say. Instantly, Hannah regretted asking.

"My younger brother Willem is kind of mad right now," she finally said.

"I think we're all a little mad right now," echoed Clara as she hooked a stitch and looked over the top of her glasses at her young friend.

"Last week they took away both my older brothers, like they did my papa before, even though they are only fifteen and sixteen," she added quietly.

The three of them sat in the silence and listened as the fire crackled and spluttered in the background. The only other noise was the clock ticking its regular reassurance.

"Mamma cries all the time now."

Hannah moved to the chair and kissed Eva gently on the top of her head. She whispered into her hair, "These times will pass. Soon you will all be together again, I'm sure."

"Jan got so mad," she continued, "that he went out into the garden and took a stick and hit the bushes and the ground hard over and over saying that he was going to kill every German when he grows up. Then Mamma shouted at him in case anybody heard and pulled him back inside." Eva's eyes became very grave. "I know I have to be strong because I'm the oldest one at home now, but can I tell you something, Miss Clara?"

Clara stopped knitting and nodded slowly.

"I'm very scared. I don't think they're going to bring my papa or my brothers back, and I think that's why Mamma cries."

Hannah took a deep breath, and Clara echoed it.

"You always have a place here, you know," said Clara, the tears catching in her throat. She leaned forward and reached out arthritic fingers to take Eva's small hand. "You can always come here to be safe. Tell your mamma that too."

Eva nodded and sipped away at her tea. They sat in a companionable silence.

Eva seemed to want to change the subject. "May I ask you something?"

"Of course," said Clara. "Anything."

"That box that you have on the fireplace," Eva said, pointing to a colorful carved box that had recently been moved there from Clara's own room. "What is that?"

"That? Well, that," responded Clara, her tone more cheerful, "is perfect for you to ask about. Hannah, pass that down."

Hannah placed it on Eva's tiny lap. Eva put her tea on a side table and stroked the box with her small hands.

"Open it," encouraged Clara. "It has a surprise inside."

Carefully, Eva undid the hook and opened the box. Inside was a brightly dressed ballerina. "Turn the key," added Hannah. "It's at the back."

Eva turned the key, and the ballerina erupted into life, pirouetting to a lilting lullaby. The ballerina looked enchanting.

"I've had that since I was a little girl." Clara smiled. "And I think it's probably time to pass it on to someone like you. Would you like that, Eva?"

Eva smiled, and then her face clouded. "I would like it, but Mamma has told us not to gather anything or take anything home now. Do you think it would be possible that I could keep it here? I think it would be safe then."

Clara nodded. "Of course you can keep it here. And when it's time, you can take it and it'll be yours, and you can pass it on to your children."

Eva looked down as if she didn't believe those words, but forced a smile. "Thank you. It's the best gift I've ever had."

"I have shortbread," said Hannah, clapping her hands together. "I completely forgot. I had to improvise without butter, but it's not bad." She brought three fingers of shortbread from the kitchen and placed them on a plate on Clara's lap. "Why don't you finish those up for us, Eva?"

Eva nibbled away and continued to chat about other things. But the heaviness of the conversation was like a mist that had descended, a thick blanket of sadness that had taken hold of the room and tainted the whole atmosphere.

As the clock chimed six, Eva jumped up. "Oh my goodness, I have to leave. Mamma says I have to be home to help with dinner and the little one. Willem is so much trouble now that he's two," she said, with a tone that obviously had been borrowed from her mother.

Hannah and Clara laughed at the young girl's inflection.

She pulled up her dark brown, ribbed tights, slipped on her worn leather shoes, and made her way out into the hallway.

Hannah helped her on with her coat and buttoned it for her. Eva was rooted to the spot.

"Is something wrong?" she asked.

Eva looked embarrassed. "Mamma said we must not use front doors anymore just in case…" Her voice trailed off.

Hannah understood at once. "Let's use the back door. Follow me. It's more fun anyway. Your mamma is wise. She knows that back-door friends are the best friends."

Hannah watched the young girl slip out the back door into the evening, her black, silken braids bobbing behind her, pockets brimming with the sweets she'd find later.

Once Eva left, Hannah made her way out into the garden, absorbed in her own thoughts. In her hands was a bike chain she'd managed to find on the university campus. She hoped it would fit the latest bicycle she'd been building. Walking out into the early evening, she was aware of something not quite right, something amiss. The hair on the back of her neck stood on end, running a chill down her spine. Quietly listening, she felt she wasn't alone, but all she could hear was an owl hooting.

She continued down the path to the shed, but as she approached, she knew something was wrong. The doors, usually latched and firmly closed, stood slightly ajar, swinging freely on its hinges, groaning in the light breeze that ruffled the trees above her.

All her senses were on guard. She hoped it was just the wind, or maybe a neighborhood cat. She moved tentatively toward the door and peered inside.

Everything appeared undisturbed. She lifted her hand to turn on the light, but something made her hesitate. There it was again, that feeling she was not alone. She stood frozen, listening to her heart pounding the blood through her ears.

All at once, from somewhere at the back of the shed, she heard someone groan. She was about to turn and run when she caught sight of something, some fabric, and instantly she recognized it. Behind a pile of crates of old parts that her father had kept in the corner of the shed, she saw a foot illuminated by a stream of late-afternoon light. The fabric on the trouser cuff was the khaki color of the Allies.

She was suspicious, but she had heard rumors of downed airmen who sometimes found their way into town. Moving through the room tentatively, she saw him. In the dusky evening light, she could see his face clearly; it was pale, as white as paper. His thin, dark lashes fluttered, his eyelids closed as he breathed rapidly in and out, beads of sweat glistening upon his forehead. As her eyes acclimated to the dark, she noticed something else. He had a gash in his side that was sticky with blood. He'd tied a crude bandage around his waist that was also smeared with dry, caked blood.

She slid down to her knees so as not to startle him, then crawled toward him and took his hand. She felt for a pulse. It was thin and thready. The airman's eyes flickered before opening sharply, as though he were about to jump into action. He looked afraid, like a wounded animal caught in a trap.

Hannah reached out to him with her voice. "You're okay. You're safe," she said in English, and then in Dutch and finally in German. The man wet his lips hastily with his tongue. As he became more consciously aware, pain stretched across his face and his hand reached involuntarily to the gash in his side.

Hannah spoke quietly to him. "Don't move. I'm going to get some supplies and something for you to drink. Be still. I'll be back."

His eyes were wild and frantic, but he seemed to understand what she was saying and nodded, sinking back down into the place he'd found in the corner.

Hannah hurried into the house. Deciding not to worry her mother, she rushed to her first-aid cupboard and pulled out what she needed. A needle and suture, bandages, some alcohol, antiseptic, and cotton to dress the wound. In the kitchen, she poured a glass of water and also some sweet tea out of the still-warm pot, knowing that may help him if he was in shock. Then she raced back to the shed.

Kneeling at the young man's side, she started to treat his injuries. He had slumped back into unconsciousness again. She cut off the fabric around his waist. He had sustained a large, shallow wound just below his ribcage, and though he had lost a lot of blood, it appeared not to have punctured any vital organs, just cut into his flesh. After cleaning the wound, she used suture and a needle to close up the gaping hole, grateful for the extra first-aid classes she had attended at the start of the war. He moaned slightly as she tended to him and slipped in and out of consciousness.

Once the wound was closed, she dressed it quickly. He moaned again in his sleep as she applied stinging antiseptic, then clean gauze and bandages. After rinsing her hands in her father's sink, she kneeled next to him, slowly bringing the glass of water up to his lips. Even though he was half awake, he drank greedily of the cooling liquid. It seemed to revive him.

Through dry, cracked lips, he finally spoke. "Am I dreaming?" he asked. "Or are you the most beautiful thing I've ever seen?"

Smiling at him, she shook her head. His accent was unmistakably American, and she marveled at his words. Even though he was apparently in a lot of pain and very dehydrated, he still managed to flirt with her.

Dabbing water on his forehead with a cloth, she whispered into his ear in English, "There is some sweet tea. I'm going to get you some bedding. You will have to stay here while I find out what I need to do for you, but you are very safe. No one comes out here but me."

The young man nodded, then groaned again as he lay back down. Going back into the house, Hannah pulled out a blanket and a pillow from her airing cupboard, then made her way back to the garden shed. She settled the man down and gave him some of the tea before he fell back into a deep sleep. She would come back the following day to re-dress his wounds, she thought, and with some rest, he would probably be okay.

His injuries were the least of her worries, though. She knew nothing of how to help him in the long term. She'd heard stories from people at the university of airmen being found and smuggled out. It had been whispered in the line as she waited for bread too, along with other tales of heroic people working in the Resistance. But Hannah didn't know how to contact anyone.

After settling the man down for the evening, she made the decision that the next morning she would find out how she could help him. After turning off the light in the workshop and closing the door firmly, she strolled up the garden. Hannah could not help Eva, but at least she might be able to help him.

Entering the house, Hannah felt a sense of purpose, a hope that she could do something. She had been learning how to make bicycles for over two years now, studying her father's books and his meticulous handwritten notes. She had long ago finished the trike her father had started, and she now also had two completed adult bicycles hidden in her shed. It was slow work, as the parts were so hard to come by, but she had made them to donate to the cause. Now she had a legitimate reason to track down the Resistance.

Chapter Seventeen

Elke looked up from her desk and glanced out the art gallery's large windows onto the streets of Amsterdam. The rain had stopped and the magnificent tree that was her main view glimmered with droplets of water that shimmered, reflected by the sun as it moved from behind darkened clouds. She was glad spring was finally here. It had felt like a long winter. She enjoyed working in the gallery, had been there for over a year since her translation work had dried up. Though it left her less time to focus on her own paintings, at least it gave her some money.

A man strode toward the door. He was a regular at the gallery. It was the art collector Helmut Janssen; his tall, chiseled features and loose-limbed stride unmistakable. He had one hand tucked carelessly into a trouser pocket of his expensive suit, and his hair was not even ruffled by the wind. He looked like a blond Adonis, she thought to herself.

A broad smile crossed his face as he walked confidently toward her desk. He had been trying to take her out for lunch since she started working at the gallery.

"Miss Dirksen," he said. "I'm glad to find you here."

Elke sat back in her seat and looked up at him. He was well over six feet. "Where else would I be?" she responded, unable to hide the sarcasm in her tone. "This is where I work." She folded her arms across her chest. "What can I do for you today, Mr. Janssen?"

Putting his other hand in a pocket, he spun around the room and surveyed the art on the walls. "Well, let's see then, Miss Dirksen. Let's see what you can help me with today." He walked boldly toward a rather large artwork and, cocking his head from side to side, surveyed it.

Begrudgingly, she stepped from behind the desk. Taking her notepad and her pen, she moved to his side. This was a game they played twice a week. She started to describe the history of the portrait, the artist's name, the inspiration. All the while, he looked at the picture with little interest.

"Sounds good," he nodded. "Why don't you put that on my bill?"

"Where would you hang it?" she said, jokily. "You've already bought so much art. Surely you don't have any space left."

"How would you know?" he responded with a glint in his eye. "If only you'd come to dinner at my house, then you'd be able to see how much space I have."

Shaking her head, she started to write down the information about the picture. "Delivered to the same address?"

He smiled. "Only if you come with it."

Shaking her head again, she turned back toward her desk.

But he held her by the shoulders and spun her around. "Seriously, Elke. When are you going to say yes? All I'm asking is to go out to dinner with you. I could take you somewhere nice. I have contacts. We all hate this blasted war, but fortunately, my family is actually doing quite well through it."

Elke was disgusted at his flippant view of the world. While so many people were suffering around her, here was Helmut in his fashionable suit, buying art he didn't need. "You are fortunate," she said before she could stop herself. "Many are not so." She went back to her desk and started to fill out the order form.

He approached her, leaning across her desk. "I didn't mean it like that. I just meant that you don't have to suffer. All I'm asking for is to take you to lunch or to dinner, even a sandwich."

He brushed her hand.

She pulled away quickly and sat back down.

"Why don't you say yes? Is there someone else?"

Elke felt her stomach contract. The sadness that swelled inside her heart and the ache that still lingered there found its way to her tightened throat. "No, there's no one else."

She had gotten used to saying that, even though her heart was still Michael's. It was easier than trying to explain who she was in love with.

Her boss, Johan Van den Berg, appeared from the back office; a short, lively man with manic energy and quick, darting eyes. He went straight to Helmut's side, extending his hand.

"Helmut, how nice to see you again. I hope Elke is taking good care of you." He glanced from one to the other, his glasses on the edge of his nose, stylish and more of a fashion statement than of any real use.

"She'd be more helpful if she would come for lunch with me," said Helmut, stressing his point. Elke rolled her eyes. "I wanted to show her my art that I have bought here."

"We'd love to see your art," exclaimed Mr. Van den Berg. "What if I were to bring Elke, be a chaperon? Maybe she is afraid of being alone with your good looks," he added, laughing heartily.

"I think it's more than that," stated Helmut. "I wonder if there's someone else in her life."

Van den Berg shook his head. "Elke? No, there's no one else, no one that I've seen anyway."

Fear gripped Elke's heart. She still felt the need to protect Michael. The need to hide him even though she knew he was probably gone, probably somewhere in Germany now in one of those work camps. The thought was unbearable. Automatically, she stiffened.

"I am not afraid of anyone's good looks," she stated sharply.

And almost before she could finish her sentence, Van den Berg took over. "Well then, it is settled. Why don't we come over for lunch one day? I would love to see your house again. I haven't been there since your father left. Elke and I would love to come. Just name the day."

Elke pondered the situation. Maybe it was best to get it over with. Go to his blasted house. He was attractive, she mused, giving him a sideways glance as he continued to chat to Mr. Van den Berg. But there was something wanting about him. Something missing. A hardness of heart, or maybe the fact he didn't seem genuine.

Elke sighed. Was she going to compare every man she met to Michael? Maybe she would never meet anybody like him again. What harm would it do to be friendly to Helmut? she thought. At least he was here. So many men had left and gone to fight the war.

"Is that okay with you, Elke?" asked Mr. Van den Berg enthusiastically.

She nodded. "I think I'll be safe with a chaperon."

"Good," responded Helmut. "Tomorrow for lunch then. Come by at, say, one o'clock. Do you have someone that can watch the gallery?"

"We'll close the gallery," said Mr. Van den Berg. "You buy most of our art anyway, and I can't wait to see how it looks in your house."

Helmut looked across at Elke intensely. "I look forward to seeing you tomorrow, Elke."

She nodded, not looking up from her paperwork. "Until tomorrow," she responded.

And with that, he turned on his heels and left the gallery.

Mr. Van de Berg scuttled behind the counter where she was seated. "You could do a lot worse than him," he reminded her, shaking his head. "You'd never have to worry."

"It's just so detestable, all that money," she responded, vehemently.

He tilted his head. "But why not have a little bit of enjoyment in your life? It has been a long war, and I hear it is not going well. Who knows how many more years we'll be in this situation. Why not have some fun?"

He tapped her shoulder reassuringly then made his way back to his office.

Elke looked out of the window and watched more raindrops fall in a steady stream. Fun? She didn't even remember what that meant anymore.

Chapter Eighteen

Ingrid stood in her sitting room, with a cigarette in one hand, studying different swatches of curtain fabric that were in the other. She held up the gold brocade toward the window and smiled to herself. She imagined it with luxurious, tasseled tiebacks. It could look beautiful, she thought.

She had moved into Heinrich's the year before, when living in her own flat had become impossible. Many of the people who had lived around her had been very anti-Nazi, and she'd had more than one altercation, which had resulted in her talking Heinrich into letting her move into his home. She still didn't understand why the Dutch people didn't see the value of the new regime. Why were they so adamant about hanging onto the old Dutch ways, when Adolf Hitler's vision and army were here to show them a better way?

It frustrated her, and she and Heinrich often spoke about it. She knew that there were a few problems within the regime but wouldn't there be with any new government? If only the Dutch would come to understand how much better life could be.

She now very rarely went on the street in her uniform, in case people she had known before the war recognized she supported the party, but traveled to and from work in Heinrich's car and changed before she went outside. Even then, she was careful about leaving the building, as it was known that a Nazi officer lived there.

Holding the curtain fabric up toward the window, she noticed her uncle moving across the square in his usual measured manner, making his way to see her.

With very little food outside the army supplies he now came to her apartment for lunch on Saturdays. Besides, she felt safer in the confines of her home. She enjoyed redecorating for Heinrich and looked forward to the day that he would take her home to Germany as a bride.

Yes, one day everything Henrich owned would belong to her as well. That would show all her friends from her old neighborhood, when she got married to her tall, handsome officer and moved to Germany with him.

She crushed her cigarette out into the ashtray and made her way into the hall to greet her uncle.

*

Josef made his way down the long dark corridor toward Ingrid's apartment and felt the usual clench in his stomach as he always did whenever he spent time with his niece; cramping that would spread through his body, giving way to a heightened sense of awareness. After the death of Mrs. Epstein, more than two years before, he was always cautious, guarded in everything he said. He had never been able to bring himself to talk to Ingrid of the older lady's death, because he felt responsible. The senseless loss of his neighbor still stung him sharply, stabbing at his conscience like a pick. He would never be that careless again. He knew that they would have found Mrs. Epstein anyway, that they'd been tipped off already. But he knew his words had helped guarantee her fate. The British had adopted a saying that he had read about in the Underground newspapers: "Careless talk cost lives." He knew, with a pained bitterness, precisely what that meant.

Ingrid opened the door, looked at him, smiled coolly, and nodded at him to come into the house. She had changed much in the last few years. The majority of the Dutch people, it seemed to him, had become more compassionate and kinder with one another through this trying time, but Ingrid had become the opposite. Hardened, calloused, and now he only saw in glimpses the kind of person he knew was deep inside her. The young girl that had so craved his love and attention had turned into a woman who demanded and got exactly what she wanted.

"Uncle, it is very pleasant to see you. Come in. I'm choosing curtains for the lounge. You can help me."

Josef removed his overcoat and tried not to show his displeasure at the futility of her request. From the shadows, Ingrid's maid appeared and took his coat. She worked during the day cleaning for Ingrid and preparing food for them during the evening. Josef knew she probably worked just for any extra food.

She nodded at Josef as Ingrid summoned her uncle. "Come."

The maid and Josef's eyes met with a mutual understanding of how they were unwilling players in the same game. Following Ingrid into her opulently decorated lounge, his heart sank as he noticed the maid had prepared a feast of sweets and cakes for him. In a world where even getting a hold of meat or bread was a luxury, her decadence was an insult, though he reminded himself he had to keep up the pretense. He had to keep coming to her house. He did not want her to have an excuse to visit *him*. It was hard enough when she'd just drop by, but fortunately, since she had moved in with Heinrich, there had been fewer reasons for her to come and see him.

"Do you like the gold?" she said, holding the curtain up to the window.

Josef nodded stiffly. "It's fine," he replied.

"I cannot decide on this or the green one." She held up another swatch. "I'm having the silk brought in from Paris."

She made it sound like there wasn't even a war on. There were things possible for her with the Third Reich that the average Dutch person hadn't seen since before the war.

With a deep sigh, she threw the samples down on the back of a chair. "Maybe I'll just order more options. I'm not sure I like either of them. How are you, Uncle?" she asked as she lit another cigarette and walked to the window to look out.

"Fine," he said. "And you, Ingrid, how are you?"

"Sick of this damn war," she snapped back, blowing out a plume of smoke. "It's really interfering with the life that Heinrich and I are trying to make for ourselves." She reeled off her list of grievances as she paced, starting with the Resistance and ending with her hatred for the Jews. "They keep Heinrich so busy. He's barely able to spend time with me anymore."

She tapped out her cigarette and automatically lit another one. Leaving the window, she arranged herself across the other side of the room on a chair as she continued to talk. "I feel like we do not see enough of each other, Uncle. Maybe we should think about getting together more. You look sad. I feel like you need someone in your life. I know a woman in the Reich offices who is about your age. Would you like me to introduce you? You could both come for dinner with Heinrich and me," she said, suddenly alight with the idea.

Josef's throat became dry and raspy; the thought of an evening with three Nazis almost overpowered him. It was hard enough being with Ingrid, but at least he could talk to her about family matters or her father or Dutch issues. Whenever Heinrich was about, he dominated the conversation, making his harsh and robust opinions known.

"No. No. I am fine. I wouldn't want you to go to that kind of trouble."

"It would be no trouble, Uncle."

Josef shook his head. "There is no one for me now. Not after…" Josef couldn't say her name.

Ingrid filled in the blank. "My aunt, Sarah. I'm sure she was a wonderful woman, but I barely remember her. I think you should think about moving on, Uncle."

Josef got up and started to move around the room. "I, uh, need to use the…" He pointed toward the bathroom and Ingrid nodded.

"I'm not going to give up on the idea, not until I see you happy with another woman," she sang after him as he made his way back into the hallway.

He moved into the bathroom and shut the door, splashing water on his face.

As he did his thoughts returned to Hannah Pender. Over the past few years, seeing her had become something he looked forward to. It sometimes felt as if he couldn't wait to pick up his mail and so he would also invent excuses to drop by her desk to ask questions. Maybe because she was married and so off limits, but listening to her laugh or watch her face light up with a smile as she told him a story was often the highlight of his day. He could still never imagine being with anyone else but Sarah. But it was good to talk to someone kind, thoughtful, and generous, nevertheless.

He waited for several minutes, hoping that by the time he returned Ingrid would have forgotten the conversation and returned to her decorating. When he finally exited the bathroom, she was talking on the telephone in the hallway. Even at a distance, he could tell that she was agitated. Putting down the telephone, she strode back toward him.

"Uncle, I have bad news. I have to leave. Once again, they have a problem at work, and Heinrich needs me to sort it out. I don't know what they would do in the office without me."

Josef nodded, pleased for any reason to be able to leave. Before she even spoke another word, the maid appeared in the hallway with his coat. Putting it on, he nodded at Ingrid as she walked him to the door.

"I'm so sorry, Uncle Josef. Maybe we can spend more time together next week. Are you sure you don't want me to invite my friend Ursula over?"

Josef shook his head a little too vigorously. Following it up with, "I'm very happy on my own. There will be nobody else for me in this world."

She gave him her usual tart smile. "We will talk more about a special friend for you at another time," she stated, opening the door.

He left without responding and made his way down the corridor.

Once he heard the door close behind him, he took in a deep breath and descended the stairs. This weekly event for him was such a trial, but he reminded himself he was doing it to keep her from his home, to keep Michael safe.

Chapter Nineteen

The following Monday, Michael stood and stretched, then made his way to the tiny cracked window in the attic. Carefully standing to the side, he pressed his face flat against the wall. His gaze stretched across the red-tiled rooftops that ran all the way to Munttoren, the medieval clock tower that chimed every fifteen minutes. Whenever he stared toward the yellow-colored numbers he would often wonder about the people who lived in the brown-and-cream buildings with their stepped gabled facades that sat in tall regimented rows between him and the tower that seemed to mock his captivity every quarter of an hour. Were other people marking time with him? he wondered. He would pay particular attention to the other attic windows—did they too hide secrets of their own? From his position he could also just about see the flowers starting to bloom in one of the neighbor's hanging baskets, gorgeous yellow tulips. He had written a poem about them the day before, and now he closed his eyes, trying to imagine how they might smell.

Before the war, having the time and space to hide away in a small room to write poetry would have been intriguing. But now, two years of doing just that had become confining and demoralizing. His whole world began and ended in this room. How he wished he could walk outdoors, smell flowers, stare at a tree, watch a bird. Surely the war will end soon, he thought to himself.

Pacing the attic, as he so often did, he sat down on one of the trunks. "Dantes," he said to his companion, "we need an adventure. We could end up dying of boredom in this room."

He threw a crumpled ball of paper toward Dantes and watched his cat bat it around before it ended up among some boxes. Michael bent down to retrieve it. As he did, his attention was drawn to a trunk tucked away in the corner of the attic. He had seen it many times before and knew that Held kept it locked, but he had never seen the professor venture into it. Feeling a little mischievous, he started to pull out the boxes that surrounded the chest so he could get a better look.

"Look, Dantes. Shall we finally see if there's treasure in it?"

He knew he shouldn't be going through the professor's things, but he was craving something, anything, to stimulate him, and it was like a sort of madness. He wanted to write a poem about something new, something not from memory. Something that he could touch and feel, look at.

He wished he could join the Resistance. He wanted to fight, but being Jewish and maybe bringing unwanted attention to the movement meant that was out of the question. He also still loved Elke and had promised her he would come back. He had to stay hidden and be strong for her. He had to stay alive so he could one day marry her. Hell, he had to stay alive just to repopulate the Jewish people. He knew that Elke had talked about converting if their relationship continued and increasingly he hoped she had really meant it. They would need to have many children if the rumors were true.

"You're not very talkative today," he informed Dantes, who promptly turned over and went to sleep.

He managed to free the trunk from its space in the far corner. It felt heavy as he slid it along the wooden floorboards. He was disappointed to find it was indeed locked firmly.

Back at his desk, dejected, he turned on the wireless so quietly it was barely audible, allowing delicate strains of Brahms to dance through the dusty room. He would just have to wait, see if he could write a poem about a locked trunk. But as he wrote, he became more and more frustrated with not knowing its contents. Unwinding a piece of wire from one of his spiral notebooks, he decided to try picking the lock. It took him a while, but eventually, the lock flipped open.

At the grinding sound of the metal hook freeing itself, Dantes jumped down from the bed and came to investigate. As Michael pushed open the lid and peered inside, the cat sprawled himself across his lap and began to purr.

"Oh, Dantes, this really is treasure."

On top lay a pair of laced gloves, carefully folded into tissue paper with a dried bridal bouquet. He lifted out items one at a time and placed them around him on the floor in amazement. Bundles of classical sheet music, letters wrapped in ribbons, a veil made of delicate cream lace, and a framed photo of a couple on their wedding day.

"Look at this," he said as he unwrapped the veil, placing it on his head and throwing the train over his shoulder. "What do you think, Dantes? Does it suit me?"

Dantes responded by stabbing a paw at the end of the gauzy fabric, catching it in a claw and flicking it up for his own entertainment.

As they continued this adventure, the delicate piano music from the wireless moved the musty air. He continued to search through the trunk, wondering what it all meant. He shuffled through a stack of photographs and scrutinized a picture of a young couple. He was shocked to recognize Professor Held.

Michael hadn't realized. Josef, *young* Josef, looked so vibrant and alive. Such a difference from the man that he knew now, but it was definitely him. Same eyes, same dark hair, but with a smile that permeated his whole face. Michael stopped and thought for a moment. Had he ever seen Josef truly happy?

Seeing the professor's arms wrapped around a beautiful woman's waist was a shock. Jarring somehow. Reminding Michael he was intruding, doing something wrong.

Moving closer to the window, he looked intently at the sepia photograph. The tiny woman was beautiful. She had long ringlets and vibrant eyes. Michael turned over the photograph. Written on the back in a delicate script, were the words "Josef and Sarah."

"Sarah," he said, rolling the name across his tongue for the first time. Who was Sarah? He and Josef had lived together for all this time, and he'd never mentioned that he'd been married.

If that's what it was, he thought, looking at the happy couple who stared back at him again. That was definitely what it looked like. He continued to shuffle through the photographs and found another one. This time Josef's hands were poised on piano keys and Sarah was lifted high on top, where she beamed, a violin snug under her chin.

"Josef played the piano." Shock traveled through Michael's body. His friend that had saved him from the Nazis whom he spoke to every single day, had not mentioned any of these things. It was unnerving.

There would be a lot of food for thought for his poetry in this trunk.

Wanting to unravel all the mysteries, Michael continued to pull out things. The rest was mainly women's clothes and a few trinkets. But at the bottom lay a violin case. Taking it carefully out of the chest, he opened it up.

Chapter Twenty

That same day, Josef left the secure warmth of his classroom and walked down the hallway. As he approached Hannah Pender's desk though, he was stopped short. In front of him, in the familiar gray uniform, a German soldier was chatting in a very animated fashion with Hannah. Josef's instinct was to feel angry. Was it because she was talking so lightly to the enemy? Or was it, he realized with some surprise, that he felt jealous? He had got used to their friendly interaction, and looked forward to stopping by her desk each day. But as she threw her head back and laughed at something the soldier had said he realized again how much he had grown to like her. Even if he still wasn't sure he could trust her.

He stayed back. Not wanting to approach. What if he asked her about the books he'd ordered for Michael, and there were questions from the soldier? He decided to wait. He turned and moved back down the hallway at a slow, metered pace, hoping it would appear he'd forgotten something.

Back in the safety of his classroom, he stood by the tall windows and took a minute to appreciate the view of the red-brick courtyard. Plants bobbed and weaved in a gentle breeze under the warmth of a late spring sun; the trees were lush, laden with an abundance of new green foliage. Sarah had loved this time of year. His chest tightened as he thought of her face, her emerald-green eyes alive with the joy of the new season. He squeezed his eyes shut, not sure if by doing so he would bring the memory of her closer or push it farther away.

Since the death of his neighbor, he had found himself unable to keep thoughts of Sarah from bubbling up to the surface. He had no choice but to live with the intense reflections of their few short years together. Initially, memories that he had repressed for over two decades seemed to burn through him like a raging wildfire. But they had, over the past two years, been tamed to glowing coals; no less hot or painful but somehow more manageable and predictable. He sometimes wished that he could move on and then would instantly feel waves of guilt. The love he still felt for her was as intense as ever. How could it have been so many years ago, yet still feel like yesterday?

As he waited, he watched a mother bird encouraging a fledgling out of a nest that was tucked high in the campus eaves. The space between the warm, wiry nest and the ground must have felt insurmountable to her tiny protégé. As he watched her coax her offspring, he reasoned that not one thing enjoyed the kind of change that challenged them out into the unknown.

After what felt like a safe amount of time, he slowly paced to the door, shut it behind him, and locked it. At an even slower rate, he turned the corner and looked to see if Hannah was alone. The Nazi was still there, but he could tell by their body language that the conversation was coming to an end.

As he approached the desk, the soldier nearly collided with him and then straightened, bobbing his head. "Professor Held."

Josef recognized him as one of the patrolling soldiers who now worked permanently on the campus. He nodded his acknowledgment.

Hannah was still smiling as he reached the desk. It made him apprehensive, as did many things these days. She spoke excellent German, and she seemed to get on well with the enemy. But her eyes brightened as she saw him approach.

"Professor," she said in her upbeat way. "You are here for your mail, no doubt. And I have a surprise for you." She leant forward and covered his hand with hers, causing him to swallow hard at her touch. Then she moved to another room and came back through the door with a heavy parcel. Putting it on the desk, she smiled, a quizzical look on her face. "Here are the books you ordered." The parcel had been opened so the Nazis could inspect it.

"Thank you, Mrs. Pender," he acknowledged, trying to keep his voice on an even keel. The soldier, who had moved farther down the desk, was still in earshot of their conversation.

Hannah playfully held onto it and appearing to want to prolong their interaction studied the pile in front of her. "Literature," she stated in an accusatory tone. "I had no idea you had an interest."

Josef froze. He was not good at lying, but he did not want her to guess the truth, so he just nodded.

But Hannah wasn't giving up. "And science," she said. "You obviously like mathematics, but I've never known you to order science books before." Her eyebrows rose. "And here's the most surprising of all," she added, picking up a smaller, thicker book. Her eyes flashed mischievously, "A book of poetry? Professor Held, it's as if I don't know you."

Josef stared at her numbly, not knowing what else to do. He felt caught. They had all become wary of any conversation that delved too deep, questioned too deliberately. Was she just being friendly or was it more? The Germans had made them all paranoid.

"My mail," he said, a little more harshly than he had intended, inadvertently forcing her to give up her game and push the books toward him. The look of disappointment that crossed her face wounded him because he realized she was only being playful, just wanting to connect. He regretted not responding in a similar vein.

Her cheeks flushed pink and she answered him in a much quieter tone. "I will get it for you, Professor."

He hadn't meant to hurt her with his brusqueness, but the reality was he had Michael to think of, and Michael's safety never left his thoughts. As she sorted through the pile of letters, he took a minute to look at her once again, dressed in a black A-line skirt and a soft cream blouse. He wondered about Mr. Pender and if he realized how fortunate he was to have such a beautiful and vivacious wife. Then he tried to recall if he had ever met him and he was sure he hadn't.

Josef swallowed hard as he felt something swell in his heart, a desire for closeness again, and with someone just like Hannah. For the briefest of moments he imagined himself kissing her and he shook the thought away, embarrassed. Surely it was just awkward nostalgia—because he had just been thinking of Sarah, missing her so much.

All at once, the soldier was by his side again, asking Hannah another question in rapid German. Josef felt the blood drain from him with the man's proximity. A gray-uniformed arm lay across the desk, inches from the bundle of books, the Wordsworth poetry book on the top. Held quickly gathered the bundle and the pile of mail together. Not even bothering to sort the stack, he turned toward the door.

It was only when he'd actually arrived at the doorway that he took a moment to look back. Hannah and the soldier were chatting and nodding once again; they didn't seem to suspect anything untoward was going on. He took a deep breath and hurried out into the late afternoon, where the spring sun warmed the ground of the courtyard.

He hurried straight home in excitement to get his gifts to his young friend. Books in hand, he forgot to tap the code and rushed up to the attic.

Chapter Twenty-One

Michael was startled when the door opened. Still engrossed in the trunk and listening to the wireless, he hadn't heard Professor Held climbing the attic stairs. "Professor, what is all—?"

But he never managed to finish his sentence before Held took in the scene and looked horrified. Lunging at Michael, he spat out, "How dare you!?"

He seized the violin and its case from Michael's lap, snatched up all the items scattered across the floor and reverently placed them back in the trunk. "Take that off!" he raged at Michael, who was wearing the wedding veil in a comedic fashion.

Michael sheepishly removed it and looked at Josef. He attempted to ask again, "What is all this?"

Professor Held stopped him short. "This is none of your business, that's what it is." For the first time, Michael heard pain underlying his friend's voice. The anguish was palpable.

"I'm sorry, Professor. I didn't think. I didn't know."

"No, you didn't," responded Held as he firmly shut the lid on the trunk and reset the lock. "You just assumed you could break into my locked trunk?"

Michael felt awful. "I'm sorry. I didn't mean to. I didn't know."

"These are her—" Held stopped, then corrected himself. "*My* private things." He was shaking now with white rage.

Michael responded quietly, "I didn't know you were married."

Held glared at him. "My life is none of your concern."

In spite of feeling guilty about breaking into Held's trunk, with these words from him Michael felt slapped, betrayed even. They had spoken every day for over two years, and he assumed Held had always been single. "Why did you never tell me?"

"You do not have the right to my life! You do not have the right to—"

All at once there was a loud knock at the front door. They were both startled, and Held immediately exited the attic. Michael quietly turned off his light and the wireless, and shut the attic door, left alone in the dark with his turbulent feelings and Held's past.

Josef raced down the attic stairs, placing the pile of books he had for Michael on one of the steps on the way down. On the ground floor, he took two deep breaths and opened the door. Waiting on the doorstep were Ingrid and Heinrich. Held tried to take a hold of himself, his emotions, heart, and thoughts still caught up in the past. Trapped in the attic. Seeing her things. Her violin had been too much for him.

Ingrid must have read something on his face. "Are you okay, Uncle?" she asked with concern.

Josef looked blankly at her. "Yes, yes," he responded. Then after a slight pause added, "Come in. Come in." He could only hope his invitation would deter her from further investigation.

He checked the streets to see if the neighbors had noticed the car. He was sure by now that they were convinced he was a Nazi sympathizer. As he closed the door, he wondered how he was going to keep up any pretense with his niece, how he was going to switch from such a deep inner stirring to socializing with Nazis.

Fortunately, Ingrid filled all the space. Throwing her arms around her uncle, she hugged him exuberantly. "We have such wonderful news, Uncle."

Josef nodded and ushered them into the front parlor. Ingrid sat on the only couch, and Heinrich stood by the fireplace. "Do you mind if I smoke?" he asked.

Held shook his head. "I will go and get an ashtray."

In the kitchen, he opened and closed cupboards loudly, feigning an attempt to search for the ashtray so he could just breathe deeply and calm himself. He was jarred, jangled. Her photograph in Michael's hand had taken him back to a time he thought was forgotten. And now it was here, all around him, the ghosts in every corner, music that he would never hear or play again, her laughter, her eyes, her soft hands on his face…

He located the ashtray and, as he took hold of it, noticed his hand shaking. He took another deep breath before walking back into the parlor and handing the ashtray to Heinrich.

"So, you have news?"

Ingrid jumped up enthusiastically. "We are getting married."

Held sat down hard on a chair and tried to digest this information. Did she mean she was going to marry the Nazi? That he was going to be related to a Nazi? It was bad enough that she was dating him. Surely she wasn't going to further humiliate herself. In response, all he could manage was, "Oh," and, realizing that was impolite, stood up, held out his hand, and offered it to Heinrich. "Congratulations."

"We have champagne," announced Ingrid. Held noticed a bottle in Heinrich's hand for the first time. "Let's open it and celebrate properly."

Josef nodded and made his way back into the kitchen, and they followed him, laughing and joking, telling the story of how Heinrich had proposed.

"It was so romantic," gushed Ingrid. "Heinrich took me out for a very expensive dinner and then for a beautiful walk along the canal, where he asked me."

"The Führer encourages family values, and your niece threatened to leave me unless there was an understanding between us. And I have become accustomed to having a woman to take care of me," Heinrich responded flatly.

"You know you wanted to ask me," said Ingrid coyly. "I just helped it along."

Josef nodded, only really half listening, his stomach knotted. In a time when food and gaiety was the last thing on most people's mind, this exuberance just seemed an insult to decency. He buried himself in the cupboard to search for glasses. Caught up in their own world, neither Heinrich or Ingrid seemed to notice his anguish.

As he returned to the table with the glasses, Heinrich slapped him hard on the back. "So, now we are to be family, Uncle Josef," he said jubilantly.

Josef stopped dead and swallowed before echoing, weakly, "Family."

They poured the champagne and Heinrich lifted his glass in a toast. "To family and to us winning this war so we can all live happily," he said, his glass high in the air. He punctuated his sentiment with, "Heil Hitler."

Ingrid parroted, "Heil Hitler."

Josef muttered something into his glass and quickly took a sip before there was any attention drawn to his lack of enthusiasm.

Ingrid fluttered about the kitchen. "As soon as this war's over, we will settle in Germany and have beautiful babies together," she preened.

Heinrich looked awkward. "Well, let's not jump ahead," he said. Josef noticed an odd look when he responded, the first time he'd seen something cloud the face of this pompous, arrogant man.

As Josef tried to assess it, Ingrid continued to twitter on. "You will of course come and live with us, Uncle."

Josef almost choked on his drink. "Uh, well, but the university…"

"But they have the finest universities in Germany. Don't they, Heinrich?"

Heinrich ignored her, seemingly wanting to move on from the conversation.

"I'm so happy," Ingrid squealed, again, as she knocked back her drink.

Suddenly, overhead, something heavy clattered to the floor. Josef, almost choking on his champagne, prayed that they hadn't heard it.

"What was that?" said Heinrich.

Josef's body went limp. "Yes, it's the, um… cat," he sputtered out. "He likes to… wander."

"I'll get him," said Ingrid, jumping up from the table. "I love Kat."

Josef got to his feet, starting to panic. "Oh no. You stay here. I'll find him."

Ingrid responded forcefully, pushing Josef back into his chair. "No, you talk to Heinrich. You have much to discuss. My wedding plans, no doubt. Because, of course, you will give me away." And before Josef could say anymore, Ingrid darted from the room, leaving him motionless, gripping his glass so tightly he was fearful of crushing it. Heinrich smiled awkwardly at him. They clearly had nothing to discuss.

Josef tried to force himself to drink calmly as he heard Ingrid's voice moving about the upstairs landing. "Here, kitty, kitty."

He could stand it no longer. Babbling something to Heinrich about a loose floorboard and some concern for Ingrid, he excused himself and raced up the stairs. When he arrived, he found Ingrid on the landing, looking up toward the attic, where books were splayed haphazardly down the stairs. The pile he had brought home for Michael. Kat must have knocked them down.

"This is where the noise came from," she said, surveying the disarray. "Look at all these books, Uncle. You should really tidy up." She started to make her way up the attic stairs. "This old attic hasn't been used for so long; I wonder if Kat is stuck in there." She continued up the stairs.

Josef moved quickly, reaching up for her hand and pulled her down the steps and into his arms for a tight, awkward hug, something he would never ordinarily do. "I'm so happy for you," he burbled into her hair. "This is not the time, Ingrid. We should be celebrating. It is your engagement party. Come on downstairs. We can do this another time."

"Oh, yes," Ingrid giggled, squeezing his arm. "You're right. He's going to make such a lovely husband, don't you think?"

"Of course he is," said Josef, and he closed the landing door, taking her by the arm and escorting her down the stairs.

They found Heinrich in the kitchen petting the cat.

"There you are, Kat," Ingrid exclaimed. She ran her hand along the cat's back before moving to pour more champagne and continue their conversation. "I think getting married and settling down is just what is needed. Heinrich has been so busy, and I know he's homesick. He's always calling Germany."

Heinrich shifted in his seat again. "It's good, yes, to have some joy. There are many unfortunate events happening right now. But when we win, everyone's life will be better."

Ingrid nuzzled into Heinrich, who looked as uncomfortable as Josef felt.

Heinrich pulled away from her, changing the subject. "Did you hear, Professor, that the registration office was burnt down yesterday?"

"Yes, I heard," Josef responded flatly. Not meeting the other man's gaze, he opted instead to stare down into the champagne glass he was only pretending to drink from.

"We're going to crack down on this," Heinrich continued. "Whoever did it, don't worry. We're going to crush this resistance. Not everyone is good like you, one of us. If you hear anything, anything at all while you're at the university, you must come to me at once. We will deal severely with these traitors. And there are rewards for those who help."

"A reward?" Josef couldn't keep the ice from his tone.

Ingrid, growing impatient, changed the subject again. "We have so much to plan for the wedding, so much we need to talk about.

Though Heinrich says we have to wait to be married until after the war," she said sullenly.

Heinrich cut her short. "We don't have time to discuss details right now. We must go, Ingrid. I have to get back to this fire inquiry." Then, knocking back the rest of his drink, he stood.

"Okay," Ingrid sighed reluctantly, following him into the hall and putting on her coat. "But we need to make time soon, Uncle Josef. We are going to have so much planning to do together. I should start coming over here much more."

Heinrich ushered her out into the street, but she managed to turn and kiss her uncle on the cheek as they exited.

Held swallowed away his fear as her words echoed in his mind, "so much planning to do together." How would he ever be able to keep Michael safe?

Chapter Twenty-Two

On Tuesday, Hannah awoke early and, while it was still dark, made her way down the garden path and out to the workshop, taking with her a cup of hot coffee and also a little food.

She didn't even pull on the light chain in the shed as she closed the door behind her, not wanting to draw the attention from her neighbors this early in the morning.

She found the airman in the corner, now sitting upright and huddled under the blankets she'd given him the first night. Reaching out to him in the darkness, she whispered, "Are you awake?" As her eyes started to adjust to the lack of light, she noticed his own were open and alert.

"Hi." His voice was raspy, but calm. "I don't think we've been formally introduced, even though you have been taking such good care of me for the last few days. My name is Joe Jankowski." He reached toward her as she dropped to her knees. In taking his hand, she was heartened that his temperature seemed cooler than it had been over the weekend.

"Hannah," she responded. "How are you feeling today?"

"Apart from being hit in the ribs by a meat hammer, I feel great," he joked.

She handed him the cup of hot coffee. "Maybe this will help a little."

He took it with a thankful nod.

Hannah studied him, carefully, as he sipped his drink. He was stocky, with dark hair and gentle brown eyes. He was only a hairsbreadth from being striking due to a broad nose.

"How did you find your way to my house?"

"It wasn't easy, I can tell you." He had a strong Brooklyn accent. She recognized its musical cadence from the New York students she knew at the university. "I came down about a mile from here. My parachute didn't open properly, which is how I managed to get this wound in the ribs when I hit a tree coming down. I hid my chute in some woodlands, under a pile of leaves. It took me hours to limp here. It's fortunate your house backs onto the woods. I just hoped if I could get to somebody that was Dutch that maybe they could lead me to the Underground."

Hannah nodded. "I don't know if I can help you, but I'm going to try." She gave him the hard lump of dark-brown bread that she'd had in the larder.

"Wow," he joked, "you guys know how to eat here in Holland."

"Trust me," Hannah chuckled in return, "that's good. Look, I will find out how to get you out. You should be safe in our workshop for a few days. Do you need anything?"

His eyes lit up as he rolled his words. "I'd love a cigarette. Would you happen to have a smoke?"

Hannah shook her head. "You'll have to be careful about the smoke. My father used to have a pipe. It must be here somewhere. Does that interest you at all?"

"A pipe?" Joe smirked. "My grandfather smokes a pipe. Do I look that old?"

"It's all I have," laughed Hannah.

"Okay, I'll take it." He sealed the negotiation by slapping his hand on his thigh.

Hannah looked about the shelves of the workshop and located her father's old pipe and a tiny amount of shredded tobacco in a tin. She handed it to him.

"Who knew that when I joined the war, they'd be rationing tobacco and turning me into Sherlock Holmes?" He comically posed with the pipe, then winced with pain.

Shaking her head, Hannah cautioned him, "Please be careful. Your body is still repairing. I will change these before I go," she added as she began to methodically unravel his bandages. "Hopefully I'll be able to find something out to help you today."

She changed and cleaned his wound and added fresh bandages to it. He watched her in awe. "You're a regular Florence Nightingale. You sure you're not a nurse?"

"I am first-aid trained. I have to be for my work," she informed him, finishing up. "Unfortunately, I have nothing for you to read," she apologized as she got up to leave. "Everything I have is in Dutch. Do you speak Dutch?"

Joe shook his head. "But I guess now would be a good time to learn," he said ruefully. "Do you have a pack of cards perhaps?"

Hannah nodded and reached up to one of her father's shelves, where he'd always kept a pack.

"My mother used to make me play solitaire when I got too boisterous," he said. "Now it might actually do me some good."

"I'll be back later," she assured him and made her way to the house to get ready for work.

Leaving before it was fully light, she walked through the dark-blue morning. The day was warm and pleasant, and the natural world was alive with the activities of spring. At Mrs. Oberon's house, new starlings called out to their parents from a tightly bound nest tucked in the eaves. Sparsely feathered heads bobbed about, their bulbous eyes, still closed, overshadowed by large open beaks waiting hungrily to be fed their breakfast.

Hannah knocked quietly at the door and waited for her old friend. Mrs. Oberon was an early riser, and if she could trust anyone who might know about the Underground, it would be Oma.

After a moment's pause, Hannah heard the woman's familiar shuffle, and in the transom above the door, a light went on. Mrs. Oberon appeared in the doorway looking concerned, and then a smile broke out across her face as she noticed who was waiting there for her on her doorstep.

"Hannah, what a lovely surprise. What are you doing here so early in the morning? Please come in." The older woman gestured Hannah inside as her two plump cats greeted Hannah at the door. Mrs. Oberon admonished the rather demonstrative tabby as it threaded its warm, furry body through Hannah's legs. "Move back, Tiger. Let our visitor in."

Mrs. Oberon ushered Hannah into her warm little kitchen, where lines of clean laundry hung from wooden drying racks and a black cast-iron kettle bubbled merrily on an open range.

"What can I do for you?" asked the older lady. Her face furrowed with concern. "Is Clara okay?"

"We are both fine. But… I wonder if you know anything about the Resistance?"

Mrs. Oberon's face lit up. "Are you planning on working for them?" she responded with glee, as though she approved.

"Not on purpose," responded Hannah, "but I may need to speak to somebody."

"Uh-huh." Mrs. Oberon nodded. "Well, I don't get out much myself. But I did hear from Mrs. Janson," she continued in a whisper, even though she lived alone, "that last year, when there was the talk of English fighters being shot down, Mr. Markus at the butchers was the one who helped get them out of the country."

"Good," responded Hannah hopefully, "that sounds like a place to start."

"Do you have time for tea?" Mrs. Oberon implored, her face alight with expectation.

Hannah, knowing Oma loved company, responded, "I would love a cup," even though she didn't really feel like another drink.

"Good." Mrs. Oberon bustled her way to the stove, where she put two large teaspoons of inky black tea into a dainty blue teapot, followed by steaming hot water from the kettle. Twenty minutes later Hannah was back on her way to work, deciding she would go to the butchers later.

*

As this was the day she only worked till lunchtime, she eventually got to the butchery around 1.30 p.m. and joined the other housewives in line. Waiting for over an hour, she listened to the neighborhood women confiding in each other the best places to get their produce to feed hungry families. Once she reached the front, she drew herself close to the counter and whispered to Mr. Markus as he weighed out some pork chops for her, "Mr. Markus? I might need some help."

The butcher's large, hairy eyebrows rose a little, seeing the need in her face. He didn't say anything but listened intently as he continued to pack the thin slivers of meat.

"I have an issue and need to talk to somebody who might be…" she tried to use her words carefully, "sympathetic toward the Allies."

Mr. Markus grunted and continued to pack her chops, moving to the back of the shop to wrap her dinner in brown paper. He stamped her ration card and handed her the tightly packed bundle. "I'm sorry, Mrs. Pender, I can't help you. I don't know how to advise you."

She was surprised at how brusque he was, how he seemed to want her to leave the shop, but when she arrived home later and unpacked the meat, she understood why. Inside the brown wrapping, he had scribbled an address and the time 5 p.m.

Chapter Twenty-Three

In the late afternoon, Hannah slipped out the back door, telling Clara she needed to finish her errands. She had decided not to worry her mother by telling her where she was going. At least Joe was doing better when she'd checked on him earlier, even starting to stand and move around. He joked about taking her dancing now he was up on his feet again.

The streets were quiet and the air crisp as she passed by a group of soldiers who waved her through on her journey into a part of Amsterdam she hadn't often ventured into. The area of the city, known for its artistic, bohemian community, experienced very little violence and offered a quiet place for poets and painters. Apart from the odd Resistance poster or eloquent graffiti-covered wall, the neighborhood hardly seemed worthy of the Nazis' time. The houses were brightly colored in the Dutch style, set back on the pavement, reaching into the sky. The smell of paint and brewing coffee scenting the air.

Hannah slipped soundlessly down a residential street with the name she had been given, turned into a narrow alleyway, and located the door with the number she had memorized from the brown butcher's paper.

From the outside the house looked unremarkable, a blue door with a pretty hanging basket of purple-and-yellow violas the only thing to mark its presence. Expecting something more ominous or clandestine, she was warmed and surprised by its disarming presentation. If she didn't know better, she could have been visiting a friend.

With her heart practically pounding out of her chest, she glanced about as she rang the bell and waited for someone to answer, not sure what to expect. But as the door opened, she was mildly surprised by the short, elderly woman who greeted her. Her hair was plaited into two braids, pinned neatly across her head. With her sparkling eyes, round face, and flat, pink cheeks, she looked more like a grandmother than a femme fatale.

The older woman nodded and smiled at Hannah as she dried her hands on a flowery tea towel. Her rumpled clothes and colorful apron showed traces of flour, presumably gathered from whatever Hannah could smell wafting down the hallway to welcome her.

Hannah looked at the number on the door again and then smiled politely at the woman who greeted her brightly.

"Can I help you?"

Hannah faltered, trying to find the words needed. She settled on, "I was sent here by my butcher."

Even to Hannah, that sounded ridiculous. But the woman didn't seem in the least surprised and just nodded, ushering her in. "I'm glad," she said pleasantly. "He is kind, thinking to invite you. You're just in time for tea."

Hannah found herself shuttled into a long, dark foyer with pretty Dutch floor tiles.

"Come this way," her new acquaintance instructed as she bounded off down the hallway, opening a kitchen door. She invited Hannah to sit at a long wooden farmhouse-style table, then moved back to her stove and, humming to herself, checked her oven. "Not many ingredients, these days," she announced dismally with a shake of her head. "But I do my best. Would you like tea, dear?"

Hannah shook her head and waited. For what, she wasn't quite sure. The woman took biscuits out of the oven and placed them on a cooling rack as the scent of cinnamon and cloves filled the kitchen. There was something quite bizarre about the whole experience.

Just then, the kitchen door opened and in came an elderly man as squat as the woman but twice as round. He had a short, dark goatee and a balding head and was scanning the front page of a newspaper as he walked in.

"We have a visitor," announced the woman in a singsong voice. "Someone from Mr. Markus."

The man looked carefully at Hannah and nodded, apparently weighing her up. "You are local?" he asked, removing his spectacles and peering at her.

"Yes. I work at the university. My name is Hannah Pender."

"The university. Very nice."

"I have somebody that I need... to help." She tried to find the correct words. "Somebody who is not from around here."

The man nodded and looked at her with kind eyes. Placing the newspaper in front of him on the table, he came to her side. "This person, who is not from around here—where is he now?"

"He is staying in my workshop at the bottom of my garden." She tried to keep it vague but also felt that she instantly trusted this man. "He is safe. No one goes in there except me."

"Aha!" the man said. "He is well?"

Hannah nodded. "He arrived with a severe flesh wound, but I managed to tend to it, stitch it, and clean it, and he appears to be making a full recovery."

Her new friend looked impressed.

Hannah continued. "Our house backs onto a wood, his plane came down and he managed to find his way to our shed. It would—I think—be fairly straightforward to get him away secretly. Especially at night."

"You live alone?"

Hannah shook her head. "With my mother. She is housebound. And... well, while I am here, I also have two bicycles in the workshop I would like to donate to the cause."

The older man's eyes lit up. "Wonderful. Please write down your address." He pushed a piece of paper toward her. "And we will take care of it for you."

While she obliged him, he went over to where the woman was cooking.

"What do we have here?" he enquired, lifting an eyebrow.

"Speculaas," she answered half-heartedly. "Well, some sort of version of it. It is complicated to cook anything without sugar."

The man took a long sniff of the fragrant cookies, then indicated something to his wife, who added a couple of them to a plate and handed it to him. Turning to Hannah, he fixed her with a smile. "Thank you for coming by. We will come in the next couple of days, once arrangements are made. Leave the door unlocked and we will take care of your problem."

Hannah knew it was time to leave. She stood and moved toward the door.

The man called after her, "You know… There's more you could do to help. Having somebody on our… side, who works at the university, is something we have discussed before. So much information, such an important job. You get to meet a lot of different people, presumably?"

She turned and gazed at him inquisitively.

"You should think about it," he added, his earnest request challenging her. "We need all the help we can get."

Hannah shook her head, looking down. "I'm not very heroic. I'm doing the best that I can, but I have my mother and the students to think of. I think that maybe I will leave such things to much braver people."

Following her out of the kitchen, the odd little man escorted her to the door and met her eyes before opening it. "One doesn't know how brave one is until the cost outweighs the fear," he said thoughtfully. "You may surprise yourself if the cost becomes something precious, worth fighting for."

As she contemplated his words, he slipped the two biscuits into a tiny basket by the door and handed it to her.

She started to protest. "I can't take your food."

He silenced her by covering her hand with his own. "It looks better when you leave." And then signaled to the door with his eyes. She understood. And his words about the cost struck her more profoundly; he was indicating to her that the house may be watched. She felt foolish and awestruck by this brave little man and his pleasant wife.

Opening the door, he said in a raised voice, "It was lovely to see you again. Please give my regards to your mother and tell her we hope to see her soon."

Hannah nodded, knowing that he meant this for the ears of anyone suspicious who might be listening. He waved to her as she stepped out into the alleyway, then closed the door behind him.

Back out in the chilly afternoon, she trotted away, looking down at the meager biscuits, and contemplated his words. Was the cost not dear enough for her already? Yes, she felt the sadness, and she felt the permanent loss. Eva's face swam into her thoughts; two of her brothers and her father so far from home already. Hannah wondered about the cruel cost it already had been to her and to her mother. Before she made her way home to check on Joe, she stopped off at a tobacconist in town.

Joe was standing in the corner of the shed looking at some of the posters on the walls. She surprised him with her gift: a packet of cigarettes and the two biscuits still in the basket. She could tell he was ecstatic, swallowing the first biscuit in one mouthful. Then he hastily lit a cigarette and took a long, generous drag of the nicotine, allowing it to fill his lungs with his eyes closed. His face showed its ecstasy as he held onto the smoke for a long moment before finally letting it filter out through his nostrils, a warm, happy smile spreading across his face.

"Beautiful!" He cast his shining eyes in Hannah's direction. Then turned and pointed to the advertisement he had been studying. "Who'd have thought we'd get so excited about old bikes? Now, this looks like a Buick to me. Anything that could get me back to Allied land does that to me now."

Hannah nodded. "I have made contact. Somebody is going to come by and rescue you."

He turned, looking encouraged. He was starting to look much better; the color had returned to his cheeks. "Rescue me? From someone as lovely as you."

She brushed him away. "Why don't you keep all that charm for the girls back home?" She raised her eyebrows. "I'm sure they're closer to your age."

Joe smiled and reached toward her, taking her hand. "Thank you, Hannah. Thank you for saving my life. I will always remember the Dutch woman and her bicycle shed."

Hannah shook his hand and then gave him a short, sharp hug. "Thank *you* for all you're doing for us." Tears started to brim in her eyes. "You men are very brave, and I know that we'll win this war because of your sacrifice."

Letting him go, she moved from the workshop quickly and shut the door behind her.

*

Two evenings later, Joe was gone, just a pile of blankets and the pack of cards to even remind her he had been there. As she gathered up the blankets and reached down to pick up the cards, she noticed that one was face upwards on the top of the deck. It was the Queen of Hearts. She smiled, knowing it was meant for her.

PART THREE

Chapter Twenty-Four

November 1944

Climbing stealthily up the usually creaky wooden staircase of the university, Josef headed toward the library on the second floor. Rarely used by students because it was rather cramped, and most preferred the more extensive library on the ground floor, this small, one-room library tended only to be used by the faculty or for one-on-one tutoring. The rubber soles of his shoes squeaked slightly as he glided along the polished corridor. It was late afternoon; the university was quiet. Slipping into the room, he closed the door behind him and listened. All was still.

He took a moment to look around, checked the back room set aside for students to collect books on hold. It was empty. So were the bays and tables where young people would sometimes bury themselves to finish homework assignments. Confident he was alone, he made his way to the bookshelf. He was pleased to see that the book he'd earmarked the day before hadn't been moved.

He added it to the pile of math books he'd brought along as a ruse and hid it within the stack. Sitting at a far desk next to a window overlooking the leafy courtyard, he glanced around carefully. From this position, he could watch for people entering the building and also see anyone coming into the room, giving him plenty of time to react if he needed to. He had to be particularly careful with this project as, even though the classes had become smaller, the Nazis were still present, vigorously patrolling the hallways and the main grounds. The slightest thing, the tiniest hint of which side you were on, which side you supported—the Fatherland or the Resistance—was taken very seriously now. The week before, an elderly professor had been marched away for having "suspicious" books in his personal library. Innocent books that encouraged young minds toward free thought. Everything that didn't fit within Hitler's narrow idea of what was acceptable was now seen as the work of the enemy.

Fortunately, because Josef's was a book about famous German painters, it had been overlooked. In it, he had found a portrait with what he needed depicted in the background of one of the works of art. Josef turned to the particular page and hastily jotted down some measurements into his notebook. That done, he placed the book back on its shelf and left.

*

Through the following weeks, he worked meticulously on his new project. He kept it downstairs, hidden in the hall closet, wanting this gift to be a surprise for Michael. Not being very adept or creative, it took him longer than he'd expected, but he was pleased when he managed to finish it by late November, just as, once again, snow began to fall on Holland.

On that day, he opened a bottle of wine, laid the table with food, and crept up the stairs. Opening the attic door, he observed Michael hunched over his desk, quietly listening to the Resistance Report as he worked on one of his poems.

"How are you, my friend?" Josef asked in a cheerful, upbeat manner.

"I desperately need a word for 'light,'" Michael grumbled, the frustration apparent from his tone. "This last line is driving me mad."

"Maybe what you need is another source of stimulation," Josef responded helpfully. "I have a surprise for you."

Turning, Michael looked suspicious. "Is it a surprise that I will like?"

"I hope so," Josef smiled. "Follow me downstairs."

"All the way downstairs?" Michael looked shocked. The house had three levels and they'd agreed he could use the second-floor bathroom, generally during the middle of the night, when he would empty his chamber pot and wash. But he hadn't been down on the ground floor since the first day he'd arrived.

Josef nodded. "All the way downstairs."

Tentatively, Michael followed Josef down from the attic but halted at the top of the landing, looking down the main staircase. "Are you sure it's okay?" He sounded like an anxious child asking permission.

"Yes, yes," encouraged Josef. "Come on. It is very late, and I know Ingrid is at a party with her Nazi, so they shouldn't trouble us tonight."

Michael bounded down the stairs. His face lit up when he reached the dimly lit kitchen and saw the food on the table, something they hadn't seen a lot of in weeks. Josef had built a warming fire and the heat permeated the whole downstairs. He had turned off the lights, and the curtains and shutters were closed fast, creating a feeling of warmth and security.

Josef poured two glasses of wine, encouraging Michael to sit down.

"How is this possible?" Michael asked incredulously.

"I have been keeping food from my visits with Ingrid. Even though we are starving, she always seem to have a supply." In the center of the table, a tea towel covered Josef's project. As Michael eyed it, Josef nodded to him. "It's for you."

Michael pulled back the towel, revealing the gift, and sat back to stare at the eight candles placed in an intricate wired arrangement. He was visibly taken aback.

"Professor, you made me a menorah?"

Josef smiled. "It took me a while, and I know it's not authentic, and it's not exactly the right day, but I wanted you to celebrate your own holiday this year."

Michael opened his mouth, but nothing came out.

"I hope it's correct." Josef beamed. "I created it without a formula."

"It's perfect," Michael acknowledged. "Thank you. I don't know what to say." Then a thought seemed to strike him. "I'll be right back."

He raced up the stairs, and Josef took a moment to admire his handiwork. It wasn't bad. You could tell it was a menorah. The candles had been harder to come by than the actual wire, but he was glad that it made Michael happy.

A few minutes later, the young man returned to the kitchen with a makeshift yarmulke on his head made out of the corner of an old black dust sheet Josef had in a discarded box in the attic.

Josef beamed.

"I found myself making this a few months ago," Michael explained. "I think I wanted to try and reconnect with… things. It's hard to spend years in solitude and not contemplate God. But I remembered the stories of Joseph and Moses and how many others of my faith have spent time in exile or were guided by God to leave their homes, and for the first time in my life, I have found comfort in those stories. As a child being Jewish was just who I was, like the color of my skin or my eyes. But hearing your reports about the ongoing persecutions and thinking what so many have suffered through the years, I believe God has helped me find peace."

Held nodded thoughtfully.

Michael then stood, lit the candles, and closed his eyes.

"Luminous," he whispered, his eyes flashing open again, the emotion evident in his tone. "The perfect word for light I was looking for upstairs."

Quieting himself again he smiled reminiscently, deep in thought, as though remembering music from long ago. Softly he sang the words of a prayer. And Josef noticed the sincerity in his tone and sat reverently until Michael had finished.

"That was beautiful."

"I'm amazed I remember it. Isn't it funny how things that you felt were forced upon you as a child can be of such comfort as you age? I also have something for you." He took out a piece of paper from his pocket and handed it to the professor.

Josef eyed it with surprise.

"Merry Christmas, Professor."

"And happy Hanukkah to you, Michael."

By the candlelight, Josef opened up his gift and read the beautiful poem that Michael had written for him.

Looking up at his young friend he asked, "Please read it for me. Read it to me as *you* would read it."

Illuminated by the flickering candlelight, Michael put his heart and soul into his words, such beautiful words, which touched Josef to his core. He felt his heart opening up in a way that it hadn't in a long time. Such beauty among so much sadness, and it was a precious gift.

Michael had grown so much through the brutality of the last few years, Josef reflected, gained so much about his character and lost something, too. The impulsive young person who wanted to take on the whole German army was now narrowed by the wisdom of his reality. Captivity had contained him long enough to hone his desire for instant gratification and channel that fiery energy into deeply profound writing and a clear-cut vision of how he wanted his future to be. Josef felt proud of him. He closed his tear-brimmed eyes as Michael continued to recite the poem.

"*You are my safe port in a turbulent ocean, the steadfast candle that guides me and when the swelling darkness threatens to overwhelm me, your light shines ever brighter. Never faltering to lead me home.*"

Something struck Josef. "It's like music," he mused.

"Music," echoed Michael. "That's what we need, music." And he raced toward the stairs.

"I'm not sure that's a good idea," Josef hissed after him. "It's after curfew."

But before he could say any more, Michael was down with the wireless in his arms. "We won't turn it up too loud."

They sat there listening to a lively version of Handel's *Messiah* for another hour, drinking and finishing the wine. Michael laughed and joked about the times he'd shared with Elke, and Josef thought about Sarah. It brought warmth to his heart for a change.

All at once, a big-band number crackled onto the wireless and Michael started to cavort around the room, dancing. Josef watched him, shaking his head.

"Come on, Professor, come and dance."

"I don't remember how to dance," Josef rebuffed.

"I will teach you then." Michael grabbed hold of him and pulled him to his feet. Both feeling the effects of the wine, they danced briefly with awkward enthusiasm before finally falling back down into their seats, out of breath.

Then they began to laugh. A long, free-flowing, barreling laugh that seemed to fill the whole house. Michael rocked back in his chair. "I haven't danced like that for so long, not since…"

"Not since this war began?" Josef suggested, out of breath.

"Elke," Michael responded. "Not since my Elke. If we both survive this war, all I can hope for, all that I dream of, is that we can marry. She spoke once of converting for me. I pray every day that she will have the chance. So that we can be together, for eternity."

"I wish I could have found her for you," Josef responded regretfully. "I asked everywhere I could think of, but it's seen as rather odd when an older man is asking about a student so fervently, and I didn't want to get her into trouble."

"Of course, I understand. But she's out there somewhere. I know she is, and she's waiting for me like I'm waiting for her. When I see her next, I'm going to hold her and I'm not going to let her go."

A sadness passed over Josef.

Michael seemed to catch it. "You're thinking about Sarah, aren't you?"

Josef felt shocked. Since the incident with Sarah's wedding veil, her name hadn't been mentioned in the house.

"Your wife," Michael corrected himself.

"Yes." His voice cracked.

"You don't have to say anything, Professor."

Josef forced out the words; he needed to say it. "We were very much in love, too."

The music continued to play softly in the background, and the air was filled with a joy that the walls of the house had not known in a long time. As the night passed, the two men continued to share with one another their hopes and dreams and stories about the people they'd loved and left behind.

Michael told the story of how he had fallen in love with Elke the first time he had seen her in the university grounds and Held told him how he and Sarah had met.

"We were practically set up by my mother. Sarah and her family were new to our village and my mother invited them to our house to eat. Aged twenty-seven, knowing of my mother's plan and resenting her interference, I had made up my mind to be very rebellious and no matter how nice this girl was I was not going to be polite, let alone fall in love with her. Little did I know Sarah had similar ideas, and so we spent a very awkward dinner trying our best to avoid speaking to each other. But as the evening passed, I started to find myself attracted to this girl with the wild red hair who seemed aloof and indifferent to me. It wasn't until we were forced to wash up side by side in the kitchen that she confessed her own mother's matchmaking plan and her distaste of it. We laughed at our predicament and made a pact to never be friends, a pact we found impossible to keep. Our parents thought the whole evening had been a disaster but the opposite was true. I knew, even as she clattered the dishes onto the draining board, that she was different. I liked her carefree independence, she was so comfortable in herself, and she just… intrigued me. We didn't let our parents know for months, and when we finally announced our engagement they were all so shocked."

Held smiled with the warmth of the memory.

By 2 a.m., they had slipped into a happy, companionable silence and were about to start winding up their evening, when they were shaken from their complacency by the jarring slam of two car doors outside. They both froze in terror. Michael grabbed hold of the wireless and bolted up the stairs. Josef heard the attic door close just as a knock came at the front door.

Frantically, he looked around the kitchen, trying to figure out where to start. As he hastily moved dishes to the sink, he heard Ingrid giggling on the doorstep as Heinrich hammered on the door again, shouting, "Come on. Let us in, I have an urgent need!"

He managed to grab the last items—the wine glasses—from the table and hide them from view before breathlessly approaching the front door.

The drunken couple stood on the doorstep singing a clumsy Christmas carol. They practically fell inside, laughing.

"Uncle Josef!" boomed Heinrich, taking him in a huge bear hug and grabbing his chin. "We are sorry to call so late but I need to use your bathroom," he slurred into the professor's face, his breath reeking of alcohol.

Josef was too concerned for Michael to allow himself the full weight of his rage. Rage that roared just under his skin and made him want to punch this man, even though he wasn't a violent person. As Heinrich stumbled into the downstairs toilet, Josef gritted his teeth and dug his nails into his palms to calm himself. Wasn't it enough that the Nazis felt they had a perfect right to oppress them on the streets and at work? What made them think they had the right to assault people in the middle of the night in their own homes?

Ingrid stared at him through her drunken stupor. "We were on our way home, but he couldn't quite make it," she slurred.

Josef pulled himself together. He would not allow this horror to snatch the joy from his heart. Instead, he chose to remain calm, dwell on his time with Michael and all the good that had taken place this evening. Once Heinrich had used the lavatory, they would be gone; Josef would not allow them to rob him as well as assault him.

Ingrid swallowed hard and he noticed she was looking a little green.

"I need some water," she garbled out and started tottering toward the kitchen.

Josef raced to keep ahead of her and double-check that the dishes were cleared away. But as he reached the kitchen all the air left his body. He had entirely forgotten the menorah. It was still lit in the middle of the table. How would he explain a Jewish menorah sitting in his kitchen?

In a split second, he ran to the table, slammed his hand down on the candles, and, hiding the menorah behind his back, turned to face Ingrid, who was tottering to the sink. Melding the wire configurations together, he attempted to mold it into a different position, fighting the desire to yell out as the hot wax burnt his fingers and ran down the back of his hands.

Ingrid drew a glass of water, and as she turned, her attention was caught by something on the ground. She stooped down to the floor and Josef followed her gaze. It was the poem that Michael had written for him. His mind raced through the words that he could remember. Was there anything, anything in his friend's poem that would alert her to the fact that someone was in the house, that Michael was his friend, that a Jewish person was still living in Amsterdam?

Heinrich appeared in the kitchen and leered over Ingrid's shoulder. "Well, well, well," he said in a derogatory tone, "what do we have here?"

He snatched the poem from Ingrid's hand and looked at Held, who was concentrating all of his effort behind his back, mashing and mangling the wires together.

"Poem for Josef?" Heinrich started to read out the poem in his harsh German tone, his alcoholic slur sullying the beauty of Michael's words. When he finished, they both looked at Josef expectantly.

Josef just stared back.

Heinrich swaggered toward him, waving the poem in an accusatory fashion. "I know what this means."

"We have suspected it for a long time, Uncle." Ingrid wobbled by Heinrich's side. "We know the truth. We know what you're hiding."

"What do you mean?" gasped Josef, trying to control the searing pain spreading through his fingers as beads of sweat collected under his spectacles and ran down his nose.

"It's time we dealt with this," Heinrich rebuked him. "You have got away with it for long enough."

"You must tell us the truth," Ingrid agreed.

Josef held his breath, then stumbled through his words. "I'm sure I don't know what you're talking about."

Heinrich towered over Josef.

"I really don't understand what you mean," said Josef, backing away.

"A little secret," responded Heinrich, slamming down his hands and bearing all of his weight upon Josef's shoulders. He pulled his face closer. The smell of alcoholic fumes was putrid, suffocating him. "You... have... a woman!" Then throwing his head back, he roared with laughter and slapped him on the back. "Good for you!"

Josef felt the tension leave his body. He had been consumed with panic, contracted, tense enough to snap. With overwhelming relief, he realized they hadn't guessed the truth, they hadn't known about Michael. Michael was still safe. That thought ran through his mind over and over again in a manic loop.

Inconspicuously, he dropped the mangled Menorah behind him on the table.

Ingrid wagged her finger at him. "I wondered when you didn't want to meet Ursula." She staggered forward and squeezed his arm. "It's about time. It has been a very long time since Aunt Sarah died."

His legs gave way then, and he found a chair and fell into it.

"Look at him," said Heinrich. "He is overcome that we have figured him out. She's not up in your bedroom right now, is she?" boomed Heinrich raucously, swaggering toward the door.

"No, no," said Josef. "She left a little while ago."

Heinrich stared at him. "A *little* while ago? I should be angry. There is a curfew, but since you are family…"

"Next time, let her stay the night," Ingrid implored. "We want to meet her. I'm so looking forward to us all being one big, happy family. We can all spend Christmas and New Year's together. I could have a party. We could also invite our friends from work."

"Ah," was all Josef could say.

Heinrich stumbled again, and Ingrid grabbed hold of him. "I think we'd better go," she said, catching Heinrich. They swayed toward the front door.

Josef followed behind them somberly.

"Good night, Uncle Josef," said Heinrich in a singsong way as he waved behind him. Ingrid staggered along, trying to hold up her fiancé even though he was twice her size.

Josef waited until he heard the car pull away then locked the door and bolted to the attic. He was surprised to see his friend sitting on the tea chest—rather than hiding—at the far end of the long dark room, staring out through the cracked window pane. He looked out upon the endless rooftops and seemed hypnotized by the luminous moon that hung heavy in the night sky.

Joining him, Josef sat next to Michael and stared out the window too. "They've gone."

"Did you manage to hide the menorah?" asked Michael, the anguish obvious in his tone. Josef looked down at his red, raw hands and nodded.

Michael looked shocked as he noticed them too.

"The minute I got back up here, it's all I could think about and the fact that if they'd seen it…"

Josef took a deep breath. "I had to destroy your menorah, Michael. I'm so sorry."

They sat in silence for a few seconds.

"It's a miracle they haven't found me yet. Have you noticed they are coming more regularly?"

Josef nodded. "And now they think I have a girlfriend."

Michael stared at him. "What?"

"They found your poem and were sure it was from a woman."

Michael started to laugh.

Josef joined in. "They want us to get together for Christmas and New Year, one big, happy family."

Michael roared. "Won't they be surprised when they get to meet me?"

The men's laughter rocked the attic.

After a while, satisfied, they slipped back to their companionable silence. Michael shook his head. "I'm tired, Professor."

Josef stood. "You should get some sleep."

"No, I mean *tired*. I'm tired of the hiding. I'm tired of the waiting. I'm tired of always having to hold my breath, hoping it'll be just one more day then I will be free."

Josef looked back out toward the moon, now partly covered by swirls of smoky gray cloud. "Who would have thought we would have done this for nearly four years? I can't believe it myself."

Michael hung his head. "Talking about Elke tonight made me realize how much I really do miss her. Most of the time I try not to think too much about her because it still hurts so much every day."

Josef nodded. He understood this pain.

"It kills me that she's just out there somewhere, and the worst of it is she doesn't even know I'm alive."

Josef stared at the floor. There was nothing that he could say, nothing he could do. They were all victims, and yet so many people had died. Being grateful to be alive was sometimes the only way he was able to face each day.

"Get some sleep," he repeated. "I'll see you in the morning."

He started to make his way out of the attic when suddenly Michael was behind him, enveloping him in a huge heartfelt hug. Turning, Josef hugged him back just as tightly.

"Thank you, Josef, for all that you've done for me. You have no idea how much I appreciate it. I never knew anyone could be this kind."

Overcome with emotion, Josef pulled out of the embrace and nodded, pushing his spectacles farther up his nose. "Well, yes. It's the least any of us can do in this horror that we are living through. I have great hope for you, Michael Blum," he added, trying to lighten the mood.

Michael nodded.

Josef turned to close the door, as Michael returned to the tea chest and staring back out the window into a world that he could see but not touch. Josef felt his pain as he moved back down the stairs.

*

The next morning, as Josef opened his eyes and looked around his bedroom, he felt the heaviness from the late night, the wine, and the food. His head pulsed and his mouth was dry. He groaned slightly as he looked at his clock. It was late, but at least it was Sunday; he didn't need to go to the university today.

He rolled out of bed, put on his slippers, and made his way downstairs to get a glass of water. A pile of dirty dishes remained in the sink, and the mangled menorah still sat on his kitchen table. His heart felt heavy for his young friend. He felt terrible that he had destroyed his Hanukkah gift. Maybe he could try to fix it today.

He made his way up to the attic, but even before he opened the door, he knew that something was wrong. There was a coldness, a chill.

Inside, everything was different. The pictures were gone from the wall. The furniture that Michael had used to create his seated area had been piled in the corner. The bookshelf was empty. And the desk that, for years, had been buried under a mass of papers was now bare, everything apparently packed away in a box in the corner, all except for one book.

Shocked, he looked to Michael's bed to make sense of it all and was surprised to find it folded up and placed against the wall.

He stumbled around the room, trying to understand, not believing what he was seeing. As he took in the sterile environment, it rendered him breathless. It was as if Michael had never been there.

Josef didn't know what to do.

Numbly, he moved to the desk, to look at the only book not packed away. An advanced calculus curriculum. Josef huffed. A joke. Michael had hated calculus. He picked it up and walked to the window, where he pulled out the tea chest and sat down to look around the bare room. As he did, something slipped from the cover of the book. A piece of paper with one word written on it. "Elke."

That's when it hit him.

Michael was truly gone.

Standing looking out of the window, he was surprised by the heavy salty tears that started to flow freely down his cheeks as he grieved, not only for the loss of his friend but for the hostile world that now awaited Michael outside the safety of the attic.

Chapter Twenty-Five

Elke crunched her way through the crispy undergrowth on her well-worn path. It was nearly December, and it was cold. She shivered and pulled her coat tighter around her shoulders. Why was she still doing this? Honestly, she didn't know, but it had become a ritual for her now. Each day after work, when it wasn't too cold or too rainy, she'd head to the woods. It was for the exercise, she liked to tell herself, and it was good for her to get out in nature. A chance to breathe and clear her head before she went home.

Though she told herself this, she knew that deep down in her heart she still held out hope that maybe Michael, one day, would be there waiting for her. It had been so long since his disappearance. She knew it was probably futile to believe that he was still alive, or still in Amsterdam, for that matter. She'd heard tales of Jews being hidden by members of the Resistance. But surely, if he were here, he would have found his way to her by now?

Still, it helped her to hold on to the familiar. The woods were known to her now, the seasonal anchor that gave her hope that one day she would walk them in a time of freedom. She circled a branch of a downed log, her feet moving at a click toward the center of the forest and the place that was significant to her. Her heart was able to pull her here with her eyes closed.

When she stopped to catch her breath for a second, she heard something behind her. Something rustling through the leaves. In all times that she'd walked here, she had never met anyone this deep in the woods. Most people stuck to the primary pathway if they were walking their dogs or getting exercise. But the path that led down to her tree was isolated, and it was always quiet. It had to be some woodland creature, she decided as she carried on walking. But just in case, she upped her pace, just a little.

Now all of her senses were on edge. Her inner radar tuned into every little sound. Stepping off the path and behind a tree to listen, she closed her eyes. Behind her, a twig snapped. Two footfalls shuffled to a stop. She was definitely being followed.

Frantically, she tried to think what to do. If it were a Nazi, there would need to be an excuse, a reason for being this deep in the woods. Worse still, it could be someone who wanted to hurt her or attack her. If someone was just taking a walk, why would they stop? Surely they would keep moving past her.

Her heart pounded as her mind scrambled, trying to figure out what to do. Making a decision, she continued on in haste, brazenly picking up a stick along the way. It probably wouldn't be much good for protecting her, but at least it made her feel a little more secure.

There it was again. There was definitely somebody behind her. With her breath coming in fast, ragged spurts, she spun around. But she could see no one there.

She took off, striding faster. The other steps also sped up. She began to run. So did the person behind her.

All at once, two hands were upon her shoulders. As she started to scream, a hand covered her mouth, turning her quickly about. She held up her branch, ready to strike, but dropped it to her side when she saw who it was. A broad smile across his face, he dropped his hand from her mouth.

"I'm sorry, I didn't mean to frighten you, I didn't want you to alert the Germans."

"Helmut," she said with some relief. "You scared the life out of me. What are you doing here?"

"I followed you," he responded playfully.

"Why?" she asked, her heart rate still struggling to return to normal.

Viewing him in this environment, she realized how out of place he looked walking through the ice and mud in his suit and expensive Italian shoes. "I noticed after work you never leave in the direction of your home and I wondered what you did with your time. So today I decided to see."

Elke felt invaded. "I like to be alone," she said curtly. "It's how I clear my head." She moved away from him at a clip.

"Please, Elke," he implored, taking hold of her arm. "Don't push me away so much. What is it? What is it that I'm not doing right? Please tell me what it is, so I can change."

His blue eyes were blazing and desperate.

What she wanted to say was, "You're not Michael. You'll never be Michael." Instead, she shook her head. "You haven't done anything wrong, Helmut. I'm just not..." She tried to find an excuse. "It's this war," she lied, shaking her head. "I just can't think about such things during such a difficult time."

"Surely," Helmut said, becoming exasperated, "that's exactly when we should be thinking of—taking care of each other, loving one another." She noticed that he said the word "loving" in such a glib way that it sounded disingenuous.

She continued to walk, and he followed her.

Over the last eighteen months, he had persistently pursued her whenever he was in town. Inviting her to parties and get-togethers, which she had politely attended at the insistence of her boss, though declined whenever possible. Fortunately, he was often gone with his work, though who could be buying art at this point in the war was a mystery to her. It had been a hard time at the gallery, and if it hadn't been for Helmut's regular purchases, she was pretty sure they would have gone under. For that she was grateful, and at least he was pleasant company, but that was all. She always felt there was something about him she couldn't trust with her heart. It felt to her that he wanted her like he wanted one of his art pieces—something to put in his apartment to look shiny and beautiful. Or that he wanted her because she had told him he couldn't have her. He never seemed to be sincere. In some way, she didn't blame him. It was the world that he'd grown up in. He wasn't a bad person, but there was definitely something wanting.

Elke and Helmut carried on walking in silence for a while, side by side. As she approached Michael's tree, her heart started to pound. She knew Michael wouldn't be there, but just being in this place, with Helmut, took her back once again to a time when this spot had meant so much to her.

Helmut kept up with her stride as she hurried past the tree to the end of the path. All at once he spun her around to face him. "I just feel you need to learn to trust me," he whispered. "Please give me a chance. That's all I'm asking." Then, without any warning, he took her in his arms and kissed her passionately on the lips, taking her breath away.

She didn't fight him. It was an incredible kiss. Warm and intense. She tried to close her eyes to enjoy it. Maybe she just needed to go with it. Why couldn't she just let herself go? Why couldn't she just accept this guy? Then the true weight of realization washed over her. No, she couldn't do that. She couldn't be cruel to him, never mind herself or her own heart. She was in no place to love anyone else.

Gently, she pushed his face away and spoke to him quietly. "Helmut, we can't do this. Not now, not here." She really meant: not here—in her and Michael's place. The place that had been so special to them. She felt her face flush.

Helmut looked crushed. "Will there ever be a right time and place for you? I don't know what else I have to do to convince you to at least give us a chance."

She shook her head, there was no good reason she could give him without telling him about Michael.

As they started walking again, she felt as desperate as he appeared, but for different reasons. They walked along in silence back toward the city. Then one last time he implored her, "Will you please think about it? Please think about us. I think we'd be really good together."

For once, she saw some sincerity in his eyes, but it wouldn't be fair. "I'm sorry," she responded. "I can't do this now." She stroked the side of his face with her hand. "Thank you for asking. It was the nicest thing that's happened to me all week."

Then, moving away from him, she pulled up the collar of her coat and started on her way home, flattered but also a little unnerved that Helmut had become so bold as to follow her.

How long would she be heartbroken? she wondered. How long would this pain last? She didn't know. What she did know was that her heart was a long way from being able to accept someone else.

"Damn you, Michael Blum," she whispered. Warm tears started to stream down her face. "Where are you?"

*

Far in the woods, near a tree carved with sweetheart initials, Michael stood concealed and shivering where he had just watched two people kissing. He knew exactly who one of them was. He would have known her from across a crowded room of a thousand people. Suddenly Michael's legs gave way and he dropped to the ground and started to sob. He had no words, no thoughts, just anger and pain. He punched the ground repeatedly with his fist as he screamed. He knew that wasn't wise. He could bring Nazis to him in a second, but he didn't care. He was going to surrender right here and just die or let them take him. He didn't care anymore, nothing mattered. He knew he had made Elke promise to move on and be happy and she had, but he hadn't realized how much the thought of her had been keeping him alive. He hadn't realized how much his faith and their love had been the hope he held onto, the things that he'd been able to count on all the years in the attic.

As he lay on the grass sobbing, he thought about the last time they'd been here, and the pain of it wrenched his heart in two. As his wailing subsided to racking sobs, he whispered her name over and over again. "Elke, Elke, Elke…"

Chapter Twenty-Six

Sitting by Heinrich's side in his car, Ingrid looked blankly out of the windows, eyes still stinging and puffy from the night before. Crying herself quietly to sleep had now become a regular occurrence as she thought of the increased strain in their relationship.

She glanced across to her fiancé, who was staring out the opposite window, and wondered what was happening to them. They'd had their first serious argument. On Saturday, they'd been out to a party, and even though Heinrich had gotten raucously drunk, they'd enjoyed themselves. He had been more like his old self. The person she had known at the beginning of the war.

Then, on Sunday morning, there had been a phone call. Even more of his troops were being pulled out of the Netherlands for a new German offensive towards Antwerp in an attempt to break through the Allied lines, which left Heinrich's own forces depleted in Amsterdam. Angry and raging that more of his soldiers were being sent away, he'd ended up taking it out on Ingrid, who had only asked about setting a date for their wedding. Why didn't Heinrich ever want to talk about their future? He'd become incredibly hostile with her, accusing her of being selfish when he had so much pressure at work.

After a huge argument, Heinrich had walked out and not returned until very late that night. Ingrid had already gone to bed, and it was apparent when he rolled in that he had been drinking. When she'd stretched across her pillow to find him, to put things right, he had pushed her away, and that had hurt. She just wished this war would be over so she could finally settle down.

Leaving the car, Ingrid shivered at the cold winter day. She lifted a pile of working files as they headed into the building. The office taken over by the Nazis at the beginning of the war used to belong to a lawyer and had the look and feel of old Holland. Heavy wooden doors and Dutch craftsmanship at its best. Their office was now assigned to handle the deployments of the troops in the city and also the logistics of the transportation of fuel and supplies in and out of Amsterdam. Heinrich strode ahead, not even pausing to hold the door open for her. She once again attempted some small talk with him in the lift, but he shut her down and they continued in the elevator in silence.

Exiting the caged doors, she galloped to keep up with her fiancé's long strides as he marched down the corridor. Approaching the office, she sensed that something felt different. Something lively that met her in the doorway. A buzz, energy, levity. She was intrigued and also a little annoyed, bearing in mind her mood.

As they entered the room, high-pitched laughter and plumes of blue cigarette smoke greeted her in the doorway. From a normally clinical, studious office, this was highly irregular. Two officers sat casually on top of one of the desks but stood up awkwardly and respectfully nodded in Heinrich's direction as he passed them. Ignoring them, Heinrich marched into his office and slammed the door, his anger echoing its presence throughout the room.

Once Heinrich was gone, the soldiers continued to converse with a woman seated with her back toward Ingrid. Her thick, curly, black hair shimmered, and her head was thrown back in laughter as she joked with the two men hovering over her.

Ingrid was livid. Who was this stranger, this woman, who had come into their office to monopolize all the other staff? Though she'd never have said it out loud, Ingrid was stung with jealousy. As she sulked to her desk, she remembered that, when she'd first arrived, soldiers had surrounded her for conversation. It struck her again how isolated she'd felt in the last few months.

Slamming down the files she'd taken home over the weekend, Ingrid glared at the woman, who still hadn't acknowledged her. As she swiveled around in her chair, Ingrid was at once taken aback by this stunning, raven-headed beauty. Luminous green eyes, dark and thick lashes, and skin as white as alabaster. A chin that hinted at elfishness gave way to a broad grin that illuminated her whole face.

Jumping to her feet, the newcomer shooed the men away from her desk and turned back toward Ingrid. She was tall, maybe five or six inches taller than her, with long, slender legs. She wore her uniform with such flair; it looked as if it had been tailor-made for her slim waist, full breasts, and curvaceous hips.

"You must be Ingrid," she stated with delight, offering her hand. "I've heard so much about you."

Ingrid shook it limply and withdrew quickly, trying not to be drawn into this woman's enthusiasm. She kept her eyes on her desk and shuffled around her files, trying to emanate importance as she nodded absently.

Not the least bit intimidated by Ingrid's flagrant dismissal of her, the new arrival continued to chat as she organized her desk. "I'm so glad to have some female company. The last office I worked in was nothing but men. And when the Major told me I'd be working with Ingrid, *the* Ingrid, *the famous* Ingrid, I was so looking forward to meeting you, and also having a good old-fashioned chat with a girlfriend."

She leaned across her desk, and Ingrid got a hint of Chanel perfume.

"I do hope we'll be great friends. Because good friends are hard to find at the moment."

Her last statement tweaked at Ingrid's heart.

The raven beauty turned her attention to her desk. "My name is Violette, by the way, but everyone calls me Vi." She smiled broadly, apparently attempting to disarm her.

"Nice to meet you," Ingrid responded, reluctantly. But inwardly, she was quite intrigued by this woman.

"Let's go out together for coffee later this morning," Vi said, picking up a stack of files and starting to move them into a pile.

"I have a lot of work to do, as you can see. I need to get caught up, and it would be wonderful to have an ally."

"I don't go out in the day," Ingrid stated, coldly.

"Well, maybe it's about time you did." Vi lifted her perfectly penciled eyebrows. "I'll show you some great places in Amsterdam. It will be fun."

Ingrid didn't respond straight away, but as the morning wore on, she started to warm to the idea. When there had been more food, she and Heinrich always used to go to lunch, but lately she often just sat in the office alone during her lunchtime, hoping Heinrich would want to spend some time with her. But he seldom did.

As the morning wore on and Ingrid interacted with Vi, she had a sense of excited anticipation, flying with ease through the list of equipment and weapons array that was her daily chore, as Vi peppered her with funny stories and jokes. By midday, she was ready to go on her new adventure as Vi announced, "Come on, Ingrid, time for a break!"

Ingrid rushed to catch up with Vi's long, high-heeled strides out the door and into the street. Feeling inconspicuous and apprehensive, Ingrid moved beside her new friend, looking carefully about her. She had barely been out alone on the street since the unfortunate incident a few years before, when people had spat at her and called her names. She preferred to just use Heinrich's car to get to and from work when he wasn't with her, and she had requested that her uncle visit her at home.

But now she was out walking during the day, so brazen, wearing her Nazi uniform. As the usual stares and snide comments came at them, Vi seemed oblivious to all of it and marched off toward the place she had picked out for them. All the while, she reminisced to Ingrid about the office she'd come from and seemed buoyant about her morning's work.

"I had to move to Amsterdam because your office was so short-staffed and the Major in Rotterdam no longer needed me."

She paused to breathe in deeply. "I love this city, so I was happy to come." She grabbed Ingrid's arm as they crossed the road. "They, of course, lost my transfer paperwork—in a bombing raid, I believe—and told me it could be weeks before they could organize it all, so I decided to come to work anyway. I hate being idle. Especially when there is so much to do."

Ingrid nodded her agreement. "It's been hard. I've been worked off my feet for months."

Vi shuttled Ingrid down a street before continuing. "And with the significant loss of life to our forces, and people being reorganized for the latest deployment, there were a lot of positions that needed filling. I was more than glad to pitch in." She turned to smile at Ingrid. "But when they told me I might get a chance to work with you, I asked if I could be assigned here. I have heard so much about you and Heinrich in the party. You are both highly thought of."

Ingrid glowed. She'd had no idea that people spoke about her and her work, and she was glad Heinrich was getting the recognition he deserved. Maybe they would send him more soldiers.

Vi headed into a brightly colored café, passing an older woman dressed in black who glared at them and spat out something about the enemy. Vi turned on her and snapped back aggressively. Ingrid was impressed, and she suddenly felt proud again, as she had at the beginning of the war. Proud to be a member of the Nazi Party.

Inside the restaurant, a couple of German soldiers passed them and made eyes at Vi. She batted her eyelashes, saying something dismissive, whispering to Ingrid on the side, "If he thinks I want to have a date with him, he's got another think coming."

Ingrid giggled as they found their way to a table.

There was no food, but there was good coffee and as Vi talked about her dreams, Ingrid felt pathetic beside her. She hadn't thought about anything apart from going to Germany with Heinrich, marrying him, and having his children. Vi, on the other hand, had full plans of all she wanted to do, she told her new friend, including traveling the world and learning to fly.

Finishing their drinks, Vi lit their cigarettes and tentatively asked Ingrid about her relationship with Heinrich. "It can't be easy for the two of you, having to live and work together with all the tension in the Reich right now."

Ingrid was surprised to feel tears well up, but she didn't feel comfortable enough to share what was really going on between her and Heinrich. He would be angry at her, always wanting to give the impression to their friends that everything in his life was perfect, so she just nodded.

"Yes, it is hard on all of us."

Vi grabbed her hand. "But we will win, don't you worry. The Führer will not be beaten."

Another couple of women walked past them and stared. Vi glared back until they walked away, then crushed out her cigarette.

"I refuse to be intimidated," she said tenaciously, combing her hand through her silky black curls. "It's bad enough being Dutch without having to stoop to their level. I'm not going to hide in the shadows. One day we will have destroyed the Resistance, and then we'll do and say whatever we want."

They walked back to the office arm-in-arm, and for the first time in a long time, Ingrid had a friend, someone she could talk to, and that felt really good.

Chapter Twenty-Seven

Watching her mother with concern, Hannah dried teacups with a tea towel in the kitchen. Clara had that faraway look again. Outwardly, she continued to function—knitting, reading, working on a jigsaw puzzle—but ever since Eva had been taken from Amsterdam, her mother had emotional lapses and would stop and stare out into space for hours, the intense pain and acute loss on her face. It was as if, as well as losing Eva, she had surrendered her hope, just given up, and little by little, moment by moment, Hannah was losing her mother.

As Hannah stared blankly out into the waning afternoon light, her thoughts again on the crushing loss in September the year before, and it was as if her heart remembered the sheer weight of the pain.

Hannah could remember that day like it was yesterday.

When she'd seen Mrs. Oberon's frantic face at the university welcome desk, it had been shocking. The older lady had never come to the university, never been to visit her there before, and Hannah knew that something was terribly wrong.

In fright, her hand had jumped to her throat, and she had managed only one word, the thing she feared the most. "Mamma?"

Mrs. Oberon shook her head. "Eva and her mother," she responded in a breathless rasp.

All at once Hannah had felt relieved about Clara, but grief-stricken for her friends.

"I went to your house, but you weren't there," Mrs. Oberon panted, wringing her hands together. "They have come for their family. All of them. They're taking all of the Jewish people from the ghetto. There will not be one of them left."

Dashing straight out of the university doors without even telling anyone where she was going, Hannah left, heading for the city with Mrs. Oberon wobbling behind her. She had to save her friends. She had raced through the streets of Amsterdam, her heart almost pounding out of her chest as she sucked hot, sticky air in and out of her lungs, her throat burning as she tried desperately to gasp for breath. No matter how she felt, she knew she couldn't stop. Must keep going, time was of the essence. Needed to know they were safe, needed to know it wasn't true.

Hannah's fear was heightened when she saw no guards on the gates into Jodenbuurt and she was able to slip in easily. She arrived at Eva's home, a place she hadn't visited since the section had been fenced off from the rest of Amsterdam. Shaking with fatigue as she grappled with the front gate, sweat poured down her face and her neck and ran between her breasts. Clinging to the gatepost, her trembling hand fumbled to operate the catch. Finally forcing it, she bounded up the pathway and banged on the front door. There was no reply, no sound. Just a deathly silence.

She knocked again, harder, and the door swung open with the force of her blows. Stepping inside, Hannah called out, but her voice returned as a hollow, futile echo bouncing off the walls.

The silence was startling. Gone was the usual happy hubbub of a house full of children or the sound of Greta at her sewing machine or dirty dishes clattering in the sink. All the cheerful sounds of home-making that had always greeted Hannah at this door before the war.

As she rushed from room to room, she assured herself they would be hiding. They had to be hiding. She had a sudden idea, one she had thought of before but hadn't had a chance to share with her friends. She would find them and take them home with her, the whole family. Maybe they could live in the workshop. Yes, she thought, suddenly optimistic, they could hide in her poppa's shed and she would find a way to get them out, just like she'd found a way to get the airman out.

She felt a sense of optimism as she desperately searched, calling their names. "Eva. Eva. Greta. Willem. Eva."

But the rooms were silent.

Her heart sank. In her frantic haste to find them, she had not seen the obvious. Beds were unmade, toys were thrown about, and clothes were strewn on the floor. Greta was always meticulous. Something awful had happened.

Downstairs, the kettle rattled on the stove, boiling dry, and a chill gripped her again. She turned off the stove and stared out the window as tears brimmed.

Mrs. Oberon was right. They had been taken.

She raced back out of the house, down the street, stopping people to frantically ask them if they'd seen Eva's family. But everyone she met appeared to be in profound shock. They just sobbed and cried and shook their heads.

Finally, one elderly man grabbed Hannah's arm and pointed to the corner of the street. "They are all down there. They're taking them, now."

She hastened down the road but was stopped halfway down as she saw her mother hobbling uncomfortably in front of her. She cried out, "Mama, what are you doing?"

The grim determination was evident on Clara's face. "I'm going to get Eva," she snapped through stilted breath. "I'm going to get Eva and Greta and their family." She winced with every step, limping so hard on her right hip, her breathing ragged and labored.

"How did you get here?" Hannah asked incredulously. Her mother hadn't left the house in ten years. "Mama, you have to stop. You'll be ill."

"I must get Eva," she growled through gritted teeth.

Hannah took hold of her mother by the shoulders. "Please, Mama, wait here. I will get her. You wait here."

Clara ground to a halt. All the fight left her face, and she nodded as she leaned heavily against a brick wall.

Hannah continued running to the end of the road, and as she turned the corner, she saw them. Hordes of people lined up, cases in pale white hands, bags slung across their backs, wrapped like scared mice in thick knit shawls, warm overcoats, and heavy shoes, even though it was only September. German trucks lined the road, hostile soldiers accompanying them and shouting angry orders as they forced families into the vehicles. Hannah pushed her way through the heaving crowd, looking frantically at the faces.

"Herzenbergs? Has anyone seen the Herzenbergs? Herzenbergs! Has anyone seen the Herzenbergs?"

People numb and dispirited looked up at her blankly, not even understanding what she was saying. Lines of startled-looking men hanging onto their wives, young women gripping bundles of clothes, sobbing, frightened children clinging to their dolls.

Hannah continued to push her way through the throng until, suddenly, she spotted Eva, her silky, black braids hanging long down her back, shining in the sunshine as a soldier lifted her roughly onto a truck.

Hannah screamed out, "Eva! Eva!" But the noise of the clamoring crowds and the revving trucks caused her voice to stop stagnant in the air, impotent and silenced.

Summoning up all of her strength, she raced to the vehicle and called again. Eva turned, her wild brown eyes afraid and full, pale white face scanning the crowd, looking for the source of the voice. Pushing with all her might, Hannah reached the front of the masses and caught hold of the corner of Eva's coat.

Eva turned and saw her and burst into tears. "Hannah! Hannah! Help us, Hannah! Please help us! They are taking us away!"

By Eva's side, Greta's frantic face gazed back as she clung onto her toddler. Locked around her waist, her other son clasped on desperately. Through his mother's skirts, he peered at Hannah, quiet and somber, wearing the little woolen hat his sister had knitted, his gray coat buttoned haphazardly.

Suddenly, Hannah was yanked backwards and her hand was ripped away from her young friend.

Inches from her face was a German, angry words spat at her. "Get back! Get back there! Do not touch anyone in the truck."

Hannah spluttered in German to him. "These are my friends. What are you doing? These are children. Where are they going?"

But the soldier ignored her and shoved her hard in the chest. "Move back now! Move back!" He was blind and deaf to her pleas. A Nazi robot, conditioned to do his superiors' bidding, insensitive to the cries of anguish all around him.

In desperation, Hannah looked at Eva again, saw the tears streaming down her young friend's face. Suddenly a steady hand was upon Hannah's shoulder. It was her mother. She had managed to limp the rest of the way, her breath coming in thick, heavy spurts.

Through the crazed, manic energy, she boomed out to Eva in a calm, reassuring tone, "You be strong for us, Eva. Do not forget who you are and what you are. We will not forget you. I will keep your knitting until you come back. You will be back soon. Do you understand me? You need to be the strong one for your family. You need to support your momma."

Hannah took hold of her mother's arm and tried to absorb some of her strength.

Eva's face took on a new boldness. "I will! I will take care of my momma, and I will find wool and knit wherever I am."

"That's a good girl, Eva," encouraged Clara. "Keep yourself busy, that's a good girl. We will keep you in our hearts and prayers until we see you again."

The back of the truck was slammed shut and the engine came to life, and as it lurched forward, Eva was thrown down into her seat. Suddenly, her porcelain cheeks were alight as she jumped back up to her feet.

"My music box!" she cried out on the air.

"It will be here," Clara shouted back over the growl of the angry engine. "When you get back. We will keep it for you, as I promised."

The young girl nodded. Through a face of dirt-smeared tears, she smiled and waved. "I will see you both soon," she said, trying to sound brave. And then, in a plume of rancid, choking blue smoke, she was gone.

Hannah and Clara stood gripping one another, staring down the street for a long time after the truck had gone, both of them unable to move. They stood there until Mrs. Oberon appeared by their side, puffing and panting. Gently, Mrs. Oberon took Clara's other arm, and between the three of them, they made their way back to their houses, quietly sobbing their way home.

Back at the kitchen window, leaving the memory behind, tears sprang to Hannah's eyes as she once again remembered that long journey home. There was no doubt that the cost had been significant. It had been heartbreaking for all of them, and their town felt decimated. But for Clara, at her age, it was overwhelming, just too much to bear. It had settled deep into her bones, forcing open a gaping void in her heart that Hannah was unable to traverse.

Hannah had gone back to Greta's house the day after they had been taken. With Greta's entire family being Jewish, there was no one left in Amsterdam to take care of the family's belongings. Reverently, she'd folded and tucked away precious possessions: well-read children's books, beloved threadbare stuffed animals, Eva's favorite sweater, Greta's wedding photographs. She'd made beds, tidied rooms, and swept the entire house; it had been therapeutic. It had to be perfect, just the way Greta liked it, clean and ready for when she brought her young family home again.

They would return, Hannah had decided, because the alternative was just too hard to bear. Lovingly packing everything into boxes, she had brought their memories home and stored them in her workshop.

Within days, the Nazis were proud to announce the Jewish 'problem' had been solved. Their pomp purposefully deaf to the cries of the eerie neighborhood streets that ached with the desolation. Joyous to be rid of their vermin, they had stripped then boarded up whole neighborhoods. Gratified to have extinguished the light of so many lives. Generations of Dutch families, their echoes of joy, love, and laughter now suffocated behind neat rows of silver nails and vast sheets of darkened wood.

For the rest of them, there was no such swift solution. Hannah had gone out of her way to buy her mother's favorite yarns and any craft project she thought she would enjoy tackling. Some of these had helped for short spells, but increasingly felt like futile acts that were no more than a different set of shiny nails and wooden boards. Because nothing was able to cover the aching, exposed emptiness ravished and beggared behind her mother's eyes.

As Hannah continued to look out of the kitchen window, a robin hopped along the icy ground in front of her, pecking the brittle earth furiously with its beak until, after many a try, it was rewarded with a juicy worm and gleefully flew away. It was going to be Christmas soon, she noted, putting her teacups away. Another Christmas under the occupation. At least they had a little extra food. Mrs. Oberon had received a Red Cross parcel and had insisted on sharing it with Hannah and Clara. Tucking flour, powdered eggs, and chocolate into Hannah's grateful hands, Oma had said, "Make something special for your mama." Having acquired a little almond paste Hannah had decided to make *banketstaaf*, her mother's preferred Christmas pastry, or a version of it.

She also had a plan, one that might cheer up Clara if she could make it happen.

Chapter Twenty-Eight

The day before St. Nicholas Eve, Elke stood on Helmut's doorstep by Mr. Van den Berg's side, shivering despite being bundled up in a warm coat. The wind howled around the doorway, freezing her ears and nose, and she stomped her feet to keep warm. As her teeth chattered, she was grateful that her boss had decided to use some of his fuel coupons to drive them to the party this evening.

The door opened, and the warmth and good cheer stretched out into the cold night air to greet them both.

"Welcome," enthused Helmut, his arms outstretched, his eyes wild and glazed, confirming he had already started drinking. Wrapping his arms warmly around Elke, he whispered into her hair, "Thank you for coming," before heartily shaking Mr. Van den Berg's hand.

In the hallway, he took their coats, and as he hung them in his cloakroom, she glanced down to check and straighten her clothes and to smooth out her tousled hair. She wasn't sure why that mattered but still found herself somewhat self-conscious about how she looked around Helmut.

The apartment inside was aglow with warm and happy people. There was the glorious sight of a string of Christmas lights and tasteful decorations, along with, unbelievably, the delicious smell of food emanating from Helmut's well-appointed kitchen. How it was possible when food was in such short supply she had no idea, it was almost as if there wasn't a war going on.

As Helmut introduced her to his friends, she felt his reassuring hand on her arm, and even though they weren't a couple, it felt nice to have the adoring attention of such a good-looking man.

Some of the people Elke already knew. These were people in the art world—dealers, artists, other gallery owners. Mr. Van den Berg quickly found an old friend and entered into a lively conversation. She mingled for a while before taking a moment to wander around the apartment looking at the artwork. Nearly every piece that hung on the wall had once hung in their gallery. She pondered the collection, still not really understanding how this man ticked.

All at once, he was by her side, offering her a glass of warm Christmas punch.

"I was just admiring *The Rain*," she remarked, referring to the picture by a new, young Dutch artist.

Helmut took in the painting as if he'd never really seen it before and nodded. "Yes. It's got nice… um… gray colors." He took a long swig of his drink.

She shook her head. He really had no appreciation of art. How he worked within his field, she didn't know. His father had been an incredibly popular and successful art dealer since before the war, and Helmut was maintaining that business here in Holland. But all this money… She just wasn't sure how he had managed to make anything during this time.

She changed the subject. "It's a beautiful apartment."

"There's so much of it you have not seen," he responded. "Remember the last time you were here? I was considering converting a room to accommodate a painting studio. Do you remember?"

Elke nodded. She had her suspicions that he hoped she would come and paint there since she had told him her last studio had been destroyed in a bombing raid.

"Come on. I will show it to you."

He took her down a long corridor and opened the door to a room that overlooked the canal. It was a very pleasant space, with high, vaulted ceilings and old wooden beams. Along one wall there were stacked easels and a table with paints and new brushes. Elke walked to the large picture window and looked out.

"Very nice," she muttered.

He joined her at the window. "I think it would be perfect for you to come and paint here."

She nodded, not committing herself either way.

"How are you spending the holiday? Maybe with the mysterious boyfriend?" he enquired, taking another swig of his drink.

"There's no mysterious boyfriend," she answered flatly.

"Then with who?"

"If you must know, with my sister and her two children, who are adorable. They are so unaware of what is happening." She gazed out at the water shimmering under a full moon. "And St. Nicholas still needs to come, no matter if there is a war on or not."

"Do they like art?" asked Helmut. "I could give you a couple of pieces."

She shook her head and laughed.

"What about Christmas or New Year? Do you have any time for us to get together to celebrate, perhaps? Just as friends," he added, qualifying an intention that sounded far from the truth.

Elke took a deep breath. "I'm really busy with my family."

His hand found her back, and he gently rubbed her shoulders. His touch felt good. Her whole body hungered to be held and loved, but she knew she couldn't lead him on. So, to stop the fact he was sending shivers down her spine, she turned and offered him her empty glass.

"Is the bathroom near here?" she asked.

Helmut moved his hand. "There's one downstairs. But there's another you can use up here, adjoined to my bedroom." There was a glint in his eye.

She smiled. "I know you will be a perfect gentleman, Helmut. Can you show me the way?"

"Just a second," he said. "I keep this end of the house locked."

They walked up a set of stairs, and he unlocked a door and pointed to the bathroom at the end of another corridor. She went in and, as soon as the door was closed behind her, sighed with relief and combed her hands through her hair, taking a minute to collect herself. She hadn't needed to use it, she just needed an escape route from a path her body seemed to want to take her down. Even though her heart and head were very much against it.

As she stared in the mirror, she noticed over her shoulder the other door slightly ajar behind her. Curious, she pushed it open. It was indeed Helmut's bedroom. She walked in and looked around. Even in the dark, it had a strong, masculine presence and more of her gallery's art pieces on the wall.

Turning to go, she tripped over something protruding from the closet. Fumbling for a light switch, it illuminated a set of art panels covered by a drop cloth. Her foot, tangled in the cloth, had accidentally exposed a corner of what lay underneath. She started to right everything when the painting at the front of the stack caught her eye. Hesitantly, she pulled back the rest of the cloth to unveil an exquisite oil painting, in vivid color and dimension, of a woman buying flowers in a market.

She knew it from somewhere. And then it came to her. This was the *Rosenthal Madonna*, a famous artwork from the nineteenth century She'd studied it at the university. It had been painted by one of the Dutch masters.

She pulled out the painting and studied it carefully. Maybe it was a copy. The signature looked original. She turned it over; the true masters could always be identified by their age. She ran her hands across the canvas; it had the coarse, heavy feel of the previous century, and the wood frame was aged too, with a little woodworm in one corner. It all spelled out to her that this may well be an original.

Why was a painting that was so valuable sitting here in Helmut's bedroom, hidden by a drop cloth?

Then it hit her. Hard. An icy feeling clenched her throat. A feeling she did not want to accept.

They'd all heard stories of art being taken, looted from Amsterdam, and sold off to the Germans for a tenth of the price or moved to Göring or Hitler's collections. Was Helmut dealing in illegal paintings and taking them out of Amsterdam for the Reich?

She covered up the canvas again and returned to the bathroom with a sickening feeling. Everything suddenly made sense. This was why Helmut was doing so well through the war. This was why his father was gone so much. They were helping the Nazis pillage Amsterdam's art; it was the only thing that made sense.

Elke thought about past conversations she'd had with Helmut, days where he was gone, supposedly visiting clients in France or Germany or Austria. He was smuggling art out of Amsterdam. Maybe "smuggling" was not the right word. Blatantly stealing it right from under everyone's noses. Apparently being paid handsomely for his time in the process.

Trying to control the anger coursing through her body, Elke marched back down the corridor, down the stairs, and straight past Helmut, who was still looking out the window. He tried to say something to her, but she shut him down. "I should get back, find Mr. Van den Berg. I am sure there are many people we need to connect with." Elke could not keep the ice from her tone, but she held back her real fury. She did not want to let Helmut know what she'd found out about him. She needed time to process this new information. Her heart and thoughts were racing. She had always suspected there was something about Helmut, something she could not quite put her finger on. And now she knew.

Elke found her boss and stayed close to him for the rest of the evening. Even though Helmut made a couple more advances toward her, she managed to brush him off with one-word answers before leaving early, feigning a headache.

On the way home, she didn't mention what she had found out to Mr. Van den Berg. He was so enamored with Helmut and had known his father a long time. However, inside she was livid and just grateful that she had not gotten involved with him. It was appalling how some people were making money on the backs of the Jewish people, and at the same time stripping their country of its wealth and beauty. She felt foolish that she had not known before. Now it all seemed obvious. All the signs were there. She would be much more careful in the future.

Chapter Twenty-Nine

On St. Nicholas Eve, Josef sat at his kitchen table, grading papers with Dantes on his lap, when there was a soft rap at his front door. His heart leaped. Michael. It had been days since his disappearance, and Josef had missed his young friend's company more than he would have expected. Hurrying through his house, he pulled open the front door with expectancy.

He was surprised to see Hannah Pender standing on his doorstep. For a moment his heart raced with the fact she was at his house, but in equal measure it sank with the disappointment that it wasn't Michael.

Apparently reading something in his expression, she enquired, "Professor, did I come at a bad time?"

Josef beamed. "No, no, of course not, Mrs. Pender." Then added in an extremely odd tone, "What a nice surprise. Please, come in."

"Call me Hannah," she insisted, with a smile.

He pushed his spectacles nervously up his nose as she stepped inside, and they stood together quietly in the hallway. Hannah looked around. "How nice and, um… tidy," she finally decided on, apparently attempting to break the silence between them.

As she stood close to him, he felt a thrill run through his whole body. There was something strangely intimate about having her here in his space, away from the safety of their day-to-day visits with her desk between them. His heart appeared to want to thump its way out of his chest and his mind raced with what that might mean.

She turned to him and for a wild second he wanted to kiss her, passionately, take her in his arms and for one moment experience her in that way, pulling her in tightly and losing himself in her soft lips and warm curves, her marriage be damned. It was as he was wrestling with his conflicting emotions that she spoke. Her caring eyes disarming him. Her words tumbling out in a jumble.

"I'm sorry to come to your house in this way. Normally I would give this to you at work, but as you know, we are closed now for the holiday and this book came for you and I wasn't sure if it was important."

He felt disappointed; for the briefest of moments he thought she might feel the same way about him and was coming here to confess.

"Oh," was all he could squeeze out under the weight of his crushed feelings as he attempted to calm his heart as it drummed in his ears like a brass band.

She handed him a package. He looked down at it curiously, then, with the full weight of remembrance, recognized it must be the other book of poetry he had ordered for Michael from the library. He'd planned to watch his young friend's face light up when he realized that Josef had listened to him about all the poets he loved.

Josef took it from her, reluctantly.

Hannah read the expression. "I'm sorry. Was I wrong to bring it over? Should I have waited until after we were open again?"

"No, no, of course not," Josef responded, overcompensating. "It was very kind of you." He tried to collect himself.

A nervous hand checked her hair as they stood side by side for a few moments. The air was statically charged between them and he had no idea what he was supposed to say or do.

The hallway clock chimed the hour, and they both glanced toward the elegant hands before returning their mutual gaze to the floor.

"Would you like a cup of coffee?" he finally asked.

"Oh, no, I can't stop," she burbled. "I was just, um, well, had to bring the package and everything. I'm just out doing errands and... you know."

Opening the door herself, she exited. Then abruptly stopped, hovering on his top step. She turned to him, squared her shoulders, and took a deep breath.

"I also brought you this," she announced, thrusting another gift into his hands. "It's Christmas *banketstaaf.* It's not really the original recipe, of course, you know how hard it is these days, but a friend had a Red Cross parcel and there were powdered eggs, and flour and I had a little almond paste and so forth." She stopped to catch her breath before adding quietly, "I thought you might like it. Happy Christmas... Professor."

Josef stared down at the wrapped gift in a basket. He was taken aback and found himself stuttering in response, "Um, thank you, Mrs. Pender. I mean Hannah. That is very... er, kind of you. For you to come to my house, from *your* house, and cook this and bring this to me and to think of me..." He sounded ridiculous, he thought to himself. Why was he babbling on like an idiot?

Hannah saved him. "Well, I'll be going. I have a lot more to do." She went down one more step and then turned again.

"Just one more thing." Her faced flushed. "I know this is last minute, but would you care to come to my home on Christmas Day? It would just be the three of us. A very simple affair, but in times like this... well, we all need company. I thought you might be interested in sharing some Christmas cheer with us, and you'd be very welcome."

Josef was tongue-tied, her invitation completely taking him off guard, and he didn't know how to respond. His heart leaped at her invitation, and then reality stepped in. What if Michael was to come back and needed him? And did he really want to share the day with Mrs. Pender and her husband? A happily married couple, no doubt. With crushing realization it dawned on him: this was why she had come, and this invitation that had come out of the blue was because Hannah felt sorry for him, and that stung him more harshly than if she had rejected him. Without Michael, he suddenly felt vulnerable, more alone than ever. For years now there had been someone. Someone to talk to, someone to care for, and he had gotten used to it.

Josef looked down at her expectant eyes and took in a sharp breath.

"Thank you, but I can't."

Her pleasant face fell in dismay. He felt instantly regretful, but before he could add any more to his apology, she marched off down his path, waving a hand at him over her shoulder, adding, with what seemed like forced merriment, "No problem. I just thought I would ask on the off chance." Then she called back behind her, "Have a lovely Christmas."

"Thank you for the gift," Josef shouted toward the echo of her shoes moving down the street.

Back in his kitchen, he opened the basket and was delighted to see the sweet-smelling loaf. He couldn't even remember the last time he had been given such a treat. He placed it in his larder and undid the string of the other package, unwrapping the book of poetry. Sitting down at the table, he turned the pages and started to read the poems. As he did, he fought the picture of Hannah's expectant face looking up at him, her kind, caring eyes, her curvaceous body moving fluidly away from him down his path. And the surprising warmth he had felt just being close to her.

Chapter Thirty

On Christmas Day, Josef sat again on his own in his kitchen. The framed picture of Sarah that he had taken from her locked trunk now sat in pride of place on the table. He put the poem that Michael had written for him next to it and quietly spoke to the photograph, a habit he had acquired since the loss of Michael.

"It's Christmastime, Sarah, and I know you loved this time of year. Unfortunately, I don't have your skills at decorating, as you can see." He smiled, his hand circling the sterile room. "Michael wrote me a poem. Remember, I told you about him? The young man I was taking care of? He wrote me a poem for Christmas. Can you imagine? If you were here, I know you would be laughing, heartily. Remember how much I used to hate poetry? Well, let's just say poetry is now following me around. Some strange fate keeps bringing it to me. I am beginning to think it's maybe a message from you, with your wild sense of humor. You are still hoping that maybe I'll grow to love it one day, as you'd always said I would."

Dantes jumped onto his lap, and Josef read an excerpt from Michael's poem aloud to Sarah and his cat, pausing on his favorite part.

"… Your quiet strength a reminder that the wind finds its voice not in tranquility, but in the roar of a stormed-lashed sea."

"Imagine that, Sarah. To see me as strong. You were always the strong one in my eyes. But now I have been able to be strong for someone else."

Chapter Thirty-One

Just after Christmas, as Ingrid sat at her desk putting away her things for the evening, Vi accosted her. Ingrid was feeling particularly blue. To celebrate the season, she had planned a very extravagant party at Heinrich's apartment, which had to be canceled at the last minute because of Heinrich's work commitments, and she had ended up spending Christmas Day alone.

Vi perched herself on the corner of Ingrid's desk, her smile dazzling. "Where are you going?"

"Home," Ingrid responded flatly.

Vi playfully crossed one leg over the other. "That sounds like fun. Will Heinrich be there?"

Ingrid shook her head. "He's coming home late every night at the moment."

Vi jumped down from the desk, took Ingrid by the shoulders, and swiveled the chair around to face her. "Then why don't you come with me?" she proposed mischievously. "Let's go out and have some fun."

Ingrid glanced across to Heinrich's office door, which was now permanently closed. She knew if she disturbed him to ask, he would only be angry with her, as he so often was these days.

"Come on," Vi baited. "We'll just go out and have one drink. He won't even know that you were out. And you can slip home and be ready to play the perfect fiancée later on."

Ingrid smiled. Vi was certainly incorrigible. And there was a side of her that wanted to do something different. She couldn't even remember the last time she had gone out.

"There is a place I know." Vi's eyes sparkled. "A little, tiny club. Honestly, we won't be longer than an hour. Put on your shoes and let's get going."

Ingrid looked down at her feet. "My shoes are on," she said, confused.

"No, your dancing shoes," Vi responded, enthusiastically pulling Ingrid to her feet and twirling her around in circles, swing dancing with her.

Ingrid giggled to herself, thinking, Surely, one drink won't matter. And Vi was right. Heinrich would never even know that she hadn't gone straight home.

"Okay," she said, "but just one."

Vi nodded and grabbed her things.

Ingrid put on her coat, reminding herself Heinrich was always gone. Out dealing with issues or staying at the office later and later into the evening. Over the last few months, he'd become moody, isolated, and didn't want to share anything with her anymore.

It made her feel lonely, and it was nice to have a friend who not only understood her situation but also supported and believed in the same ideals as she did. All of her other friends had dropped away when she'd become involved in the Third Reich. Working in the offices was the only life she had now.

Following Vi out, she felt smug. Yes, it would do Heinrich good to see how it felt to be left alone, to be the one waiting—if he even made it home before her. And if he didn't, so what? She would have some fun with this new friend.

The girls walked arm in arm through the city of Amsterdam, chatting about their workday. Vi led her down a tiny street and winding stone stairs into a dark, smoky bar. Energetic jazz music greeted them on the way down, and the atmosphere was alive and pulsing.

"I didn't even know this place existed," Ingrid remarked, looking around in awe. The room was a hollowed-out brick cavern with black-painted walls and subdued lighting. On a corner stage, a small jazz band played upbeat music to the Nazis that filled the bar—soldiers and officers alike, all laughing, drinking, and smoking together.

As the girls entered the room, they caused a stir. There were long approving glances in their direction. Ingrid liked how that made her feel. She loved the power that it gave her, and instantly she felt more confident.

Vi pushed her way through the crowds, ignoring the wolf whistles and comments as she went. A drunken Nazi stepped in front of her. "Would you like to dance, Fräulein?" he slurred.

She grabbed both of his cheeks and squeezed them. "Maybe later, soldier, but right now I am thirsty." She pushed him down into a chair, and his friends around him roared at the display.

Vi led Ingrid to a little table away from the band, and Ingrid followed eagerly. "Who owns this place?" she asked, taking off her coat.

"They're the good Dutch," responded Vi. "They believe in what we are doing. Not everyone in Holland is a traitor."

A wiry little Dutch woman wearing a starched white apron arrived at the table to take their order. She greeted them enthusiastically. "I'm so glad that you came here, ladies. Thank you for the work that you're doing for the war. I know we will soon have a victory. Heil Hitler."

"Heil Hitler," Vi responded earnestly. "And we would have anything fabulous you've got to eat."

Ingrid blinked in confusion. "They have food?"

"Don't ask where they got it," Vi said conspiratorially "And two very stiff gins," she added to the order.

Ingrid tried to stop her. "I don't drink hard alcohol."

"You will tonight. It is Christmastime. Have a glass of gin. You look like you need it."

After the waitress had left the table, Vi sat back on her seat and eyed Ingrid with interest.

"You have never told me much about yourself," she said, pulling a cigarette from a silver case with her long red fingernails and extending one to Ingrid, who took it. "Are you from Amsterdam?" She lit the tips and snapped the case closed.

"Yes, but I moved around a lot." Ingrid became pensive. "My parents died when I was very young."

Vi blew out a plume of smoke. "I'm sorry, that must have been very hard for you."

"Yes. Yes, it was," Ingrid said quietly. "But now I have Heinrich, and we will have our own family." She tried to sound optimistic.

"Of course." Vi took another long, deep drag. "Tell me about you and Heinrich. Where did you meet?"

Ingrid smiled, remembering happier times. The times that seemed so distant to her now. The beginning of the occupation, when everything had felt so much more positive. Now there was nothing but work and pressure.

"He swept me off my feet," she giggled. "I started working for the Third Reich at the beginning of the occupation and enjoyed it immensely. But it has been hard in the last year."

"I know," Vi responded. "I can't wait for this to be over, too." Ingrid nodded.

"Do you intend to go to Germany after the war is over?" Vi asked as their drinks and food arrived.

"Of course," Ingrid said.

"So, you get on well with his family, then?"

Ingrid looked down and quickly took a slug of her gin before answering. Not used to hard liquor, it stung the back of her throat, but it did give her the courage she needed.

"No, they are a long way away, and Heinrich means to keep them safe."

"You've not spoken to them?" Vi sounded surprised.

"I will when I get there. We will all be a family together. I look forward to those days."

"How intriguing. That doesn't bother you?"

Ingrid felt the sting but shook her head. "I just think he likes to keep things to himself. I'm hoping that once we're married, he'll be more open. Then we can settle in Germany."

As they finished eating, two soldiers sidled up to them. "Would you ladies like to dance?" one of them slurred.

Vi pushed her chair back. "Come on, Ingrid. If we don't dance, they're going to keep bothering us."

"Oh no," Ingrid said, blushing. "I don't think Heinrich would like it."

"They didn't ask Heinrich, they asked you," Vi said jovially. "Heinrich isn't here. Come on."

She grabbed Ingrid's hand and pulled her to her feet. Ingrid knocked back the rest of her drink before she was pulled onto the dance floor, twirling with a young officer with blue eyes and white-blond hair. He stared at her intently, smiling at her through his drunken glare. She did have fun, though, as he whirled her in circles and spun her around.

One dance and one partner followed another. She soon lost track of time. Exhausted, she finally collapsed down at her table with her friend. They compared notes about their dance partners and laughed heartily. It was many drinks later when Ingrid finally noticed the time.

"I must get going," she said as she tried to focus on her wristwatch. "Heinrich will be home anytime, and I must get back to him."

Vi nodded. "Well, if your master is waiting, we should go." She pulled Ingrid to her feet, and Ingrid swayed with the effects of the alcohol, which suddenly seemed to have hit her. Vi grabbed her friend before she toppled over and insisted on walking her home.

"I'll be fine," mumbled Ingrid. "I can find my own way back."

"I know you can, but I'm sure Heinrich will never forgive me if something happened to you on the way there. He is my boss too."

Ingrid giggled. "Okay," she agreed, hanging onto Vi's arm.

All the way through town, they acknowledged the Nazis on patrol, knowing most of them by sight. And those who didn't know them noticed their German uniforms and waved them on.

When they arrived at Ingrid's building, Vi kissed her on both cheeks and Ingrid giggled. "See you tomorrow, Ingrid," she sang out. "And remember, don't let Heinrich give you a hard time."

Ingrid grinned. "No, I won't," she shouted back as she stumbled into the building.

She felt less confident as she went up in the lift. On the way up, she attempted to smooth out her hair and straighten her clothes, knowing that Heinrich would notice. Hopefully he was not back yet. Maybe she would go straight to bed.

But as she opened the door, she sensed his presence. He was in the hallway, pacing angrily. He had taken off his jacket, and his shirtsleeves were rolled up. He had a drink in one hand and a cigarette in the other.

"You finally came home," he snapped. "Thank you so much for doing that."

Ingrid shut the door meekly and leaned against it to stop herself from falling over as Heinrich continued to berate her.

"How dare you disrespect me like this? Where have you been till this time?"

Ingrid tried to sound as sober as she could. "I just went out for a drink with a friend." Even though she concentrated, she could still hear the slight slur in her words.

"What friend?" he snapped back, his eyes blazing.

"The new girl from the office. You know, Vi."

"And what do you mean by not telling me?" he shouted into her face.

"Don't yell at me, Heinrich," she hollered back, feeling emboldened by the alcohol still coursing through her body. "You are gone every single night. You never tell me where you've been. I just wanted to go out and have a little bit of fun."

He appeared shocked at her forthright comeback but continued on his rant. "You're an embarrassment to me. Look at you. Look at the state of you." He looked her up and down in disgust. "Your hair is unkempt, and look at your clothes. Your makeup looks terrible. You're an embarrassment to that uniform. You shouldn't be out there looking that way."

Ingrid automatically felt shame; she looked down, her eyes taking in her disheveled clothing. How could he make her feel that way? She tried to respond, though her voice had lost its power. "I don't care what you say. I've had a good night, and it's about time I did."

"Well," he said menacingly, "if you're going to continue to be with me, you're going to have to learn to be more considerate. Such as telling me where you are and who you're with. We have a critical job to do here. Do you understand? Do you know that we are in the middle of a war?" And with that he strode away from her.

"How will I ever forget that? One that we seem to be losing," she spat back at him.

Suddenly, Heinrich raced back to her and took her by the shoulders and started to shake her. She was shocked by the aggression. He'd never done anything like that before.

"Do not shame me!" he shouted, his face inches from hers. "Do you understand? I will not be shamed."

Shocked by the violent turn their altercation had taken, Ingrid backed down. "Yes, okay. Sorry, Heinrich. I did not realize that this would shame you. That is the last thing I want to do," she whispered, desperately trying to control the panic rising in her throat and wanting to get out of his grasp.

Her words seemed to calm him. He let go of her shoulders and walked to the bedroom, yelling over his shoulder as he went, "You will come home on time tomorrow. Do you understand? And you will never go anywhere without telling me first." He slammed the door.

"Yes," she whispered quietly to the closed door, making her way to the bathroom.

She suddenly felt angry. How dare he treat her this way? Weren't they meant to be engaged? Wasn't he supposed to love her? This wasn't how this was supposed to be. But everybody had ups and downs, Ingrid reminded herself as she washed the makeup from her face. And the war was so stressful. Everybody's nerves were short. He wouldn't have hit her, would he? She considered the rage in his eyes and the way he'd taken hold of her. Her shoulders still hurt from where he'd grabbed them. Of course not. Heinrich loved her and he wasn't that kind of a man.

Ingrid took a moment to pull herself together before she made her way into the bedroom. He was already lying down with his back to her as she slipped under the covers. Her head continued to swim with the effects of the alcohol and her own tormented emotions. Looking up at the ceiling, she felt hopeless. This wasn't the life that she'd envisioned for herself. She would try harder, make it up to Heinrich. Ingrid turned off the light and closed her eyes, though sleep eluded her until the early hours of morning.

Chapter Thirty-Two

On the last day of 1944, Josef sauntered along the icy sidewalk and turned down his pathway, flexing his chilly red knuckles a couple of times before placing the key in the lock. The snow had come down without warning and swirled into accumulating drifts. Light, fluffy, and whipped up in the wind, it circled and spun its cotton-candied dance around the bushes and shrubs in his tiny garden before finally gathering at the roots.

Dantes was waiting patiently for him at the door. But instead of his usual warm welcome, he seemed agitated and meowed loudly at his master. Removing his damp coat, scarf, and hat, Josef spoke to his pet. "Are you hungry, Dantes? I did manage to get you some fish." He went into the kitchen and started his evening routine.

He was surprised when the cat showed no interest in the bowl of food he placed on the floor. Instead, Dantes circled the kitchen, agitated, meowing urgently. Then he trotted purposefully to the back door, which was also surprising. The cat was not a fan of the cold. Josef opened up the door, which led into an alleyway and spoke softly. "You won't want to go out, Dantes. It's freezing."

Dantes stood and peered out into the frozen night, complaining incessantly. Josef chuckled to himself as he began to close the door. Suddenly, a fierce gust of wind picked up and ripped it from his hand. The door squealed angrily on its hinges as it was wrenched wide open, allowing a circle of turbulent snow to dance around his kitchen, chilling Josef to the bone. As the windows in the kitchen rattled their own displeasure, Josef grabbed hold of the door and wrestled against the wind to shut it.

That was when he noticed something outside. Something dark that lay partially buried by a snowdrift. At first he thought it was a bundle of ragged clothes. But then it seemed to move, and he realized that it was alive. A black dog curled up in a ball, perhaps? Pulling on a jacket he ventured back out into the frigid, howling weather.

As he drew closer, he realized it wasn't a dog at all, but a person, lying face down. Hurriedly rolling them over, he realized with a jolt, this icy, bone-thin creature with a gray complexion and filthy, matted hair was, in fact, Michael.

Falling to his knees, he rubbed the young man's frozen cheeks, calling his name over and over again. "Michael. Michael, can you hear me?"

He picked up the limp hand, and the chill shocked him. The skin was blue and frozen. He felt for a pulse. It was slow, but he was alive. He pulled Michael to his feet and dragged him inside, noting how light he was, just a bundle of clothes and bones. He laid his friend on the kitchen floor and started to rub his body vigorously. His hands, his arms, his shoulders, his chest.

"Michael," he called out frantically, over and over again. "Can you hear me?"

Once inside the warmth of the house, the young man started to shiver uncontrollably, and Josef rushed to get him some blankets and smothered him with them, then lit a fire and went upstairs and started to fill the bath with warm water so as not to shock him too much. When the water was in the tub, Josef whispered to his friend, "There is a bath for you."

There was no response, so Josef carried him upstairs into the bathroom as Dantes followed and stood at the door, watching with curiosity. The steam from the bath brought Michael back to some sort of awareness. His eyes opened a couple of times, though he still looked dazed. Even so, he seemed to understand Josef's words when he told him to get undressed. He fumbled for his shirt buttons, but his numb and frozen hands were unable to complete the task.

Gently, Josef started to unbutton and then remove his shirt. Michael, whose eyes were still shut, mumbled through his semi-consciousness, "I hope you're a brunette. I'm very partial to brunettes." Josef shook his head, amazed at his friend's sense of humor even though he was barely alive. He took it as a good sign.

Josef finished undressing him and then lifted Michael into the bath. As he was lowered down into the heat of the water, the shock of it seemed to sting him, and he cried out in pain.

Josef reassured him, "It's okay, my friend, it's okay." Cradling Michael's head, he started to scoop up the water and pour it gently down his body.

The young man's eyes flashed open in terror. "Where am I?"

"You are here, Michael. You are home."

Michael seemed to understand and slowly his eyes focused on the person in front of him.

"Professor," he slurred in recognition. "I bet you thought you'd got rid of me."

Josef shook his head and continued to lap water over his frozen flesh; slowly Michael started to thaw.

Josef looked at his young friend's body. It was painfully thin, covered in dirt, marked with untreated cuts, bites, and bruises that confirmed he had probably been sleeping rough the whole time. Taking a piece of soap, Josef rubbed it into a lather and then slowly started to wash Michael, paying particular attention to his hands and feet, which were caked in the grime of weeks out in the elements. Then he carefully washed Michael's hair, un-matting the clumps in his thick, dark curls and pulling out the burrs that had buried themselves there. His anger began to rise.

"Why did you not come back before?" he demanded. "You could've come back at any time."

Michael opened his eyes and fixed his older friend with his sadness, the hurt and pain evident on his face. "I had something I needed to do, something I needed to come to terms with. And, honestly, toward the end, I just wanted to die."

Josef listened. In time, he knew, Michael would tell him everything.

As Josef rinsed his hair, Michael relaxed, the soap and water revitalizing him. When he was clean and sufficiently warm, Josef helped him out of the bath, wrapped him in a dressing gown, and supported him down the stairs to a seat in front of the fire. He fetched Michael a brandy, stoked the fire until it was roaring, then made him a bowl of thin soup, all he had. By the time the food was ready, Michael was looking more alert. Josef placed the tray of food in front of him.

"You must eat now and get well," he stated plainly, noticing Michael had started sweating profusely. He hoped he didn't have pneumonia.

As Michael attempted to take a spoonful of soup, his eyes rolled back and closed again as he mumbled, almost to himself, "It was impossible out there. The whole of Holland is like a barricade. There's no way out."

"Thank goodness you weren't caught. It was a perilous thing to do."

As the fire crackled happily in the grate, they found a peaceable silence.

"Michael?"

Michael opened his eyes slightly. "Yes, Professor?"

"Please stay. Please stay to the end. It's much safer here."

All of Michael's fight appeared to have left him as he whispered back his response, "I have nowhere else... *no one else* to go to." There was anguish in his words, and Josef wondered if there was more he was not saying. He could only imagine what the young man had gone through. The streets of Amsterdam, in fact of the whole world, were a dangerous place to be in this dark time.

After Michael had forced down half a bowl of soup, Josef guided his friend back up to the attic, made up his bed, and added more blankets. The young man melted into it with a deep sigh.

All at once, from outside, the air-raid siren screeched into life. Josef turned out the lights and looked over at his friend, who was already fast asleep. There wasn't any way he could take him to the shelter under the house and he wasn't going anywhere without him.

So they remained side by side in the darkness while bombs dropped down upon Amsterdam, one after another. The whole house shook with the force of the detonations from the Allied bombing campaign, and the sky continually lit up as if with fireworks. The smell of smoke, the sound of glass smashing, and the constant drone of ambulance bells filled the streets.

One bomb dropped a couple of streets away, shaking dust and plaster from the rafters and waking Michael from his deep slumber. He reached out a hand and grabbed frantically in the darkness. "Josef!" he cried out.

"Yes, I'm here." Josef took a firm hold of Michael's hands.

"Thank you."

"I'm glad you're back."

Michael answered in just above a whisper, "Me too."

Chapter Thirty-Three

Ingrid and Vi's relationship fell into a comfortable rhythm as the war escalated on the outside. The girls relieved their day-to-day stresses by going out two or three times a week, much to Heinrich's begrudging displeasure. But with the continued lack of troops and the war being fought on multiple fronts, he was always distracted and appeared to prefer that Ingrid was not demanding anything of him.

Often they would go to the little jazz bar in town, making their way through the dark, dreary streets down into the solace of the smoke-filled bar with the haunting sounds of jazz piano, trombones, and trumpets in order to dance their cares away.

Ingrid realized how lonely she had been before Vi. She and Heinrich had been so much happier at the start of the war. There had been plenty of time for parties and to be together. But now, as things had intensified, she felt more and more isolated from him. He had become suspicious of everybody around him, keeping secrets and coming home angry every evening, always refusing to share with her why he was so upset.

Their lovemaking, which had been so magical in the beginning of their relationship, had become dry, clinical, and loveless; a physical act to distract him from some deeper need that wasn't being met for him out in the world. She felt more like a dress-up doll, waiting at home in beautiful clothes for him to play with if he had the need. But the rest of the time she was no more than a piece of furniture.

On the other hand, Vi was exciting and fun-loving. Ingrid shared her fears and her life openly with her new friend and had planned to ask Vi to be her bridesmaid when they went back to Germany, after the Reich had won.

One evening her friend arrived at her desk. "We're going out," she announced with a gleeful glint in her eye. "Somewhere different."

Ingrid packed away her things quickly and grabbed her coat. As she linked arms with Vi, she confirmed, "We're not going to the bar?"

"No," Vi responded enthusiastically. "A friend of mine is holding a party. There'll be music, dancing, and alcohol," she declared as they bounded off into the night.

They arrived at an impressive-looking townhouse and entered a long, winding staircase that took them up to the top of the building. As they reached the top landing, it was evident from the music vibrating its way out into the corridor that the party was in full swing. The apartment inside was alive with raucous laughter and a blur of familiar faces they knew from the bar and the Reich offices. It was jam-packed with people; the hallway was so tiny they could barely move. A band played in a corner.

Vi shouted to her friend over the hubbub, "Why don't you wait here? I'm dying for a drink. I'll get us something and be back in a minute." She dove off into the heaving mass, pushing her way through toward the makeshift bar.

Ingrid felt awkward and alone without her confident friend's presence. She heard Vi's laughter from the bar and knew she was already in the full social swing of the party.

As she looked around to see if she knew anybody else, a voice spoke behind her. "Fräulein Ingrid, isn't it?"

Ingrid's body stiffened and then shivered. She knew who it was, and fear consumed her entire being. Turning around swiftly, she confirmed her suspicions. Heinrich's Lieutenant Colonel stood in his intimidating black uniform, his hooked nose prominent, his black, beady eyes shining and feasting on her as if she were something good to eat. She automatically tried to step away from him, but the crowded, narrow corridor prevented her from moving very far.

"Lieutenant Colonel," she responded coolly, trying to keep her voice steady, remembering how afraid she had been when his hand had fondled her thigh the evening she had toured his house.

Now, packed in so tightly, he leered over her. "How wonderful to see you again, Fräulein. I noticed that the dashing Heinrich is not with you." Then he added sarcastically, with a twist of his lips, "Not here to rescue you today, I see."

Ingrid glanced around nervously and could just about see Vi across the room. She was talking to three men and smoking a cigarette, and wasn't aware of what was happening in the hall.

"He's busy," she responded, trying to keep a brave, conversational tone. "So we'll not be staying that late," she added, briskly, "as I need to get home to be with him."

This man sickened her, but she still needed to be pleasant. This was Heinrich's superior, after all.

She turned back toward the wall, pretending to look at a picture hanging there. He picked up on her observation.

"A nice piece," he stated flatly. He pointed at another one across the hallway. It was of a naked woman lying across a bed. "I prefer that one. That would be beautiful in my bedroom, don't you think?" he purred into her ear.

The insinuation wasn't lost on Ingrid. Why was Vi taking so long? She desperately needed rescuing. There were so many people and she couldn't move forward, and was now pinned against a wall as he towered over her.

"I don't know much about art," she stated robotically, stepping in the only direction she could manage to go, backwards toward the front door. She pretended to gaze intently at another painting of wheat fields as though there was something in there that was going to jump out and speak to her.

Suddenly, someone pushed past them, and she was rammed against a hall doorway and the Officer was forced upon her. She recoiled as his arms went forward to steady himself and ended up around her waist. He drooled at her. "If you wanted to get close, you should have just asked."

All at once, he opened the door behind her and pushed her through it. For a second she didn't know where she was or what had happened. Then she realized she was in a bedroom as she heard the door close behind her in the darkness. Fear shot up her back and squeezed the back of her neck as a voice screamed in her head, *Get out, get out now!*

"I need to find my friend Vi," Ingrid snapped, speaking in the direction she knew the officer had to be. "And then I need to go home to Heinrich."

"Not so fast," he sneered back. "I feel like we have some unfinished business from the last time we were together."

"I don't remember any unfinished business." Her voice quivered as she desperately looked around for a way of escape. Her eyes started to adjust to the dark. There was a window, no other doors in the room, and one bed. "I really do need to go," she protested, attempting to push past him.

But his intimidating presence loomed ominously over her, his feet rooted to the spot. Fear and shock rose in her throat as his hands were suddenly upon her, grabbing and pawing at her body, and then the horrific sensation of his lips upon her neck. Violently, she jerked away from him. He responded by grabbing her by the throat and slamming her against the door. The door handle jabbed harshly into her back, and she screamed out in pain and fear. He stepped back and slapped her hard across the face with full force. Her head exploded, whipped backward, ricocheting off the door, cracking on contact. It felt as if it had been ripped from her body and she nearly blacked out as the blinding, searing pain spread through her skull and across her cheek and nose.

Pinning her arms to her sides, he lifted her up and slammed her down onto the bed. He kept her in place with his knee and grabbed a chunk of her hair to stop her from wrestling out from under him. She gasped for breath as her lungs emptied with the force of assault. Then, aware of his body on top of her, she felt sheer panic course through her veins like an electric shock, her heart trying to pound its way out of her chest. The realization of what was about to happen terrified her, along with the knowledge that she was powerless to stop it.

He grappled with her clothes, his hand thrusting inside her silk blouse as he pulled aggressively at her bra.

She started to beg. "Please, don't do this. I don't want to do this."

He grabbed her face and squeezed her cheeks together to stop her speaking, spitting out, "You will be quiet and do as you're told. Remember, you Dutch whores are here for our pleasure. Heinrich has spoiled you keeping you all to himself. Well, we need to remedy that now, don't we? And if you tell anybody, I will kill you. Not to mention, I will make sure Heinrich knows that it was you, his whore, who came on to me."

His hand thrust up her skirt and he started to tear at her underwear. She sobbed, silent tears streaming down her face, her body shaking uncontrollably.

All at once the bedroom door was flung open and the light flicked on. A couple fell in, giggling, a young soldier and a Dutch woman. They stopped dead when they saw what was going on. Then the man stuttered, "Lieutenant Colonel, we just need to get our coats from the bed. We didn't mean to disturb you."

As the officer turned his attention to respond, he rolled his weight to the side and released Ingrid's face and hair for just a second. It was all she needed. With all of her might, she pushed him from her and rolled onto the floor. The Lieutenant Colonel grabbed for her arm and ripped off her bracelet instead as she jerked it away from him, scattering beads across the floor. She didn't stop to pick them up. Instead she leaped to her feet and ran through the open door. She grabbed her purse, which she'd dropped in the hallway as he'd forced her into the room, and scrambled through the throng of people, stumbling to the farthest point away from the bedroom.

She could still feel his grip on her throat as it continued to throb. Her head was splitting with the pain, her neck and jaw ached, and she was sure her face would be a mass of bruises in the morning. Grabbing at the edges of her gaping blouse, she fought her way back up the hallway, her head pounding and his voice still ringing in her ears. *If you tell anybody, I will kill you… I will make sure Heinrich knows that it was you, his whore, who came on to me.*

Once in the safety of a room full of people, she pressed her back against the wall to steady herself before her legs collapsed from under her. She tried to calm her breathing. The heat from her body melded with the hot, sticky wall as a trickle of sweat ran down between her shoulder blades, causing her delicate silk shirt to cling to her back. She looked down at her clothes and was shocked to see the top of her lacy cream bra. Her hands shook as she buttoned up her shirt.

As feeling returned to her legs, Ingrid made her way rapidly through the rooms, trying to find a bathroom; she needed to clean herself up before she spoke to anyone. The building was a mass of staircases and landings. She spotted Vi over by the bar, still talking to a young soldier, her head thrown back laughing at something he had just said, a cigarette held high in her hand. Feeling as if she was no longer in her body, Ingrid stared around in amazement. How could everything seem so normal around her? How could no one know what had just happened to her?

She eventually found a bathroom. Once she locked the door, Ingrid reached out to the stark tiled wall, her hand needing its reassuring presence. As the cold stone permeated her skin, she caught a glance of herself in the mirror. She was shocked at the face that greeted her. It was filled with terror, her eyes staring out, almost paralyzed with fear.

She readjusted her skirt and underwear back into position, rinsed her face with water, and dabbed at her cheeks. Tears collected in her eyes, and her throat was dry as she fought down the need to scream. She had to keep it together. She couldn't let him win. This couldn't get back to Heinrich. Things between them were already so complicated; he was so angry all of the time. He might not even believe her word, especially against someone higher up in the party than he was. She wanted it all just to go away.

Fumbling through her purse, she found some makeup and quickly reapplied her crimson lipstick. Her hands shook so violently she could barely draw a straight line; she used her other hand to attempt to steady her trembling fingers as she tried desperately to pull together a semblance of order. After her lipstick, she carefully cleaned the streaks of mascara running in two black tram lines down her face. She combed her hair into smooth waves from its twisted, mangled clumps, trying not to wince from the throbbing pain where he'd slammed her head against the door and then grabbed handfuls of her hair. As reality began to sink in, she couldn't believe this had happened to her, and even though she tried to fight it, tears rolled down her cheeks in hot, thick waves.

When she felt that she could maybe face the world again, she carefully dried her eyes and went back out to find Vi. From a far corner, she sensed *him* watching her, his eyes boring into her as she walked across the room. Even though she didn't meet his gaze, it was as if, with each step, his words echoed in her head. *Heinrich's whore.* Ingrid straightened up. She wasn't going to give him the pleasure of thinking he'd intimidated her. She wasn't going to let him believe that he had broken her spirit.

Vi was suddenly by her side. "Hey, there you are. I've been looking for you."

"I was in the bathroom," Ingrid responded, not wanting to talk about what had just happened.

Vi seemed to sense something. "So, do you need a drink?" she enquired.

Ingrid nodded. "I would like something very strong."

"Okay." Vi quirked her eyebrows and had the barman pour Ingrid a large gin. "Here, this should be strong enough." She handed Ingrid the brimming glass, which she drained.

Ingrid took a slow, deep breath, allowing the warm, intoxicating liquid to smooth her ruffled nerves.

Somehow, Ingrid managed to make her way through the rest of the evening without revealing the emotional turmoil deep inside. She couldn't bring herself to tell Vi what had happened; it just felt surreal, too horrible to confess out loud. Perhaps not dwelling on it would make it all just go away. Ingrid continued to stay close to Vi, before feigning a headache and asking her if they could leave early. Perpetual fear raged through her being, informing her that her body was injured at a much deeper level than the pain and bruises now massing under her skin. She thanked God the Lieutenant Colonel had been interrupted, but still, she felt immense shame. She felt violated.

As she stood alone waiting for Vi to fetch her coat, fear gripped her again as if she were still trapped in that room with him. She could still smell his breath, hot and rancid on her face. She could still hear his words as he had spat into her ear. She could still feel his hands on her body, tugging at her clothes, pulling her hair. It took everything in her to concentrate all of her energy on something else, just to stop the screaming that wanted to erupt from the pit of her stomach. She allowed thoughts of Heinrich, and the life they would have once the war was over, to fill her as she smiled at people and made light conversation.

Vi walked her home, chattering to her obliviously as Ingrid hung onto her friend's arm. The full force of what had happened kept washing over her in nauseating waves, paralyzing her. Once back in the safety of her apartment, she couldn't hold it together for one more minute. Breaking down into tears, she fell to her knees and sobbed. She clamped both hands over her mouth to muffle her desperate cries. The last thing she wanted to do was wake her fiancé.

She stumbled to the bathroom, stripped off her clothes, lit the boiler and ran a bath. Submerged in the hot water, she allowed her tears to flow freely. She scrubbed furiously at her skin with her nails and soap until she was red raw, staying in the water until it turned cold. Then she wrapped herself in a thick white towel and sat down on the toilet seat.

Her whole body ached and she felt desperate about her life. She wished that she and Heinrich were closer. Ingrid wanted them to have the kind of relationship where she could tell him what had just happened. But as she contemplated that possibility, the reality hit her hard: Heinrich wasn't that kind of man.

As fresh tears slid down her cheeks, she wondered what she needed to do to make him love her again. If only she could figure out what she'd done wrong.

When there were no tears left, she slipped out of the bathroom put on her nightgown and, wincing in pain, limped slowly into the bedroom. She hovered on the edge of the bed, not wanting to disturb Heinrich. As she carefully pulled back the covers, he turned away from her, moaning in his sleep. She desperately wanted to hold him or to have him hold her, but he would be so angry if she woke him. So instead, she drew her feet under the covers and, clutching her pillow, slipped into a fretful sleep as her battered body gave way to exhaustion.

Chapter Thirty-Four

It had been two days since he had found Michael in the alley and, seated on the trunk in the attic, Josef watched as the young man tentatively sipped his soup, Dantes curled up in a perfect furry ball at the end of the bed. He studied his young friend with grave concern as he labored through his food, his pale face ashen and haggard. It spoke not only of the severity, but also the extent of his ordeal, which he had still barely hinted at to Josef.

"Are you starting to feel better at all?" Josef attempted to sound hopeful but couldn't hide the heightened concern in his tone.

Michael waved a pathetic hand dismissively. "I'll be fine," he croaked. The words petered out as he punctuated his declaration with a prolonged and wracking cough.

Josef's heart sank as a blanket of impending fear wrapped its way around his body. He tried hard not to allow the alarm to show on his face, but couldn't disguise the tremble in his voice. "Would you like some tea, perhaps?"

Michael shook his head and closed his eyes, gasping for breath, the mere act of eating seeming to exhaust him. "I just need to rest," he said wearily as his head sank into his pillow. The spoon in his hand fell to the bed as he dropped into a deep sleep.

As Josef removed the bowl and spoon from Michael's hand, he could hear his rasping breath and feel the heat emanating from his body. He stood to his full height, hesitating, trying to decide what to do. All of his being wanted to sit down beside Michael and watch him breathe in and out, monitor any sign of distress. With a heavy heart, he realized he must go to work.

The Nazis at the university had become hyper-vigilant. Anything out of the ordinary was weighed and scrutinized as their paranoia saw plots and resistance everywhere. He shook his head. He would put Michael in danger if they were to search his house. He had to go on pretending everything was normal, move through his day predictably, blending in the way he had for most of his life.

That day at the university was excruciatingly long. In between classes, Josef went to the library and read through books about illnesses similar to Michael's, then piled up a stack to take home with him. As soon as the day was over, he hurried home without even stopping for his mail or to get his meager weekly ration of potatoes.

He ran up the stairs and into the attic, hoping for the best. But his mood shifted as he lit the tiny light and caught sight of Michael. He looked worse. His thick, dark hair was matted and damp across his forehead. Beads of perspiration glistened on his face, and he muttered in his sleep.

Quickly going for the jug that he'd placed out that morning, Josef poured a glass of water and touched it to Michael's lips. "Michael, Michael, it's me."

Michael started in his sleep, then rolled his eyes a couple of times before opening them. As he looked at Josef, he seemed to have trouble focusing, screwing up his eyes. Finally, he spoke.

"Professor, can you turn out the light?" There was pain in his voice. "It's hurting my eyes."

Josef snapped off the light and came back to join his friend in the darkness at the side of his bed. Even in the gloom, he could see that Michael's pajamas were soaked with sweat. "I will get you a cloth," he said, feeling hopeless.

Downstairs, he soaked a cloth in cold water. He glanced at his reflection in the kitchen window, shocked at the person staring back. He didn't even recognize himself. When had he aged so much?

He hurried back upstairs. Once in the cold, dark attic, he dropped to his knees and gently wiped his patient's face and neck. Unbuttoning Michael's pajama top, he was shocked at the angry rash spreading across Michael's chest. Josef's gut tightened. If only he was a doctor, not a mathematician.

As he continued to mop the young man's brow, Michael rolled in and out of consciousness. Josef made a decision. He brought a chair into the attic to sleep by his friend's side that night.

Both men slept fitfully, and whenever Josef woke, he continued to nurse Michael, who was feverish and delirious. At about three o'clock, the fear and helplessness overpowered him. To relieve his tension, he paced the attic in circles, ending up finally at the cracked window looking out at the pale moon, somber in the night's sky. A slight breeze moved through the pane and stirred him. He closed his eyes and whispered, "Tell me what I should do, Sarah, please."

But all he could see in his mind's eye was her face, her green eyes shining as she giggled at him and shook loose her mane of copper curls. He wished he could talk to somebody, confide in anybody, but he had to keep Michael safe. He couldn't allow anyone to know about his secret guest.

Eventually, he moved back to his chair to read through more of the medical books he had brought home before he fell asleep, only to be woken an hour later by Michael's wracking cough. Josef made him some hot water with lemon and brought it back up to the attic. Rechecking Michael's temperature, he shook his head. It was still so very high. How long could a body go through such an ordeal? He could not lose him; he could not lose someone again.

As the first dawn of light transformed the darkness to a royal blue, he reached over to his friend. "I must get you some medicine," he whispered into his ear.

Michael nodded.

"I won't be long."

The young man turned his head and opened his eyes. "I'll be fine, Professor," he said meekly, the sheer act of speaking exhausting him. He dissolved into a coughing fit that ended with him vomiting into the chamber pot beside the bed.

Josef cleaned him up and laid his head carefully back on the pillow.

"I'm going to the chemist as soon as it's open. I'll bring some medicine. It must be some kind of influenza. Please lie still and drink lots of water. That will help."

Michael nodded but appeared to be incoherent as he closed his eyes again.

Josef made his way into the silent street, forgetting his scarf in his haste. He paced the icy sidewalk outside of the chemist until the door opened and almost knocked the man out of the way as he pushed himself inside.

"I need something for my son. He has influenza. What do you recommend?"

The chemist—a thin, stooped eagle of a man, obviously proud of his position in life—strode back to his counter and did not attempt to answer until he was behind it. "How old is your son?" he asked stiffly.

"Twenty-six."

The chemist lifted his eyebrows. "I'm very short on supplies. I have to save medicine for the old people and the young."

Behind him, a doorbell tinkled and someone else entered the shop.

Josef lowered his voice. "But he had a dreadful night."

"Well, he should see the doctor and get a prescription," snapped the chemist. The chemist moved away from the counter dismissively and started to stack boxes of pills onto a shelf.

Josef sucked in breath to calm himself. He wasn't going to leave without something. "I will need something for the fever. Can you at least give me something for that?"

The chemist sighed deeply. "You need a prescription."

"I'm not leaving," challenged Josef, his resolve unwavering. "I know you have something you can give me. I cannot get a prescription. I need to get something for my son, now."

The chemist peered at Josef and, apparently sensing his customer's defiance, turned from behind the counter, put a key into the lock of a drawer, and opened it. He pulled out one small bottle of pills, measured a few out, and placed them in a paper envelope. "You can give him those, but you must take him to the doctor."

Josef nodded, relieved to get anything. He put them in his pocket and paid for them.

Arriving back at the attic he administered a couple of the aspirin to Michael, who forced them down with water. As Josef wiped sweat from Michael's chest, he noticed that the rash that had appeared the day before was now a deep, angry purple.

Michael's eyes opened as he watched his friend. "Professor, thank you."

Josef nodded and stood to his feet, feeling some sense of hope that the aspirin might bring down Michael's temperature. And it did, in fact, seem to help a little, as his friend settled.

He sat beside Michael's bed again. "It's very odd. Why am I not sick, too?" He spoke more to himself than to Michael. "If it's influenza, surely I would be sick as well. If I was sick, I could get you medicine. But they won't let me have anything. We need to think of a way to get you to a doctor."

Michael's eyes creased in concern. "Did you forget I was Jewish?" he said, barely above a whisper.

"Maybe they won't notice," said Josef, trying to sound optimistic. "Your features aren't so Jewish-looking," he lied.

Beside him, Michael's dry lips attempted the hint of a smile. "Not look Jewish? I could play Moses," he whispered. "Besides, there are other ways to know I am Jewish that are harder to disguise." He lifted his eyebrows, showing a little of his usual humor. "I think, unless there was a miracle there, visiting a doctor is out of the question."

Chapter Thirty-Five

At 4 a.m., Josef dropped the third medical book that had confirmed the diagnosis. The rash, the cough, the temperature, and the bites—it could only be one thing, and that explained why Michael was not getting better.

As soon as it was light, Josef rushed out without even having a drink. Going directly to the hospital, he walked up to the desk, swallowing down the panic sweeping over him. Through a dusty window, a dry-looking nurse peered up at him.

"I need to see a doctor."

"Please take a seat. We have many patients today," she stated, curtly.

"You don't understand; my son is very sick."

She screwed up her eyes and looked around the room. "Where is he?"

"He is too sick to bring here, but I believe I know what he has. I need to see a doctor and get the medicine."

The nurse let out a long, slow sigh. "Sit down. We'll get to you when we can."

After an anguished, two-hour wait, Josef's name was finally called and he was ushered into one of the consulting rooms. A weary doctor writing on a chart didn't even look up.

"How may I help you?"

"It's not for me." Josef couldn't bring himself to sit, instead pacing the room and turning the brim of his hat in his hand nervously. "I need medicine. My son has murine typhus."

The doctor stopped writing, taken back, and then peered at Josef, apparently weighing him up as to whether he was medically trained or just a hypochondriac.

"Who gave you that diagnosis?" he enquired gravely.

Josef looked about him nervously. "I have books."

"Well, there's a reason I have a degree in medicine," the doctor rebuked stiffly. "Books can't replace the right care or consultancy. Bring your son in for an appointment and I will check to see what he has."

The doctor turned his back as if to dismiss him.

Josef did not back down. "But I need the medicine. I need to take the medicine home to him, today."

"You will have to bring your son in," the doctor repeated sternly. "I can't just give out medicine for something when I don't know what it is. I have ethics. If he does indeed have typhus, then we will have to do the proper tests. Make an appointment with my nurse at the front desk."

Josef's anger and frustration boiled. He could never bring Michael in; it was just too dangerous. He tried a different tactic. "Can you not just give me something to tide him over until I can bring him here?"

The doctor looked exasperated. "I think I've been very clear, Mr. Held. You bring your son in. I will do the tests, and once we have the results, then I will treat him. That's how these things work."

He then stood, marched to the consulting-room door, opened it, and ushered out the professor with a sweep of his hand.

Josef shuffled from the room despondently, stopping in the doorway for one final appeal. "But he's really sick."

"Then he needs to be in the hospital," snapped the doctor.

Held moved back out into the waiting room and wandered aimlessly through the hospital corridors, worrying. As he did, he observed doctors and nurses caring for patients and administering medicine. All at once, he had an idea, and finding the right door, he waited for his opportunity.

Staff went in and out for about an hour before he got his chance. A nurse unlocked the supply closet and was pulling out a roll of bandages when a doctor called to her. She moved out into the corridor to speak to him and, behind her back, Josef crept stealthily to the closet. He grabbed a few hypodermic needles, shoved them into his pocket, and then slipped past the nurse, unnoticed.

Arriving home, he went straight to the attic. His young friend was sleeping fitfully; his fever was even higher. Josef went outside, scooped a pile of snow into a large bowl, and, folding it into cloths, packed them around Michael to try to cool him down. Then, while his patient coughed and moaned, he settled to reread the chapter he had marked in one of the textbooks.

Dantes sat on Josef's lap looking over at Michael with concern. "Yes, Dantes, I know."

The professor closed the book and then stood. He knew what he had to do.

Opening another of the textbooks to a different page, he read carefully the chapter on how to draw blood. Beads of sweat blurred his vision as he talked to himself. "I can do this. I can do this."

Michael rolled over and looked at him bleary-eyed. "You can do what, Professor?"

Josef looked at his young friend and then at the needle in his hand. "Are you okay?"

"I need to draw some of your blood." Josef closed his eyes and took two deep breaths. "And I do have a confession I should probably tell you about."

Michael stared up at him.

"I have always had a great fear of needles and... of blood."

Michael rolled back on his pillow, murmuring, "I don't think this is going to work."

"I just need a minute."

Josef paced the attic, breathing deeply. When that failed to calm his nerves, he walked briskly out of the room, descended the two flights of stairs, and strode out the kitchen door. Standing in the snow, he breathed deeply in the frigid air. As the cold assaulted his lungs, he found the courage he needed. This was his friend's last hope. There was no other way.

Back in the kitchen, he scrubbed his hands thoroughly and then collected a clean white linen cloth and a small porcelain bowl before returning to the attic. Then he practiced injecting with the needles he'd stolen by inserting one into a small leather ball. As he did, all the blood rushed from his face.

Michael watched with concern.

Josef took the used needle and dropped it into the bowl. His hands were now shaking. "I can do this, I can," he reaffirmed.

"Are you sure?" Michael swallowed. "You can't even inject the ball."

Josef looked back at the medical chapter and reread it. He took a deep breath and tried again as Michael coughed violently. He turned to his patient, his hands still trembling.

Josef tied a thin cord around Michael's arm and then swabbed it with vodka. Michael turned his face away so as not to witness Josef's attempt to plunge in the needle. On the first attempt, Josef missed the vein. Michael winced.

"I'm so sorry."

"Can't get much worse," Michael responded, before starting another set of rattling coughs.

Josef tried again and then again. Each time he missed the vein. He stood up, closed his eyes, and took a deep swig of the vodka. Removing his glasses, he wiped the sweat from his brow with his shirtsleeve before replacing them and turning back to try again.

This time, thick red blood filled the syringe.

As he withdrew the amount he needed, Michael's face was ashen. "Are you taking it to the hospital now?"

"No, not exactly," Josef responded, fighting the urge to vomit.

Then, extending his own arm, he plunged the needle deep, injecting the infected blood into his own body. The last thing he heard before he passed out across Michael's bed was, "Oh my God, Professor!"

Chapter Thirty-Six

Josef took his temperature; it was normal. Staring at his face in the bathroom mirror, he rubbed his eyes. Wouldn't he be showing symptoms by now? Surely he would be starting to feel ill, feverish, anything. A gnawing fear ground like broken glass deep in the pit of his stomach. What if his plan hadn't worked? The situation felt hopeless.

As if to remind him of the cost, Michael erupted into a coughing fit in the attic. It had gotten worse over the last day or so and was now presenting as dry and rasping. This new development concerned Josef not only with the progress of the illness, but a concern about keeping him hidden.

He hurried to his bedroom to dress. It was Saturday, and he was due to go and see Ingrid. Every fiber of his being wanted to stay with Michael, but the reality was if he didn't turn up, Ingrid may just stop by to check on him, and with Michael being so ill, he couldn't risk having his Nazi niece at the house.

Before leaving, he checked on his patient one more time, hovering over him with concern, watching him breathe in and out, his pallid skin a deep gray. Drawing closer, he whispered, "I'll be back as soon as I can." From his close proximity, he could feel the heat radiating from his friend and hear the rasp in his lungs.

Michael didn't respond.

*

Arriving at Ingrid's apartment, he looked about him before he entered. He always felt wary. He was sure that when this war was over, Nazi sympathizers might not be treated too kindly, and he didn't want to give anyone that impression of him.

He knew it was a careful tightrope he was walking, but for Michael's sake, he needed to keep everything on an even keel. Thinking of Ingrid, he fought to remember the little girl lost somewhere inside the woman who had become so harsh and callous over the years. He knew deep down that she was as unhappy as everybody else. Yes, she still believed she was living in a fairy tale, but from the Resistance Report on the wireless it appeared that the war wasn't going well for the Germans, and he suspected, and indeed hoped, it wouldn't be long before her fairy tale came to an end.

She opened the door to him and gave him a sad smile.

"Uncle, thank you for coming." Her tone was despondent. She didn't even kiss him on the cheek.

She slunk up the hallway, and he followed her. Once in the front room, she didn't settle but seemed preoccupied, staring out of the window as she addressed him.

"I'm glad you could come," she offered offhandedly, snatching at a packet on the table and lighting a cigarette.

Josef nodded, noting she seemed worn, tired, with none of her usual brazen self-confidence. He didn't have time to contemplate this because as he settled himself on the sofa, his head started to swim. Dare he hope that he was getting sick? It had been two days since he had injected himself with Michael's blood.

A bead of sweat trickled down his temple, and as Ingrid droned on about her life with Heinrich, he took stock of his symptoms. He was warm—not a roaring temperature but definitely warmer than usual. His throat was dry, and he was having trouble focusing. He mopped at his brow and pushed away a bowl of snacks Ingrid had waiting on the table as his stomach lurched.

When he put his head in his hands, Ingrid finally noticed. "Uncle, are you all right?"

"I'm not feeling well," he announced, standing abruptly, then feeling as if he might faint, he quickly sat back down.

Ingrid got him some water, and his hand shook as he took the glass and started to drink. At last, he would be able to help Michael.

Ingrid sat back away from him, eying him, warily. "We should get you home, Uncle." She placed a handkerchief to her mouth. "I can't have you here sick."

"No, I do not want to go home. I need to go to the hospital."

Ingrid looked alarmed. "Then my driver should take you in the car."

"I can make my own way there."

"Nonsense, my driver will take you."

Josef was uncomfortable, but he was also glad that he was ill: it was all part of his plan. The driver was away on an errand and didn't arrive back for a while. When he did, Josef was sweating profusely.

"We must be taken directly to the hospital," Ingrid instructed the driver as he came to Josef's side to help him.

It was still cold outside, and Josef was glad there were not many people about. The last thing he wanted was for anyone to see him being driven in a Nazi car.

At the hospital, Ingrid walked to the main desk and demanded to see a doctor. And even with all her protesting and threatening, they still had to wait a good hour before Josef was finally called. As he was helped into the consulting room, she sat outside, her handkerchief covering her mouth and nose.

"Do not feel the need to stay," he coughed as the door closed.

"I need to make sure you are well, Uncle," she shouted back through the closed door. "You nearly fainted in the car."

A different duty doctor walked into the examination room. "What seem to be your symptoms?" he asked dryly, looking down at a chart.

"I need a test now."

"Mr. Held, I need to continue to ask you a few more questions before I consider that option." The doctor scribbled something on the chart.

Josef opened his shirt and revealed a rash starting to form. He was covered in it. "A rash, look!" he said jubilantly. "I have a rash!"

The doctor looked hesitantly at him. "Please calm down. I need to examine you properly."

"I need a test," stated Josef, shouting, probably for the first time in his life. "And I need it now! I believe I have murine typhus and I need a test to prove it."

With the outburst, Ingrid rapped on the door. "Are you okay, Uncle?" she shouted through the wood panel.

The doctor called in his nurse. "Please prepare a test for this patient," he said sternly.

The blonde nurse nodded and dashed out.

Ingrid wandered into the room and stood at a distance away from the bed. "Is my uncle okay?" she asked warily.

The doctor stepped from behind the curtain. "He's a little hysterical. I think it's probably his temperature. We're going to give him something."

Josef lay down on the bed and looked at the ceiling. He felt the weight of the last few days starting to lift from his shoulders. They would find out he had murine typhus. Then he would get medicine, and he could treat Michael with it. For the first time in a long time, he felt he had hope.

The pretty blonde nurse arrived behind the curtain with a kidney-shaped enamel dish. Josef's euphoria was short-lived as she picked up the syringe, and before she'd even injected him, he passed out.

The next thing he remembered was being awoken by the same nurse, and something cold being administered to his forehead. "Can you hear me, Mr. Held?" she asked him.

He nodded. "Sorry," he croaked. "I have a terrible fear of needles."

The doctor's face swam into view. "We will test you, and the results will be ready in a couple of days."

Josef felt distraught. "A couple of days?" he repeated desperately, rising to his elbows, which made his head swim again. "What do you mean a couple of days? He might not have... I mean *I* might not have a couple of days."

The doctor shook his head. "You're in the early stages of whatever this is. We have to make sure we give you the right treatment. You do not want to be misdiagnosed."

Ingrid was back by his side, a handkerchief still covering her mouth and nose. "The doctor said you might need to stay here for a day or two. I can go back to your house later today and pack you some things if you wish."

Josef became alarmed. "I cannot stay. I have things to do." He raised himself up and his head swam with the fever.

The nurse spoke rapidly to Ingrid, ushering her out the room. Josef could still hear their murmured conversation out in the hall. "We will take care of him, have no fear. I will prepare him a bed, and you can visit him later."

The doctor departed, and the nurse came over and smiled at Josef.

"You need to lie here. I will come back when your bed is ready. Do you need some water?"

"No, I'm fine," said Josef, mopping at his brow.

The minute the nurse was out of the room, he swung his legs off the bed. He felt hot, and his whole body trembled. He needed to get back to Michael. He pulled on his shirt, doing up his buttons roughly, put on his coat, and pushed on his shoes. Opening the door of the hospital room, he looked about the corridor. It was clear. Slowly, he shuffled out into the hallway. His lungs felt tight and his legs felt as if they might collapse under him at any moment. He made his way cautiously past the reception desk, but just as he turned a corner, his head swam again, and he steadied himself against a wall. He stumbled and a hand reached out to catch him. He looked up gratefully and was surprised to see Hannah Pender holding his arm.

"Professor Held, are you okay?" Her concern was evident on her face.

"Mrs. Pender. Hannah." He tried to pull himself up to his full height but found himself wobbling. "What are you doing here?"

"My mother had a turn. She has been allowed home, but I needed to pick up some medication to help her sleep."

He didn't want her to see him so unwell and tried to move past her, but Hannah took hold of Josef's arm and started to walk with him. "I will help you. Where are you going?"

Josef was grateful for her reassuring presence and once again, even with a fever, he felt the attraction that was always there between them.

"I need to get home," he rasped. "It's important that I get home."

She eyed him nervously, shaking her head. "Are you sure? You look very sick. Maybe you should stay."

"No, no. I need to go home," he demanded, thinking he had to beat Ingrid there, and started to shuffle toward the door.

Hannah didn't let go of her grip and continued to hold his arm as she ushered him out into the cold morning air. She supported his slow walk through the town. He was too exhausted to protest her help and found himself leaning on her arm more than he wanted to. Every step became arduous as he tried to fight for breath. "Are you sure you shouldn't be in the hospital?" she asked again quietly as they approached his house.

He shook his head. "There's nothing they can do until they know what is wrong. I just need to go to bed."

She nodded as they crossed the street.

"I have to take care of Mich… my cat," Josef corrected himself. In his delirium, he was not thinking clearly.

"I could always feed your cat for you," Hannah offered.

They reached his front door. Hannah helped him put the key in the lock, and he sighed with relief as they entered. "Thank you for getting me home."

Hannah shook her head. "Well, I'm still not certain it was the right decision, but I'd like to make you a cup of tea if that's okay."

Before Josef could respond, she had already bustled past him into the hallway and had taken off her coat.

Josef tried to protest, but all the fight had left him. He sank into a chair and closed his eyes. Faint coughing drifted down from above. He projected his own cough to cover the sound as Hannah came back into the room.

She handed him a cup of tea and tried to make him more comfortable. "Are you sure you wouldn't like me to stay with you?" she asked.

His head spun. Under different circumstances there was nothing he would have wanted more but he found himself saying, "No, no. Thank you, Mrs. Pender. You've been very kind. I will just go straight to bed once I've drunk my tea."

She nodded but didn't look convinced. "I could check in on you tomorrow."

He shook his head. "That won't be necessary."

"Are you sure there is nothing else I can do?" She looked around the room, as if searching for something.

"No, truly, I am fine, thank you."

Hannah smiled. Taking his hand, she gently stroked it. Her touch startled him, and his heart started to pound again, but he didn't withdraw. He allowed her warm touch to envelop him. Once again he reminded himself that as much as he was attracted to her, he still wasn't sure she could be trusted. Wasn't sure he could trust anyone these days. Michael's life was too precious to gamble with.

After Hannah left, he locked the door behind her and struggled upstairs toward his bedroom. He decided to visit Michael first. Michael's eyes opened briefly as Josef entered.

"You are sick," croaked Michael.

"Yes." Josef smiled and patted Michael's arm.

"I wouldn't be that happy," he responded dryly. "Trust me, you're not going to like it."

"But now I can help you," Josef whispered. "All we have to do is wait. Soon I'll have medicine, just a couple of days."

"A couple of days?" Josef heard the desperation in Michael's tone. "I'm not sure I have a couple of days." Michael reached a feverish hand out to grab his friend's arm. "I can't believe you did it. But thank you, Josef."

Josef suddenly became giddy. "I'm so tired, maybe I'll rest a bit here." He slumped into the chair. Michael covered him with a blanket. Josef drifted off to sleep, listening to his patient struggle to breathe next to him.

Chapter Thirty-Seven

Josef's walk back to the hospital, two days later, was long and labored. He had to stop a few times to lean against fences and walls to retrieve the breath that no longer seemed to want to fill his lungs. As he coughed uncontrollably, passersby kept a careful distance, needing to navigate their own survival through a long brutal war.

Arriving at the hospital, he went to the front desk and asked to see the doctor. The same dry, inhospitable nurse was in the midst of telling him he would have to wait when a rather dramatic fit of rolling coughs convinced her to rush him in. In a stark consulting room, no bigger than a closet, the same doctor he'd seen two days before arrived and knotted his eyebrows as he examined the rash, now an angry purple.

"Where did you go?" he enquired with obvious annoyance. "I thought you were still in the hospital."

"I had something I needed to do."

"More important than your health?" the doctor enquired. "What you have is very dangerous."

"I am not infectious, though, am I right?"

The doctor shook his head. "Still, you need to have the right medicine, and at your age, there can be…" He paused to find a word he was comfortable with. "Complications." Looking carefully at the results, he shook his head in mild disbelief. "I wouldn't have believed it, but you were right. You have murine typhus."

A huge weight lifted from Josef's shoulders. As he laid his head down on the pillow, tears sprang to his eyes, a mixture of joy, sadness, and relief.

Mistaking it for fear, the doctor's manner continued in a more amicable fashion. "Don't worry, Mr. Held. We will take good care of you here. How did you know it was typhus?"

"Research," Josef responded before another set of rolling coughs.

"Have you been anywhere near rats?"

"Rats?" Josef repeated. His head was starting to swim. He couldn't stand all these questions.

"This illness is regularly spread by vermin."

"Vermin." Josef smiled to himself, seeing the irony in that statement. "At the university."

"We'll need to make a report. This could be very serious. It could be an outbreak." The doctor turned to the nurse next to him who had a clipboard in hand. "Nurse, please prepare a bed for our patient, and then some medicine. Let's give him a double dose to start with. We have a new type of treatment called penicillin, Mr. Held. We do not have a lot of it and have to use it very sparingly, but in your case I feel it is warranted."

Josef decided he would come back and steal more, later. "You will need to take all the medication, but I have to warn you, this is not an easy illness to fight."

When the nurse returned, she gave Josef two of the tablets to swallow as he waited anxiously on the end of the examination bed.

"I could do with some more water to take them." Josef pointed at the jug he had just emptied into a potted plant. He was getting better at lying.

Once she'd gone, he struggled to his feet, grabbed the bottle she had left, and after placing the two tablets in his pocket, walked out of the room.

The journey home was more arduous than before, but at least this time he was spurred on by the fact he had Michael's medicine. By the time he reached his house, he was wheezing badly and had to pause for a second in the hall before he caught his breath. Then, slowly, he made his way up the stairs, one labored step at a time.

The attic was silent. Deadly silent. In the last twelve hours, he had become more fearful of the lengthy silences than the coughing fits.

He found Michael lying on the pillow, so still, looking so young, like a child. Black wavy hair, matted with sweat, clung in wet curls to his forehead.

"Michael," he rasped. "Michael!" Fear rose in his throat.

Michael stirred a little but didn't wake up.

Josef shook him, vigorously. "Michael, wake up. I've got the medicine."

He finally opened his eyes. "There you are," he muttered. "I was having a wonderful dream."

Josef took the medication from his pocket.

"Here, I have your medicine." Looking inside the bottle, he was disappointed to find barely enough medicine for three days for one person. He decided Michael would have it all.

"I think it is probably too late for me, Professor. You should take the medication. I fear I am slipping from this world."

"No," Josef said forcefully. "We have not come this far for it to end here in this attic. You must stay alive. You have your whole life ahead of you."

"Some life."

"It will be." He placed two tablets in Michael's mouth and gave him water, then tentatively waited until he saw him swallow before asking, softly, "Tell me about your dream."

"I was with my family," Michael croaked.

"Yes?" Josef coughed, listening intently.

"My mother was so beautiful."

"When did you see her last?"

"Just a few minutes ago."

"No, I mean…"

Michael nodded. "I know what you mean. I was barely a man when she became ill. And my father, the renegade, died during the Great War. Even though we were neutral, he wanted to fight.

After my mother's death, my grandmother raised me, and I lost her, too, just before the occupation." He sighed, adding wistfully, "Her one dream was that I would graduate university. It was for her I was completing your mathematics course."

"I'm so sorry," responded Josef.

Michael shook his head. "I'm not. I'm glad they're all gone. That they never had to witness this atrocity." He looked exhausted from talking and closed his eyes. His anguish was palpable and, wracked with pain, he turned his face to Josef. "Please, Professor, talk to me, about anything else other than illness."

Josef nodded. He went to the other side of the attic and unlocked the chest, which was now tucked neatly away. He came back to the bedside with the picture of him and his wife. He began talking as though it was the beginning of a fairytale.

"My wife Sarah and I," he said tenderly, "we were very much in love. And years ago, in a whole other lifetime, she and I played music together."

Michael stared down at the photograph, eyes unfocused. "You *did* play piano then." Josef nodded, but Michael must have caught a glimpse of pain on his face because he went on to ask, "You don't want to play anymore?"

Josef shook his head and tried to find the right words. "It's a long story."

Michael began to cough and took a little sip of water. "I have nothing but time, Professor," he said sarcastically.

Josef stared out across the room, lost in his memories. Finally, he continued his story.

"My father thought I was going to be some incredible classical pianist." He laughed to himself. "From a very young age, I showed such promise they were calling me a prodigy. My mother was a pianist, and every day they would school me and drill me in the art of playing the piano. But even though playing came naturally to me, I found myself becoming resentful. Every evening after school, my brother Marcus—Ingrid's father—and all our friends were playing outside while I was sweating over the finer points of Mozart's most difficult symphonies. So, when I got older, I just stopped playing. Then I met Sarah. And she encouraged me to play again. This time it was different. She had so much joy, and it was something we did together."

"You look so happy," Michael said, studying the photograph.

Josef swallowed hard before he spoke in a whisper. "We were. I was. But after she left me…"

He couldn't manage any more words and just shook his head to signify his ongoing pain. Then, feeling the intrusion into his private world was too much for him to bear, he stood.

Michael stared up at him, an expression of sadness and compassion on his face, and Josef wasn't sure if he was comfortable with this new feeling of exposure. It was too close to the pain he was always trying to avoid—the true reason his wife had died. So once again, he quickly changed the subject, pushing away his thoughts from long ago.

"Rest now. Let the medicine do its work so you can fulfill your grandmother's wishes."

"Professor, don't forget to take some medicine for yourself."

"Yes, of course," Josef lied.

Josef sat and watched Michael as he fell into another deep sleep.

*

For three days, Josef nursed his patient, battling his own feverish symptoms. But instead of getting better, Michael seemed to grow worse. On the morning of the fourth day, the bottle was empty.

"I need to get more medicine. I'll be back soon," he whispered, more to himself than to his slumbering patient.

Another wracking cough took hold of him as he descended the stairs and went out into the street. His delirium was intense. The whole world swam in front of his eyes as he attempted to put one foot in front of the other. His legs felt like lead.

"I have got to get Michael his medicine," he reminded himself over and over again, weaving back and forth but willing himself to keep moving, one excruciating footstep at a time. "Just a bit farther."

As he turned a corner, it started to snow again, and he became disoriented as a vagueness consumed him. Where was he? What was he doing? He couldn't even remember who he was. Just one burning compulsion drove him. If only he could remember what it was...

He stared up into the darkening sky, but the leaden clouds only echoed back their own unknowing. He paused, gazing up as the urgent snowflakes rained down upon him, coating his face in an icy veil. He was tired, bone-wearily tired. He closed his eyes to rest them for just a moment. A smothering darkness hovered on the precipice of his awareness for a second before creeping across the divide to devour him.

Then a feeling of weightlessness, the carefree release of falling through the air, followed by searing pain and ice, stone, coldness as the harsh ground rose up to meet him. Alarmed, he tried urgently to rouse himself. He needed to open his eyes, but it was impossible. The weight, the heaviness spreading through his body, held him captive.

As he fought to keep breathing, feathery snowflakes continued to float down onto his face, coating his eyelashes. All at once, the jarring screech of an air-raid siren shrilled out into the air all around him, persistent and compelling. He tried to anchor himself by focusing on the shrieking sound. But the siren started to fade. Soon it was far away, then it disappeared as he slipped off quietly and his world turned dark.

*

Josef became aware of an intoxicating fragrance swirling around him. A delicate bouquet he instantly recognized: tulips. He inhaled the scent freely, realizing with great relief that there was no tightness in his chest anymore, just the provocative promise of spring filling his lungs. As well as the evocative aroma, the cold chill of the day was far behind him. Instead, drenching its way all the way into his bones, was an enveloping warmth.

Even with his eyes closed, he knew he was outside and the sun was shining in the sky. He could see and feel its radiant heat as it reflected its red glow on the inside of his eyelids. He absorbed it all for a long moment before blinking his eyes open to stare up. It had been a long time since he'd really enjoyed the sun's heat, and he reveled in it. The sky above him stretched out, a taut canvas, Wedgewood blue splashed with wisps of white-cotton clouds. He smiled to himself, aware of exactly where he was. In the middle of a tulip field.

Taking another deep breath and closing his eyes again, he allowed the sunlight to creep across his cheeks and warm his face. He didn't care how he'd gotten here; he just wanted to bask for a moment.

Then, from above him, someone giggled. The sound was gentle and childlike, and it was familiar to him. Resting up on his elbows, he looked about him, but couldn't see anyone.

The laughter came again, now, from beside him.

Curious, he sat up to survey the whole field. It was breathtaking. Yellow, pink, red, and white tulips stretched forth in every direction. They gently waved in the breeze that ruffled his own hair, but though he looked about him, he appeared to be alone.

A voice boomed from above, coming through the clouds. He recognized it instantly as the slow, deliberate words poured forth.

How will I keep my soul from touching yours?
How shall I lift it out beyond you toward other things?

Josef rose to his feet, closed his eyes again, and listened. It was his father's voice and he was reading to him, the poem he'd read aloud on his wedding day to Sarah.

All at once he became aware of another presence; someone was behind him. Turning swiftly around, his heart leaped in knowing, even before he saw her.

"Sarah," he whispered, fearful that if he spoke her name too loudly, she would disappear. She was as beautiful as he remembered her on the day they had married. Her heart-shaped face framed by the copper curls, her large emerald eyes staring lovingly up at him.

He reached toward her, wanting to take her in his arms but so afraid. It had been so long. Tentatively, he drew the back of his hand down her face, tracing her cheekbone. She shivered at his touch, her face glowing as she tipped her head up to him with expectation.

Unable to hold back any longer, he pulled her to him desperately and hugged her tightly. His world stopped. Stopped right in the middle of that moment. His body entwined with hers, their hearts beating as one. He let out a long, slow breath he had been holding for so many years and then inhaled her scent, his face buried deep in her hair, her body pressed close to his.

When he finally drew away, he searched her eyes. "How? Why?"

She shook her head, and her strawberry-gold curls shimmered in the light of the sun. She answered him by tracing his lips with her tiny fingers.

Urgently, he took her in his arms and kissed her, passionately, holding her so tightly he was afraid he might break her. Not wanting to let her go. His legs buckled, and a carpet of tulips softened their fall. He continued to cover her face with kisses as she giggled. Then, exhausted, he looked down at her.

"I've missed you so much," he muttered breathlessly.

"I've missed you, too," she whispered back.

He wrapped himself around her body, and they held each other very close for a very long time, savoring the feeling of completeness.

After what seemed like an eternity, he released her, and she ran her hands through his hair as he lay staring down at her in awe. "I have so much to tell you," he began. "So much has happened since you left."

She nodded. "I know. But, Josef, it's time."

"Time?"

"Time for you to let me go. Time for you to forgive me, forgive yourself. You cannot remain in the place that you have been. There are new things for you ahead. More love, more joy."

Panic gripped hold of him as he sat bolt upright and searched her face. "You can't leave me. Please tell me you won't leave me again, Sarah."

"I never left you, Josef," she uttered, just above a whisper. "I have always been with you. But you must promise me now you will forgive yourself."

"How can I? It was my fault that you died."

"No," she responded forcefully. "It was no one's fault."

"I killed our son," he spluttered out, feeling the weight of his words stinging the back of his throat.

She shook her head. "I should have told you that the contractions were coming. I just thought it was my body practicing."

"No! I should have noticed, should have taken a moment to see, to look at you. I was so caught up in preparing for the math exam, I didn't even remember looking into your face that morning or kissing you goodbye." Tears caught in his throat. "I *didn't even* kiss you goodbye."

"Shhhh," she comforted him. "I knew how much you loved me. I didn't need one kiss to tell me that. I saw it every day in your eyes, in your care for us, in your smile."

Josef buried his face deep in her hair again, needing to say it all. "When I found you that afternoon, there was already so much blood. I knew it couldn't be right. I wanted to go for help, but I was so paralyzed with fear. I knew if I left you, you would slip from me and, selfishly, I wanted every last minute with you, holding you, kissing you. But if I had gone right then, I could have saved our son. I could have saved him."

"You don't know that." She placed her tiny hands on the sides of his face. "No more regrets. Just love. Just love from now on. Now you have to live for yourself. Live for me and live for Jacob."

His heart jumped at the mention of his son's name.

"Promise me, Josef. Promise me you will forgive yourself." Tears brimmed in the corners of her emerald eyes. "It's the only way you'll ever be able to remember the joy, not just the pain. Other people need you now."

He knew she was talking of Michael.

She drew him in with an intoxicating kiss as his own salty tears flowed freely down his cheeks and mingled with hers.

Before he knew it, she was gone.

He started to panic. He had to find her. He jumped to his feet again, looking frantically around him. He caught sight of something rippling in the wind, the veil from her wedding day. She was wearing it, and it streamed out ahead of him then disappeared in the glint of the sun.

He leaped frantically over the tulips, scattering and crushing multicolored petals beneath his feet, barreling toward the place he had seen the veil.

He caught sight of it again; it was just ahead of him. He stretched forward to grab it, but it slid through his fingertips. He lurched at it, snatching at it again and again, but each time it slipped from his grasp, growing longer and longer each time.

Now, she was so far away he could no longer see her. He continued racing after the train, toward a windmill that marked the corner of the field. As he did, its ancient sails began to spin faster and faster, matching the pace of the heady terror running frantically through his mind. He lunged forward one more time, his fingers managed to latch on tightly to the veil. He yanked hard, but Sarah was gone. There was nothing left of her but the gauzy fabric in his hands.

Josef continued to look frantically about him. The strains of violin music drifted out to him along the wind. He looked up above him and there was Sarah, now perched on the top of the windmill, playing her violin in frantic time, matching the pace of the sails. Suddenly, all around him were dozens of windmills and dozens of Sarahs. Which one was his? He raced from one to the other calling out her name.

He heard her voice all around him, reciting her beloved Rilke.

And yet everything which touches us, you and me,
takes us together like a single bow,
drawing out from two strings but one voice.

He turned around frantically. The sun burned in his eyes, but through the glare, he saw a silhouette. He reached for it. If he could just touch her, he knew he could hold on. Gratefully, he felt her fingers. He gripped hold tightly of her hand then and was not going to let it go. Yes, she was there. Suddenly the day went black and the sun faded. The light was gone but she was there. He could feel her fingers in his.

He felt exhausted, his breath was suddenly labored, and he was sweating. Through the darkness, a ceiling swam into his view. It was unfamiliar. Where was he now? Where was the beautiful sky? His eyes tried to focus. He was not in his own bed. There was no crack above him in his ceiling. But he could still feel Sarah's hand. He turned quickly to her. A lamp came on by the side of his bed. He was startled to see Hannah Pender looking down at him, looking alarmed, and he was gripping her hand so tightly it was white.

"Are you okay, Professor?" she asked with great concern.

Chapter Thirty-Eight

"Where am I?" Josef croaked, releasing Hannah's hand. His throat was parched and dry. Hannah reached for a glass of water and drew it to his lips. He drank urgently.

"You are in the hospital," she whispered back. "You were found on the street after collapsing during an air raid."

Josef tried to take in the information. "How did you know?" he asked, feeling embarrassed that he had been gripping a married woman's hand so tightly.

"I came to your house to check on you yesterday, and I could hear the cat meowing very loudly at the front door. And I was concerned when you didn't open it, so I came to the hospital just to check, and I found you here."

"What do you mean yesterday? How long have I been here?"

"Four days. The doctor says you are lucky to be alive."

"Four days!" He closed his eyes to absorb the news. Then they flashed open again in terror. Michael! He had to get back to Michael. How would he have survived so long alone?

He struggled to sit up. "I have to go," he insisted.

Hannah laid her hand on his shoulder. "You need to rest."

"But I have to check on my… cat."

Hannah spoke with calm assurance. "Don't worry about your cat. When I found you here, I managed to contact your niece. She was listed as your next of kin at the university. And we found your key in your belongings. Don't worry. She is feeding your cat."

"She is what!?" Josef pulled himself to a sitting position, trying desperately not to give into the suffocating fear. "I have to get home," he persisted. "I have to get home now!"

"That's not a very good idea," Hannah warned. "I'm sure the doctor will not want you to leave yet. You're still very weak."

But he wasn't listening to her and had already started to move his body out of the bed, rocking up onto unstable feet. He clung desperately to the bed frame, breathing heavily, his head swimming as he tried to regain his balance.

"Please, Professor," Hannah implored, "you really do need to rest."

"I'm going home," he responded in such a firm tone that she backed down. Apparently she knew she wasn't going to be able to argue with him. He stumbled to his wardrobe in the hospital room and, gasping for breath, pulled out his shirt. "You can help me or you can watch me, but either way I am going to dress."

Hannah's cheeks pinked a little as he unbuttoned his pajama top the hospital staff had clothed him in and pulled it off revealing his chest, still covered with the rash. Reluctantly, she reached for the rest of his clothes in the wardrobe and helped him dress.

"I think we should at least find a doctor to look at you before you leave," she said.

In response, Josef left the room and shuffled down the corridor.

Hannah's voice followed after him. "Please, Professor, you need to get back into bed. You may still be hallucinating."

"I'm going to go home."

"Well, I won't help you," she stated as he continued to drag himself down the hallway. "You need to stay in the hospital."

Ten minutes later, a very disgruntled Hannah supported Josef as he struggled along the road toward his home. His breathing was raspy and labored as he walked one foot in front of the other, once again leaning on her heavily. All of her reservations fell on deaf ears.

As they finally turned the corner to his street, Josef was relieved to see his front door. But not for long. Parked outside of his house was a distinct black car. He recognized it instantly. It was Heinrich's.

Both of them stopped and stared at it. Terror ran through Josef's veins. They must have found him, found Michael. Ingrid and the Nazi. Why else would he be here?

Hannah looked confused and echoed his own fear. "Why is there a German here?"

Josef shook his head, with no energy to explain or even to speculate. He hurried down his path. As they approached the open door, from inside he could hear voices raised in anger. A chilling fear spread through his whole being, and he started to shake uncontrollably. "Oh my God," he muttered hopelessly.

As they entered the hallway, Josef saw Ingrid; she was downcast, sheepish, her face crimson as Heinrich marched up and down, yelling at her. Noticing the new arrivals, the Major barreled up the hallway with great agitation.

"Now here's Uncle Josef!" he snapped sarcastically. "You brought me all this way and he is here to feed his own damn cat." His voice boomed throughout the whole hallway, vibrating with his anger.

Hannah clung a little tighter to Josef's arm, visibly shocked by the encounter as Heinrich continued to berate his fiancée. "*Uncle* Josef?" Hannah questioned, staring at him with great concern. "You are related to him?"

Josef was speechless, unable to answer her.

Ingrid tried to cover up her embarrassment at their argument by racing down the hallway to hug him at the door. "Uncle Josef, you shouldn't be home yet. Why did they send you home so early?" she enquired, concerned.

Heinrich followed her, continuing his tyrannical rant. "He's obviously better," he snapped. "And look, his woman is here to take care of him."

Heinrich took a long moment to look Hannah up and down as everyone shifted uncomfortably.

"Have we met?" he asked suspiciously.

Hannah shook her head vigorously. "I don't believe so," she responded. There was conviction in her tone, but there was also a slight tremor that Josef picked up.

"So, this is your special friend," Heinrich stated, with obvious anger that he had been troubled to come when there was someone else to take care of the professor's home. His gray uniform and yelling in an unpleasant tone felt intimidating in the quiet comfort of Josef's house.

Hannah's eyes found Josef's with expectancy and her cheeks reddened as she tried to understand what Heinrich was insinuating. Straightening herself to her full height, her voice became level. "I need to get Josef settled. He needs his rest." And turning her back on the Major, she took a firm hold of Josef's arm and carefully helped him into a chair.

Josef, weakened by the whole experience, was grateful but agitated. He just wanted everybody to leave so he could check on Michael.

Hannah read the concern on his face. "I'll make you a cup of tea," she whispered to him as she moved back out into the hallway.

"I'm going to feed the cat," Ingrid announced, following Hannah into the kitchen.

Left alone, Heinrich strode into the front room and slammed a heavy hand upon the mantelpiece. His anger still brimmed below the surface. Thrusting his hand into his pocket, he pulled out a packet of cigarettes. Without even asking, he snatched one out and lit it, angrily blowing out a plume of gray smoke. Then he continued to pace the room, complaining as he practically wore a groove in the carpet. "She thinks I am her little lapdog," he spat out, thrusting his cigarettes back into his pocket. "I command hundreds of men every day. I have to make life-and-death decisions. She thinks all that is easy and has no idea what I have to deal with!" Then, gripping the mantel for a second, he spat out under his breath, "Nor what I am capable of."

Josef closed his eyes and tried desperately to will his pounding heart, shaking limbs, and spinning mind to calm.

Heinrich continued to pace. "She lives in her little world," he snapped, "with no idea of the problems I have. The Dutch people are horrendous to deal with on a daily basis."

Josef continued to concentrate on his breathing. He dared not point out that Heinrich seemed to have forgotten that he too was Dutch.

Ingrid called out in a soft voice, "Hey, kitty, kitty, where are you hiding today?"

Suddenly, above his head, there was a loud thud, which sounded like either a bird hitting a window or a book falling to the floor. Josef held his breath as everyone in the house went silent, focused on the sound above them.

Heinrich took a deep drag of his cigarette as he peered at the ceiling.

Josef began pleading to God. Please, please... Please don't let him go upstairs.

Ingrid's voice called up the hallway, "So, you're upstairs again, are you? I know where you're hiding."

From where he was seated in the front room Josef saw her tiptoe up the stairs. He watched, paralyzed to do anything, the weight of his illness like a shackle pinning his body to the chair.

Hannah bustled into the front room with a tea tray, and Heinrich continued on his rampage as he took another deep drag of his cigarette. "And don't even get me started on the so-called Resistance," he snapped.

Hannah dropped the tray down on the table a little heavier than appropriate, her face flushed as she moved quickly from the room. "I forgot something," she said absently.

Josef was only vaguely aware of what was going on around him, as all of his concentration and his senses were tuned into the sounds above his head. He registered every single creak of stair and floorboard as Ingrid moved along the landing. He followed her in his mind's eye as she traveled from room to room, as doors and bed springs creaked and she searched in wardrobes and cupboards, with just the whisper of her voice drifting down through the ceiling.

"Come on, I have your dinner."

Josef was only half aware of Heinrich relaying a very animated story to him, and in the midst of it he took out his pistol to illustrate what had happened the day before. Josef didn't notice because he was following the sound of the lower attic door opening, and as a dry breath caught in his throat, he closed his eyes to listen more intently.

When he opened his eyes again, he was staring down the barrel of Heinrich's gun as he used it as a prop to tell his story. All Josef could see was Mrs. Epstein's face. All he could hear was the sound of that pistol shot, and all he could smell was the stench of cordite. He winced, keeping his eyes closed as he prepared for the Major to shoot him, prepared to die.

Just then, Hannah moved back toward the front room. She must have caught sight of the gun, because she screamed and dropped a jug. It crashed to the floor, shattering into a hundred pieces. Josef opened his eyes as Heinrich holstered his pistol.

Hannah rushed back into the kitchen then a second later screamed again.

She suddenly appeared at the foot of the stairs, a furry bundle in her arms. "I found the cat!" she shouted up to Ingrid, the tremor in her voice very obvious. "He was hiding in the cupboard. I found him when I pulled out a broom."

With a great sense of relief, Josef heard Ingrid close the lower attic door and her feet patter along the landing and back down the stairs. He laid his head on the back of the chair. Sweat poured down the side of his face, puddling at the collar of his shirt. His hands were clammy and damp. He took off his spectacles, carefully wiped them, and replaced them one hooked wire at a time, his hands shaking the entire time.

Her task completed, Ingrid made her way into the hallway, and Heinrich joined her side, impatiently ready to leave. Josef watched them through the window as Hannah saw them out.

She approached him, and kneeling down beside him took his hand, and even with all the extreme tension coursing through his body he felt that familiar connection. He wanted more than anything to tell her about Michael, but something Heinrich had just said, about maybe knowing her, put all his senses on guard.

It was as if she sensed his thoughts though. "Are you telling me everything, Professor? I want to help you in any way I can. I greatly value our..." she searched to find the right word and then settled on, "friendship."

Kneeling next to him, her face was so close to his it was unbearable and he could smell the scent of her hair. But he reminded himself there was a Mr. Pender somewhere and really all he could think of was Michael and getting her out the house without her suspecting anything.

"I am very tired and just want to rest here for a while, thank you for your kindness," he whispered.

She nodded, understanding that he wanted to be alone, and only lingered momentarily at the door to the room before nodding and vowing to check on him the next day.

After he heard the front door close Josef pulled himself to his feet and, exerting all of his energy, shuffled into the hallway and up the stairs. Four days! He couldn't believe he'd been unconscious for that long.

As he reached the landing, he had to stop for a second to catch his breath. Peering up toward the attic door, he prayed with all his might that Michael would still be alive. Dantes wove in and out of his legs nervously, as if he too was wondering the same thing.

Slowly, Josef clawed his way up the last set of stairs, breathing heavily. As he stretched toward the doorknob, his hand shook, not only with the exertion but also with the fear of what awaited him on the other side. Slowly, he turned the knob and pushed it open.

The room was dark and the air hung heavy with the mantle of illness. Not even daring to put the light on, he listened, holding his breath. Hoping for any signs of life.

Josef dropped to his knees beside the bed. Michael's face was ashen, his dark hair matted on the pillow. He couldn't see if he was breathing or not. He feared to even take his hand to find out.

Dantes bound into the room and jumped upon the bed, landing heavily on Michael's chest. "Oh, that damn cat," Michael mumbled in a dry rasp.

Josef's heart leaped with joy. Had he imagined it or had Michael really spoken? He drew close to his young friend and gently covered his hand with his own. Michael opened his eyes and tried to focus.

He seemed to have aged since Josef had seen him last, but his eyes were bright with some of their familiar twinkle. "Professor, it's you."

Josef took both his hands in his own with joy.

"What happened to you? Where did you go? Why didn't you come back?" Michael asked.

"I collapsed, four days ago."

Michael shook his head in disbelief. "I thought you were dead."

"I thought the same about you."

"Four days?" Michael repeated incredulously. "I thought one or maybe two. I've been somewhere else."

"The dreams," Josef said. "Did you have the dreams?"

Michael nodded.

Josef felt Michael's forehead. "You're cooler," he confirmed. "I think the medicine is working, even though you didn't have much of it."

Michael began to cough, and Josef poured him a glass of water from the jug that was still by his side. He drank thirstily and then, closing his eyes, lay back on the pillow.

"The air raids." Michael swallowed. "They were terrible." He gestured toward the end of the attic. Josef looked around him for the first time. In one corner, crumbled masonry and stone debris were scattered about the room, and a thin film of dust covered Michael's desk and chair.

All at once, there was a noise on the stairs behind them, the sound of footsteps. Both men froze in terror. There was no time and nowhere to hide. Josef instantly berated himself for not locking the front door. If Ingrid found them…

Slowly, the attic door swung open, and Hannah Pender stood in the doorway. Taking in the sights around her, she nodded to herself, as if something was falling into place for her. The men were stunned into silence, and the air was thick with fear.

"I wouldn't exactly call this resting," she stated with a smile on her face. "You forgot your medicine. The front door was open, and I was just going to leave your medication in the bedroom, but I was surprised to see you not in there. Then I heard voices coming from up here. I wanted to make sure that you weren't hallucinating. Your temperature's still pretty high."

All the times Josef had seen her talking to the Nazis, laughing and joking at a desk in the hallway, flashed across his mind. Now he would know for sure if she was working for the enemy.

"Mrs. Pender?" Michael spluttered out.

"Michael Blum?" she questioned. "Yes, I remember you. You were at the university a few years ago. Before…"

She stopped to find the right words and Michael filled in the blanks.

"Before I became vermin," he said with a half-cocked smile.

Hannah blushed a little at the insinuation. "I wouldn't have put it quite that way," she responded softly. She nodded to the wireless on Michael's desk. "Glad to see that you're using my gift."

"It was from you?" Josef responded, standing up.

Hannah nodded. "I knew your wireless meant a lot to you, and let's just say I acquired one. Well, Michael, the professor spoke a lot about you while he was in the hospital."

Josef blinked in surprise.

"In your sleep," she confirmed.

He became alarmed. "Did anybody hear?"

"Only the nurses. I wasn't sure who Michael was, but I knew you lived alone and I knew you probably wouldn't want questions. I just told them that he was your nephew."

She handed the medication bottle to Josef.

"Michael needs it," he responded firmly, shaking out a tablet and giving it straight to Michael with a glass of water.

"You both need it," she contested, taking the bottle and administering another to Josef himself. "I will go to the hospital tomorrow to get more."

Josef nodded. He felt his exhaustion again.

Hannah helped him downstairs. Then once he was in bed, she brought him a jug of water and poured him a glass. As he sipped it, she sat on the end of his bed.

"How long have you had him here?" she asked with great surprise.

"From 1941," he answered, grateful to be able to talk to somebody about it.

"I am astonished. I had no idea you were hiding someone in your attic. I've heard of this happening elsewhere in Amsterdam. But… I didn't expect it of you."

"It has not been easy to keep him hidden, especially when my niece decided to become engaged to the enemy."

She nodded. "We have all had to do so much more than we believed we were capable of. I have had my own illnesses to deal with at home too."

"Mr. Pender has been unwell?" he enquired.

She looked taken aback and shook her head. "My mother, Professor. There hasn't been a Mr. Pender in my life for many years, not since the Great War."

Josef's hope soared. He'd never for a moment suspected she wasn't married, and no one had ever talked at the university about her being widowed. This new realization stirred something deep within him. He started to quickly review all of their interactions over the years. The times they had been together in his classroom or at her desk and the way he had felt drawn to her, had she too, been attracted to him? He tried to think through all the times she may have displayed anything more than a passing friendship. Through this new lens he saw everything differently. The times she had touched his hand or watched him leave the university, had there been more to those interactions? Her invitation at Christmas and the disappointment on her face when he had refused to go, and now the gift of the wireless. Thinking she was married, he had barely given her kindness a second thought. But now that he was able to indulge the thought that she was single, he started to realize that there might be a chance his feelings were reciprocated. Though could he even ask her? With Sarah they had practically been thrown together, he didn't really know how to talk to a woman in those terms. He looked expectantly into her large, concerned blue eyes, framed by soft, shiny brown curls, and he felt in over his head.

Seemingly unaware he was studying her, she stood up and smoothed down her skirt. "I will take a key and lock the door on the way out. I'll come back tomorrow to see you and bring you both some soup."

Josef nodded, feeling his heart starting to pound once again. Sarah's face danced into his thoughts, along with her words of encouragement to live life. He had to do something, anything that communicated his feelings. Then, for the first time in decades, he reached forward and purposefully grabbed a woman's hand, *her* hand. Hannah looked down surprised.

"Thank you, for not reporting Michael—and me—to the authorities" he said. "You have no idea how much your kindness over the years has meant to me, and now more than ever for keeping my secret and my friend safe." He wanted to say more, much more, but he was so out of practice and literally couldn't think of anything else to say.

Nevertheless, when her eyes met his, something genuine passed between them. A knowing, a connection on a deeper level. Without saying a word, they both heard the echo of one another's stories. They had both been lonely for so long, courageously enduring hardships within their own worlds, and somehow they had survived and were now reaching out to one another.

She swallowed hard before nodding and leaving the room.

Josef's head swam as he lay back down on his pillow and looked at the familiar crack in his ceiling. He closed his eyes, he was going to have to do better than that, if he hoped to win her heart, which he realized in that instant—he really did. But in the meantime, he was grateful to be experiencing something new, just a sliver, a hint of happiness. Something he hadn't felt in a long time, even before the war. And he realized his wife had been right. As he chose to live and forgive himself, he felt lighter. When he drifted off to sleep that evening, there was no pain as he thought about Sarah one more time, before Hannah's face was the last thing in his thoughts.

Chapter Thirty-Nine

Over the next couple of days Hannah came to visit them each day, bringing any food she could manage from home. She also administered medicine and cups of tea, taking care of them both. After a week, Michael turned a corner and Josef didn't seem to be far behind him.

One evening, Hannah entered the attic with a steaming bowl of food and some clean sheets for Michael's bed. She fussed over him, and he scooped soup from a bowl as he watched her.

"You're a much better cook than the professor," he stated. "You also smell better," he added as she leaned forward to tuck his sheets into the bed. She stopped and considered him for a moment, the fact he was here and alive such a miracle, when so many had not been spared.

He smiled at her. "Do you know, you're the first woman I've seen up close in years?"

Hannah blushed. "You're still a rascal, Michael Blum. I remember you and all your charisma when you were at the university. Always having a charming comeback for never having the right form filled in, continually losing your books and skipping classes. Some students I will never forget, but I will remind you I'm almost old enough to be your mother."

"But not the professor's," he remarked playfully. "You like him, don't you?"

Hannah stopped tucking, a little taken aback. She had not admitted her feelings toward Josef to anyone but herself over the years, keeping her secret hidden in her heart. So having a virtual stranger blurt this out to her was disconcerting.

She swallowed down her embarrassment, trying to find the right words. Not ready to share the feelings in her heart, without knowing if there was a chance of them being reciprocated.

"I am amazed at his strength, what he has done here with you. Keeping you alive, risking his life, it is as if I don't know him at all. He has been so brave in such a quiet way. I have always been very..." she looked for a safe word, "fond of him." Then she added quickly, in case it exposed her, "He is one of my favorite professors."

Even so, Michael seemed to sense her true feelings and his face broke out into a mischievous grin. "*Fond* of him?"

She blushed and followed up with, "Anyway, I don't think it's like that for him. He barely seems to notice me. We have worked together for years now."

Michael put his dish down and folded his arms behind his head. "Don't be fooled by his indifference. He sees everything."

Hannah blushed again and busied herself tidying around the attic before leaving. Enjoying that she had a legitimate reason to spend time with Josef, even if he was sick and could barely acknowledge her presence.

As she opened the door to Josef's bedroom, she noticed he looked worn and tired. The illness had affected him, leaving his body languid and his face gaunt. He opened his eyes slowly as she entered.

"I brought you some soup," she whispered. "And some fresh water to take your pills with."

He nodded as he crawled out from under his sheets. Hannah administered the medicine.

Josef shook his head. "How did you get them to give you more medication?"

"I went back to the hospital and informed them I was an old friend," she explained. "Then I told them you had a fear of hospitals and that I would be taking care of you from now on."

As she moved around his bed tucking in wayward sheets, she noticed that he watched her carefully, as if he felt exposed. Perhaps he felt it was too intimate, her being among his personal things in his bedroom.

"Mrs. Pender, Hannah."

She stopped and her eyes met his. He seemed to struggle with the words he wanted to say, as if he had been practicing something he wanted to communicate. He finally settled on, "You are very resourceful."

She smiled, and nodded, a little disappointed. The way he had said her name with such intention she'd hoped for something more personal. Not a declaration of love or anything, but maybe something that hinted at more than just admiration.

But as she looked into his eyes she saw something warm there, something reaching out to her, as if he wanted to say something else that he was unable to quite vocalize.

As he took a sip of his soup, his usual awkward aloofness seemed drawn aside for a moment, and he genuinely seemed to be interested in conversing with her.

"You look better today."

"I feel better," he stated, taking a rather large spoonful of the soup.

"I'm sorry it's just cabbage," she apologized. "Food is getting scarcer. I fear that soon there won't be anything left to eat in Holland."

"It tastes like a feast to me."

Once he had finished eating, she stood to leave. As she did, she stopped in the doorway and as she turned, she caught him watching her intently again.

She took the opportunity to say something that had been on her mind for a while. "You're very brave, you know, Professor." He looked shocked. "What you did for Michael. What you continue to do for him. That was, and is, a heroic thing to do."

Josef batted away the comment. "Other people are doing far more than me. Risking and losing their lives for our freedom. I just did what any person would do."

"Not anyone," Hannah responded. "There are a lot of people who wouldn't see the value, let alone have the desire, to risk everything to save a Jewish person."

He was silent for a moment, seemingly lost in that thought. Then, barely above a whisper, he responded, "In many ways, Michael saved me."

Chapter Forty

The next day, Hannah didn't arrive as usual, and Josef found he was disappointed. He had been working on the right words to say to her about his feelings, practicing them in his mind. Nothing too sentimental, just something that would open the door up to a conversation, so he could see if she shared any of the same feelings. So, when she didn't come, he wondered if even the few words he had managed to say in that direction had frightened her off. If she had only taken care of him out of kindness, maybe even him taking her hand had been too forward. He felt sadness as the day wore on without her light and presence to illuminate it. He had started to enjoy seeing her each day and looked forward to it. But when she hadn't arrived by three o'clock, he reminded himself she also had her own life with her mother.

Not wanting to wallow, and after checking on Michael, Josef made the decision that it was time for him to get some fresh air today, just a short walk up and down the street and back. He had been inside for so long. So, with much effort, he dressed, put on his overcoat, hat, and scarf, and, taking his time, made his way out into the early afternoon light.

It was the perfect winter's day, not too cold, but crisp, and the sky was blue. As he hobbled down the street, he stopped outside Mrs. Epstein's house with dismay. Her beautiful brown mahogany piano was out on her pathway.

Running his fingers across the lid, he noticed that, though dusty, it had been well cared for. He could just imagine the studious little woman humming to herself as she buffed it to a shine with an ample amount of beeswax.

He wondered why it had not been taken when the house had been emptied after she had been murdered. Probably too heavy for the Nazis to move. But now it appeared they were using her house for storage, and clearly it had got in the way.

He closed his eyes and took a moment to remember all the music he'd heard on this piano and all the joy it had brought him.

Moving past it down the street, he was filled with sadness. Sadness at the length of the war, the sadness of the many years of Amsterdam's captivity, and the pain of Mrs. Epstein's loss, still so raw to him even after all this time. As he sauntered slowly on his way, he longed for the day when they would all be free.

With his newly regained strength, Josef made his way up to the attic and was heartened to see Michael moving around the room. Still painfully thin, his body was a jumble of bones, his skin a sickly yellow, and even though Michael was still in his twenties, he looked far older, with gray hair already starting to appear at his temples. This war had aged them all. He watched Michael shuffle across the room to the box in the corner in which he'd placed all of his things before he had left. Evidently he was slowly unpacking his books and poems that he'd hidden among a pile of Josef's old clothes.

"I didn't think I'd be back here again," he whispered.

Josef came across to join him and seated himself at the desk as he watched him unpack. "I am glad you're back—and safe. Even though I know that you desperately want to be free."

Balancing a pile of books, Michael got to his feet and walked toward the desk, stacking them similarly to how they'd been before he left. "Freedom wasn't quite what I expected," he said as he flicked through one of the editions.

"Did you find Elke?"

Her name was enough to create a pained reaction, which told Josef that it hadn't been the reunion Michael had hoped for.

"She is a woman who keeps her promises. I asked her to find love and she did. I thought I'd felt the deepest loss being separated from her, but it was nothing compared to knowing she didn't love me anymore."

"Did you speak to her?"

Michael shook his head and continued back to the box to unload some more of his poems. "There was no need. I watched her from a distance and I know what I saw."

"So, she still doesn't know you're alive? Maybe things would be different if she did."

Michael continued to unpack as he shook his head. "I'm not alive anymore. Not inside. My heart might still be beating, but there's nothing left of me. Amsterdam, out there, is a hollow shell of what it was, it was shocking to me after being in here for so long. I walked past Jodenbuurt, it was like a ghost town and I wondered about all the people I knew from there. But there was no one left, not one person. It has made me question everything again. How can a loving God allow all this? I sometimes think that if it wasn't for the kindness I see in you, I would find no goodness to dwell on in this life. The world is a cold, harsh place, especially now without even the hope of love from the only woman I will ever care about."

Josef understood the pain. His thoughts went to when he had lost Sarah; he hadn't wanted to go on living either. He'd felt that hollow, aching emptiness of being. He didn't want to share with Michael that it could last a very long time. "I think I'll get us some tea," he said, getting to his feet. "For some reason, Mrs. Pender didn't come today. I'm thinking maybe she has other fires she is fighting in her own life."

Michael nodded. "Tea sounds wonderful. I can't wait to see what you make it out of."

"Ah, I will surprise you," said Josef as he shuffled toward the door. "It'll at least be warming."

Josef closed the door behind him. He stood for a minute listening to Michael as he moved around the attic, feeling his pain and wanting to help him in any way he could. He may have saved his life, but saving him from his heartache was beyond him.

Chapter Forty-One

When Hannah walked home on the last afternoon she'd visited Josef's, her spirit had been buoyant. Not only due to the attraction that was growing in her toward Josef, but also thinking about the courage he had shown, in such an unassuming way. However, when she would look back on this day in the many months to come, she'd remember that afternoon as the last day that she'd genuinely felt happy for a long time.

When Hannah arrived home, she realized something was wrong. Clara wasn't sitting in her usual chair by the fire, and the house was so still and quiet. Removing her hat and coat, she moved into her front room, calling out to her mama. She called out over and over again, but no response came back. She searched from room to room before finding Clara lying in bed. The room was dark, and a heavy oppression seemed to seep from the walls themselves.

Moving quickly to her mother's side, she took her hand. "Mama, are you okay?" she asked, unable to keep the fearful tone from her voice.

Clara's eyes drifted open, and Hannah could see that she was seriously unwell. Clara had suffered from a dry cough for a while, but now her chest rattled as she breathed in and out. Hannah felt her forehead and realized that her mother had a temperature.

With her body shaking, Hannah called for the doctor. He arrived promptly.

"I'm not happy with the sound of her chest," he informed Hannah as he stood in their little front parlor talking in hushed tones. "She has a severe chest infection and will need a long recovery time. With her age and her already depressive condition, I'm not sure she has much fight in her for this illness, and if we are not careful, it could turn into pneumonia."

Hannah nodded, but she was adamant she would do all she could to keep Clara alive.

She nursed her mother day and night, hardly sleeping, barely even leaving the house, willing her mama to survive. Mrs. Oberon came by each day with supplies and to talk to her old friend. Hannah and Oma took turns reading to Clara, doing jigsaws, and telling her stories about what they would do when the war was over. But no matter what she did or said, Clara would look at her daughter, her runny eyes signifying her desire to pass to a better place.

In late February, Clara took a turn for the worse. With so little food for anyone to eat and the fact that the Germans gave the Dutch such meager rations, Hannah didn't even have the ingredients to make a warming soup for her mother. It was also so cold, people were chopping down trees and burning their own furniture just to keep warm. As well as being ill, Clara started to lose weight rapidly. Hannah tried everything to coax her, to encourage her, but deep down she knew her mother's will was strong. If she did not want to be part of this world anymore, there was nothing Hannah could do to stop her.

It was on a bright day in early spring that Hannah arrived home and knew that something was very wrong. She'd been out all morning serving at one of the many soup kitchens. So many people were starving in Holland; eating tulip bulbs and even the wallpaper off the walls. Hannah heard the stories and wondered how long they could go on like this. Taking care of Clara and surviving was all she had the energy for each day. She now only went to the university a few hours a week. Many of the professors were still not back, including Professor Held, as the university was barely open due to lack of power. There was virtually no gas or electricity getting through, and they didn't even have hot water. Hannah did like to go to work a couple of times a week just to keep on top of the mail. That day, when she walked into her home, it seemed quieter than ever before. Almost as though the very walls themselves were waiting for her return, waiting quietly for Hannah to see what had been happening in the house while she was gone.

She called to her mama, "It's me. I'm back."

The silence from the darkened bedroom was deafening. She made her way quickly to her mother's bedside. As her eyes adjusted to the dark, she noticed something was odd. Instead of lying under the covers, her mother lay out on top of the bed, and instead of being in her nightgown, somehow she had managed to dress in her traditional Dutch dress, which Hannah remembered from her childhood. Clara had been saving it for Eva when she grew up. No one had worn such outfits since before the war, but Clara had been fiercely proud to be Dutch and had been married in hers. Beside her on the bedside table, the music box had been playing. Hannah ran to the bed and grabbed Clara's cold hand. She felt urgently for a pulse, but she knew it was too late. Clara had slipped quietly from this world.

Sobbing into the pillow, she whispered, "Why, Mama, why?" over and over again. Clara had been weak that morning, but no better or worse than the day before. What had turned her mother's condition downhill so rapidly? Then she saw the sleeping tablets the doctor had prescribed to help ease Clara's nights. They had been high out of the way in a kitchen cupboard. Clara must have somehow made her way in there to find them.

On the bedside table there was an envelope addressed to Hannah in Clara's shaky hand. Hannah refused to accept that her mother was gone and quickly called the doctor, but there was nothing he could do. Many older people were dying from hunger, he informed her with sadness, reminding Hannah how grim his job was right now.

After he left, Hannah sat by the fire, drinking a stiff brandy. She opened the letter that her mother had left her, hoping for any kind of answer to why Clara had taken her life.

The note was short and must have taken great effort. Hannah then realized that in order for all of this to take place in one morning, Clara must have been preparing for days. In the note, Clara talked about how she wanted to save the food for Hannah and that without the will to live there was nothing left for her to fight for; that Hannah would have to fight for both of them now.

Hannah went to bed that night sobbing, knowing that nothing would ever be quite the same again.

PART FOUR

Chapter Forty-Two

Spring 1945

Over the weeks, as they continued to recover, Josef often sat by Michael's bed and was relieved that they both continued to get well. With the lingering illness and the lack of food, they had both lost a great deal of weight; though now and again, Ingrid did give Josef extra food, as the Germans received more rations. There was no more talk from Michael of leaving, especially as stories of the concentration camps became more widely known, though they still felt the risk of their situation, particularly since Ingrid had told Josef the story of how the Gestapo had found two entire Jewish families in an attic hidden behind a bookcase in an office building the previous summer.

Hannah tried to visit Josef, but her priority had been her mother while she was ill, and then since her death Josef understood she was grieving. And, really, everyone was preoccupied with surviving. Since the start of winter, the Germans had ordered the blocking of food supplies designed for the civilian population in retaliation to a Dutch rail-workers strike the year before, and it had caused a famine across the country.

Josef eyed his cat. Dantes was the only one who seemed to fare well through the time, converting back to his natural instincts and hunting rats and mice. Josef was always wary of letting him outdoors now, though; people were becoming so desperate that they had stooped to eating cats and dogs.

By the late winter, he had no longer attended the university, which had been closed because of the war. Each day he tried to find food and conserve his energy, and every evening he and Michael sat huddled around the wireless, desperate to follow all the advances of the Allies. This night was no different.

"Not long now, I hope," Michael stated after a very encouraging message. "Then I will be able to leave this attic."

"Yes," stated Josef, then adding dryly, "and you can go back to university and finish your advanced mathematics course."

Michael rolled his eyes. "What about you, Professor? What do you plan to do?"

Josef shook his head. "I haven't given it much thought."

"Maybe take out the lovely Mrs. Pender," Michael teased.

Josef choked on his bitter chicory coffee, spluttering out, "What?"

"Well, she likes you."

"She told you that?"

"Not in so many words, but I can tell."

Josef, uncomfortable with the turn the conversation had taken and not wanting to expose his own feelings, became embarrassed, and tried to brush him off. "I can assure you I haven't even considered such things. In times like these, that is a very frivolous occupation."

Michael just beamed. "Why can't we think of these things? One day the war will be over and you can go out drinking and dancing again."

Josef glared at him sternly, hopefully conveying that he had never taken on such endeavors even before the war.

"Why not ask her out?" Michael persisted.

"You forget that I am not the dashing Mr. Blum. I wouldn't even know where to start."

"It's not hard. You just ask her to go for a walk, or you could ask her to join you for dinner."

Josef chuckled to himself as he gathered their empty cups. "To dinner? If we ever have any food again, maybe I will do that."

He wandered out of the attic, shaking his head, but felt renewed optimism with Michael's words. Since his health had improved, he had not seen much of Hannah, and had convinced himself that what she felt for him was simply friendship. But maybe when they weren't all so busy surviving there would be more time to explore these emotions.

*

As the war continued its forward thrust through 1945, Josef and Michael listened with great interest to their little wireless, wondering if there would ever be an end. They took in every detail of the battle being waged on all fronts around Holland. As the Nazis tried desperately to keep a stranglehold on Amsterdam, the Allies fought back on both sides, continuing a vigorous bombing campaign.

During the raids, Josef would go to a shelter. He had created as safe a hiding place as he could in the attic for Michael, a place he could crawl into that'd be safe from shattering glass or explosions. It was just too dangerous to bring him outside.

One particularly perilous night in the midst of an extensive campaign, a stray bomb dropped on the street right outside Josef's house.

The professor had just returned from the shelter and thought that the bombing had stopped when the sheer force of the blast from an explosion shook the whole of the house.

As Josef's ears rang with the percussion, he was flattened first against the wall then thrown to the floor. He scrambled under the table for cover, attempting to get back his breath as he looked around the kitchen to survey the damage. His wooden shutters had been blown wide open, and shattered glass covered the floor and counters. His back door hung limply on its hinges, and pots and pans were splayed across the floor having been blasted out of their cupboards.

Michael. He had to get up and check on Michael. Finding new strength from his aching body, he made his way quickly to the attic through the household debris scattered around the floor and stairs. It was as though everything in the whole house had been thrown every which way. Moving up the attic stairs, he got to the door and pushed it open. The room itself showed hallmarks of the blast; plaster, stonemasonry, and dust scattered the attic, and splintered wood formed a mosaic of shrapnel on the floor. Fortunately, Michael was still in his safe space and crawled out from below the hardened structure that Josef had created for him under the eaves.

All the lights were out in the house, but fires that raged close by illuminated the room, which now sat in an eerie silence.

"Are you okay?" asked Josef, helping Michael out of his shelter. Michael nodded and then moved to the far end of the attic, away from the window. From a distance, they could hear the sound of ambulance bells and firefighters on their way.

Suddenly, another bomb exploded in mid-air above them, lighting up the room as if it were a firework, and the two men dove onto the floor again. They lay there, very still, until finally the all-clear siren screeched its assurance.

While Michael recovered on his bed, breathing heavily, Josef went down to find a candle. Upstairs swirls of brick dust still circled, and one end of the attic was mangled where a beam from the ceiling had given way and fallen.

As they surveyed the damage together, Josef's breath caught in his throat when he noticed Sarah's trunk. The wood was splintered in two, and the trunk was broken open. Quickly the two men pulled it away from the crumbling walls and dragged it farther down the attic to Michael's bed, which was relatively debris-free.

Sitting on the bed, Josef looked at the trunk, and great emotions welled up inside of him. Without saying anything, Michael crossed the room and pulled out an empty box, brought it to Josef, and sat on the bed next to him.

"I'm sure we can save some things," he said quietly. Josef nodded and tentatively started to peel away the wood and brass, now a mangled heap that hardly resembled a chest. On the top, though many of her delicate things were broken, the photos of Sarah beaming out were miraculously unscathed.

Josef picked up the photos lovingly and dusting them clean with his hands. He placed them gently on the bed next to him. He leaned down into the box and noticed the violin case had been damaged in the blast. But miraculously, when he opened the case, the violin itself was still intact. He ran his fingers along the wood and the strings, enjoying its smooth and shiny veneer; memories of a different era.

"She loved to play this," he informed Michael, who understood the gravity of the situation and nodded his head. Cradling the neck, Josef shook off some of the dust that had settled on it. "Unlike me, she loved to play music." He smiled. "She had to beg her father to allow her to play the violin. Her family was the opposite of mine. Mine were passionate creatives. Hers were academics. It took much persuasion on Sarah's part. Finally, her father gave in and allowed her to play, and later she managed to talk me into playing with her too. And even though at first I begrudgingly took up the piano again, she took so much joy in us playing together that I found myself falling in love with her enthusiasm. Playing the piano with her was one of the happiest times in my life."

He placed the violin reverently on the bed next to him. Next, he unpacked the veil, shaking off the brick dust. He unraveled it, stroking the gauzy fabric. Josef smiled, remembering the day of their wedding and how he had chased Sarah through the tulip fields. There were her shoes in there too, and her clothes. And a bundle of letters.

Josef lovingly took the bundle that was wrapped in a pink velvet ribbon and placed it next to the violin. "This is all I have left, just dusty things."

"But you have your strength and your great capacity to love. Only a person that loved so deeply and has been loved back like this could be as selfless as you have been with me. That is so much more than just dusty memories," Michael said to him sincerely.

Josef nodded, unsure what to do with his friend's praise. He didn't see himself as anything much. He had been so broken for so long he had even wondered about his ability to ever love again. At least he was able to think of these good memories of Sarah. It had been hard to access them over the years with that one final day of her life being so sad and shocking. He hoped, one day soon, that he would be able to transform that negative memory and walk through the darkened doorway, and just remember the love that they had shared together.

He saw something in Michael's eyes then as they continued to pack the box. He knew he owed his friend an explanation. They had not talked about Sarah since Michael had been ill. Someday soon, he knew he would share with him the whole story of her life and also her death. It would be hard to talk about, but they had already shared so much together. It only seemed right that he share that part of his life, too.

Chapter Forty-Three

Ingrid had her head down, working at her desk when he entered, so she didn't see him straight away, though the hair on the back of her neck informed her something wasn't right. When she looked up, all her breath caught in her throat. It had been months since the party, since he had attacked her, since she'd nearly been raped.

Arrogantly striding into the office flanked by two of his officers, he surveyed the room with disdain. As she watched him, it took all of her strength not to jump up and run from the building. She couldn't believe how terrifying it was for her to see him again.

Heinrich appeared at his office door and strode over to shake the Lieutenant Colonel's hand as they spoke in respectful, clipped German.

All at once, they were walking toward her, and panic seared through her body. As she stood to her feet, her knees buckled from under her, causing her to cling onto the desk to stop herself from collapsing.

"Lieutenant Colonel, you remember my fiancée," Heinrich stated.

The officer pierced Ingrid with an icy glare, his eyes assaulting her with his coldness and indifference. He paused while his gaze traveled purposefully up and down her body, allowing his eyes to rest on her breasts.

"Yes, I think I have met her before," he said with a cruel curl of his lip. "Ingrid, yes? The lovely Ingrid."

He stretched out his hand and Ingrid froze. She looked down at it in front of her. The hand that had grabbed her around the throat, that had thrust her against a door and practically torn off her underwear.

The flashback took the breath from her lungs. Everything inside of her wanted to scream. Frozen in fear, she just stood there, staring at his outstretched hand. Apparently longer than was acceptable, because Heinrich spoke sternly to her. "Ingrid, do you remember my Lieutenant Colonel?"

"Of course." Her voice quivered as she placed a cold, white hand in his.

"I believe the last time we met was at a party," he snarled.

Ingrid looked at him in terror. Surely he wasn't going to reveal what had happened between them here in the office with Heinrich standing right there.

The Lieutenant Colonel seemed to enjoy taunting her, as he paused before adding, "A few years ago when you both came to my house." He squeezed her hand very hard before he let it go. A sinister smile returned to his lips, as if reminding her that somehow she was his, something of her still belonged to him. "Lovely to see you again, Ingrid. I hope to see a lot more of you as our offices work together over the next few months."

Ingrid looked helplessly at Heinrich for confirmation.

"Yes," reiterated Heinrich. "We are hoping to accomplish much more working together. We could even give you an office here, sir, if you would like that."

"We will see," he murmured, not taking his eyes from Ingrid, obviously teasing her. "Though there is no doubt it would be nice to be…"—he paused before saying the last word with added emphasis—"closer."

Terror rushed through Ingrid's body. She started to shake uncontrollably and clung again to the desk, hoping Heinrich hadn't seen evidence of the emotions raging within her. *Heinrich's whore.* The words echoed in her head.

The Lieutenant Colonel turned from her desk and marched toward Heinrich's office. As the door slammed shut, she just managed to make it into her chair before she collapsed.

Vi, who had been close by, noticed straight away. "What is wrong?" she enquired with concern.

"I need to go to the bathroom," Ingrid spluttered, grabbing her purse and rushing out of the room.

In the bathroom, she stared at herself in the mirror as she ran water into the bowl and tried desperately to catch a breath.

All at once there was someone behind her. She spun around in fear. But it was only Vi.

"What's wrong, Ingrid?" she asked again. "Something is going on. I know it is."

Ingrid couldn't hold on any longer. She started to sob uncontrollably as the fear and experience of that night washed over her in violent and horrific flashbacks.

Vi was instantly by her side with her arms around her as Ingrid wept on her shoulder.

After a long cry, she confessed to Vi what had happened, and her friend was horrified. Ingrid explained how she had managed to hide the ring of angry black bruises on her face and neck the following morning with makeup, but the pain of not telling anyone of her anguish had overwhelmed her.

"What about Heinrich? Can't you talk to him about this?" implored her friend.

Ingrid shook her head as she dabbed at her eyes. "He wouldn't understand. I'm not even sure he would believe me. I need to make this relationship work, and he is very busy with his job and is so distant from me right now."

Vi stood staring at her, shaking her head. "Surely if he loved you he would care about this and want to at least do everything in his power to keep you away from this animal."

Ingrid shook her head. "The Lieutenant Colonel is his superior and everyone is so stressed right now since the south of Holland fell to the enemy. There are rumors they could make substantial advances into all of Holland, and Heinrich is so tense. I need to do something for him right now, to bring him back to me."

Vi placed her arm around Ingrid's shoulders again. "We will think of something, Ingrid. We will not let this despicable human being win, and we will also think of a way to get you and Heinrich back on track."

Ingrid blew her nose, feeling heartened from talking with her friend. She should have spoken to her about this before, and for once in a long time, she had a glimmer of hope. A sliver of optimism that maybe there was a way she could heal the gap between her and Heinrich.

That evening, Vi took Ingrid to their little jazz club in town. The starvation all over Holland had intensified, leaving very little to eat, even for the German's. The club stayed open for members of the Third Reich to continue to meet, but Ingrid noticed business had been dwindling as more forces were stretched to fight the war on so many fronts. There were rumors of soldiers dying from malnutrition. But still, a few evenings a week, they sat at their favorite table, that was usually lit with a single red candle thrust into an ancient wine bottle, layered in dripped wax, while the little jazz band played. It was here, a few days after Ingrid's confession to Vi, that they came up with their plan.

Ingrid took a long, slow drag on her cigarette. "I'm not even sure if he loves me anymore, but I'm afraid to leave now. Where would I go? All of my old friends here have rejected me. Any chance of leaving for Germany to be with Heinrich's family is now impossible with the enemy surrounding the Netherlands."

Vi nodded. "It's a difficult time for all of us, but maybe there is something we can do about your relationship. What is making Heinrich so stressed? Perhaps we can help him."

"Oh, that's easy," responded Ingrid. "He complains all the time about the Resistance and how they're stopping him from getting any work done." She sighed. "Lately, they have done so much damage. He is sure there are spies within the Reich, maybe even in our office. Helping them cripple the Nazi advances."

"What if we were to find them for him?" Vi suggested, her eyes alight with the adventure of it all.

"What do you mean?"

"You could talk to Heinrich and find out what kind of operation is coming up," Vi responded with a smirk. "Then you and I can use all our savvy to watch for any suspicious activity related to that operation in our office: people who are listening in, that sort of thing."

Ingrid nodded, feeling encouraged. "That's an excellent idea. If I could find a traitor, especially in our office, I know Heinrich would be so proud of me. But how would I find out what he is working on? He hardly speaks to me anymore."

"Well, we shall have to find a way for you to get his attention. I have a few friends working in the black market who could, say, obtain some food. Maybe you could cook him a nice dinner."

Ingrid was taken aback. "You have food?" she whispered.

"Let's just say I have a certain soldier friend whose job it is to confiscate food obtained by the black market. He has a hard time saying no to me," Vi said with a wink. "What does Heinrich like to eat?"

"Duck is his favorite, but we haven't seen duck for nearly a year. Do you really think you could get me some?"

"Leave it with me." Vi stubbed out her cigarette. "We will see if we can win over Herr von Strauss for you by winning over his stomach."

*

Vi was good for her word and a few days later handed over the food. Ingrid decided to talk to Heinrich that evening.

She arranged for her housekeeper's daughter to cook duck *à l'orange*, Heinrich's favorite, promising the girl's family any leftover food. Arriving home early, she dressed in the tight black dress he had always said he loved her in and dabbed the musky perfume he had bought her behind her ears.

Her fiancé came home late that evening. Exhausted, he shuffled inside, his head and shoulders weighed down with the burden of an endless war.

Ingrid greeted him at the door, looking ravishing, if she did say so herself. He appeared surprised.

"You're going out again tonight?" he sneered, as he took in her attire.

"No," she responded, laying on all her charm. "I decided to stay home and have dinner with you."

She took off his jacket and led him by the hand into the dining room; he was taken aback by her preparations. The table was laid with fresh flowers and the best crystal was glistening by candlelight. Music played on the gramophone.

"What is this?" he enquired suspiciously.

Ingrid seated him at the end of the table and poured him a glass of red wine. "I feel like we're growing apart and we need to spend more time together. This war has hurt all of us."

Heinrich was about to respond when the cook arrived with the duck *à l'orange*. He looked at it in awe.

"How is this possible? How did you get this food?" he spluttered, his usual need to interrogate her overtaken by his desire to eat.

Ingrid took a sip of her wine and smiled. Her plan was working; Heinrich looked impressed.

"A friend of mine got it for me. I told her my fiancé is doing a critical job for the Third Reich and needed to be rewarded."

Heinrich didn't waste any time and started to eat hungrily.

Throughout the dinner, he was quiet, and Ingrid spent the time reassuring him of the excellent job he was doing.

"Tell me about your work," she asked as the housekeeper brought in their dessert. "What are you doing at the moment?"

He drained his glass of wine and sighed. "You know I can't talk about that. You know everything is top secret."

"I know," she pouted, "but I'm sure there must be something we can talk about that I could help you with."

Heinrich scoffed. "Killing everyone in the entire Resistance would be good. Or at least stopping them blowing up our fuel trains so we could fire off our V2 rockets once in a while."

Ingrid didn't get to respond to him because the telephone rang and he left the table to answer it. But she started thinking. Maybe if she knew when the fuel trains were coming in, she could help, somehow.

When he returned, he looked grave. "There has been an incident I have to attend to. I must go." He picked up his jacket and moved toward the door. Just before he exited the room, he turned to her, his indifference thawed for a moment. "I enjoyed our dinner."

Then he left and didn't return until she was already asleep in bed. But his early departure had given her the whole evening to come up with a plan.

*

The next day she hurried to work and pulled Vi from her desk to the bathroom to tell her about her idea. Vi checked that the stalls were empty before Ingrid started speaking in a hushed tone.

"I think we should try to uncover who is blowing up the fuel trains. Heinrich is so stretched right now, he doesn't have the manpower to conduct a full investigation just for that. But maybe we can do it for him. The Resistance must be getting their information from somewhere. It could easily be someone in our office. We should start by looking into it here. There are only a few people who handle the fuel trains, and it would be easy for us to keep an eye on them."

"Surely Heinrich would have ruled out that possibility," Vi whispered back. "Besides, the dates and times of the trains are all kept secret. Virtually no one knows when they are coming in."

"Heinrich does," stated Ingrid, her face glowing. "I bet the information is in his safe, and I know the combination."

Vi looked at her friend in awe. "Are you planning what I think you are planning?" she whispered, her eyes wide with anticipation. Suddenly a clerk from one of the other offices came through the door and both Ingrid and Vi pretended to be preening in the mirror until she left with a nod, uttering a "Heil Hitler" to them both.

"You're not planning on confronting the Resistance fighters yourself, are you? That could be so dangerous."

Ingrid shook her head. "Of course not, I just plan on uncovering the spy for him. It might mean following someone, I suppose. But only so I can report who they are to Heinrich and he can take action and look like the hero. That way everybody wins—he looks good to his own Lieutenant Colonel *and* he sees the value in having me in his life. I think we should start by watching people in the office for suspicious activity." Ingrid squealed. "I can't wait to see his face when he finds out what an asset I can be to him. I want to make him so proud of me."

"Okay," said Vi, "I will help you. I reckon I know exactly which of our office workers we need to keep an eye on. And, hopefully, help save your love life."

Chapter Forty-Four

After her mother's death, Hannah found that her life and purpose took on new meaning. She worked tirelessly against the regime, mainly on restoring bicycles for Resistance fighters to use. They were basic, and there was no rubber for tires, most people just rode on the metal frames, but they served a purpose.

The Resistance leader, Henri, whom she'd met all those years before, had connected her with salvage people all over Amsterdam. Bicycle parts were found and smuggled to her. She would also sometimes use her job at the university to hold falsified documents for people who needed them. Even though the university was officially closed, she still volunteered to keep on top of the mail. The couple of afternoons she was there, she would hide the documents in empty pigeonholes, and then, at the right time, she would slip them into the outgoing mail to another member of the faculty who was also working for the Underground.

One evening, she had received in her usual small pile of Resistance mail a note for her to attend one of the Underground's meetings. It was worded very carefully as an invitation for tea with an old friend, but she knew exactly what it meant.

The next afternoon she arrived at the door the butcher had sent her to years before, and the same woman opened it. Gone were the wafts of cooking smells. The buxom woman of years earlier had lost much weight and looked drawn and pale. But her eyes brightened when she saw Hannah and ushered her into a dark back room. A hush fell on the room as she entered. A small group of freedom fighters was gathered there.

The Resistance leader introduced her to the group. "This is Hannah," he informed them. "She is here to ensure bicycles arrive in the hands of our agents when they need them."

The group nodded their hello, and Hannah stood back in a darkened corner to listen as they discussed the latest plot. To keep all of them safe, everyone only knew the barest of information about the plan in case either there was a traitor among them or the Gestapo captured one of them and they were tortured.

It was evident as they descended back into their debate that Hannah's entrance had stopped them in the midst of an intense discussion.

"They're rounding up members of CS6 and shooting them," a despondent-looking member of the group reminded them all. "The Gestapo are watching. It's dangerous for any of us to do anything right now. Aart was picked up two days ago, and we have no one to ride the latest package out to the location."

The group continued to have a heated debate, and Hannah felt something bubble up inside her as she listened. She saw her mother knitting hats. She saw Michael Blum battling for his life and Josef being willing to sacrifice his own to save him. She saw Eva's young face the last time she had seen her and how she'd promised to be brave. Suddenly, something pushed her forward.

"I can do it," she said, moving into the circle of men gathered there. "I can cycle there."

A mustached man, Erik, showed his displeasure. "You don't realize this is hazardous work."

"I will take my chances," Hannah responded.

"You are sure?" Henri enquired, looking concerned. "This is very dangerous, Hannah. If they found you, you would be arrested, tortured, maybe killed."

Hannah swallowed down her fear. "I find that the need far outweighs the cost."

A flicker of recognition registered in Henri's eyes, and he nodded.

Hannah continued, "No one is going to question a middle-aged woman on a bicycle. My role in the Resistance has been so small I am confident I am not known to them. Please let me try."

"What you have to do is very important," snapped back a willowy man with a day's worth of beard growth. He looked uneasy about Hannah's confidence. "If they capture you, you cannot tell anyone about us or this meeting, do you understand?"

Hannah nodded with determination. "I know that, and I'm willing to take this information to my grave."

Henri shook his head. "I don't think we have much choice. Our inside agent, known to us as Cuckoo, has received credible information. We have to act fast. Everything is already in place, apart from the carrier."

The group looked at Hannah as if they were each weighing her up. Then, reluctantly, one by one, they nodded or shrugged their resignation.

Henri beckoned Hannah to the table, where he turned on a light and flattened out a map in front of him, pointing to and then drawing his finger along a route.

"You will meet up with our operatives, who will take the package from you. But you will need to go here first." He tapped a place on the map. "Ernst's house is a long way out on the outskirts of Amsterdam. There will be washing on the line to signify it is safe, two pairs of socks, a pair of gray trousers, and one white handkerchief. He will give you the package, which you will hide in a medical bag. You have medical training, right?"

Hannah nodded. "I looked after my ailing mother for many years."

"Yes, I remember. Good," he said, nervously fingering his chin. "We can give you papers that stipulate that you have permission to ride the bicycle as a nurse in case you are stopped in and around the city. There is a false bottom in the bag where you can hide the package once you receive it at Ernst's house. If anyone asks where you are going, you can say you are visiting a patient. You will pick up the package, then you will head to here." He circled a place along the route in the woods. "There is a cottage there, right on the edge of the town, with three pairs of trousers and two white handkerchiefs on the line."

You will knock on the door and say the doctor has sent you. If he answers, 'Doctor Horst?' you know you are in the right place. Go inside and hand over the package. Wait about fifteen minutes and then leave and come back here. I can't give you this map, in case you are stopped, so you need to memorize your route."

Hannah looked carefully at the map and then nodded. "I won't let you down."

He covered her hand with his. "I know you won't. Do you think you can make it in an hour?"

Hannah smiled. "I will be back before the curfew, don't worry."

"Then my wife," he pointed at the woman she had first met years before, who had just entered the room and was drying her hands on a tea towel, "will give you your papers and medical bag."

Hannah followed the lively woman to the kitchen, where she tipped over a flour container filled with sand into a bowl and pulled out a bundle of documents from a cloth bag.

Hannah was amazed as she watched the little round woman retrieve a leather medical bag from underneath a floorboard. Moving around the kitchen with the ease of an experienced chef, she gathered various pieces of medical equipment hidden in different food containers and sacks.

She finished her task then handed the bag to Hannah. Finally, she took something from a metal canister and placed it in Hannah's hand. It was a small scone.

"For you to eat before your journey," she said, closing Hannah's hand over it and squeezing it. "Don't ask me where I got the flour."

Hannah nodded thankfully, said her goodbyes, then accompanied by the sweet Dutch woman with the candy-floss white hair, moved down the hall to the front door and slipped out into the street.

Chapter Forty-Five

A few days after their conversation, Vi approached Ingrid's desk, her eyes wide. "We need to go to the bathroom," she said in a hushed tone.

Ingrid knotted her eyebrows. "What do you mean?" she responded with irritation, not looking up or wanting to be distracted from her work.

Vi leaned in close and whispered into her friend's ear, "I've found out something. We need to go, now!" She jerked her head toward the corridor.

Ingrid understood. She put down her work and followed her friend out the door.

Once in the ladies' restroom, Vi checked all of the stalls to make sure nobody else was there before turning to face Ingrid.

"What did you find?" Ingrid enquired expectantly.

"You're never going to believe this," Vi whispered. "I found something in Herr Mautner's drawer. I've been watching him for a while, and there was something about him I just didn't trust. Today, I had to deliver some files to him, and I just happened to drop a couple on the floor." She smiled slyly. "And while I was down there picking them up, I slipped open the bottom drawer he keeps locked whenever he's not in his office and found this."

She handed Ingrid a folded piece of paper. On it were the details of a location.

"What is it?" Ingrid asked.

"I think this is where the Resistance is planning to blow up the fuel train. It's on the route, next to the tracks."

"This was in Herr Mautner's office?" Ingrid responded incredulously. "I would never have thought of him as a traitor, but it makes sense. His job is coordinating all the ammunition coming in and out of Amsterdam."

"It's always the person you least expect," Vi stated, her eyebrows raised.

Ingrid thought about the studious, diligent little man, who was always impeccably dressed, with his egg-shaped head and heavily grooved forehead, his rat-like eyes staring out from horn-rimmed glasses, beady and expressionless. He had always been somewhat cold with Ingrid, and he seemed to begrudge the fact she and Heinrich had a special relationship.

"This is unbelievable," she muttered. "I'm going to go straight to Heinrich to tell him."

She made for the bathroom door, but Vi stopped her. "But he will just deny it! I think we need to catch him in the act. And didn't you say you wanted to make Heinrich see you as heroic?"

Intrigued, Ingrid turned. "What do you mean?"

Vi moved swiftly to her side. "What if you were actually to go there and spy on them? What if you were to go before they plant the explosives? Then you could go straight to Heinrich, and he could come and catch them in the act. Then, instead of exposing one traitor, you'd be catching a whole group. Wouldn't that really help him?"

Ingrid thought for a minute. It certainly sounded appealing. She imagined how happy Heinrich would be when she had been the one to uncover members of the Resistance. He would be so proud of her.

"It's a perfect idea," Ingrid responded. "What do I need to do?"

Vi thought for a moment. "First, I think we have to find out when the fuel train is coming in so we know when to be there," she explained. "Then we can go to these coordinates and wait. I will come with you if you like, so you're not alone. We could get there early and spy on those people. Then we can race back to the nearest station, and call Heinrich to get him to meet you there with the police."

"I love this idea," Ingrid said. "Thank you so much." She threw her arms around her friend's neck. "You are the best friend ever."

Vi pulled away. "We all have to do what we have to do for the war effort," she said, more seriously.

Ingrid nodded and happily left for her desk. She now had a plan.

*

The next day, Ingrid slipped into Heinrich's office when he was meeting with city officials and closed the door. She was glad she knew the code to the safe—he had given it to her years before when there had been a lot less security. She hoped he hadn't changed it. Moving stealthily inside, she turned it to the numbers she knew and was delighted when the heavy metal door creaked open. She pulled out Heinrich's master file and flicked through the pages to locate the information she needed—the times and arrivals of all the inbound trains. She determined all the trains for the next month and smiled. She put back the ledger, closed the safe, and returned to the offices.

Eying Vi, she walked to her desk and whispered in her ear. "Friday afternoon at 6.30 p.m., there is a fuel train coming in from Germany."

Vi nodded. "I will start watching the office for Resistance activity. We will make a hero out of you, no doubt, Miss Held."

Ingrid nodded. Excitement filled her as she returned to her desk. The only thing on her mind was what she and Heinrich would do once the war was over.

Chapter Forty-Six

That week, the desperation of the famine had been lessened by humanitarian food drops that were organized by the Allies. Instead of bombs, the mighty Lancasters released care packages filled with tinned food, flour, peas, coffee, sugar, dried egg powder and chocolate. Grateful Dutch rushed out into the fields to greet the planes, waving flags and holding up their signs of thanks.

Josef was in his kitchen opening an unlabeled can. Earlier that day Hannah had dropped around a small food parcel but had rushed off soon after arriving. He was idly wondering what the can might contain when he happened to glance up at his calendar. Since leaving the university, one day had merged into another without the precise schedule that he had adhered to in academic life. When he saw the date, his heart stopped for a second, and he couldn't believe it. It was his wedding anniversary, and he hadn't even been aware of it. Every year since her death until now, he would feel an overwhelming gloom setting in days before, and would often take the day itself off from the university to place flowers on her grave. But it was here, and he had nearly forgotten it.

He stopped opening his can, which he could now see was tinned meat, and stared out of his window as he remembered her voice.

"We will always celebrate our anniversaries, won't we, Josef?" she had whispered into his ear on their first. She had been wearing a brooch in the shape of a tulip, her favorite flower, that he had bought her as a gift.

"Of course, my love," he'd answered her. "We'll always remember." And now here he was already halfway through the day, and he'd barely given her a thought. He wanted and needed to tell somebody about her life. There was only one person—it was finally time to share his story with Michael.

He had been contemplating it ever since the day that Sarah's chest had been broken open during the air raid. Even though it was the middle of the day he poured himself a small glass of wine, he had managed to save through the difficult winter, and lifted it toward the framed picture of his wife that he now kept downstairs and wished her a happy anniversary.

"Twenty-four years, Sarah. Twenty-four years since you became my wife and made me the happiest of men. From the time we met I have thought about you every day, and even though you were only with me for such a short time, I still love you, and part of me always will."

He took a sip of his drink and thought about the young girl with the copper curls and the dancing emerald eyes. Where had the years gone? To him, time had stood still for so long, though he'd noticed a change in himself since the day of the illness when he had dreamed about her. Things had started to shift within him. He didn't feel so constricted. He knew, with his temperature so high, that the dream was probably nothing more than a hallucination, but it had been such a vivid experience that it had stayed with him in a genuine way, a comforting arm around his shoulders, making him feel as if everything was going to be all right.

He remembered her words of reassurance, and each day he reminded himself that he'd been given a gift and that Sarah had encouraged him to focus on taking care of Michael now.

He poured a glass of wine for Michael and, carrying the open can of meat, he climbed to the attic. Michael was lying on his bed, reading a book of poetry. Josef handed the food and glass of wine to him.

"Are we celebrating?" he enquired, quirking an eyebrow.

"Yes," affirmed Josef as he seated himself in the old armchair in the corner. The same chair that he had placed there while Michael had been sick. It had remained next to Michael's bed and had become a favorite place for them to converse, with Michael lying on his bed and Josef seated next to him.

"Did the Germans finally leave town?"

Josef looked down at his glass before responding in a quieter tone. "I'm afraid nothing that exciting. But it is my wedding anniversary." Josef could tell by his expression that Michael instantly understood his mixed feelings. "I would have been married twenty-four years today," he continued. "And it's been over twenty years since Sarah's death. She was just twenty-two when I married her and I still love her."

"The same age as Elke when I met her," Michael mused. "What was she like?"

Josef took another swig of the wine. It would take a little courage to tell Michael the story he needed to tell him.

"She was the brightest, funniest, most alive person I've ever met, and why she fell for an awkward, skinny mathematics teacher, I will never know. In many ways, you remind me of her." He smiled. "Your devil-may-care attitude. Your desire to live the best life you can live… Your passion."

Michael swung his legs around and sat up on the bed, clearly sensing Josef needed a moment before he continued his story. "Ah, I wonder about that passion. I wonder about who I'm going to be after this war. Everything seemed so easy, before. I had a dream of becoming a poet, of spending my life creating beautiful words, maybe even being a scholar. And after this war, if we even win, I'm probably just going to be nothing more than a Jew."

Josef wished he could assure him that it wouldn't be the case, but the world had gone mad and no one could predict what peacetime would look like.

"I had a dream the other night that I was free, and so was Elke. And we were able to be together. It was so real. When I woke up, I was surprised to see she was not there with me."

Josef sat back in his seat. "I had a dream, too… when I was sick. Sarah came to me in that dream, and she talked to me about my life and our life together. She made it clear to me there were things in my life I needed to forgive. Forgive her, forgive myself, and each day since then, I have tried to get to that place of forgiveness."

Michael looked up and spoke gently, "Can I ask—how did you lose her?"

Josef took in a breath and held it for a long time before slowly letting it out and taking another sip of his wine.

"She was the most beautiful pregnant woman I have ever seen. Some women, you know, get sick or pale during their pregnancies. Not Sarah. Sarah seemed to get more beautiful by the day, even when she became very heavy. It was the summertime, and there were many festivals and music concerts, and she wanted to go to all of them. I was apprehensive, but Sarah didn't seem to care. She danced to music and walked around barefoot and happy, her skin browned by the sun. Just a month before the baby was due to be born, she had started to get some back pain. I had been very busy. We had final exams for many of the students, and I must admit, I was preoccupied with my work. And because Sarah was really content, I took it in my stride that everything was well."

"When you talk about her your whole being lights up," Michael observed.

"It is hard not to, just remembering. She was so happy to be having our first child. She loved to feel the baby moving in her stomach and was excited, telling me that she believed another professor was waiting to be born. I didn't care as long as it was healthy, but my wife…" He stopped to think, and finally settled on, "She *celebrated* who I was. As the days wore on and she grew closer to her due date, her sister, Yvette, agreed to come from the countryside to help with the delivery. But it wasn't so easy to travel. Something detained her, and she was unable to come at the agreed time and instead put her trip off for a few days. But Sarah wasn't the least bit concerned.

"One morning, I was preparing for the exams and fretting about everything I needed to do, and I didn't happen to notice how quiet Sarah was. When I look back now, I should have seen it, but I didn't. Now when I think about it, she was probably in pain and keeping it from me because she knew my students had exams and how important the day was to me, but how I wish she would have told me."

Josef stood to his feet, for the next part of his story would be challenging to recall. He paced to the attic window to collect himself, then added, "I didn't even remember kissing her goodbye that morning. It's the small things like that that I have such regrets about. But when I left, there was a moment at the door when I saw something cross her face. Was it fear, anguish, or pain? It was there for just a second, then it was gone."

Josef's voice started to quiver, and Michael got up and joined him at his side, placing a reassuring hand on his shoulder, knowing the importance of Josef telling this story.

"I never took the time to ask her, and instead, I left, busy with the thoughts of my day and everything that I needed to achieve… So many regrets."

In a whisper, Michael answered him, "We all have those, Professor. I will never see my friend David again in this life. He gave his life to save me, to warn me. How can I ever come to terms with that?"

The two men shared a look that reassured the other that they both understood this kind of pain. The pain of never being able to go back and right a wrong, a mistake that had cost somebody dear to them their life.

Josef moved back to his chair and poured himself and Michael another glass of wine before continuing, the deep connection of understanding with Michael encouraging him to finish his story.

"I was late arriving back that day, so much work to do. The exams had gone well, and I was ready to relax at home. But as soon as I walked into the house, I knew something was wrong. There were none of the cooking smells that usually greeted me at the door, and the house felt cold, even though it was sunny outside. I called out to Sarah, but she did not call back. I eventually found her in the kitchen, lying on the floor, her face reddened, and she was panting hard.

"I rushed to her side and was shocked to see..." Josef stopped to gather his breath. Then in a whisper, "So much blood. I asked her how long she'd been like this and she just shook her head. I don't think she even knew. I think she was just waiting for me to get home. Her hair was matted, stuck to her forehead, her clothes dripping with sweat. I knew I needed to get help, get a doctor, anyone, but the midwife who was meant to be taking care of Sarah lived right across town. And she begged me to stay with her. She was so afraid.

"As I held her in my arms, it was obvious Sarah was about to deliver. But I knew something was very wrong. She was so ashen and felt clammy, and even though I knew nothing about delivering babies, I was sure there shouldn't be that much blood. And I knew, I knew without a shadow of a doubt, that I was about to lose her.

"All at once her body became limp, as if it was already moving away from me. I gripped hold of her, willing her to stay with me, willing her to stay alive. When the baby was finally born, he was tiny. A month early. Perfect, but not breathing.

"I tried everything I could to resuscitate him. I willed Sarah to stay with me, but she too slipped away, and I'll never forget the look in her eyes. Her eyes that had always danced with joy and laughter were suddenly lifeless and dark."

Josef stopped then as the tears caught in his throat. Michael nodded, and Josef took another gulp of his wine.

Michael spoke barely above a whisper, "And the dream you said you had?"

Josef took a breath. "In it she met me in a place special to us and told me that it wasn't my fault. She said… that I had other things to do in this world. And I realized that I had been holding onto the pain, holding onto the loss, because I was afraid that if I let go, that somehow I would dishonor her memory and would lose even more of her. But now I realize after so many years of the grief and hurt, that the opposite is true and by holding onto the pain, I have not allowed any love back into my life. I have survived. But now I have to learn to *live*."

"Maybe we both do," added Michael, thoughtfully.

They sat in companionable silence as the weight of Josef's story found its place between them. Josef's head started to spin with the effects of the alcohol. He hadn't touched the food and needed to eat something more substantial. Gathering the glasses and the empty bottle, he got to his feet.

"I will try to find something more to eat," he said, feeling emotionally drained. As he headed for the door, Michael called after him. Josef turned. Getting to his feet, he hugged Josef.

"Thank you for sharing your story with me. I know how hard that was."

Josef nodded. "It was the right time."

Moving downstairs, Josef noted he actually felt somehow lighter.

Chapter Forty-Seven

The day after the meeting at Henri's house, Hannah was nervous as she prepared for her mission. After a restless night, she got up early and spent her morning going over the route in her head, oiling her bike chain, and packing and repacking the medical bag. She dropped off a parcel of food to Josef, but made her excuses when he'd offered her tea, rushing back home to continue her wait. When the fear gripped too tight in her, she would instead focus on thoughts of Eva, on her mother, on Josef. All of these people, the most unlikely of heroes, had somehow managed to find the courage within themselves to do the extraordinary, stand up for what was right, and hold onto their humanity in a world where human life was of such little value.

The words of Henri, the Resistance leader, said to her a few years ago, stirred in her once again: "One doesn't know how brave one is until the cost outweighs the fear."

So many people round her had been prepared to pay that cost, she would take comfort from their strength today.

In the afternoon, she made herself a cup of tea and anxiously watched it turn cold in her hand as she waited to go. The orders from Henri had been to leave no earlier than 4 p.m., so she sat for a whole hour, waiting for the grandfather clock in the hall to strike its permission. As its deep, dulcet tones droned out the four o'clock hour, she jumped to her feet. A calm assurance descended upon her, filling her body in a glowing warmth. She suddenly sensed her mother's presence in the room, nodding her encouragement from her chair by the fireside, and it filled her with hope.

Hannah put on her coat and hat and moved rapidly out of the house to the workshop. Grabbing her bicycle, she knocked it against a shelf, and the deck of cards she had balanced up there toppled down, splaying out across the floor. Every one of the deck landed face down. Except one. The queen of hearts. She smiled. The forces of good around her were working together today to give her the strength she needed.

As she gathered up the cards, she thought of Joe from Brooklyn, so out of place, a stranger in her world, yet he had been willing to sacrifice everything so she could be free. That emboldening thought was what she needed. She owed this to all of them, all the people sacrificing their lives and liberty for her. Her minor mission just a fragment, a tiny puzzle piece of a new-world picture that, through determination and sacrifice, they were creating together with the unwavering hope for a bright new tomorrow.

She left her back garden, pedaling slowly down the back streets of Amsterdam, keeping her chin down to not draw attention to herself. Even as perilous as this mission was, she was surprised to feel a sensation she hadn't in a long time: wild abandonment. She, like most Dutch children, had learned to ride bicycles at a young age, and it had become part of her identity throughout her life, part of what made all of them Dutch. She hadn't ridden a bike openly in almost four years. As she pedaled through the cold afternoon, she reveled in the air rushing past her ears, freeing wisps of her hair from beneath her hat, and chilling her cheeks. And as she leaned into the experience, for the briefest amount of time she could actually taste that freedom that one day she believed they would know again.

Turning onto Damrak, she became cautious again. To get to the other side of town, there was no avoiding traveling this way. But she knew this would be the most likely place she might be stopped.

As she became hyper-vigilant, she noticed with relief that the Allies' victories were really starting to affect the Nazis' presence on the streets. Recalled for more critical battles, as well as sickness from hunger or fatigue, had resulted in a thinning out of troops everywhere.

Passing street after street, she started to feel confident that she would make it the whole way through Amsterdam without being stopped. Until, just before the outskirts, a German officer stepped out in front of her and raised his hand.

"Halt."

She pulled on her brakes and braced herself.

"Good evening, Fräulein," he snapped sharply as he eyed her suspiciously. "Where are you going on this bicycle?"

Meeting his steely gaze, she swallowed down her nerves before she answered him. "I am a nurse, and I'm on my way to visit a couple of patients on the outside of town. I want to make it back by the curfew, so I'm taking a bicycle." Then she added, quickly, "I have approval to have one."

The soldier peered at her, apparently weighing her up before asking her for her papers.

She fumbled in her case for the forged documents and, tensing her arm to stop it from shaking, handed them to the young soldier. While he read them, he looked back at her more than once, as if he was trying to look for cracks in her meticulously controlled calmness.

"The curfew is soon. Do you think you'll make it in time?" he snapped.

"If I can get on with my journey," she responded, trying to feign a little irritation.

He ignored her and examined the bicycle. "What do you have in your bag?"

"Just my medical equipment." She managed to keep her voice level.

"Open it for me."

Slowly, Hannah walked to the front of her bike and took it off the rack where she had it strapped and clicked it open.

The soldier shuffled through it, picking up the stethoscope and some bandages before seeming satisfied with what he saw. He thrust her papers back at her.

"You must return quickly," he growled and waved her on. "Be back well before the curfew."

"Of course," she answered, smiling sweetly and strapping the bag back on her bicycle. She rode away with her heart beating so hard she would have sworn he must have been able to hear it.

As the city limits gave way to the countryside, she started to breathe easier and picked up her pace. On just the rims, it was a very uncomfortable ride. Visualizing the map in her head, she followed the route, exactly. As a tiny pink cottage came into view, she was relieved to see the house that Henri had described to her. Even from a distance, she could see the washing line with the laundry flapping in the wind—two pairs of socks, a pair of gray trousers, and one white handkerchief. The exact clothes Henri had informed her would be there as a sign of all-clear.

Pulling to a stop outside the cottage, she opened the gate and wheeled her bicycle up the path. As she waited for her contact to answer, her heart thumped again in her chest and she glanced around to make sure no one had followed her.

A rather thin man, dressed casually in turned up trousers and an open-necked shirt that displayed his grubby undershirt, opened the door to her. Only the briefest hint of surprise showed on his bony face, sporting more than a few days of stubble. He had not been at the Resistance meeting, and seemed to have expected a man, not this woman standing before him. They exchanged code words. Once she had passed his test, he opened the side door leading into his garage and encouraged her to wheel her bicycle inside, chatting in a friendly manner to her about his health. But as soon as the door was bolted with them inside, all of his carefree demeanor changed.

"What happened to Aart?" he hissed through clenched teeth.

"He was picked up three days ago," Hannah responded in a whisper. "Henri sent me instead."

Ernst looked at her with amusement and a little apprehension. "A woman? You do know what you need to do?"

Hannah nodded.

"It is dangerous, you know."

"I am aware of that," responded Hannah, more than a little frustrated at his tone.

Ernst shrugged and made his way through the garage toward a door that led into the house, whispering over his shoulder to her, "Bring the bag!"

Hannah unbuckled it and followed him through the cottage to the back of the house and into a bedroom. Against one wall was a sizable, shabby wardrobe. He opened the creaking doors and removed two panels to reveal a false back. Tucked neatly inside was a mass of explosives.

Quickly opening the doctor's bag, he removed its false bottom, then gently and slowly took the explosives from the back of the wardrobe, wrapped them in an old cloth, and carefully replaced the bottom and the medical equipment on top.

Once everything was tucked away, his attention turned back to Hannah. "You know where you have to go, right?"

"Yes, Erik's house, half a mile down the road, with three pairs of trousers and two white handkerchiefs on the line."

He nodded at her and carefully picked up the bag. "Please be careful with the explosive, they are sensitive. We need to wait for ten minutes," he informed her as they made their way back to the kitchen, "just in case anybody is watching the house. We don't want you to leave too soon."

She nodded, and they waited in an awkward silence. A dripping tap and a perky little yellow kitchen clock attempted to break the tension between them, both working rhythmically against one another in a race to have command over the silence.

As she waited, she glanced around the chilly room. She was sure this man lived alone. Dirty water formed a ring around the sink, and clothes were heaped across all the chairs. The windows needed washing, and a strong smell of mildew emanated from the dripping sills.

After ten minutes, he nodded to her. "If you are asked, you took my temperature and listened to my chest, advising me to continue with my medication."

She nodded and followed him back through the shed, where she strapped the bag on the bicycle and wheeled it back outside.

"Thank you, nurse," he shouted to her. "I'll see you again in a month's time."

"Remember to take your medication," she responded, playing her part.

"I will, I will," he said, laughing and shutting the door.

Hannah mounted her bike and set off down the road, her pounding heart now reverberating all the way to her throat as she obsessively watched the bag in front of her. Somehow, in all of the planning of this, it had not entered her mind that she would actually be riding down the street with dangerous explosives rattling in a bag in front of her. All of her previous fear had been directed at being stopped or captured by Nazis, but now, as she slowly made her way on her clattering rims, her focus was concentrated in one direction, with one thought only: how to ensure the smoothest ride possible.

As she crept her way haltingly along the road, beads of sweat gathered around the brim of her hat and across her forehead, trickling down behind her ears. The half a mile she had to travel to Erik's house felt like an eternity.

About halfway there, her fear was compounded as two Nazi trucks loaded with soldiers sped by her on a seemingly urgent mission somewhere. They barely gave her a second glance as they barreled past her, but the shock of seeing them, coupled with the slipstream they created behind them, forced her to grip even tighter to the handlebars as her unstable bicycle threatened to wobble itself into a ditch.

Righting herself, she stopped for a second to catch her breath. She could do this. She *had* to do this.

She moved off again. As she rounded a bend, she was grateful to see another house come into view. And there was washing on the line; though from this distance it was hard to make out what it was. She was nearly there, but as she drew nearer, she was horrified to see that the two trucks of soldiers were parked outside. Unconsciously, she gripped the handlebars even tighter, causing her to lose feeling in her hands. Her beating heart, coupled with a sense of nausea and overwhelming lightheadedness, threatened to cause her to faint.

What should she do? Return to Ernst? Henri had only mentioned in passing any change to the plans, and that was if the washing was not on the line. But undoubtedly a Nazi raid trumped that. She made up her mind. She would keep her head down and cycle right past the house. If anyone stopped her, she would say her patient was farther up the road and pray they didn't ask her who or where. If she was to turn her bicycle around, she was sure that would bring more attention.

As she got closer to the house, she prayed under her breath, willing herself to keep moving forward, forcing herself not to stare at her bag. Instead, she fixed her sights on a spot on the horizon and continued to pedal mechanically toward the enemy.

As she reached the farmhouse, she heard a woman scream and raised voices inside, followed by the sound of glass shattering. Outside the gate, two soldiers stood guard, and she could feel their eyes boring into her as she continued on her path. Speeding up just a little, she forced herself not to meet their gaze or even acknowledge them. She pedaled past them before either of them had a chance to stop her.

Somehow her plan worked and, once out of view, she picked up her pace to put as much distance between herself and Erik's house as possible. How had the Nazis known? Had it been just a wild coincidence, or had someone tipped them off?

The sound of furniture being broken and more glass shattering behind her grew fainter. She decided she would get off her bicycle in the wooded area up ahead to recover and watch from a safe distance until they left. She thought about hiding the explosives in the woods but decided against it. After all, if this had cost Erik his freedom, maybe even his life, it was imperative that the mission went ahead as arranged to make it worthwhile.

At a safe distance, she dismounted her bike. Her legs shook uncontrollably, weak from fear and exertion. She grounded herself against a tree trunk to catch her breath. Why hadn't she thought to bring some water?

Suddenly, from behind her, a branch snapped underfoot. Turning quickly, Hannah sensed she wasn't alone. She snatched at her bicycle and attempted to mount it when someone grabbed her from behind by both arms.

"Hannah," he snarled.

She struggled within his grip and fought the desire to scream.

"Hannah, stop!" the voice ordered her, and she relaxed, recognizing who it belonged to. She turned to look into the eyes of Erik. "Quickly," he snapped, bidding her to follow him deeper into the bushes.

She went along behind him as he wheeled her bicycle out of sight. Under the cover of canopy, she met the terror and determination in his eyes.

"Your house…" she spat out in panted spurts. "Raided. How? Why?"

"I don't know," he responded woefully. "Someone must have tipped them off. I got out just in time. My mother is strong; she won't tell them anything. Hannah, do you think you can finish this?"

Hannah swallowed, hard. Her throat was desperately dry. She tried to make sense of what he was saying. She *had* finished it. Her job was to deliver the explosives to him, and he was here.

As if he were reading her thoughts, he continued, "They will be on the lookout for me. I can't continue. It could jeopardize the mission. Hannah, do you think you can take the explosives on to the operatives who will plant them?"

Everything inside of her wanted to say, "No." She had proved not only to herself but to anyone around who could see her shaking limbs that being that level of heroic was way beyond her capabilities. What she wanted was to go home, lock her door, and not leave until the war was over. But she saw something cross Erik's face, and she knew instantly that he wasn't just asking her; at this point, she was their only hope. Eva's upturned, smiling face flashed into her mind. So instead of saying what made total sense to her, Hannah found herself saying, "What do I need to do?" And was surprised at how calm she sounded. Her mama would have been proud.

He pointed down toward the road. "Continue about half a mile until you come to a tree with a branch recently ripped from a trunk. Check underneath it. If there is no branch below it, you are in the right place. Walk back behind it and look for the limb. It will be placed farther in the forest, in the direction you need to follow. Continue on that course. If there is a need for a change of direction, a tree trunk will have two fresh slashes on it to signify a left turn and one for a right turn. Keep heading in the direction they specify until you come out onto the railway. The operatives will meet you there. Wait there until you hear three short whistles. They should be there in the next hour or so."

Hannah felt she had earned the right to know more of the plan.

"What are they planning to do with the explosives?"

Erik eyed her warily, as if trying to decide if he could trust her.

Hannah persisted. "I need to know in case someone else is apprehended and I have to change the plan again. I am putting my own life at risk here."

Erik blew out air and relented. "They are going to blow up the next fuel train."

Hannah's eyes widened, realizing the impact of her mission and how debilitating it could be to thwart the Nazis' relentless bombing campaign of England.

She nodded, understanding, and Erik pushed the bike back toward her, indicating she should go. Then he dove back into the thick of the forest and disappeared.

Hannah moved back out to the roadway, her heart starting to pound again. Mounting her bike, she set off.

It didn't take long for her to find the tree with the torn off branch, and as Erik had stipulated, there was no sign of the limb at the base of the tree. She hid her bike in some shrubs, carefully unstrapped the doctor's bag, and started through the trees.

Unfortunately, this part of the forest was dense, and it wasn't long before she was tripping on roots and undergrowth that knit its way around her ankles and shackled itself to her arms. The bulky doctor's bag proved utterly impractical to carry through it all. Stopping for a moment to catch her breath and wipe sweat from her brow, she made a decision. She tentatively opened the bag and removed the false bottom, then she gently tucked the bundle of explosives under her arm and continued her journey. As she hacked her way through the bracken with one hand, she tried hard not to imagine what might happen if she was to trigger, by mistake, the explosives nestled next to her body.

After about twenty minutes, she finally saw light streaming through the trees and also the glint of railway tracks. Making her way to the edge of the forest, she crouched down next to some bushes to await the signal.

Chapter Forty-Eight

Ingrid paced up and down the street angrily. Where on earth was Vi? They had gone over the plan only that morning, and her friend had assured her that she would meet her outside the office no later than five o'clock. Ingrid looked at her watch again. It was ten past five, and the fuel train was due into Amsterdam at six thirty. She would barely have enough time to get out to the countryside, to confirm the Resistance were indeed going to target this specific train, then travel back and get word back to Heinrich so the train could be stopped and the Resistance members arrested. She couldn't afford to wait any longer.

Rushing to her car, she jumped in and gave her driver the directions. A look of mild confusion crossed his face, but nevertheless, he started the car and made his way out of the city.

Ingrid looked out of the window as they traveled. Heinrich had forbidden her from taking any unnecessary trips in the car due to the oil and gas shortage, but this would be worthwhile, especially seeing Heinrich's face when he found out how brave she had been. Maybe it was good that Vi had been late. At least this way Ingrid could get all the recognition. Not that she wasn't grateful to her friend and the information that she'd helped her uncover, but this would work out better.

As they reached the outskirts of Amsterdam, she smiled to herself. This was what their relationship needed, for him to know that she was on his side. She'd always sensed there was a small part of him that kept himself back from her because she was Dutch. This would prove once and for all that they were fighting together.

But when the car arrived at the location she had been given, she was confused. There was nothing here but thick woods. She'd expected to be able to see the train tracks, maybe not even have to leave her vehicle to confirm the suspicious activity, before going straight to Heinrich. The driver looked at her through his rearview mirror, waiting to see what she wanted to do as she checked the coordinates in her pocket against her map.

"There is supposed to be a train track here," she informed him.

"I believe there may be, somewhere in there," he said in a dull tone as he pointed into the thicket.

She sighed deeply, realizing her shoes were not going to last very well in mud and sodden leaves. But she didn't have much choice if she wanted to do this.

"Wait for me here," she commanded him, and pulling her coat tightly around herself, she stepped out into the cold afternoon.

Through the thick undergrowth, she tentatively followed a beaten path that seemed to have been created recently. Before long, she arrived at the tracks and was grateful to see she was early, as no one else seemed to be there yet. Suddenly, from behind her, she heard someone coming in haste and drew herself behind a bush to observe who it might be.

Chapter Forty-Nine

Crouched within the bushes, Hannah looked down at the explosives with concern. They were starting to weigh heavily in her hands, and now that she had stopped, she had plenty of time to imagine what might happen if she accidentally set off an explosion.

She heard someone approaching. Holding her breath, she flattened herself against a tree. Three clear whistles rang out, about a hundred feet to her left. She carefully got up and headed toward where she'd heard the sound.

Suddenly, someone grabbed Hannah from behind. She just stopped herself from screaming in time, almost dropping the explosives as a heavy hand clamped down upon her shoulder and turned her around briskly. Three other men jumped up from their hiding place in the undergrowth. They wore flat caps thrust down firmly on their heads and thick scarves wrapped around their faces, just allowing their eyes to show. She saw their apprehension at her presence.

"My name is Hannah," she said hastily before anybody could react. "Henri sent me."

The hostility around the circle calmed a little as they looked warily from one to the other, and then the apparent leader stepped forward.

"Where is Erik?" he questioned her.

"His house was raided. I was just supposed to transport the explosives from Ernst's house. But when I got to Erik's, the Germans were there. He managed to make contact with me and gave me directions to get here, as he was afraid he'd be picked up on the road."

"You have the package?" demanded one of the others.

Her hand shaking, she held out the explosives wrapped in the rag. The leader nodded at her, taking them from her as the group moved away with haste.

The relief must have been obvious on her face because before he disappeared back into the undergrowth, the leader turned to her. And even though she couldn't see his mouth, she sensed he was smiling as his eyes wrinkled. "You did well, Hannah. You did a good job," he reassured her before he, too, left to follow the others.

Hannah took a deep breath. She couldn't believe she'd managed to do it.

She made her way back slowly through the forest, following the path she had created. She would still have to make good time to return before the curfew. Finding her doctor's bag on the way, she re-strapped it onto her bicycle and headed toward the city.

Chapter Fifty

Ingrid tried to remain out of sight, but as she moved backwards, the heel of her stiletto caught on a branch and it snapped underfoot. The footsteps halted. A hand pulled aside the branches covering where she was hiding. She prepared to deal with the enemy, but was instead surprised to see a group of German soldiers in front of her.

She was momentarily relieved. Vi must have realized she'd made Ingrid late and decided to send Heinrich. She was dismayed, however, to see that it wasn't Heinrich or his soldiers who had arrived. She had so hoped to tell him of the plot and watch his face as she described what she had done. These soldiers were the Gestapo.

The officer in charge looked suspiciously at Ingrid. "What are you doing here?" he asked brusquely.

She stood to her full height. "My name is Ingrid Held. I work for the Third Reich, in the offices of Heinrich von Strauss. There are Resistance members planning to blow up the train tracks from this location this evening."

He peered at her with disdain.

She continued, sensing his skepticism. "If you don't believe me, send your men to the tracks just up ahead. I believe they should be along any minute."

He nodded to his men who headed off. But instead of being overjoyed or even grateful, he just peered at her with contempt. "Our men have been in the woods for a while. We have seen no one but you. What are you doing here, really?"

Ingrid was confused. "I told you what I'm doing here."

In response, he grabbed her roughly by the arm and began marching her out of the forest.

"What are you doing!?" she yelled at him.

"We had an anonymous tip that a member of the Resistance would be working out here this evening, and you are the only person we have found."

Ingrid attempted to shake herself from his grasp. "Do not treat me like this," she snapped. "I am Heinrich von Strauss's fiancée and—"

She never got any further in her conversation because just then, about a mile away, a loud explosion erupted. All of the soldiers froze, looking toward the noise as an enormous fireball and a plume of angry black smoke billowed into the air, obviously the fuel train.

The officer was livid. "We've been sent on a wild goose chase and you, Fräulein, I believe, are a part of it."

He pulled her roughly to the roadway, gripping her arm so tightly, he was hurting her. He dragged her toward his car. Ingrid looked over at her own car and Heinrich's driver, who looked on dumbfounded.

"You just don't understand," she snapped again. "My fiancé will be so angry with you when he finds out what you have done to me."

"And the high command will be very angry with you when they find out what you have done to our fuel train," he snapped back at her as he threw her into the car and slammed the door.

They traveled back into Amsterdam as the evening started to set in, and she was horrified to realize they were taking her to a place where they held prisoners; a cold, miserable stone building, that was dark and smelt of mildew. Heinrich is going to be furious, she thought.

They marched her down an endless corridor with nothing to warm it except gray light reflecting off the blue, chalky wall, giving the entire walkway a luminescent, eerie quality. Then they threw her into a darkened cell. The smell of urine and damp inside made her heave. "You will be so sorry," she spat at the guard as he slammed the door shut and locked her in.

Chapter Fifty-One

As Hannah traveled home, her initial relief was replaced with an awareness of something she had not thought about before, something that in her determination had not even entered her head until now. Who would be traveling on the train? The driver? Other railway workers and soldiers too? When she'd set out to complete the mission, she hadn't even thought about the impact of her actions, only the need and her compulsion to make things right in Holland. Now she was struck with a terrible thought that, somewhere out there, someone was about to die. Someone who maybe had children and parents. And she'd helped to murder them.

The immense sense of guilt almost overwhelmed her. She felt the weight of that and tried to imagine how soldiers on the battlefield felt having to deal with this guilt and loss on a daily basis. There was something so wrong about war, something so horrific and soul-destroying that she hadn't ever contemplated, until now, as the senseless loss of life crushed her. On one side you were crippled by it; on the other side you were the perpetrator of it. There were no winners in this awful reality.

Putting her bike away in the workshop, she could have sworn she heard an explosion far away, but maybe it was just in her imagination. As she turned to close the door, someone grabbed her arm in the dark. But before she could react, the person stepped quickly from the shadows. It was Henri.

"Hannah, we have to talk."

*

As soon as Josef saw the soldiers racing down his street, he knew something was wrong. He had been on his way home after getting a few meager rations as they had rushed past and surged up his path.

It had to be about Michael. Someone had seen him, heard him, reported something unusual. There was no other explanation. As he ran to catch up with them, he wracked his brains trying to figure out when he had been so careless.

Breathlessly, he made it to his pathway as they started to hammer on his door. Thrusting himself through the mass of heaving soldiers, he reached the door just in time to watch them crash through. A wave of gray uniforms poured into his house like termites. This was a very different search to what they had done before, the first day Michael had arrived. They careened from room to room, pulling out drawers, tearing down curtains, and smashing his possessions as they went. In shock, he saw his mother's vase shatter on the floor, cast from the hand of a soldier as if it were litter to be discarded. He looked frantically around, trying to decide what to save. But he realized the only valuable thing he had was hidden in the attic.

Suddenly a stern voice greeted him from behind.

"Well, if it isn't Professor Held."

Josef turned to stare into the face of his enemy. Heinrich von Strauss marched toward him with all the intimidating pomp that his stature and uniform conveyed. The terrorizing Nazi that stood in front of him with such hate and anger in his eyes was very different to the one who'd been presented to him before. And Josef understood with a chilling realization that he had never really known this man.

The only word Josef was able to mumble out was, "Why?"

Heinrich was fast to spit back, "You know why! Because you are a traitor!"

The words lashed Josef like a slap in the face. Heinrich knew about Michael. There was no other explanation. He didn't even try to defend himself because, in seeing a group of soldiers racing up his stairs, he immediately knew it was all over. There was no point in giving the appearance of innocence anymore. But he did want to see Michael one last time.

Sprinting up the stairs and reaching the landing, as he heard the thundering feet of soldiers as they headed up the staircase to the attic, he was momentarily halted by the devastation in his home. He was numb, paralyzed. Bedroom drawers were splintered like matchsticks and he heard one of his mirrors shatter into what sounded like a million pieces. He couldn't believe it. After all they had done, after all they had come through, it was going to end like this. And when victory for the Allies, for Holland, was surely in their sights.

Within seconds of entering the attic, a soldier shouted back down to Heinrich, "In here, there is someone in here!"

Josef suddenly found the strength he needed to move. Mrs. Epstein's terrified face swam into his thoughts and he decided this time he would fight. They would not take Michael unless it was over his own dead body. Forcing himself past the soldiers on the landing and up the stairs, he pushed his way into the attic, ready for a battle. But never would he have been prepared for what greeted him in there.

As he stood staring, his mouth agape, Heinrich arrived behind him in the attic.

"What is this person doing here?" Heinrich commanded.

Josef was struck dumb. He scanned the attic, trying to understand what was going on. But he was at a total loss.

"I asked you what this person is doing here!" Heinrich spat out at him.

But it was Hannah who answered. "I am cleaning. I thought that would be obvious."

Josef again tried to make sense of it. Michael was gone, the attic was without any trace of him, and Hannah stood in the middle of the room with a duster in her hand. Thirty minutes before, when

Josef had left the house, Michael had been here. Michael's whole life had been here. Now the attic was empty, and it was if he had never been.

"Is this true?" snapped Heinrich.

"Of course it's true," responded Josef, without wavering for even a second despite his whole body trembling with shock and relief.

Heinrich commanded them to keep looking as he made his way down the stairs.

Josef fixed his eyes on Hannah as she nodded ever so slightly to signify all was well. He fought to hide the waves of relief washing through his body.

When their raid turned up nothing significant, the soldiers headed back downstairs. Heinrich commanded his troops to leave, and then turned to face Josef. "Your niece has shown her true colors, and it is only a matter of time before I find out anything you might be hiding. So be aware, this is just the beginning of your trouble."

"No," Josef coldly said, stepping forward and standing up once and for all to this bully. "I'm afraid, Herr von Strauss, that this just might be the end."

The Major looked taken aback but, instead of retaliating, turned on his heels and marched out of the house, slamming the door behind him.

When he'd left, Josef locked the door and raced to the attic. Hannah was standing at the window looking across the rooftops toward the road watching them leave. She smiled at him, just a hint of mischief at the corners of her mouth, and then turned to continue cleaning the dirty, broken window pane.

"Where is he?" Josef spluttered out.

She turned. "He got out just in time. I got word from the Resistance that your house was to be raided and I managed to get here before the soldiers. Fortunately, I still had your spare key."

"The Resistance? How do they know you know me?"

"They followed me here once while you were sick. Checking to make sure I wasn't a double agent. They found out all about you but weren't sure about my connection, until today. I'm afraid Ingrid may be in some trouble, which is what triggered your raid."

Josef sat down on the tea chest to take it all in. "Where did Michael go?"

"I'm not sure. There wasn't any time to arrange a safe house for him. And it would be too dangerous for him to come back here. You are sure to be on their watch list now." She put her hand into her pocket. "He left you this." She handed him a piece of paper and, appearing to sense his need to be alone, excused herself, saying she would make some tea.

Josef opened the hastily written note: *Find the man who used to play the piano.*

He stared at the words and knew precisely what Michael meant, but he wasn't even sure that person existed anymore. And with this current blow, he wasn't sure he would ever find him again.

Chapter Fifty-Two

Ingrid was taken from the cell and brought to an interrogation room. The room was small and dark, with just a single bulb hanging in the center of the ceiling. She was placed on a metal chair in front of a metal table. A low-level official entered the room and started to interrogate her, asking her over and over again why she had misled the Gestapo. Ingrid told him everything she knew. But still he continued to ask the same questions over and over again, until she was exhausted. After a couple of hours, without even giving her anything to eat or drink, they dragged her back to her cell and threw her inside.

Hours later, Ingrid sat quietly fuming on the very edge of the wooden bed, all her pleas to speak to Heinrich unheeded, when the heavy metal door swung open. An officer stood in the shadows. Finally, she thought, Heinrich had cleared up the mistake and they had come to release her. But then the officer stepped from the shadows into the light, and she froze as she heard a familiar voice she'd hoped she would never hear again.

"Well, if it isn't Heinrich's whore."

Terrified, she jumped to her feet, attempting to run past him out of the cell, but he caught hold of her with ease.

"Not so fast," he taunted her. "I believe you and I have some unfinished business. I think I may have to see to that tomorrow." He then shoved her back into the cell and slammed the door shut.

*

The next day, with the crunch of metal upon metal, the door to Ingrid's dark, cramped cell swung open again. Light from the hallway streamed in, blinding her. She cowered against the slimy brick wall as heavy footfalls echoed into the room. Had the monster returned for her?

But instead of her torturer, an angular-looking soldier marched into the room. His sharp-edged frame filled the doorway, snuffing out all but a halo of light around him. From the intimidating silhouette came a gruff order, "You will come with me, Fräulein."

Reluctantly, Ingrid gathered herself up from her bed and slowly shuffled toward him. Everything in her body hurt from a rough night's sleep and inside her spirit felt crushed. She urgently needed to find Heinrich; why had he not come for her? He couldn't know she had been arrested and was probably sick with worry. She wanted his comfort; she needed desperately to feel his arms around her.

She attempted to straighten out her soiled, creased clothes. The soldier lost his patience, grabbing her roughly by the arm and yanking her out into the dreary corridor, the same one she had been dragged down the night before.

"My fiancé, Heinrich von Strauss, will be very angry with you when he hears what you have all done to me," she rasped, her lips and throat cracked from a night without water.

The guard sneered. "Major von Strauss is the person who instructed me to get you. He knows all about what you have done."

"Heinrich is here?" Ingrid cried out with relief. "Oh thank God."

The guard continued to drag her at a clip and seemed to relish his next biting revelation. "He has been here for hours. He only just got around to dealing with you."

Ingrid was confused. Hours? If he was here, why had he not come himself to get her?

They continued down the dismal corridor toward a different room than the one she had been interrogated in the night before. A nagging concern gnawed her insides. Something was wrong.

The guard opened a door and roughly pushed her into another gloomy room that smelt of sweat and mildew. Once again, a single light bulb dangled on a chain from the ceiling, where a wayward moth tapped an ominous rhythm; its fluttering wings thrumming like fingertips on a window pane. As her eyes acclimatized to the darkness, she noticed this room was bigger than the first, but held a similar metal chair in the center of the room.

At the far end, three officers were seated behind a long, sterile desk. Her heart leaped. Heinrich was one of them.

"Heinrich!" she cried out hysterically.

But he didn't look up or acknowledge her. He was engrossed in writing notes.

"Ah, Miss Held," stated one of the other SS officers dryly, peering up at her.

Ingrid moved toward the table imploringly. "Heinrich, it's me, Ingrid!"

But Heinrich didn't waver from his task.

"You will only speak when you're spoken to," the third officer yelled sharply. "You'll sit down and listen to what we have to say."

She was rooted to the spot, paralyzed by a new kind of fear, a fear that was much more acute—the fear of rejection. Responding to his superior's request, the guard forced Ingrid down into the chair.

A silent desperation weighed on her, like a heavy, damp fog that chilled her to the bone, along with the feeling of utter bewilderment. Why was Heinrich ignoring her? What had she done that was so bad they were treating her like a criminal?

The first officer spoke again, his eyes fixed on her with disdain. "I believe you were interrogated last night by the Gestapo?"

Ingrid shuddered with the memory.

"Yes," she responded meekly. Maybe if she got this over with quickly, Heinrich would take her home. She reasoned that he obviously had to keep up this charade of indifference toward her in front of the other officers.

"You were accused of working with the Resistance to cause a diversionary tactic that resulted in one of our trains being destroyed," he stated coldly, reading from a document.

"I don't understand," she said in confusion. When she'd been arrested, she had heard the explosion but wasn't sure that the Resistance mission had succeeded. "As I told the officer last night, I obtained information that the Resistance would be there, but they weren't. How could I have known why the train blew up where it did?"

The third officer got to his feet and marched toward her, towering over her in such a menacing way that she flinched in her chair.

"We ask the questions. You were present during a deception which cost us lives and a significant advancement against our enemies. How do we know you were not behind this? You say you had obtained information about the Resistance. But why did you not come straight to your commanding officer with this information?"

She looked across at Heinrich as his eyes flicked up briefly to meet hers. The chill she felt from his gaze shook her to the core. They conveyed so much hatred for her. She still couldn't understand what they thought she had done.

"I wasn't, I swear. I thought I would be helping. I was going to try and find them myself then call you to arrest them. I wanted that train to make it to the depot." She swallowed hard, looking past the officer to Heinrich again. "I know how important the V2 missiles are to the war effort. I wouldn't have jeopardized that for anything."

"We would like to believe you, Fräulein," the officer said, "but there are a few things we don't understand. How did you know when the train would be arriving at the depot? That information is top secret."

Ingrid swallowed hard again, distracted by the moth. She watched as it beat against the light bulb, the very thing it desired over and over again, only to get burned for its trouble. She knew that in telling the truth, she could also get Heinrich into trouble. But if she didn't tell the truth, they could think she was Resistance.

She looked down at her hands and whispered, "I got it from a book in the safe, in Heinrich's… I mean, Major von Strauss's office."

Heinrich jumped to his feet and marched toward her. She looked up at him, desperate for any kind of reassurance that he still loved her. But he glared at her with nothing but contempt burning in his eyes.

"What were you doing in my safe?" he demanded. "How dare you go in there without permission?"

"I was trying to help, Heinrich. We had this idea of finding the Resistance for you. We had a lead that they would be at the place alongside the railway to blow it up. I wanted to stop them. You have to believe me."

Heinrich raised his hand as if he was going to strike her, and she recoiled like a fearful animal. But he stopped and spat at her, "You disgust me."

She looked up at him, trying desperately to see anything of the man she had fallen in love with, but all she saw was a beast. A monster created by the desperate and deplorable acts that he had become accustomed to inflicting on others on a daily basis. That's when it struck her. The ideals that they had all felt so pompous about, so self-righteous indulging in, the superior world they were creating for the fatherland, was nothing more than a tragic illusion. An illusion that shattered in front of her as she looked up into his terrifying eyes. She realized in that instant what they had all become. This war had done this to all of them, and she despised it. She despised herself.

Heinrich turned and strode back to the desk and sat back down. The third officer stepped forward. His tone cold and cutting. He picked up from his last question as if the exchange between her and Heinrich hadn't taken place.

"You said *we*, Fräulein. Who is *we*?"

"My friend Vi and I," she stated solemnly. "Did you have to interrogate her too?"

The officer quirked an eyebrow. "Vi? Who is this Vi?"

"She works with me, with us, at the office. Violette. She was helping me."

"Helping you?" he scoffed. "It appears that you were misinformed about her being your friend. Violette Schmit, who was in your office, is a member of the Resistance. She disappeared yesterday, and the place she lived in was empty. When you were picked up, all of the working staff in Major von Strauss's office were checked, and she, Fräulein, has gone."

Ingrid felt distraught. Vi was gone and also working for the Resistance? Her world had gone mad. This new revelation multiplied her anguish and pain. Did no one in the world care about her? She just couldn't believe what she was hearing.

The officer continued matter-of-factly. "Through our intensive investigations, we have now established this Violette as the renegade known as the Cuckoo. She had left Rotterdam months ago, where she had created much chaos for us. She was smuggled into Amsterdam and placed right under our noses. Very plucky, but also very foolish, as now we know exactly who she is. We will find her, don't you worry. She will pay for her crimes. Then she apparently tricked you into finding out the delivery day and time of the train for her. This resulted in our fuel for our V2 missiles being destroyed by your foolishness."

Ingrid started to weep as the weight of it all overwhelmed her. "I'm so sorry. I was just trying to help."

The second officer pierced her with his steely gaze. "We should shoot you for this terrible indiscretion, but knowing the Cuckoo's skills and the work you have done for us over the years, plus taking into consideration other factors..." He glanced over at Heinrich, who was looking down at the desk, his face burning with fury. "We have decided in this instance to be lenient in your case. You will remain in custody until we decide what to do with you. Do you understand?"

Ingrid nodded through her whimpers.

The officers stood and exited the room. As Heinrich passed her, she grabbed at him, gripping hold of the fabric of his trouser leg. "Heinrich," she wailed, "I love you."

He recoiled from her as if she were a serpent, slapping her hand away from him.

She reached out to him again in desperation. "But I am your fiancée!"

He stretched his hand toward her, and for a moment she thought he was going to take her hand. Instead, he roughly pulled the ring from her finger.

"You are a traitor," he spat back. "You are nothing to me." And with that, he strode from the room.

The guard pulled her up again by the arm and attempted to drag her back out the door. But her legs collapsed from under her and he had to carry her. From deep within her gut came a sound she could not control, not unlike a wounded animal snared in a painful trap. Her wail reverberated around the stark corridor as he dragged her back to her cell.

"You will have to stay here until the right documentation is signed," he spat at her as he pushed her roughly back into the cell.

She collapsed on the floor, blubbering. Defensively she wrapped her hands around her stomach.

The guard moved toward the door and hesitated for a moment to look back at her. His lips curled in a sneer. "You shouldn't feel so bad about the major, Fräulein. He would have rejected you once this war is over anyway. I'm pretty sure his wife and two children are waiting eagerly for his return to Germany."

Ingrid couldn't stand it any longer. Unable to hear one more dreadful thing, she pressed her hands hard against her ears and howled as she was plunged back into the darkness with the clang of the heavy cell door.

Chapter Fifty-Three

Elke stood in the kitchen and looked around her houseboat. It had been months since she'd been here. And the place felt sad and unloved. With her brother-in-law away fighting the war, her sister had been grateful for Elke's help taking care of her children as they pooled their rations. It had been so hard without Michael. Even to this day Elke felt the loss of him. But she was grateful for her loving family, and with the joy and innocence of her sister's young children to buoy her up, she had survived, somehow.

However, whenever she came back to visit the houseboat, she always felt a little heartbroken. It was still alive with too many painful memories of Michael. His poems scattered about the room, a pile of his books he had managed to smuggle in, his clothes in her wardrobe, his socks in her drawer, his razor, dusty and discarded on her bathroom shelf.

Leaning against the bedroom wall was her guitar, placed there the last time he'd played it. Sometimes she would run her fingers along the strings, hoping that a little of his presence still lingered there.

Elke had, finally, changed the sheets on the bed, but the pillow-case he had last slept on went with her everywhere. Though it was probably just in her imagination, she believed she could still smell the fragrance of soap from the final time he'd laid down his head.

Sighing again, Elke rolled up her sleeves, preparing to clear away the debris from the latest bombing campaign. As she did, she thought about the first time she'd visited the houseboat after Michael had disappeared.

She'd kept away for an extended period of time to be safe and had finally made her way back nearly a month later. Opening the door after such a long absence, the first thing to greet her had been the smell of mildew and rotting food. The stack of dirty dishes they had left in the sink was covered in green, furry mold. It had been the perfect illustration of how she had felt. Time had stopped for her too, and nothing was left in her world but decay. She'd looked at her moldy dishes, and instead of washing them, she'd thrown them away. Elke knew this was extravagant in wartime but was unable to bear the sadness of the last time she and Michael had been together.

After clearing the bomb dust from the latest raid, she looked about the houseboat, so much of the furniture she had sold during the last winter in exchange for food. It had been a desperate time, and she and her sister had gone to any extreme to get them something to eat. Things had become so desperate, and she hated hearing her sister's children going to sleep crying with the pains of hunger.

As Elke searched through her belongings, she found a picture of her mother. And she thought about her, then. The houseboat had belonged to her, and Elke had inherited it. An excellent painter, her mother Christina had used it as an artist's studio, especially after her father had died following a short illness ten years before. The photo had caught her in the midst of painting, sitting in front of her easel, a paintbrush in one hand to capture the spirit of her subject. Always self-assured, she had instilled in her girls the need to seek truth and beauty and love, and always to be brave. Christina's wry smile and intense gaze reached and assured Elke that everything was going to be all right. Acknowledging her mother's encouraging smile, she nodded. Maybe one day she'd come back and live here when all this was over. Maybe one day she'd find the joy in this place again.

All at once, Elke felt the ground shift beneath her, and as the houseboat swayed slightly to the right, she reflected that she'd entirely forgotten the feeling of living on the water. A larger boat had probably created a rolling wake, she surmised. But when it came a second time, Elke wondered if someone was actually on the gangplank. She was curious, as no one knew she would be there that day.

Going back into the kitchen, she looked out of the window but couldn't see anybody about on the towpath. It was quiet. Elke went back to the bedroom to continue her search when a sudden chill found its way down her neck and around the back of her legs, as if someone had opened the door. Turning back into the kitchen, she saw a silhouette framed in the doorway.

Elke should have been fearful but because she had seen him so many times in her dreams, she didn't react right away, but instead blinked, trying to clear her vision. And when the shadowy figure stepped forward into the light, the breath caught in her throat. This person really did look just like Michael, just as she had always pictured him standing there one day. This person was thinner, older, but it was an uncanny resemblance.

Her next thoughts happened in quick succession. She first convinced herself it was a trick of the light, someone else that looked like him; that it was her imagination, lack of food, anything but the truth. Then she'd questioned her imagination, as he was older, more assured, his early boyishness gone. Why would she imagine him differently than how she'd remembered him? Elke finally settled on him being a hallucination. But all notions of that disappeared as he rushed to her and took her in his arms. Taking her breath away, he enveloped her and covered her face with frantic kisses, running his hand through her hair and muttering in half sentences.

"I was going to be calm… give you a chance to get used to the idea that I was alive… let you tell me about the man you are in love with. But I had nowhere else to go. I have been staying… somewhere and the Nazis came. And my only thought was to get back to you. And then, when I saw you, I couldn't stop myself. Forgive me, sweet Elke. You can slap my face if you want… but I fear I cannot stop."

Elke responded to his kisses in kind but was struck dumb; she was afraid to speak in case this incredible hallucination disappeared. She breathed in the scent of his skin, was enraptured by the feel of his mouth on her face, his hair brushing her cheek, his arms crushing her body. Slowly it started to sink in, and finally she pulled away to look closely at him.

She found words. "Is it really you?"

Michael smiled, and then she knew. It was him. Her Michael. Back from the dead and in her arms.

She couldn't believe it. She hugged him so tightly that her arms started to lose sensation, but she dared not let him go. She couldn't get close enough to him, wanting their bodies to meld together, wanting to climb under his skin and stay there, for the rest of her life. For the first time in over four years, Elke felt a burning desire course through her body, and she finally felt alive, again.

After what seemed like an eternity she released her grip. "I missed you so much," she whispered into his neck.

He pulled back, and she felt his body stiffen a little, the pain evident on his face.

"I know there is someone else," he responded, his voice cracking. "I just wanted to believe for a moment that what we'd had was real, that somewhere in your heart there was still a small space for me. And even if we can't be together, I just wanted you to know that I never gave up and that I always loved you."

A chill ran through her body. "What are you talking about, Michael?"

"I saw you in the woods," he said flatly, the pain creating agony on his face. "I saw you kissing someone there."

Elke wracked her brains for what he could mean. When had she been in the woods with a man? She was always there alone. Then suddenly she remembered, and her face flushed. The time she had been with Helmut.

"You were there in the woods that night?"

He nodded.

"Oh my God. Why didn't you tell me you were there?"

"It was a little difficult while you were kissing another man," he responded, the smallest hint of a smile drifting across his lips. "Besides, he was taller, blonder, and more Aryan-looking than me," he joked. In seeing how mortified she was, he then added more seriously, "I did tell you to be happy. How could I take that from you?"

"You don't understand," she spluttered out. "That was a misunderstanding. Helmut and I are over. In fact, we barely began. He wanted a relationship, but I did not love him. I could not love him because I was in love with someone else. And it was unfair to him to keep the relationship going."

She saw the relief then, and she felt his tense body slacken in her arms.

"Michael, I was then, and I am now, still head over heels in love with you. I was so scared that you were dead and that I would never truly feel happy again."

Elke led him into the bedroom then, and on her bed, they started to make love. Gone was the intense passion of their youth and the last time they had been together. This time everything was precious. And as the world around them became timeless, they took great care caressing each other. His mouth brushed her with tiny, gentle kisses that searched and covered every inch of her face and neck. Finally, he kissed her slowly and deeply on the lips, and she kept her eyes open to take in every contour of his face. As their kissing intensified, she felt the thrill of pure joy, and warm tears of ecstasy and relief ran down her face and mingled with his own, dripping from his chin and running down between her breasts.

Slowly, they began to undress. When he nervously tried to unbutton her blouse, she replaced his shaking fingers with her own to complete the task. Once they were both naked, they touched and stroked every inch of one another, marveling at every discovery as if it were for the first time. Until, unable to hold back any longer, they made love over and over again until they were exhausted. Then, entwined tightly in each other's arms, they fell into a deep, blissful sleep.

*

A few hours later, someone hammered on the front door. Sitting bolt upright, fear coursed through Elke's body as her mind flashed back in horror. Surely fate couldn't be this cruel to them twice.

"I must have been followed," Michael stated, his voice only above a whisper.

Terrified, she clung to him. "You're not leaving me again," she hissed defiantly. "I couldn't ever be without you. Where you go, I will go, and whatever happens to us, we'll face it together."

He kissed her passionately then, as if he didn't have the strength to let her go either.

The thumping on the door came again. They started to dress, watching one another intently, not wanting to waste a moment thinking of anything else. Whoever was on the other side of the door could not be a friend. Every Jewish person they knew was gone, and her sister never came down to the boat. With a calm assurance, she realized that if it was the Nazis coming to take him, she was just overwhelmingly grateful for this one last time with him, and they would face whatever it was together. Slowly, hand in hand, they walked to the door, and she opened it.

Someone stepped inside, and Elke gasped when she saw who it was.

"So this is why you never wanted me! You had him, hiding somewhere, and by the looks of him I am guessing he is a Jew. I'm sure the authorities will be very excited to meet the very last Jew in Amsterdam." Helmut's face was red with fury. "I went to see you at your sister's house. She said you were down here. I suppose she has no idea either."

Helmut turned to leave, and Elke strode up to him.

"I wouldn't tell anyone if I was you. It could be very bad for you."

Helmut turned and scowled at her.

Elke continued. "I know what you have been doing through the war, giving art to the Nazis, and when this is over—and we know it will be soon—I think there will be some Allied authorities who will be most excited to meet you."

"You can't prove anything," he spat back.

"Ah, and that is where you are wrong. The last time we hung a picture for you in your apartment, when you were in Berlin, do you remember, you gave us the key to hang it for you? Well, someone had to go with the art to supervise and while I was there I needed the bathroom and managed to find some very interesting reading in your bedroom—correspondence, receipts, addresses. I must admit to keeping a couple of interesting documents just in case I ever needed to alert the authorities when we won this war."

Helmut looked crestfallen. "You would have done that? To me? Why? This was just business, surely you understand that. I loved you!"

"Helmut, you know as well as I do that those were Dutch masterpieces. They are our country's treasures—stolen and acquired or sold at a fraction of their worth."

He became defensive. "Why is that my fault? Isn't that just business?"

Elke shook her head. "Where is your humanity, and sense of honor? And now you plan to wreck my life too? I never thought even you could stoop so low. I always intended to report you, but now I have a proposition. Help Michael and me escape to France or England and when we are safe I will write to my sister and tell her where those papers are hidden and have her burn them."

He eyed her nervously.

"Sneak a Jew out, that is impossible."

"Surely you have made friends at the checkpoints. They know you, and what you are doing. On your next run into Germany, drop us close to Allied lines, take us hidden in your van below the pictures. And no one but God will know about your crimes."

*

Two days later, at what would be their final checkpoint, something unusual transpired. Up until that point, the van had stopped, they had heard Helmut talking in a concise and fast back-and-forth exchange, and then they had continued again. But this time, they heard Helmut open the door and get out and slam it behind him. Michael could hear the muffled conversation going on outside of the van, but had no idea what was being conveyed. Even in the darkness he could see the fear in Elke's eyes. He reached out to her and took her hand and squeezed it, mouthing the words, "I love you."

She nodded, but both of them recognized that this was not a good sign. Suddenly, the rear door of van was wrenched open. Bright sunlight streamed in and almost blinded them, but in silhouette, they could see German soldiers pointing rifles at them.

"Get out. Get out, both of you."

Stunned, they scrambled out of the van and Michael looked across at Helmut, knowing at once he had never intended to take them to freedom.

All at once, Helmut blurted out. "He's a Jew; this one is a Jew! He threatened me and forced my girlfriend to stay with him in the back of the van; otherwise he said he would kill me."

Helmut's eyes were wild with his lie, and his voice was high-pitched and shrill. Michael looked across at Elke, her own eyes wild with a mixture of fear and outrage.

She turned on Helmut. "How dare you, Helmut? How can you be this cruel?"

Suddenly two soldiers seized hold of Michael, and they rough-housed him toward the building at the checkpoint as another officer took hold of Elke's arm.

Helmut called out, "She can come with me. It is not her fault; she's my girlfriend." He sounded pitiful.

Even in her terror, Elke found the words she spat out, "He is not my boyfriend. I do not know him. Obviously, I've never known him."

What took place after that, was in such quick succession that Michael wasn't sure it was real for a moment. He had turned to glance at Elke, her rapid movement catching his attention. He saw her grappling with the officer who had hold of her arm. Evidently the guard, assuming he had the easier prisoner, had not grasped her tightly enough.

Suddenly, she whirled around at her captor and snatched his rifle from him, and then cracked him on the skull with it, after which he slumped to the ground. The two guards who were holding Michael in front of her pivoted and for a moment, time stood still as they all stood in shock, taking in the scene.

That was, everyone except Elke. Masterfully she pointed the gun at one of the soldiers holding Michael, and a shot rang out, followed by the scream of the man who clutched at his stomach. He sank to his knees and fell forward in pain. As the other guard reached for his weapon to fire back at Elke, for a moment he let go of Michael.

She cried out to him, "Run, Michael, run!" As she dropped the gun and sprinted away from the checkpoint. Michael, now free of the officer's restraint, raced behind her.

"Elke, Elke stop! We can't do this. They want me, not you. Please come back."

But Elke just kept running. It was a magnificent day, the sun was high and warm, and as she leaped through a field of tall grass, feeling like she was racing to the very edges of Holland itself, there was something about the scene that felt timeless to Michael as he chased her. His thoughts returned momentarily to their initial meeting, as they had raced through the streets of Amsterdam on her bicycle, her head thrown back as she laughed, and him pedaling at speed, the wind rushing through their hair, and for just a moment he wondered if they would make it, if the Nazis would let them go.

Two shots rang out, and he watched her body crumple to the ground. The terror that started in his stomach ripped through his body in an animalistic scream he didn't recognize as his own voice. When he reached where her body had fallen he dropped to his knees and looked into her eyes, that were filled with panic and pain. He pulled her into his arms. "No! Elke, no!" He held her even closer, trying to use his fingers to stop the bleeding gushing from a wound in her chest, but he knew it was futile. Her breathing was coming in fast ragged spurts, and he could see her life slipping from her.

Somewhere in the distance, he heard someone screaming to him, yelling at him to drop her, come back, or they would shoot him, too. He didn't care, didn't care about anything but looking into her beautiful face.

"I love you, Elke," he whispered.

She gently nodded her response, unable to speak.

He knew that he had to be close to the border and no doubt Allied troops, maybe even a doctor. He picked her up tenderly in his arms and carried her, wading through the grass as the angry voices called out to him again.

Another shot rang out, and the pain that seared through his body was unimaginable. He didn't realize he could feel such pain exploding inside of him. He dropped to his knees, breathless, knowing someone had shot him too. But he didn't let her go. Holding her tightly to him, he clung to her, they would die together. It would only last a moment, he told himself, and all the pain, and all the suffering would be gone. And he could be with Elke forever.

He fell forward, still holding her tightly, and the last thing he remembered before he blacked out was hearing her stilted breath in his ear as she rasped, "At least we found each other again. And I would rather die in your arms than live without you."

Chapter Fifty-Four

The echoing loneliness Josef had felt after losing Sarah returned to haunt him with the loss once more of Michael. Everything around him now was a painful reminder, and he felt desolate and bereft. The disappearance of Ingrid after his house was raided had added to his concern, and even though he had asked and searched for her, the Nazis acted as if she had never existed. But the loss of Michael was what haunted him most. He wandered the house, mainly at night, remembering everything they had been through together.

The kitchen, the place where they had celebrated Hanukkah; the bathroom, where hot water had brought his friend back to life; the front room, where they had first talked and grieved together; and the attic, where they had formed the bond of the most profound friendship.

As he wandered aimlessly from room to room, he was tortured by how empty his life felt without someone in it to care for. In the middle of the night, when he could not sleep with the weight of his insignificance, he would often find solace walking the attic boards, staring through the cracked pane, across the red rooftops often bathed in moonlight, reading Michael's poems.

Opening Michael's journal, he continued to read his poem "Invincible."

> … *I am battle-worn without lifting a weapon*
> *And scarred without a cut to my flesh*
> *But still I will lift up my head. Still I will not give up the fight.*

Josef was surprised at how Michael's words comforted him and gave him great solace in his darkest moments. Furthermore, he saw with true clarity now what Michael's imprisonment had been like. And that, while he had been free to come and go, he too had been a captive, but of his own making; enslaved to the guilt of the past, invisible shackles restraining him from embracing any good things of this world. And somehow, the words of the young poet became the keys to him understanding the walls that had imprisoned him.

That evening, something miraculous took place. Reading Michael's poetry once more, the tears started to flow freely down his cheeks. Removing his spectacles, he wept openly: first with deep sadness of what he had lost, then with tears of overwhelming joy of what he had gained. Jumping to his feet, he bellowed out to the world through the cracked attic window pane, "I understand! I understand! Sarah, I understand! I know now what you tried to tell me and what I couldn't hear. You were right. Music and poetry… That is the real formula.'

He thought of his father and the pages and pages of poetic words committed to his own memory. Fresh tears rolled down his cheeks as he started to recite verses that he had heard his father utter with such reverence. And he realized that it had taken him many years, but those words he had read over and over again had finally completed their long, slow journey from his head to his heart.

And as he gazed up through the glass pane toward the half-crescent of a new moon, he pictured Michael, hoping he was somewhere safe and warm. Now he knew for sure why he had been sent to his house that night so many years before. He had hoped that Josef would save him, when in fact Josef had been the one who had needed saving. When he'd taken in that young student so long ago, he hadn't known it, but he was about to become the pupil and Michael was to be his teacher. Without Josef realizing it, the young man's passion and enthusiasm for love and life had slowly worn down the bricks and mortar of his internment, like a relentless ocean on a seawall. Even in the confinement of an attic, Michael had drunk larger and deeper from the well of life than

Josef ever had. He had taken all of his fearless vitality and lust for life and had honed it into his craft. And as Josef dwelt on this, it humbled him to realize how much of life he had been asleep to. Numbly moving through a world of hurt and sadness, he hadn't taken even a moment to absorb anything of good around him. And there was so much good, even in the depths of a desperate war.

All at once his thoughts turned to Hannah, her smile, her eyes, the thought of her body close to his. He realized with great surprise how desperately he needed to touch her and feel her close to him. For the first time as he thought on these things it was not coupled with guilt toward the memory of Sarah, but just a need to feel the passion and the love Michael had so often captured on the page, like his love for Elke, and indeed Josef's love for Sarah. Hannah's mother had just died so he wanted to be respectful and wait, the timing never seemed to be right, but he would tell her how he really felt, soon.

Every morning he woke up with the hope of Michael returning, and every night he went to sleep feeling lonelier than ever. But in between those hours, he made a conscious effort to be thankful. Thankful for the life he had been given and thankful for everything he had learned. When his isolation threatened to overwhelm him, he turned to Michael's poems, and the poetry Michael had loved. The words, so beautifully crafted together, somehow brought a stillness to his thumping heart and a feeling of comfort and relief as he was gently coaxed from his darkness.

He had seen Hannah once since Michael had disappeared, and he ached to spend some time alone with her to confess his feelings to her, but as the Allies advanced on Amsterdam, her work in the Underground kept her busy. When he'd seen her for that fleeting moment, he had asked if there was any word of Michael, but there was no news. As far as she knew, none of the Underground had helped him or even made contact with him. The fear that he was dead was left unsaid. It was a thought that threatened to crush him. But he also had to trust in a higher power, the higher power that had kept the young man alive until now, from the inscription in the book of Rilke's poems to the illness and their recovery, to his miraculous escape. Surely a person who had been kept alive by such unique twists of fate was destined for much greater things in this world?

Chapter Fifty-Five

One morning, while walking down his road to take some exercise, Josef stopped to watch the migrating birds returning and noticed, with great joy, that the one tree left in his neighborhood where so many had been cut down for firewood was budding with the pink-and-white flowers of spring.

As he approached his house, he noticed Mrs. Epstein's piano was still outside. Tucked well under the eaves of her house, it had been spared from the worst of the weather, but still, it was a sad sight, pushed out onto the uneven pavement, bereft and impoverished. Stopping in front of it, he stared at it for a long moment, remembering all the beauty of the music it had brought to him. Now it was missing a wheel, and its highly polished mahogany veneer was cracked, smoky white in places. Sadness seeped from its every corner with no loving owner to take care of it.

All at once, something bubbled up inside of him, something that compelled him. He went inside and arrived back a few minutes later, in his hand the crumpled sheet music he'd pulled from his bushes four years before.

Tenderly, he lifted the lid and, placing the music in the music holder, seated himself on the piano stool. He paused for a moment to close his eyes in a silent prayer as Chopin's spellbinding nocturnes and Mrs. Epstein's lively piano concertos played in his thoughts. He thought of Michael's last words to him in his note: "Find the man who used to play the piano."

Opening his eyes, he ran his hand along the smooth surface of the keyboard, gently caressing and sampling a few notes, and finding it miraculously still almost in tune. And as the reverberating sound rewarded him, he felt the joy of the resonance that pulsed through his fingers to delight him.

Then, following Mrs. Epstein's spidery handwritten script, he started to play her composition. Slowly and cautiously at first, wondering if his middle-aged fingers would remember and be nimble enough to find their place. But as they sank into their familiarity, he opened himself up to reckless abandonment, bringing life to the music on the page and playing her musical creation as though his heart was breaking. Its lively, dancing rhythm stretched fingers of warmth out into the chilly afternoon, filling every corner, every space of the dark and sadness with its love, light, and hope of a better tomorrow.

Up and down the street, people couldn't help but be drawn to their windows and open wide their front doors to huddle together on their doorsteps. Even on the street corner, the two soldiers paused from checking papers, their bleak faces lifted upwards in apparent remembrance; whisked back to a world beyond the bounds of war, a time and place where they all were neither hunted nor hunter, neither friend nor foe, but just human beings dwelling together in a world of beauty.

Josef continued to play. After Mrs. Epstein's composition, then every tune he could remember—Chopin, Mozart, Beethoven. Anything that danced its way from his heart to his fingers he delighted in, indulging himself until he was utterly spent. At the end, he was tired but overjoyed, and somewhere in between Mozart and Beethoven, he felt himself smiling.

Resting his hands on the keyboard, he whispered to the piano, "Thank you, Mrs. Epstein. Thank you for your beautiful music."

Then he was struck by a thought. Even years after her death, she still somehow managed to reach forward into his present and once again give him a gift. It wasn't lost on him that he was still powerless to give her anything back in return.

With that thought, he gathered the music reverently from the stand and, closing the lid, ran his hands once more over the smooth veneer. Then, he gently mounted the steps to his home, stood on his top step, and turned to look out onto his street. "My Amsterdam!" he yelled out into the frozen air. "*My Amsterdam!*" he proclaimed again to the sky as he lifted his eyes heavenwards to smile at the two women who had given and gone before him.

Chapter Fifty-Six

May 5th, 1945

One morning, Ingrid stumbled out of her bunk and moved toward the cell door. The jail had been silent overnight, which confused her. Usually, the echoing footsteps of marching feet down the corridor and slamming doors kept her awake, but the night before her world had been silent. As yet, no one had come to her cell with food, as the guards usually did in the morning. Though "food" was hardly what she could call it—a handful of rice if she was lucky, or a piece of stale, dark bread. The rations that even the party had known from time to time on the outside seemed luxurious to what they gave prisoners in jail.

She placed her ear against the door, listening; all was silent. She put her fingers on the handle and noticed that it gave way underneath her grasp. Normally locked from the outside, now it was moving freely. Gingerly, she slid it to its fully open position and the creaking door swung open. Why had they not locked it?

Looking tentatively down the corridor, she heard hasty footsteps approaching. Withdrawing back into her cell, she kept the door cracked a little so she could see the person coming, afraid to move out in case it was a guard. She had already found out first-hand what happened when she was disobedient, and her jaw still didn't feel aligned after the slap she had received for answering back to one of her captors. But as she kept her eyes on the man approaching her, it was apparent this wasn't a Nazi. He was dressed in disheveled civilian clothes, walking with a slight limp, and his bruised face had more than a day's worth of beard growth. Hesitantly, she opened the door farther, so she could get a better view.

Across his cheek was an angry, red scar, and when he caught sight of Ingrid, he smiled, showing two cracked teeth. He spoke to her in perfect Dutch.

"Hello, fellow prisoner."

She opened the door a little wider, apprehensive. "Where are the guards?"

"Gone." He beamed. "Scampered like rats in the middle of the night, left us. At least they left the doors open. I'm guessing that the Allies have made their way to Amsterdam and they got out before they had to pay the price of their crimes."

Ingrid dared not to hope. Could she be free? Could she, at last, be free of this nightmare? She tried to figure out in her head how long she had been in jail. Was it a month? Was it six weeks? One day was the same as the next, and one week had turned into another. She was numb and cold after weeks of deprivation in squalor and the heartache of losing Heinrich and everything that she held so dear.

Slowly making her way out of her cell, she noticed more people starting to filter out into the corridor, all looking as bewildered and disheveled as herself.

"This way," someone shouted farther down the hall.

Straightening her dirty, creased clothes, she followed the group toward the open door.

As Ingrid shuffled outside on her unsteady legs, she couldn't believe she was free. Her eyes squinted as she came out into the sunshine for the first time in over a month. Her bones ached, and when she looked down at her body, she knew she'd lost a lot of weight. She couldn't wait to get home.

All at once she realized that she couldn't go back home. Home had been Heinrich's apartment. Where would she go? She didn't know. Maybe she could go to one of her friends from where she used to live. Ingrid hadn't seen them for a long time, but there was no one else. Vi was gone, and there was no Heinrich. Suddenly her world had become very small.

Carefully she started to make her way down the street to the area she'd left so long ago. Maybe she could ask one of the women in the block of flats she had once lived in to let her in to take a bath. Halfway there, a woman she'd known from her old neighborhood recognized her.

"Ingrid? Ingrid Held?" she said, the sarcasm strong in her tone. "Here is Ingrid Held," she shouted to a group of women who were with her. "Ingrid Held loved the Nazis."

Ingrid was bewildered. Couldn't they see she'd suffered at the hands of the Nazis too? She stood frozen as the angry mob moved to surround her. Too hungry and weak to run, she had no other choice but to await her fate.

The woman grabbed her by the wrist and pulled her into the crowd. "Ingrid Held loved the Nazis. She even slept with one of them, said she was going to marry him."

The women surrounded her, shouting and screaming names at her and pulling at her body, pulling at her clothes, pushing her, slapping her. Ingrid couldn't believe this was happening. She'd spent all this time in jail, and now that she was free, she was being beaten yet again.

Suddenly she was thrust into a chair, and somebody came toward her face with scissors. What were they going to do to her? Were they going to cut her face? She closed her eyes tightly as the nightmare unfolding in front of her overwhelmed her. But instead of her face, the woman with the scissors grabbed hold of a chunk of her hair and started to cut savagely all the way to the root.

Ingrid tried to scream again, but no sound came out. Nothing. She was too shocked. She waited in horror as she felt another woman take a razor to the back of her head. All the time they taunted her, screaming about their husbands, boyfriends, and children who had suffered at the hands of the Nazis while she had lived under their protection.

"We shall color you orange, the color of the Resistance so everybody will know you are a traitor," said another woman with an angry glint in her eye. "You, Nazi lover, you will be shown for who you really are."

A stream of hot, salty tears ran down her cheeks as she felt the weight of what she had done become real to her, and she watched in anguish as another woman approached her with a rusted can of paint.

*

As he approached his home, Josef had been thinking of Hannah. With the war over there was nothing to hold him back from pursuing a relationship with her, or at least finding out if she had any feelings for him. He was in a jubilant mood, buoyant with the celebrations of the end of the war, marveling at the atmosphere all around him. The streets had been flooded with British and Canadian soldiers, and people from all over the city had come out to welcome them into Amsterdam. The Allies had been handing out food packages on the street, and he was excited to get home and eat something nourishing. But as he opened the front door, something didn't feel right. Carefully, he walked into his house and closed the door. There seemed to be a draft. Where was it coming from? Maybe he'd left a window open, he thought, as he slowly moved about the downstairs.

When he entered the kitchen, he realized what was wrong. A small window had been smashed and somebody had forced open his back door. At first, he was concerned about looters, but after a quick investigation of his house, nothing seemed disturbed. Not that the Nazis had left a lot to be stolen after they had raided his home the month before. He continued to move through his house hesitantly. Then a thought hit him. Michael. What if it was Michael? Hastily he raced upstairs to the attic. But only a hollow emptiness greeted him. With a heavy heart, he moved back down to the kitchen to prepare food.

All at once, a thud came from behind him, and he noticed Dantes crouched down on the floor peering at the pantry in a curious way. With all of his senses on edge, Josef moved toward the door. Unlatching it carefully, he looked inside the darkened cupboard.

Someone was there, he was sure of it now. He could see their outline and hear the sound of air rushing in and out of their lungs in short, hot spurts. It had to be his former student. Flinging open the door, he cried out Michael's name. But his joy was short-lived as he flicked on the lights and realized he was wrong. The person cowering in the corner was not his dark-haired friend at all but someone he didn't recognize. They looked terrified, painfully thin, their clothes ripped and smeared with mud, and their face a mass of cuts and bruises. But what was most shocking was their head. It appeared that where hair used to be there was now stubble that was painted bright orange.

Suddenly, with a jolt, he realized who it was. "Ingrid?" he asked haltingly. "Is that... you?"

Crouching down so as not to scare her, he held out his hand, as if approaching a timid animal. In seeing him, she howled uncontrollably, reaching up for him to hold her. He took her in his arms and rocked her gently, the smell of paint almost overpowering him.

"What happened to you? Where were you for so long?" he asked her gently. But she could do and say nothing in response but sob in his arms.

He took her into the front room and placed her in the same chair Michael had sat in so many years before. Giving her a glass of brandy, he brought down a blanket to wrap her in. Even though the weather was positively balmy outside, she was shivering, so he lit a fire and prepared food, waiting for her to calm.

She sipped at her brandy and tasted a little of the food. Her sobbing subsided. Then she started to tell him the tale of what had happened to her.

Josef listened quietly to her story and thought about the sadness of her life, and compassion welled up in his heart. As much as she'd been stubborn and foolish following the Nazis, he could see that she'd paid a hard price for her decisions.

She turned her watery eyes toward him. "And the worst of it all," she croaked, "is Heinrich no longer loves me, and apparently, he has a wife and children in Germany that he has gone back to." Her voice cracked with the sheer agony, and she crumpled forward, weeping into her hands again.

Josef nodded. He had suspected something like that. Whenever they talked about Germany, a look had crossed that man's face, and Josef had been aware of it.

After she finished her drink, he decided to run her a bath. She struggled up to the bathroom and sat huddled next to him. As he poured in hot water, he noticed that there was a tear in her dress, and her elbow hung out of a gaping hole.

He started to make his way out of the bathroom, but turned again to look at her. She seemed pitiful, smaller and more pathetic somehow as she sat staring at the water. She was not so different to how she had been when she was a little girl, with the same look of desolate abandonment on her face. Slowly he walked back over to her and tentatively picked up the corner of the torn fabric that hung down raggedly, exposing the skin at her elbow. He lifted it gently and smoothed the material across the gaping hole. He was suddenly transported back to the time when she was small and had just lost her parents, and he had placed her on a train with a similar hole in her dress. This time he couldn't abandon her again. This time he would do the right thing.

"I will make sure that your dress is repaired," he informed her, a lump finding its way to his throat. With that, he left the room and shut the door. He knew precisely what he needed to do.

*

The next morning Josef woke very early, before it was even light, and lit a fire. Even though it was late spring, he felt the need to warm himself. He moved about his house, gathering his last few things. Ingrid would not be safe in Amsterdam. He would have to take her somewhere else.

He thought about Sarah's sister, Yvette. And though he had not spoken to her in a very long time, he knew she and the rest of Sarah's family would welcome him with open arms. They lived in the country, in the south, far away from the high emotion in Amsterdam.

Waking Ingrid, he informed her of his plan.

"We need to leave, Ingrid. Now that the city is open, I need to take you away so you can be safe. I will find you some of Sarah's clothes, and we will put a headscarf upon you and tell people that you have lost your hair because of an illness. We cannot stay here. Too many people know who you are, and this could happen to you again. I know Sarah's family will take care of you."

Without reservation, Ingrid agreed, and Josef went down to prepare them some of the food from the Allies packages. He packed more food for their travel and looked out of his kitchen window one last time. A furry body threaded its way through his legs. Dantes would have to come too, he was still as spritely as ever.

Picking up his cat he whispered into his velvety ear, "There will be plenty of mice for you in the country, Dantes, my friend."

Josef thought about Mrs. Epstein and wished he could rewind the clock and hear her music one last time through his window. He thought about Michael and hoped, wherever he was, he was safe. He couldn't think of the alternative. It was too hard. His only hope: that with the war ending, Michael had made it through somehow into Allied land. He wished he could wait and stay to see if Michael returned to him. But he also knew that Ingrid needed him now. He had let her down once before, when she was a little girl, and he would not do it again. He would make sure she was taken care of this time.

Maybe after this experience she'd be able to connect in a more honest way, heal and maybe even find love again. She had more chance of survival away from the city. It was her only hope. Emotions were high in Amsterdam, and he had to leave as soon as possible, fearing the longer he lingered the more dangerous it would become for his niece.

He brought some of Sarah's clothes down from the attic and Ingrid dressed. And while it was still dark, he finished up what needed to be done in the house, and locked the doors. The last person he thought about as he secured the shutters at the windows was Hannah and his heart felt like a stone in his chest. Since his feelings had become clear in the last few months there had not been a good opportunity to tell her how he felt. He cursed himself for not just blurting it out instead of waiting for the right time. But that right time had never come, and now he had more pressing needs. Maybe after he settled Ingrid he could come back and tell her? Or he could write her a letter? But then he realized he couldn't risk bringing Ingrid's shame down onto anyone else. That would be unfair. He didn't know how her dishonor would play out. There could be a trial, even a prison sentence, her disgrace could last a long time. He was prepared to endure that, but he could not do that to the woman he loved. If one day he and Hannah were meant to be, it would happen at the right time. But for now his priority had to be to care for Ingrid.

He stepped back from the window realizing what he had just thought, he had never admitted it before, even to himself. Josef loved Hannah, and even though they had never had a chance to explore a relationship, that was how he felt. The feelings had crept up on him because he hadn't recognized them, he hadn't recognized them because it hadn't been like the love with Sarah; that young, passionate devil-may-care love that is only reserved for the young without years of real life to color it. This was different; deep and meaningful but still as strong and in some ways so much more real. He wished he'd had an opportunity to explore it, but the war seemed to have endless ways of derailing people's plans and his love life seemed a small price to pay in view of what so many had lost of far greater value.

Taking Dantes in a basket, Josef and Ingrid moved through the streets of Amsterdam, which were still recovering from the celebrations of the day before.

As they left, the roads were strewn with flags and "Welcome" messages for the troops, and the peaceful tranquility of Allied life passed them by. Canadian soldiers on patrol waved at them as they traveled along. For just a moment, Josef paused and looked around at his ravaged city and thought how different the morning felt after so many years under Hitler's regime. It was as if the whole of Amsterdam was purring its content. It felt peaceful at last. Then, taking Ingrid's arm, as they hurried toward the train station, he felt relieved he could finally breathe again.

Chapter Fifty-Seven

Hannah woke up and thought about the day before. She had been at home when she heard the commotion on the streets. The war had ended. After years of desolate silence, it sounded strange to hear people shouting, laughing, and cheering. She raced to Oma's, and her friend's tearful, ruddy face beamed as she hugged Hannah so tightly she thought she might crack one of her ribs.

"We can finally start to live again," her old friend said, squeezing Hannah's hand, "instead of just surviving."

After a celebratory cup of tea, Hannah, overcome with emotion, headed home. She opened her front door to her grandfather clock chiming its message of endurance, and she felt stinging loneliness. She wished more than anything that Clara could have been here to share the news. The memories of her and Eva, and her family, and so many friends that she had been robbed of stung her. What had it all been about? What had it all been for? Somehow to her, the victory felt hollow, some cruel joke of freedom when all she felt was bound. Bound to a past and to people who no longer existed except in her heart.

She thought of Josef. Once her mother had become ill, she had barely left her side, needing to use all of her own will to keep Clara alive. They both became cocooned in their own sadness as she dealt with the death of her mother and then he had to cope with the trauma of Michael's complete disappearance on the day his house was raided. Both preoccupied with their own grief, it felt as if it had consumed all the air between them.

If they'd had the chance to get to know one another better, maybe she would have felt she could have wept on his shoulder or he could have opened up to talk about his own loss. But there had been no understanding between them, and she didn't know how he felt. She had seen something in his eyes from time to time, but he had never given her any confidence to believe that this was anything more than a friendship. She knew how she felt about *him*, she had known for a long time. But she had been careful over the years, sensing the journey his heart had been on. She had heard rumors from other members of staff over the years about the tragic death of his wife and had watched him go from being very closed down to so much stronger, more open. Particularly in his act of hiding Michael and even contracting a deadly illness to save his life, showed her how brave and strong he was. And in all that time she had loved him. Surely now they could put this war behind them and maybe finally explore a relationship together? She had pictured him kissing her so many times, him holding her in his arms and now—if he loved her too—there was nothing to hold them back.

She decided on a plan. In all this time she had waited for him to make the first move but now she was going to take matters into her own hands. She would go to his house the very next day and invite him out for coffee. Then she would tell him once and for all how she felt about him and let the cards fall where they may. During the war, with there being no absolute certainty of it been won by the Allies, she had barely considered happiness for herself and had only looked to ways that she could serve. But now she wanted to be selfish. Now she desired to be loved. And Josef was that person for her.

*

The next day, Hannah was nervous. As she got close to Josef's house, an excitement fluttered in her chest with the weight of her feelings for him.

She made her way up his path and knocked at the door. There was no reply, and with a heavy heart, she decided to return later.

But when she returned that evening, there was still silence. Suddenly, a fear gripped her. What if he was inside and had become sick again or was incapacitated from hunger? She shouted through the door but couldn't even hear the cat. Using the key that she still had, she walked hesitantly into the cold and empty house.

As she moved from room to room calling his name, she noticed the starkness around her. Always sparsely decorated, it was completely barren now. Whatever little had been there earlier that had not been broken or destroyed by the Nazis, Josef had obviously swapped for food during the winter.

She made her way hurriedly upstairs and knocked gently on his bedroom door. It swung open. Creeping inside, she was surprised to see that his bed was stripped and his wardrobe was open and empty. What did it mean? Could it be that Michael had returned and he had taken him somewhere safe? But Amsterdam was safe now. And why would he pack a case? Not to mention where was the cat?

She went down to the kitchen and sat at the table for a second as the weight of the quiet engulfed her. Josef was gone. She didn't know why or where but she had this terrible sinking feeling that she might never see him again.

Closing and locking the front door behind her, as she made her way home that evening she rebuked herself for not talking to him earlier about how she'd felt. She knew she'd seen something in his eyes, but she'd not questioned it then. And now, she realized despondently, there might never be the opportunity.

Chapter Fifty-Eight

Six weeks later

The days after the war were a roller-coaster of joy and tragedy accompanied by hard work as the nation tried to get back on its feet. One quiet Friday evening Hannah heard a knock at her front door. She had been preparing schoolwork for the young children of the neighborhood who she was tutoring individually to help with their studies while the school system was still being reconstructed.

Assuming it was a student, Hannah had opened the door. But she didn't recognize the young woman standing on her doorstep. Even by Dutch standards, where people had lost so much weight, this young girl was shockingly thin. She could see the bones in her slender arms, and her collarbones were protruding through the blouse she was wearing. Her dark cropped hair didn't seem to match her body, and her cheekbones were hollowed out, framing dark eyes that peered out at her in bewilderment and with a sense of fear.

The young woman threw herself into Hannah's arms as something familiar seemed to register deep in Hannah, that she had dared not consider. But, when a tiny voice filtered through from beneath the layers of her clothes, it confirmed it.

"Hannah, it is me, Eva."

The young girl clung to Hannah desperately. But how could this tiny fragile young woman, barely more than bones and fear, be the same child she had known so many years before?

She hugged Eva back tightly, hoping that this wasn't a dream, that Eva had truly come back to her. They remained like that on the doorstep, for how long Hannah did not know. When Eva finally drew away, and Hannah looked at her clearly for the first time, she was euphoric, someone, someone she cherished had made it back alive from the concentration camps. How had Eva managed to make it through the war when they'd lost so many? There had been terribly high numbers in the newspaper of people who had been killed and fewer than a quarter of the Dutch Jewish people who had been sent to the German death camps had returned. Hannah had ultimately given up hope of ever seeing the Herzenbergs again. But here was a miracle right in front of her.

She led Eva into the front room and into her usual armchair. Then she built a fire even though it wasn't cold; she felt a desire to nurture and mother this young woman.

"I will put on the kettle, Eva, and we will drink tea!" she sung out, realizing immediately how ridiculous it sounded, but not knowing what else to do, needing to create normality, a sense of where they'd left off.

Eva nodded, and once in the kitchen, Hannah allowed her tears to continue to stream freely down her face as she said out loud over and over again, "Thank you, God. Thank you for this miracle, God."

Once she had composed herself and the kettle was warming on the stove, Hannah returned to the room, observing her young friend who was staring mindlessly at the fire. When their eyes met, Eva's bottom lip trembled as she finally spoke again.

"They're all gone, Hannah. All of them have gone. Willem, the baby, the boys, my father, my mother. I went back to the house first, and I waited. I've been waiting for days. I didn't know where else to go."

Her voice cracked as Hannah sat down hard into an armchair and shook her head in disbelief as this new pain gripped her chest like a vice. Hannah wasn't even sure how to respond to such over-whelming grief; she felt helpless to comfort her. It was too much pain all at once and with immense sorrow she realized Greta was gone along with her whole family. Everyone, except Eva.

Leaning forward, she gently took hold of both of her young friend's hands. "You were right to come here. I am overjoyed to see you, Eva. You are alive and this is a miracle."

"They didn't kill me because I kept myself busy. I thought about Clara's words." Eva stopped and looked about her then as if she expected Hannah's mother to come in at any moment. "Where is she? Is she here? I want to tell her that her words kept me alive. The Germans didn't kill me because I would sew for their wives and knit for them. But I still never believed that I would make it out alive. But then one day I was free and I need to tell Clara about it all."

Hannah shook her head, despising the fact she was dealing this young woman yet another blow. She couldn't say the words, but Eva sensed them automatically. It appeared this was news she was used to receiving. "Oh," was all Eva could utter as fresh tears appeared in her eyes.

The kettle whistled and Hannah was grateful for a brief respite to give both of them a moment to deal with the grief that was settling in the room like a shroud.

They were quiet as Eva sipped her tea and then as she finished her drink she said, "I went to the authorities too. They say they have had considerable trouble locating... anyone in my family. They are not sure," and then she filtered to a whisper, "if there is anyone left."

Hannah took Eva in her arms again and held her tightly, whispering into her ear, "We are family. *We* are a family. And my mother will take care of all of them in the next life. Clara will be there with them, and you and I will be a new family."

Eva's body melted into Hannah's as if those were the words she'd been waiting to hear, as though she had been desperately searching to find a soft place to fall that she could call home, and she sobbed into Hannah's shoulder. Hannah stroked the dry bristles of her hair as she tried not to imagine what she had been through.

After that day, Eva moved into Clara's old room and didn't leave Hannah's home. She had slowly unpacked the story of the last days with her family. Then as time went on she began to open up about her painful experience that echoed so many that Hannah was hearing about, terrifying things, inhuman atrocities that had been done to so many people. Even though Eva was relieved to be safe, fear seemed to cling to her and her childlike optimism never surfaced again. She suffered terrible nightmares, and Hannah would often find her staring out of the window, as if looking for those people who would never come home again.

One gift Hannah had been able to bestow was the Herzenbergs' boxes she'd gathered, after Eva's family had been arrested and before the Germans had raided their home. Eva had been so grateful for everything. Every tiny memory, every scrap of fabric, every child-hood toy gave her a sense of comfort. She had especially savored her mother's letters and the photographs of her family, which she kept in her most precious possession of all—Clara's music box.

And it was the melody of Clara's box that became the music that somehow represented their journey of healing. Hannah would wind it up and sit next to Eva on the bed and the two of them would lie, arms wrapped around one another, listening to it play over and over again as they would remember with great joy and sadness the people they'd loved and lost. And as Hannah tucked Eva in every evening she would marvel at the miracle of having her back in her life. That out of great tragedy had come some light.

Chapter Fifty-Nine

September 1947

Hannah shuffled through the pile of mail that had gathered on the mat in front of her door. Alongside the usual collection of bills, she noticed a white linen envelope and turned it over in her hand. It was from the university. Slipping it open, she pulled out a smooth white card. It was an invitation to an evening of music to benefit the Jewish refugees. Hannah nodded her approval; it was so sad that so many of them had been so traumatized by their experiences that they still feared reprisals from their own countries. For their safety and security, many of them had been placed in refugee camps throughout Europe, including several near Amsterdam.

She propped the elegant card against her mantel clock in the sitting room, its methodical ticking lulling her back in time, pulling her thoughts back to her days at the beginning of the war, days spent at the university. Through veiled memory, she could still see the classrooms and halls filled with eager students full of the optimism and gaiety of youth. The halls were always teeming with life, echoing in raucous laughter or serious debates. Year after year she had watched them blossom before her eyes, going from awkward freshman to well-rounded seniors, now even returning as faculty. She had been proud to work there with committed educators, many of them brilliant, dedicated to their craft and the honing of young minds.

Once the university had reopened, the faculty had contacted her to resume her position, but she had declined. Having a new life and freedom every day had challenged her to reach for more. She had never regretted her decision. Hannah loved the work that she did now, teaching young children. After so many tumultuous years, their keen young minds were more than ready to learn about mathematics and the art of creating words for the page. Twice a week she even taught them how to knit. It gave her great joy to pass on her mother's skills, and in a way, it helped her to honor her memory.

As she listened to the continuous, lyrical thrum of the clock, Josef's face drifted into her thoughts, and his quiet, gentle presence surrounded her like a shawl.

*

On the day of the concert, Hannah left Eva writing in her diary, as she did most days, and made her way through the streets of Amsterdam on a now infrequent but well-remembered path. Approaching Mrs. Oberon's house, she marveled again at the fact that Oma had miraculously made it through the *Hongerwinter*. Even though Clara's death had been hard on her old friend, she had gone on to adopt a number of the neighborhood children who had lost their parents. One of them was Hannah's little friend, Albert, now a robust young adolescent with all of his adult teeth. He had lost his father in one of the labor camps and his mother had died just after the war of pneumonia, her body weakened by the winter of 1944. As Hannah passed Mrs. Oberon's house, she thought of the life those orphans had in the tiny red-brick home. Days spent wrapped in the security of the floury lap of the woman with the florid cheeks and eyes that twinkled with tears whenever she laughed.

Arriving at the university, Hannah entered the familiar limestone entrance. The sight and sounds that greeted her filled her with pleasure. If she closed her eyes, it was as if she had never left. The main foyer was freshly painted in a warm yellow that complemented the wood paneling perfectly, and the timber floor she had walked so many times was newly polished and smelt of beeswax and lemon.

Thrusting her hands deep into her coat pockets, she echoed down the hallway, glancing over only briefly at the welcome desk where she had spent those years of her life. It seemed so small now, an insignificant space, like a hat check or a ticket booth. A place you passed by on your way somewhere else, somewhere more important, without even giving it a second thought. She had no idea how she had lived so long in that one tiny life as the whole world had silently passed before her.

Arriving at the main concert hall, she took off her coat and slipped into a row just as the university president got up and creaked along the wooden stage to the podium. He greeted the crowd, enthusing about the musical performance and the need to raise money for Jewish refugees. She felt the usual twinge of sadness that always accompanied her now with the loss they all felt. Every day she woke up thankful to be alive, but the rebuilding of those lives had taken a lot longer than the reconstruction of their town. The loss of so many lives and their naïveté had come at a cost. During the war years, they had found the best of themselves, but had exchanged it for the loss of their innocence. Everything was now less complicated, but nothing was simple.

However, she had refused to feel sorry for herself in the last few years, supporting the reconstruction process by continuing to rebuild bicycles for Holland and working with the war refugees. And now she had Eva, the greatest gift.

It was because she sat there, deep in thought, that at first she didn't see the person seated on the stage, waiting patiently to begin his concert. Even when she looked up, it took her a moment to realize who it was. With his piercing, blue eyes, and dark features, her heart caught in her throat. It was Josef.

She was near the back, so she was sure that he couldn't see her. But she watched with interest as he stood and walked to the front of the stage, and even from her great distance, she could see that his whole countenance was different to before. The man who always tried to make himself smaller, shrink from the world, now filled the space behind the podium.

He was still softly spoken and purposeful in his speech, but he talked with a new boldness about the music he was going to perform at the piano. He warmly acknowledged the faculty and the university, and she watched with eager anticipation as he seated himself in front of the piano.

As he started his performance, she knew instantly that something was different. Something about him was now liberated. The man who had been so locked away, so unapproachable, found abandon as he played, taking them all to heights of exquisite ecstasy with his powerful musical renditions. After thirty minutes of breathtaking music, he stood to his feet again, came back to the front of the stage, and scanned the crowd.

"I taught mathematics here at the university for many years. But before that time, I used to create beautiful music with my beloved wife, who passed away. Her name was Sarah." He paused for a moment to gather himself after uttering her name, but then continued. "I didn't play for many years after she died, but one thing that loss has taught me is that keeping a gift locked away only brings harm. It is essential to express ourselves. Walls and doors keep out not just the bad but also the good. It is our job to own the keys of our freedom, and to be able to open those doors. I spent many years behind a closed door without knowing where to find the key to my life, but thanks to my music, I am now finding my way out. To quote an extraordinary but lesser-known philosopher, my late wife Sarah Held, 'What is life without the beauty of art or music or poetry to help us interpret it, encourage us to know how to feel, how to love and how to live?' In music I see the darkness, the light, the messiness, the beauty, and the complexities of life that simply can't be summed up like an equation. Music, for me, helps bring down the walls, to open those locked doors. And I hope it has been that way for you too, tonight."

The audience applauded warmly, and Hannah's eyes filled with tears as she tried to reconcile the man who stood before her with the one she had known for so many years. Since finding out about Michael she'd known Josef's depths, but the inspiring human being who now stood before her had indeed finally stepped out from his self-imposed captivity, and recognized them himself.

As the clapping subsided, Josef continued. "The last piece that I want to play for you holds an exceptional place in my heart." His voice started to quiver. "It is an original composition written by a dear Dutch woman who was barely known, even to me. Though now I know her full name was Mrs. Florence Epstein, and she was a private person who led a quiet, sedate life, teaching piano to Dutch children. Unfortunately, she was also Jewish."

An icy hush filled the air as everyone took a moment to absorb that information.

Wrestling with his emotion, Josef continued. "All that has survived of her ordinary yet valuable life are the memories in her students' hearts and this beautiful piece of music that she composed and that I would like to play for you this evening. It is entitled, 'My Amsterdam.'"

He sat down at the piano and put his fingers upon the keys. Tears rolled down Hannah's cheeks as she listened to him fill the space with his rendition of Mrs. Epstein's joyful composition, and she closed her eyes as the music lifted to the ceiling. It felt familiar, somehow capturing in its rhythms her joyous city, the free spirit of the people, their strong endurance, and their sense of community. All and more were embedded in the notes that he played passionately.

Chapter Sixty

Josef rested his hands on the keys, grateful he had made it to the end. Having played refugee concerts for over a year now, he was surprised at how much tonight had affected him. Maybe it was being back here, back at the university where he had spent so many years of his life. Standing to take his bow, he looked around the room at all the faces looking at him encouragingly. So many people he knew whom he had never really let know him. They stood to their feet to honor him with a standing ovation, and he felt humbled.

Josef had come of age twice in this building. First as a student, then years later as a middle-aged mathematics professor. The first time with the hope of a successful academic future and a loving wife to support his journey, and the second time many years later when his real purpose had become visible. Never had he been happier than with the work he was doing now.

As he started his encore performance, he imagined his father's face smiling at him and his words echoed in his mind: "One day you will be a fine pianist, my son. You have great skill, and one day you will find the passion to match it."

Josef recalled the headstrong young man whose only determination had been to be the opposite of all that his parents expected. And mathematics had been a suitable punishment to his creatively biased family. While he had only reluctantly played in his youth to please his father, it was with his wife that he had first derived great joy from music, seeing the pleasure it gave her. But now was different, as even though he played to honor Mrs. Epstein's memory, he also played for himself. The happiness he felt deep inside of him for the many gifts he had been given brought him to tears, and he channeled all of that thankfulness back into his music.

After the performance, he tucked away his papers, including Mrs. Epstein's crumpled, yellowing sheets. He could have copied them in his own hand onto fresh paper, but with so little of Mrs. Epstein's legacy to preserve, it seemed undignified to do so.

He moved quickly from the stage, stopping to shake a couple of hands before disappearing out of a side door. He still was not entirely comfortable in large groups, especially as he had spent the last two years in near seclusion in the country with Sarah's family taking care of Ingrid.

Hurrying through the throngs of excited concertgoers, he made his way to the exit, but on his path to the main door, his heart was pulled down a familiar corridor and he found himself outside his old classroom. It was empty and quiet. Opening the door, he was greeted by the usual creak of wood and smell of chalk dust.

Looking around the room he beamed. "Hello, dear friend," he said out loud.

Nothing but the old meticulously ticking clock returned his greeting.

Walking to the darkened windows, he looked out into the night. How many times had he stood just here, looking out to a world he had barely been a part of?

All at once, the door creaked behind him and someone put on the light. It was Hannah. She looked as if she had been running, her cheeks flushed red and her breath stilted.

"I thought I had missed you," she rasped. Then added with a smile, "Hello, Professor."

Josef gasped. She was still as beautiful as he'd remembered. In the two and a half years since he'd last seen her, a day hadn't gone by when he hadn't pictured her, thought about her, and wondered about what could have been between them. As soon as he'd arrived at the university that evening, the first thing he'd done was go to her desk, only to be greeted by someone else. The young woman, Isabelle, who Hannah had been training so many years before, curtly informed him that Hannah no longer worked there. He had felt crushing regret that he hadn't written or come back sooner. But now here she was.

As she approached him, the thrill of just being in the same room with her ran through his body like a charge, tightening his throat, making his heart thud, and rendering him tongue-tied. He finally managed to whisper, "They told me you'd left."

She smiled, catching her breath. "I have. I did. I am just back for the concert."

He found himself dumbstruck and all he could manage was, "Ah."

As she joined him at the window, he felt coy, self-conscious. A million thoughts went through his mind. He wanted to tell her exactly how he felt about her, but he wasn't sure how to start the conversation. She saved him with a question.

"Did you ever hear from Michael again?" she asked, concern in her tone.

He shook his head and returned his gaze to the blackened sky. "I have enquired at many of the refugee camps, but nothing yet."

She nodded in understanding. So many people were still missing and presumed dead.

"How is Ingrid?" she enquired. "Did she leave Amsterdam with you? I imagined it was difficult for her after the war."

He nodded. "Yes, I accompanied her, she had to leave and wasn't strong enough to go alone. She is much better, now. She was very wounded by her experiences during the occupation, but I took her to a remote village in the south and we stayed with Sarah's sister to help with her recovery. She met a nice young man, a farmhand. Not quite as cavalier as Major von Strauss, but he is kind and adores her and is exactly what she needs. They were married a few months ago, and already she is expecting my first grand-nephew or niece." Josef beamed.

He looked over at Hannah. He had to do or say something, anything that conveyed all the feelings he'd felt for her, still felt for her.

He forced out the words, "I'm very grateful to you, Hannah." And reached forward and covered her hand with his own, as another thrill raced through his body.

She looked down, obviously surprised at his forthrightness. He desperately hoped that she could see in his face everything that he wanted to say but couldn't vocalize. He never wanted to ever let go of her hand again. He took in a deep breath and decided he was just going to say it, tell her he loved her and didn't want to go one more day without her being in his life.

Just then a voice called to them from the door. "Professor Held, here you are." They turned to look into the businesslike face of Isabelle. "I am glad I caught you."

He withdrew his hand, not wanting to embarrass Hannah. This had been her employee, after all. Gone was the awkward young girl. Now she was a woman who took her job and position very seriously.

"Hello, Isabelle," Hannah said. "How is the desk?"

Isabelle responded almost a little defensively, as if Hannah may be back to judge her efficiency. "All is in order," she snapped. "I have something for the professor, his mail. I will go and get it."

"Mail! Mrs. Pender, can you imagine?" he responded in mock horror. "There is still mail!"

They both laughed warmly as Isabelle strode away to complete her task.

He wanted to get back to what he had to say but Hannah was making nervous small talk. "Maybe it is a new algebra course. I remember you saying the one you used was ancient."

Isabelle returned quickly with a small brown package and placed it on the desk. The postmark was from America. Then she left the room to continue with her duties.

"You have friends in the USA?" Hannah enquired, noting the confused expression on his face.

He shook his head and silently unwrapped the parcel. Two pieces of paper slipped out. One appeared to be a letter, the other a math equation he recognized from so long ago, on a fresh sheet of paper. Completed. He opened the letter and read the first line, then collapsed into the chair at the desk, overcome.

Hannah became concerned. "Is it bad news?" she enquired, hesitantly.

Josef couldn't speak and handed her the letter. "Read it, can you?" he asked hoarsely.

She took the letter and read it out loud.

"Hello, Professor. It's me, Michael!" She paused then, understanding Josef's show of emotion, feeling it herself. He nodded at her to continue as tears filled his eyes.

I know you thought that you had finally got rid of me, but here I am. I am resending this package, as the one I sent to your house was returned and I'm hoping that you are still at the university. I didn't know how else to contact you.

It was important for me to get this gift to you. I will never have the words or actions to thank you for all that you did for me during the war. I know I will never meet a finer, kinder human being than you. I can only hope that when I am faced with similar challenges that I can be up to the task set by your example.

After I escaped that day, I went to find my dear sweet Elke. I cannot talk about this, even in writing, without the pain being almost too acute for me. All I will tell you is she saved my life by sacrificing her own. They tried to kill me too, but before they could Allied forces in the area intercepted them and pulled my unconscious body to safety.

I would not find out Elke was dead until I awoke weeks later in a hospital in America where I got taken, and my recovery felt like a mixture of crippling sadness and elation to be free at last. It has been a hard road, Professor, I will not pretend. But Elke lost her life to save me. And you risked yours in so many ways to save me too. And I knew I owed it to both of you to live. I threw my emotions into my writing and over the last few months I have once again begun to open up to love and there is the beginning of something beautiful again. I have thought many times over the last year of you and Sarah, and realized once again how brave it is to face our feelings, our losses, and our grief, and you taught me how to do that. It was a long and heart-wrenching emotional journey, but none of it would have been possible if you hadn't taken care of me for so long, and I will never forget our friendship.

I am thankful daily to you, Hannah Pender, to God, and to Rainer Maria Rilke, all of whom, in an odd twist of fate, contributed to my salvation. Please do write back. I would love so much to hear from you.

Your sincere friend, Michael.

P.S. I thought you might like to know, I just passed my advanced mathematics course, with an A in algebra. And you thought I would never make it!"

Josef smiled at the last comment, removing his spectacles and wiping away the tears. With his shaking hands, he opened the rest of the parcel. It was a published book of poetry by Michael Blum called *Miji Held*—My Hero. He turned to the front page and read the inscription.

This book is dedicated to my hero, my friend, and my professor, Josef Held, who taught me algebra but also taught me in the darkest nights of my soul the true meaning of the words, "Sometimes the most courageous love is whispered in the quietest moments."

Overcome, Josef handed the book to Hannah, who read aloud the first poem in the book, also called "Miji Held," which told a story of protection, quiet strength, and courage.

After she was finished, tears brimming in her eyes, she closed the cover of the book. There was a long silence between them. And then, reading the atmosphere, she decided maybe he needed to be left alone with his thoughts. He was only vaguely aware of her calling out from the door, "It was lovely to see you again, Professor," as she moved out into the corridor.

Josef continued to sit for a long moment, absorbing everything that had happened. Michael was safe. *Michael was safe*.

Suddenly he was stirred from his reverie, Hannah's words suddenly finding their way into his consciousness. She had left and he might never get a chance again. Remembering something Michael had once suggested to him long ago, he raced to the door. The hall was now filled with people, young students and faculty, and on seeing him, they automatically came to the classroom door to congratulate him on his performance. Trapped in the classroom, he looked about frantically and finally saw her moving toward the main exit.

Josef took a deep breath and tried to speak. But no sound came out.

He tried again. This time his voice boomed down the hall. "Mrs. Pender!"

She didn't hear him.

So he called again even louder, "Hannah!"

Apparently taken aback by his use of her first name, she turned to see who called to her. When she saw it was Josef, she started to walk back.

He didn't even wait until she reached him. Josef wasn't going to let her slip from his life again. He continued to shout over the crowd, "Hannah, I was wondering... no, I was hoping that you might wish to join me for dinner, this evening... and then maybe... for the rest of my life."

Hannah stopped, surprised by his words, but also emotional, tears brimming. "I would love to," she mouthed back, walking slowly toward him.

And he felt—for the first time in so long—warm and light. Her smile was a gentle glow warming and reminding him of the sun on the rooftops after the rain. As he looked down at her he saw reflected in her eyes his whole life stretched out before him and he felt complete. It had been a long and harrowing journey back to his heart and to loving again and now it was here he would not let it go. He enfolded her gently in his arms, drew her in close so he could feel her heart beating, her breath grazing his cheek. Closing his eyes so he could fully experience the feeling of the woman he loved in his arms, he drew in a long, slow, contented breath knowing, finally, he was home.

A Letter from Suzanne

Dear Reader,

I want to say a huge thank you for choosing to read *A View Across the Rooftops*. If you did enjoy it, and want to keep up-to-date with all my latest releases, just sign up at the following link. Your email address will never be shared and you can unsubscribe at any time.

www.bookouture.com/suzanne-kelman

This story is incredibly close to my heart, and is inspired by a true story of a man who risked everything to save another, and by the courageous acts of the Dutch people. You can read on for a little more about the story behind the story.

In the meantime, if you loved *A View Across the Rooftops*, I would be enormously grateful if you could write a review. I'd love to hear what you think, and it makes such a difference helping new readers to discover one of my books for the first time.

I love hearing from my readers—you can get in touch on my Facebook page, through Twitter, Goodreads or my website.

Thanks,
Suzanne Kelman

[f] suzkelman

[twitter] @suzkelman

[website] www.suzannekelmanauthor.com

The Story Behind
A View Across the Rooftops

Sometimes a story takes hold of you and it just won't let go until you've written it. *A View Across the Rooftops* was exactly like that for me. Back in 2010 I was talking to another writer, my friend Susannah, discussing writing and stories we had been profoundly touched by. As we sat sipping pink wine, she told me about a true story that had moved her ten years before, that she had never written and that still truly touched her.

She'd been researching Holocaust stories for a theatre show she was directing and by chance unearthed a story—a plaque on the wall of a museum, telling the story of a man who'd deliberately contracted a deadly disease just to get medicine for the Jewish person he was hiding. It had such an impact on her, this one courageous act that one person had done for another, that she wrote it down on a napkin and carried it around in her handbag for months until it got lost, though she never forgot the story. I sat on the edge of my seat as she went on to describe this one quiet heroic act.

When she left that evening I found I couldn't sleep and, as I paced my kitchen, what kept me awake wasn't just this one man's selfless act, but the fact I recognized I wasn't capable of it. A much deeper question then haunted me: Just how far would I be willing to go to save another person's life?

The very next morning I called Susannah and that started a journey that has lasted ten years for me. Not because it has taken that long to tell but because it turns out this story had its own idea of how it wanted to be told.

Originally, in 2010, we decided to write the screenplay together, and there were significant challenges, but also uplifting moments. As we started to read about Amsterdam, it was hard not to become overwhelmed at the volume of unsung hero stories, particularly from ordinary Dutch people. Overthrown in just five days, Holland was one of the countries most viciously policed by the Nazis. But their people were also one of the most vocal about the unethical treatment of the Jewish population. Even so, the Netherlands lost some of the highest numbers of Jewish citizens; there were 140,000 Jewish people living in Holland before the war and devastatingly fewer than 25 per cent survived, with only approximately 5,000 returning home from the death and labor camps.

What was amazing, however, was that a staggering further 30,000 Jews survived the war by hiding in people's basements, attics, and barns. We probably all know the story of Anne Frank and her family, but whilst like so many her story ended in tragedy, a huge number of lives were saved. And if it hadn't been for the quiet courage of ordinary Dutch citizens who continued to keep their former neighbors safe even in the face of starvation during the brutal *Hongerwinter* where many were forced to eat tulip bulbs and wallpaper just to survive, nearly a whole nation of Dutch Jews would have been lost.

Something astonishing happened as we wrote. A script in the first draft typically takes me three to four months to complete. But the story that was then called *Held*—the Dutch word for hero, and of course our fictional hero Josef's surname—wrote itself in only one week. It was as if this story needed to be told.

The original screenplay did really well. It won many awards and was even placed in the top ten of the Academy of Motion Pictures Nichols Fellowship, winning its place over 8,000 other scripts. But still, even though we tried many avenues for a number of years, and it went into pre-production twice, it is yet to be made as a movie.

Both Susannah and I went on to work separately on other projects but this story never entirely left me. Flash forward a few years, and I was telling the story to my literary agent, and it also touched her in a profound way, and she asked me to write it again, this time as a novel.

So over the last two years that grain of a story became *A View Across the Rooftops* and has grown into something so much bigger than I could have imagined. Still though, at the center of this story, is that single act of heroism that touches my heart to this day.

The wonderful thing that emerged as I wrote this book, was that with over 100,000 words I had so much more latitude to explore everyday people and their simple acts of bravery—from Hannah and her work for the Resistance, to Vi (or Cuckoo) bravely concealing herself in Nazi High Command, even to Clara and Oma whose quiet resistance and parenting taught those around them the difference between right and wrong. And their voices came forth in the work, too. I have also realized that before I started telling this story, I had some sort of blind idea that heroes existed only on the battlefield charging to their death, when the truth is so many people show quiet heroism we will never know about. This is one of those stories, and I'm just grateful that I could be the one to give it a voice.

Nations of heroes do not exist. But there were among the Dutch tens of thousands of ordinary beings, men and women, who did save the country's soul.

—*Louis de Jong*

Acknowledgements

I couldn't have written this book without the myriad of people who helped me along the way. Firstly, I have to thank Susannah Rose Woods, thank you for bringing this amazing story into my life and also for being gracious enough to trust me to tell it one more time.

Secondly, I have to thank my partner, my love, my husband, Matthew Wilson, who as I am writing this, is sat right next to me re-checking links and historical facts one more time. He has been my rock and constant supporter. Thank you so much, honey. Not only for being my historian but also for being a soft place to fall and answering the question over and over again when I was bone-tired, "Why am I doing this again?"

I would also like to thank my son Christopher, whose editing and linguistic skills are throughout this book, and for his gift of humor that keeps me going every day. I'm indeed fortunate to not only have you as my son but also as my friend.

Thanks also goes to my team: my agent, Andrea Hurst, and editors, Jeri Walker, Audrey Makaman and Cameron Chandler, you all helped add something special to this story.

With my publishers, Bookouture, I was indeed fortunate to have found a champion of this work in Isobel Akenhead, who not only got the heart of this story right away, but her skilled development made my writing shine. I'm also grateful to the rest of the editorial team at Bookouture, as well as Oliver Rhodes, Peta Nightingale, Noelle Holten, Kim Nash, and all the other supporters at Bookouture and Hachette UK. Lots of thanks also go to Abby Parsons, the editor over at Little, Brown Books, for also loving this story and publishing the paperback.

To my own circle of cozies, Melinda Mack, Kim Wetherell, Eric Mulholland, and Shauna Soule, thank you for keeping me sane through this process. To my favorite writer pal, K.J. Waters, who is always my number-one writing cheerleader. I couldn't do this without your support, thank you so much.

Also, I need to recognize Phillip Thoman who always believed in the power of this story.

And lastly, thanks to you, the reader. I hope that you'll be as touched by the heart of this story as I was, and it will help you forever recognize the quiet hero who resides in all of us.

Research

The Holocaust Centre for Humanity in Seattle

www.abmceducation.org/sites/default/files/Swenson_Timeline_MajorWWII_Events_handout.pdf

www.historyplace.com/worldwar2/holocaust/timeline.html

http://faculty.webster.edu/woolflm/netherlands.html

https://en.wikipedia.org/wiki/February_strike

http://seehiddenamsterdam.com/tag/nazi-occupation/

www.verzetsmuseum.org/museum/en/exhibitions/the-netherlands-in-ww2

https://ww2gravestone.com/1941-2526-february-strike-also-known-strike-february-1941

https://en.wikipedia.org/wiki/History_of_the_Jews_in_Amsterdam

www.ushmm.org/wlc/en/article.php?ModuleId=10005434

www.ushmm.org/learn/timeline-of-events/1942-1945/deportation-of-dutch-jews

www.annefrank.org/en/Subsites/Annes-Amsterdam/

https://en.wikipedia.org/wiki/Hannie_Schaft

https://en.wikipedia.org/wiki/Dutch_resistance#References

www.ushmm.org/wlc/en/article.php?ModuleId=10005436

www.jta.org/2017/07/03/news-opinion/world/
in-holland-the-nazis-built-a-luxury-camp-to-lull-the-jews-
before-murdering-them

www.iamsterdam.com/en/about-amsterdam/amsterdam-
neighbourhoods

https://en.wikipedia.org/wiki/Netherlands_in_World_War_
II#Life_in_the_occupied_Netherlands

https://en.wikipedia.org/wiki/Dutch_famine_of_1944–45

https://en.wikipedia.org/wiki/Operation_Silbertanne

www.wikiwand.com/en/Amsterdam-Centrum

www.wikiwand.com/en/Jodenbuurt

www.ilholocaustmuseum.org/wp-content/uploads/2016/06/
Netherlands-Holocaust-History.pdf

https://dirkdeklein.net/tag/holocaust/

www.utm.utoronto.ca/~dwhite/101/28.htm

www.netinnederland.nl/en/artikelen/dossiers/overzicht/tweede-
wereldoorlog.html

www.rafmuseum.org.uk/blog/operation-manna-29th-april-to-
8th-may-1945/

Made in the USA
Columbia, SC
11 January 2021

30603786R00238